THE THRILL BOOK

Sept. 1, 1919 Issue

(Volume Two, Number Five)

THE THRILL BOOK

Sept. 1, 1919 issue

Pulp Classics #10

Series editor: John Gregory Betancourt

New elements copyright © 2004 by Wildside Press.

Published by:

Wildside Press
P.O. Box 301
Holicong, PA 18928-0301 USA
www.wildsidepress.com

THE THRILL BOOK

SEMIMONTHLY

:: :: :: ::

Vol. II   CONTENTS FOR SEPTEMBER 1, 1919   No. 5

Publication Issued Semimonthly by Street & Smith Corporation, 70-89 Seventh Avenue, New York City. ORMOND G. SMITH, President; GEORGE C. SMITH, Secretary and Treasurer. Copyright, 1919, by Street & Smith Corporation, New York. Copyright, 1919, by Street & Smith Corporation. Great Britain. All Rights Reserved. Publishers everywhere are cautioned against using any of the contents of this Magazine either wholly or in part. Entered as Second-class Matter, February 15, 1919, at the Post Office at New York, N. Y., under Act of Congress of March 3, 1879. Canadian subscription, $3.82. Foreign, $5.04.

WARNING—Do not subscribe through agents unknown to you. Complaints are daily made by persons thus victimized.

IMPORTANT—Authors, agents and publishers are requested to note that this firm does not hold itself responsible for loss of unsolicited manuscripts while at this office or in transit; and that it cannot undertake to hold uncalled for manuscripts for a longer period than six months. If the return of manuscript is expected, postage should be inclosed.

YEARLY SUBSCRIPTION, $3.60   **SINGLE COPIES, 75 CENTS**

The Thrill Book

Semi-Monthly

| Vol. II | SEPTEMBER 1, 1919 | No. 5 |

The Silver Menace

By Murray Leinster

THE yacht was plowing through the calm waters with a steady throbbing of the engines. The soft washing of the waves along the sides, the murmur of the wind through the light rigging aloft, and the occasional light footstep of the navigating officer on the bridge were the only sounds.

The long white vessel swept on through the night in silence. Here and there a light showed from some porthole or window, but for the most part the whole boat was dark and silent. For once the yacht contained no merry party of guests to one-step on the wide decks and fill all the obscurer corners with accurately paired couples.

Alexander Morrison, millionaire steamship magnate, and his daughter Nita had the ship to themselves. They were sitting in two of the big wicker chairs on the after deck, and the glow of Morrison's cigar was the only light.

"Getting chilly, Nita," he remarked casually. "Are you warm enough?"

"Yes, indeed." Nita was silent for a moment, gazing off into the darkness. "It's nice," she said reflectively, "to be by one's self for a while. I'm glad you didn't invite a lot of people to come back with us."

Her father smiled.

"Judging by the way you behaved along the Riviera," he reminded her, "you didn't mind company. I never saw any one quite so run after as you were."

Nita shook her head.

"They were running after you, daddy," she said lightly. "I was just a means of approach."

Her father puffed on his cigar for a moment in silence.

"It is a disadvantage, having a millionaire for a father," he admitted. "It's hard to tell who is in love with you, and who is in love with your father's money."

"So the thing to do, I suppose," said Nita amusedly, "is just to fall in love with some one yourself, and pay no attention to his motives."

"Where do you get your notions?" asked her father. "That's cynicism. You haven't been practicing on that theory, have you?"

"Not I," said Nita with a little silvery laugh. "But you know, daddy, it isn't nice to feel like a money bag with a lot of people looking at you all the time, some of them enviously and some of them covetously, but none of them regarding you just like a human being."

"I don't see," declared her father, with real affection, "how any normal young man who looked at you could stop thinking about you long enough to think about your money."

"I rise and bow," said Nita mischievously. "May I return the compliment, substituting 'young woman' for 'young man?'"

"Don't try to fool your father," that gentleman said with a smile. He added with something of conscious pride: "I don't suppose there are two other men in America as homely as I am."

"Daddy!" protested Nita, laughing. "You're lovely to look at! I wouldn't have you look a bit different for worlds."

"Neither would I have myself look different," her father admitted cheerfully. "I've gotten used to myself this way. I like to look at myself this way.

It's an acquired taste like olives, but once you learn to like me this way—why, there you are."

Nita laughed and was silent. Suddenly she began to look a little bit puzzled.

"Do you notice anything funny?" she asked in a moment or so. "Somehow, the boat doesn't seem to be traveling just right."

Her father listened. Only the usual sounds came to his ears. The washing of the waves along the sides, however, had a peculiar timbre. Then he noticed that the boat seemed to be checking a little in its speed. There was an odd, velvety quality in the checking, very much like the soft breaking effect felt when a motor boat runs into a patch of weed.

"Queer," said Morrison. "We'll ask the captain."

The two of them walked down the deck arm in arm until they came to the stair ladder leading up to the bridge. The gentle checking continued. The boat seemed to be gradually slowing up, though the engines throbbed on as before.

"What's the matter, captain?" asked Morrison.

His first mate answered:

"I've sent for the captain, sir. Our speed has fallen off three knots in the past five minutes."

The captain came hastily up on the bridge, buttoning up his coat as he came.

"What's the matter, Mr. Harrison?"

The first mate turned a worried face to him.

"Our speed has dropped off three knots in five minutes, sir, and seems to be still slackening. I thought it best to send for you."

The captain called up the engine room.

"All right down there?"

"Per-rhaps," came the answer in a thick Scotch burr. "Ah was aboot to ask ye the same mysel'. We're usin' twenty perr cent more steam for the same number of rrevolutions."

"We might have run into a big patch of seaweed," suggested the first mate.

"Unship the searchlight," said the captain crisply.

A seaman came up to the bridge. He had been sent back to look at the patent log.

"We're logging eight knots now, sir."

The first mate uttered an exclamation.

"That's six knots off what we were making ten minutes ago!"

No one spoke for a moment or so, while one or two seamen worked at the lashing of the cover on the searchlight.

"Do any of you smell anything?" asked Nita suddenly.

A faint but distinct odor came to their nostrils. It was the odor of slime and mud, with a tinge of musk. It was the scent of foul things from the water. It was a damp and humid smell, indistinctly musklike and disgusting.

"Like deep-sea mud," said one of the seamen to the other. "Like somethin' come up from Gawd knows what soundin'."

Nita gasped a little. The searchlight sputtered and then a long, white pencil of light shot out over the water. It wavered, and sank to a point just beside the bow of the boat. It showed —nothing.

The bow wave rose reluctantly and traveled but a little distance before it subsided into level sea. There were no waves. The water was calm as an inland lake.

"No seaweed there," said the captain sharply. "Look on the other side."

The searchlight swept across the deck and to the water on the other side. Nothing. The water seemed to be turgidly white, but that was all. It was not clear; it was rather muddy and almost milklike, as if a little finely di-

vided chalk had been stirred in it. There was no disturbance of its placid surface. Only the reluctant bow wave surged away from the sharp prow of the yacht.

The seaman returned from a second trip to the patent log.

"We're logging five knots now, sir."

"Nine knots off," said the first mate with a white face. "We were making fourteen."

"We'll take a look all around," said the captain sharply.

The searchlight obediently swept the surface of the water. Every one on the bridge followed its exploring beam with anxious eyes. That musky, musty smell of things from unthinkable depths and the mysterious retardation of their vessel filled them with apprehension.

There was not one of them, from the ignorant seamen to the supereducated Morrison, who did not look fearfully where the light beam went.

The hand laid on the vessel—that in a calm sea had slowed from fourteen knots to five, despite the mighty engines within the hull—that force seemed of such malignant power that none of them would have been greatly surprised to see the huge bulk of some fabled Kraken rearing itself above the water, preparing to engulf the yacht with a sweep of some colossal tentacle.

The sea was calm. As far as the searchlight could light up its surface not a wave broke its calm placidity.

The seaman returned from his third visit to the patent log.

"Two knots, sir!"

The movement of the yacht became slower and slower as it gradually checked in its sweep through the water. The throbbing of the engines grew louder as they labored with increasing effort to master the mysterious Thing that was holding them back.

The boat was barely creeping now. It seemed to be struggling against some invisible force that gripped gently but relentlessly, some infinitely patient force that from the very patience of its operation was the more evidently inexorable.

The engines were working in panic-stricken tempo now. The chief engineer had given them all the steam they would take, and the propellers thrashed the water mightily, but the ship slowed, slowed.

At last it was still, while the engines seemed to be trying to rack themselves to pieces in their terrific attempt to drive the ship against the Thing that held it back.

The captain watched with a set face, then ordered the engines reversed. There was an instant's pause, and the propellers took up their thrashing of the water again. For a moment it seemed that they would have some effect. The yacht shivered and moved slightly backward, but then stopped again with the same soft gentleness.

The seamen inspected the water all around the ship with lanterns lowered to the water's edge. They found nothing. A sounding line was thrown overboard, and sank for two hundred fathoms without reaching bottom.

The searchlight played endlessly over the water, trying to find some turmoil that might indicate the presence of a monster whose tentacles had fastened upon the ship, but without result. The surface of the water was like glass.

Again and again the engines struggled mightily to move the ship. Again and again the propellers beat the water at the stern into froth and foam, but never did the yacht move by as much as an inch.

The sea was calm and placid. The stars looked down from the moonless sky and were reflected by the still surface of the water.

The yacht struggled like a living thing to break free from the mysterious force that held her fast, while all about her there hung that faintly disgusting odor

of slime from the depths of the sea, an indistinctly musky odor as of something unclean.

At last the wireless began to crackle a frantic appeal for help, giving the details of what was happening on board the yacht. Hardly had the message finished when the yacht began to rock slightly, as from a faint ground swell.

II.

BUT, Theodore, old pet," said Davis amiably. "The fact that a plane won't loop the loop or make nose dives at ninety degrees doesn't make it hopeless as a battleplane."

He was affectionately expounding the good points of a monster seaplane drawn up in its hangar by the beach.

Davis wore the insignia of a flight commander of the aviation corps and the ribbons of half a dozen orders bestowed on him after the destruction of the Black Flyer, destroyed by Teddy Gerrod and himself some six months before.

Teddy Gerrod was in civilian clothes, but was earnestly, though cheerfully, disputing everything his friend said.

"A two-seater like the one we used six months ago," he pointed out, "could fly rings around this bus of yours, and with a decent shot at the machine gun could smash it in no time."

"Fly rings around it? Not noticeably," said Davis confidently. "Since our idea of platinum plating the cylinders everybody's doing it. Using picro gasoline, as you and I did, we get a hundred and eighty miles an hour from this 'bus' you're trying to disparage. And, furthermore, if you try to damage this particular ship with machine-gun bullets you're going to be disappointed."

"Armor?"

"Precisely. I admit cheerfully that you may know a lot about physics and cold bombs and liquid gases and such things, but when it comes to flying machines—my dear chap, you simply aren't there."

Gerrod laughed.

"Perhaps not. But I'd rather dance around in a more lively fashion in a little two-seater."

"And privately," admitted Davis, "so would I. The next war we have I'm going to arrange for you to be my machine gunner."

"Delighted," said Gerrod. "But what would Evelyn say?"

He was referring to his wife. Davis waved his hand.

"Oh, she'd say there aren't going to be any more wars."

"That reminds me," said Gerrod. "We want you down for the next week-end. No other guests."

Davis nodded abstractedly. A messenger was coming over to the hangar at double time.

"Thanks. I'll be glad to come. onder what this chap wants?"

The messenger came up, saluted, and handed Davis a yellow slip. Davis tore it open and read:

Steam yacht *Mariposita*, Alexander Morrison of New York, owner, reports position 33°11"N55°10"W, wants immediate assistance. Engines and hull perfect condition, not aground, no derelict or obstacle discoverable. Unable to move any direction. Sea calm. Only possible explanation has been seized by sea monster. Flt. Comm. Richard Davis ordered to make reconnaissance of situation in seaplane. Reported condition considered incredible, but no naval vessels in immediate vicinity. Flt. Comm. Richard Davis will make immediate investigation and report.

Davis whistled.

"Here's something pretty!" he remarked. "Take a look."

He handed the order to Gerrod and went quickly to the door leading into the workshop attached to the hangar.

In a few crisp sentences he had ordered the big plane prepared for an extended flight, with provisions and as much fuel as it would carry. He returned to find Gerrod thinking busily.

"May I come along on this trip?"

"It's against regulations, of course," said Davis, "but no one will kick if *you* go. You're privileged."

He cried an order or so at the workmen, who were now swarming over the machine.

Although the wireless message had been sent from the yacht after nightfall, the sun was barely setting on the coast, where the hangar was placed.

The vessel in distress was some thirty degrees east of the coast, and consequently the sun set two hours before it sank on the coastal line.

Gerrod phoned a hasty message to his wife and went to Davis' quarters, where he borrowed heavy flying clothes from Davis' wardrobe. The mechanics and helpers worked with desperate haste.

The aëroplane would be flying all night long, but it was desirable that *it* take off while there was yet some light. The long fuel tank was filled, and the motors run some ten or fifteen minutes, while critical ears listened for the faintest irregularity in their bellowing roar.

Two engineers and a junior pilot were to go with Davis in the big aircraft, and they were hastily summoned and told to prepare to leave in as short a time as possible.

It was hardly more than half an hour from the time the telegraphed order was received before Gerrod preceded Davis up the ladder and into the inclosed cabin of the seaplane.

The motors were cranked—two men tugging at the blade of each of the huge propellers—and the plane slid slowly down the ways and into the water.

Davis maneuvered carefully until he was clear of all possible entanglements. Then he gave the motors more gas and more. Their harsh bellow rose to a deafening sound, and the long, boatlike body began to surge through the waves with gradually increasing speed.

For a few yards the spray blew upon

and spattered the glass windows of the cabin. Then the planes began to exert their lifting power and the plane began to ride the waves instead of plowing through them.

The speed increased again, and suddenly the shocks of the waves beating on its under surface ceased. The plane rode upon air with a smooth and velvety motion that was sure and firm.

Davis rose gradually to five thousand feet and headed accurately to the east. A southerly wind, reported by wireless from a ship at sea, would carry him slightly to the south, and the sum of the two motions should bring him, by dawn, very close to the spot from which the yacht had sent out her wireless call.

Davis was not pushing the plane to its utmost. He would need light by which to descend, and had no intention of reaching the spot where the *Marisposita* was in distress until dawn.

From their altitude the ocean seemed only a dark, unfathomable mass below them. The stars twinkled down from the arch of the sky in all their myriads of sizes and tints.

There was no moon. Those in the closed car of the big seaplane could only see the star-strewn firmament above them and upon all sides, which sank down, and abruptly was not.

Save for the cessation of the star clusters, the horizon was invisible. The sea was obscure and mysterious, like some mighty chasm over which they flew precariously.

The dark wings of the plane stretched out from the sides of the body with a mighty sweep. The plane was over a hundred feet across, and with the powerful motors it possessed was capable of lifting an immense weight. Even now more than two tons of fuel were contained in the huge tanks in the tail.

Davis drove steadily on through the night for a long time. His face was intent and keen. He made little or no attempt to look out of the windows before him.

His eyes were fixed almost continuously upon the instruments before him: the altometer, which was a barometer graduated to read in feet and with means for correcting the indication by barometric readings from sea level; the inclinometer, which showed the angle at which the plane was traveling with regard to the earth's surface, and the compass.

The compass was one of the very latest developments of the gyroscopic compass and showed the true north without regard for magnetic deviations.

Davis felt out his machine thoroughly and then turned it over to his junior pilot. The younger man—and to be younger than Davis meant that he was very young indeed—slipped into the driver's seat, quickly ascertained the course, speed, and altitude, and settled back to continue Davis' task, while Davis curled himself up in a chair and went instantly to sleep.

It was chilly in the car, but Davis slept the sleep of the just, ignoring the roaring of the motors outside, which was only slightly muffled by the windows of the car.

Gerrod had gone to sleep some time before, and one of the two engineers was similarly curled up on the floor of the roomy and comfortable car.

Hours passed, while the big seaplane winged its way steadily through the night. It roared its way across the vast chasm of the dark ocean below, an incarnation of energy at which the placid stars looked down in mild surprise.

The exhausts roared continuously, the stays hummed musically, and the great wings cut through the air with resistless force.

Within the dark body of the plane three men slept peacefully, one sat up sleepily, listening to the motors, and prepared to wake into alertness at the slightest sign of irregularity in the action of any of them, and one man sat quietly at the controls, his eyes fixed on the instruments before him, lighted by tiny, hooded electric bulbs.

Course, due east. Altitude, five thousand feet. Speed, one hundred and fifteen miles. Twice during the night Davis woke and made sure that all was well.

In leaving the navigation of the machine to his assistant, he was not throwing the major part of the work on him. The work would come in the morning, when they found the yacht.

If there were anything in the talk of a sea monster having seized the yacht, Davis would need to be fresh for the search and possible battle that would follow.

He was taking the most sensible precaution possible. And, in any event, he had driven for the first four hours, during which the younger man had rested.

The first gray light began to appear in the east. The pilot of the plane had not looked away from his instruments for an hour, and not until a faint light outside called his attention to the approach of dawn did he think to glance through the windows.

A dimly white glow was showing as an irregular splotch toward the east. The pilot saw it and noticed something odd about its appearance, but did not stop to examine it closely.

He called Davis, as he had been ordered to do. Davis sat up, rubbed his eyes, and was thoroughly awake.

"All right?" he asked.

The pilot nodded.

"Sunrise," he said. "You said to call you."

"Right you are." Davis stood up and stretched his muscles. "Here, Teddy, wake up."

Gerrod stirred, and in a moment was awake. Davis deftly prepared coffee and sandwiches.

"Rescuers like ourselves need to be fed," he observed with a smile. "I wonder what is actually the matter with that person Morrison?"

"Millionaires are timid folk," Gerrod agreed. "I'll bet we've had a wild-goose chase."

"Funny, though," said Davis ruminatively. "People don't usually send out wild wireless messages like that. They probably ran into a big bunch of seaweed."

He bit into a sandwich. The two engineers, with complete democracy, were already eating. The man at the controls suddenly uttered an exclamation.

"What's the matter?" asked Davis quickly.

"Look out the window," said the pilot in a tone indicating that he could not believe his eyes.

Davis looked, and his mouth dropped partly open. Before them the white patch of light had turned golden and then yellow. A bank of clouds lay before them, behind which the sun was evidently hidden.

That had not caused Davis' exclamation, however. He was not amazed at anything he saw, but at the lack of something he did not see—the ocean. The cloud bank was illuminated by the sun. It covered half of the sky before them, *and below them!*

There was no ocean below them. There was no land below them. Above, the rapidly graying sky could be seen. Below them was rapidly graying sky! There was no horizon, there was no land, there was no sea.

There was only sky. They seemed to be alone in an illimitable firmament, a derelict in open space, adrift in some unthinkable ether in which there was no landing space or any solid thing except themselves.

Above them and below them, before them and behind them, on their right side and their left side was sky, and nothing but sky. There was not one bit of solid matter visible on either side, ahead or behind, up or down.

It was as if they had gone aloft, and while they flew the earth had been destroyed. Only the incredibility of such a catastrophe kept them from believing it instantly.

"Teddy," said Davis in a moment or two, trying to jest, though his voice was shaking, "you're our tame scientist. What's happened to our well-beloved earth? Has it gone off and left us in the lurch? Have we flown off into space?"

Gerrod was looking with all his eyes. He looked down into a blue bowl that was the exact counterpart of the dome above.

"Which way is down?" he asked quietly. "Is it that way, or that way?" He pointed over his head and at his feet. "Are we flying right side up, or upside down, or what?"

The plane banked sharply and sideslipped for a moment before it recovered.

"Steady!" said Davis to the man at the controls. "Steady——"

The machine banked again, then shot upward, stalled, and slipped on again.

"Straighten out!" said Davis sharply. "Up with the joy stick!"

"I don't know what's what," said the white-faced pilot desperately, obeying as he spoke. "Great God! What's happening now?"

The plane seemed to be standing on its tail, and the three men standing in in the car slid toward the rear. Davis seized a seat and clambered toward the controls. As he made his way toward the instruments the plane seemed to go mad.

It twisted, turned, stood upon its head and darted forward, and then seemed to be wallowing in the air. Davis seized the controls, and with his eye solely on the inclinometer worked madly for a moment. The plane stopped its antics and drove on steadily.

"It's like driving in a fog," he said over his shoulder. "All right back there now?"

"Yes." Gerrod was answering. "What happened?"

"With nothing to tell which was up and which down, we lost our level and couldn't find it again. I've flown upside down for five minutes, going through a cloud, and didn't know it until my barometer dropped upward. We're all right, but what's happened to the earth?"

Gerrod cautiously made his way to a point beside Davis, who was driving with his eyes glued to the instruments. That incredible vastness into which the machine seemed to be boring was appalling. They seemed to be speeding madly from nothingness into nothingness, with nothing below them and nothing above.

They were alone in a universe of air. Gerrod stared ahead at the cloud bank behind which the sun seemed to be hiding.

"There's the sun, all right. What's our barometer reading?"

"Eight thousand feet."

"Try dipping, by the inclinometer."

Davis did so. Though there was not the slightest change in the appearance of the sky that compassed them all about, the barometer quivered from eight thousand feet to seven, and then to six. Gerrod suddenly uttered an exclamation:

"The sun's coming out!"

The fiery disk of the sun peered slowly from behind the edge of the cloud bank.

"There's *another!*"

From the opposite side of the cloud bank a second sun could be seen, slowly appearing as had the first. The two suns swam away from the fringe of the cloud and glared at each other.

"I've got it!" Gerrod struck his knee with his hand. "What fools we are!"

"I'm glad we're only fools," said

Davis mildly. "I've been afraid we had gone mad. What's happened?"

"Why, the water," Gerrod said excitedly, "the water is perfectly calm and reflects like a mirror. We don't see the sky below us. We see the reflection of the sky. And that isn't a second sun," he pointed; "that's the reflection of the sun."

"Only, the water doesn't reflect like that," said Davis. "At least, not from straight overhead. Open a side window and look directly downward."

Gerrod did so, and exclaimed again: "I'm right, I tell you! Directly under us I can see the reflection of our plane, flying upside down."

Davis took a quick glance.

"I guess you are right, after all," he admitted, "but the water doesn't reflect like that normally. Something queer must have happened." He was silent a moment, while his eyes swept the distance before them keenly. "Here's another proof you're right. There's the yacht we're looking for."

Far away, its white hull turned to red gold by the first rays of the sun, they saw the yacht, motionless on the water. And in striking corroboration of Gerrod's hypothesis, they saw every line and every spar reflected in the water below.

Davis shifted his course to bear for the yacht and dipped down until he was only five hundred feet above the strange, mirrorlike surface of the sea. Below them they could see the spreading wings of their seaplane reflected from the still water.

They swept up to the yacht and circled above it. The junior pilot unshipped the tiny wireless set of the aeroplane, and it crackled busily for a few moments.

"All right to alight," he reported. "They say nothing has happened all night, but they're still unable to move."

The plane swept around the yacht in a wide circle, coming lower and lower.

It was quite impossible to judge where the surface of the water might be, but Davis kept his eye on the deck of the yacht, to get the level from that.

At last he made his decision. Being quite unable to tell exactly where the surface was, he could not land in the usual fashion. He slowed in mid-air until the machine was moving at the lowest speed at which it would keep aloft.

Then, by a jerk of the joy stick, he headed it upward at an angle it was unable to make at that speed. The result was that the machine stalled precisely like a motor car on an upgrade and, with next to no headway, "pancaked," sank vertically—downward.

"Sit tight!" he ordered as the plane sank.

Next moment every one of them clutched wildly at the nearest object to keep himself from falling. The plane had struck the surface, but instead of skimming forward, as its slight remaining headway made it try to do, it was brought to a sudden standstill as if by a mighty brake.

Only a miracle kept it from overturning. Davis opened a window of the cabin and shouted:

"Throw us a rope and haul us alongside!"

The men on the deck of the yacht heard him, and a rope came hurtling through the air, to fall across one of the wings. Davis scrambled out and made it fast. Those on the yacht hauled, but the plane did not move. Half a dozen men grasped the slender line and threw their united weight upon it. The rope broke with a snap.

"What the——" exclaimed Davis in astonishment.

A second rope was thrown. The captain of the yacht called from the bridge:

"Haul a heavy line to you and make that fast!"

Wondering, those on the seaplane obeyed. The sailors on the yacht made the other end of the stouter line fast to a capstan and manned it. Slowly and reluctantly the seaplane was drawn toward the white vessel.

It was Gerrod who looked behind them. Where the float of the seaplane had been he saw a deep depression in the surface of the water, which, as he watched, slowly filled.

"The sea is turned to jelly!" he exclaimed, and he was right.

They found the truth of the matter when they clambered on board the yacht. With the morning, the members of the crew were able to make a more thorough investigation of what had happened.

They lowered boats, and the boats stuck fast. When oars were dipped into the strangely whitened or silvered water the oars were drawn out coated with a sticky, silvery mass of a jellylike substance.

From the deck of the yacht the altered appearance of the sea was as remarkable as from the air. All of the ocean seemed to have been changed to a semisolid mass of silver.

The horizon had vanished or ended into the sky imperceptibly so it could not be distinguished. The captain discussed the matter with them.

"I've never seen anything like this before," he said perplexedly. "I've been on a ship that traveled two hundred miles on a milk sea, but never anything like this."

"What do you think it is?" asked Davis. "Something on the order of a milk sea?"

The captain nodded.

"You know a milk sea is caused by a multitude of little animals that color the water milky white. They're phosphorescent at night. This must be something on that order, only these cluster together until the water is made into a jelly. And they have a queer, slimy smell."

"They aren't phosphorescent," said Davis.

"No, of course not."

Nita Morrison had joined the little group. Her father was beside her, looking rather worried.

"Well," said Nita anxiously, "what's to be done? How are we going to get the yacht free?"

"I'm afraid we aren't," said Davis, smiling. "The telegraphed orders that brought me here told me simply to make an examination and make a report. My plane can't do anything for the yacht, of course."

"Then what——"

"I'll go back and report," Davis explained, "and they'll send boats to try to get in to you people. There doesn't seem to be any immediate danger, and at worst you can all be taken off by aëroplane, if we can rise again from that jelly mess."

Nita wrinkled her small nose.

"I know we aren't in danger," she said, "or at least I know it now, but are we going to have to stay here and smell that horrid smell until the government gets ready to rescue us?"

The odor of the jellylike animalcules was far from pleasant. It was an unclean scent, as of slime dredged from the bottom of the sea.

"Well-l," said Davis thoughtfully. "I dare say we can accommodate two more people. It isn't quite regular, but that's a detail."

"But the crew?" Morrison looked inquiringly at the captain of the yacht.

"Milk seas always break up, sir," said the captain. "I have no doubt this silver sea will break up as well. We can wait and see, and at worst we have our wireless."

"Then it's settled," said Nita joyfully. From sheer gratitude she smiled at Davis.

"Always providing we can get aloft again," said Davis.

"The propellers of the ship, sir," suggested the captain, "though they can't move the yacht, yet manage to thrash a fair-sized patch of this jelly into liquid."

"A good idea," said Davis heartily. "We'll haul the plane around to the stern, and you'll set your engines running."

In a very little time this was done. The great propellers of the yacht thrashed mightily, and a narrow patch of open water opened in the silver sea. The seaplane was laboriously hauled around to the stern of the yacht, and the party was lowered on board.

With some difficulty the motors were cranked again and the plane scuttled madly down the lane of water. With a quick jerk of the joy stick Davis lifted the plane from the water just as the open water ended and the silver sea began.

The big plane circled in the air, rising steadily as it circled, and at last headed for the west again, still flying in that incredible appearance of sky above and sky below, with the reflected sun glaring upward just as fiercely as the real sun beat down.

III.

NITA sat in the seat beside Davis' control chair, pointing to the instruments one by one.

"And that's the inclinometer," she repeated, "to tell you the angle at which the plane is climbing or descending. That's the barometer, which reads—let me see—seventy-four hundred feet. We're over a mile high, aren't we?"

"We are," said Davis, "though by the looks of things we are ten thousand miles from anywhere."

The silver sea was still beneath them, and they still seemed to be floating in a universe of air. Nita paid no attention.

"And that's the compass dial, and that—— What did you call it?"

"An anenometer," said Davis again, smiling. "It's the speedometer of the air—or the patent log, whichever you like to call it."

"You only have to learn one syllable," said Nita. "They all end in ometer. It's convenient that they're named like that."

Davis smiled.

"I never thought of that before, but it is convenient."

"But how do you balance the plane?" Nita demanded.

"In straightaway flight it balances itself," Davis explained. "It's one of the new inherently stable designs. For turning, the wing tips work automatically. We've a gyroscopic affair that attends to them."

Nita subsided for a moment, then demanded further information.

"What's that lever for? To change speeds?"

Davis laughed.

"Well, no. We haven't but one speed forward and no reverse——"

"You're making fun of me!"

"That's the joy stick," said Davis, chuckling. "We dive and climb with it. Pull it back and we go up Push it forward and we dive."

"Mmmmm," said Nita interestedly.

Her father took his cigar out of his mouth long enough to join in Davis' chuckle at Nita's absorbed air.

"Don't talk to the motorman, Nita," he said. "He may run past a switch."

Nita turned around and smiled at him. The car was rather crowded with seven people in it. Gerrod was looking curiously at a bit of the silvery jelly, with which he had filled several pails before leaving the yacht. He took a bit of it between his thumb and forefinger and rolled it back and forth speculatively.

It seemed faintly granular to the touch, but at the slightest pressure underwent a change that felt like crumbling, and was nothing but watery liquid.

"I'll bet anything you care to name," he said thoughtfully, "that this is just a mass of little animalcules with little silvery shells. The silvery shells would account for the reflection we see."

"The captain of my yacht," observed Morrison, "said that he thought it was like a milk sea. That's a mass of little animals that glow like phosphorus in the dark."

"Perhaps," said Gerrod meditatively. "I'd like to look at this stuff under a microscope."

"Oh some of it will go to the government chemists," said Morrison with a large air, "and they'll figure out a way to kill the little beasts. There's a cure for everything."

"Perhaps," said Gerrod.

The plane flew on steadily, Davis finding some amusement in gratifying Nita's suddenly aroused curiosity about every part of the seaplane. When her curiosity about the plane was satisfied, however, and she began to make inquiries about himself, Davis was much less comfortable.

He tried to be evasive, but she pinned him down, and was filled with excitement when she found that he was the same man who, as Lieutenant Davis, had flown the two-seated flying machine that had destroyed the Black Flyer and with it Varrhus' menace to the liberty of the world.

She tried very hard indeed to get him to tell her the story of that fight, but he blushed and said there was nothing to tell. It would be hard to say to what lengths she would have gone had not something outside the plane caught her attention.

"There's the horizon!" she exclaimed. "We've come to the edge of the silver sea, and from here on it's just the plain, good, old-fashioned ocean."

The line that marked the point where sea and sky joined was indeed visible, and a gradually widening bank of darker blue showed that the silver sea had indeed come to an end.

As the seaplane flew onward the darker, wave-tossed ocean came toward them and passed below, but blended so gradually with the jellied ocean that it was impossible to tell where the silver sea ended and blue water began. It was evident that the silver sea was still growing.

Then, for a long time, the seaplane sped onward over the blue waters, while Nita tried ingeniously to extract from Davis the details of the fight with the Black Flyer.

Davis was acutely uncomfortable, but nevertheless he felt strangely disappointed when the dim line of the coast appeared ahead. He hovered a moment to get his bearings, and then sped northward toward the aviation station to which he was attached.

Nita, too, seemed disappointed. She had enjoyed tormenting Davis, and he impressed her very favorably. After the plane had swooped downward and come to rest on the water a scant two hundred yards from the hangar in which it was kept, she turned to Davis.

"Well," she announced, "since I haven't been able to make you tell me what I want to know this time I warn you I shall make you tell me next time."

Davis smiled.

"May I hope there will be a next time?"

Nita smiled at him.

"I shall be angry if there isn't," she said demurely.

The launch came up to tow them ashore, and Davis was busy for a few moments, but before Nita and her father climbed into the motor car they had commandeered to take them to the city he found time to make a more definite arrangement and learned he was expected to call at the Morrison mansion "very, very soon."

The description of the silver sea aroused but little attention in the newspapers. A particularly pathetic murder trial was filling the public mind, and small paragraphs in obscure corners, describing the plight of the yacht, contained all that the public learned.

Every one seemed to dismiss the matter as a natural curiosity which would probably disappear in a little while. An aggregation of tiny animalcules which had clustered together until they formed a jellylike mass did not promise much in the way of drama, and our newspapers are essentially purveyors of drama.

Obscure notices in the shipping news, however, told of the growth of the silvery patch, and at last there was a ripple of interest caused by the news that the crew of the yacht claimed that the jellylike creatures were clambering up the sides of the ship and threatening to overwhelm the vessel.

Seaplanes put out from shore and took the crew off, and then public interest lapsed again. An almost uneventful accident to the yacht of a steamship magnate was good material for society news, but not for the pages devoted to items of general interest.

To Davis, however, anything pertaining to Nita had become of surpassing interest. He practically haunted her house, and Nita seemed not at all unwilling to have him there. Her father was as cordial as Nita at first, but later began to watch Davis' frequent appearances with something of disquiet.

Davis was sufficiently well known from his Black Flyer episode to be considered socially eligible anywhere, but he was far from rich. He had consistently refused the numerous offers from motion-picture companies and book publishers to enact or relate his exploits, though the acceptance of any of those offers would have meant a small fortune.

Davis was instinctively unwilling to commercialize his reputation. Morrison could find no fault with him personally, but he could not quite believe that Davis' increasingly evident infatuation for Nita was real—that he was actually more than a fortune hunter.

The shipping news continued to give sparsely phrased notice of the location and size of the silver sea. Two naval vessels were assigned to observe it, reporting regularly to the meteorological bureau.

It must be recorded to the credit of that much-maligned department of weather forecasts and maritime information that it was probably the first body to see the possibilities of evil that lay in the silver sea.

It had quantities of the silvery mass of animalcules brought to it for study, and set its scientists to work to try and find a means of destroying them. Fish would not eat them. They seemed to possess some repulsive taste that led all the carnivorous fishes to avoid them at all costs. Placed in an aquarium with a huge sea bass that was exceptional for its voracity, the sea bass avoided the tiny, jellylike mass as it would the plague.

The silver globule of jelly multiplied in size, and still the sea bass avoided it, retreating to the farthest corners of its tank to keep from coming in contact with the little animalcules. At last the aquarium was a shimmering mass of silvery, sticky jelly, and the bass was unable to retreat farther. It was found gasping out its life outside the tank, having leaped from the water to escape from the omnipresent silver menace.

The silver sea grew in size. It began to figure in the news again, when passengers on the transatlantic liners noticed that the steamers were taking a route much farther to the north than was customary. It was admitted at the steamship offices that the detour was made for the purpose of avoiding the now vast silver sea.

Late in March people along the eastern coast of the United States began to remark upon a musklike, slimy smell that was faintly discernible in the sea breeze. A steamer, going from New York to Bermuda, reported seeing a patch of the silvery jelly only three hundred miles from the eastern coast. The disagreeable, musklike smell was strong and noticeable.

The newspapers woke to the possibilities of the silver sea. Ships could not navigate in its jellied waters, nor fish swim. It covered thousands of square miles now, and was growing with an ominous steadiness that foreboded ill.

The seaside resorts along the Atlantic coast were practically abandoned. Tourists would not stay where that foul, slimy, musklike scent was borne to them constantly on the sea breeze. The patches that were the forerunners of the silver sea itself appeared along the coast. At last the horizon disappeared.

The silver sea had come close, indeed, to the shore. Then every newspaper burst into huge headlines. For the different papers they were phrased differently, but the burden of each, displayed in the largest possible type, was

COASTAL NAVIGATION STOPPED!

America's Communication With the World Cut Off By Silver Sea.—Harbor Blocked from Maine to Georgia.—Authorities Helpless to Fight Silver Menace.

Then the world began to be afraid.

IV.

DAVIS was unwontedly silent as Gerrod drove him out to the tiny cottage to which he had been invited.

"Evelyn's expecting you," said Gerrod as the little motor car wound up a hill between banks of fragrant trees that line the road on either side. "We rather looked for you last week, but you wired, you know."

"Yes, I know," said Davis gloomily. "I went somewhere else."

Gerrod smiled. Davis was sufficiently his friend to break an engagement and admit it frankly, and besides Gerrod more than suspected where Davis had gone.

"How is Miss Morrison?" he asked.

"She's all right," said Davis still more gloomily. "But damn her father!"

Gerrod raised his eyebrows and said nothing until they arrived at the cottage with the little built-on laboratory. Evelyn came out at the sound of the motor and shook hands with Davis.

"We were beginning to be afraid the competition was too much for us," she said with a smile.

Davis looked at her and tried to smile in return, but the result was a dismal failure.

"Oh, I'm glad to be here now," he said dolefully.

Gerrod made a sign to Evelyn not to refer to Nita again until he could speak to her, and helped Davis carry his two suit cases into the house.

"Your usual room, of course," he said cheerfully. "Dinner is served at the same hour as before, and you can do just as you please until you feel like coming down. I'll be in the laboratory."

Davis went heavily upstairs, his usually cheerful face suffused with gloom. Evelyn glanced at Gerrod.

"What's the matter?" she asked quickly. "Has he quarreled with Nita?"

Gerrod shook his head, smiling.

"I asked about her, and he answered by damning her father. I suspect he has run against a little paternal opposition."

Evelyn's eyes twinkled and she laughed.

"Best thing in the world for them,"

she declared. "When he's ripe for it I'll take a hand. Nita Morrison was a classmate of mine in college and I know her well enough to help along."

Gerrod chuckled.

"He was like a funeral all the way out. We'll let him alone until he wants to talk, and then you can advise him all you like. But just now I want to get back at those small animals that are raising so much particular Cain."

He went into the laboratory and slipped off his coat. He had a number of test tubes full of the silvery animalcules and was examining them under all sorts of test conditions to determine their rate of growth and multiplication.

He was rather hopeful that he would be able to demonstrate that after a certain period they would—because of their extremely close packing together —either die from inability to obtain nourishment or be poisoned from their own secretions.

He was looking curiously at a phenomenon that always puzzled him when Davis came into the room. His expression was that of a man utterly without hope.

"What've you got there?" he asked listlessly.

"Some of our silvery little pets," said Gerrod cheerfully. "I'm studying them in their native lair. Have you looked at them under a microscope?"

"No."

Gerrod smeared a bit of the silvery mess on a glass slide and put it under a microscope. He worked busily for a moment or so, adjusting the focus, and then waved Davis toward the eyepiece.

"They're funny little beasts. Look them over."

Davis looked uninterestedly, but in a moment even his gloom was lightened by the interest of the sight he saw. The enlargement of the microscope was so great that only a few of the tiny animals were visible, but each of them was clearly and brilliantly outlined.

They were little jellylike creatures, roughly spherical in shape, with their bodies protected by almost infinitely thin, silicious shells that possessed a silvery luster. From dozens of holes in the fragile shells protruded fat, jellylike tentacles that waved and moved restlessly, forever in search of food.

Under the microscope the shells were partly transparent, and within the jellylike body inside the shell could be seen a single dark spot.

"That blotch in their shells seems to be the nucleus, or else their stomach. I can't quite make out if they're one-celled animals like amœbæ, or if they're really complex creatures."

"Rum little beggars," said Davis without removing his gaze from the eyepiece. "They're separate animals, anyway. Odd that they should make a jellylike mass."

"Move the slide about a little," suggested Gerrod. "You'll see how they do that. You're looking at individuals now. Sometimes—and I think it's when food gets scarce—they twine their tentacles together and the tentacles actually seem to join, as if they were welded into one. In fact, as far as nourishment goes, they do seem to become a single organism. That's when they're so noticeably jellylike."

Davis watched them curiously for a few moments, and then straightened up. He moved restlessly about the room.

"The funny thing," said Gerrod cheerfully, ignoring Davis' evident gloom, "is that they seem to be able to move about. See this test tube? They've climbed up the sides of the glass until they almost reach the top.'

"I know," said Davis uninterestedly. "When we took the crew off that yacht they showed us where the jellylike mass seemed to be slowly creeping up the sides of the ship. Looked like exaggerated capillary action."

Gerrod listened with a thoughtful frown.

"I wonder——" he began, but Davis turned to him suddenly.

"Look here, Teddy, I'm in a mess. I want your advice."

Gerrod put down his test tubes and sat on one of the tables in the laboratory, swinging his legs and preparing to be properly sympathetic with Davis' plight, which he already knew perfectly well.

"Go ahead."

"It's like this," said Davis reluctantly. "I liked Nita tremendously the first time I saw her, and she seemed to like me, too. I called on her, and she seemed to like me better. And I kept on calling. I must have pretty well infested her house, but she didn't seem to mind it, you know——"

Gerrod nodded sympathetically.

"I know."

"Well," said Davis savagely, "I found out I was pretty badly gone on her, and last week I was just getting up the nerve to propose—and I *know* she wouldn't have been displeased—when that infernal father of hers began to interfere."

"He asked you quite pleasantly," said Gerrod with a faint smile, "exactly why it was that you were coming around so often."

"And I told him," said Davis, suddenly plunged into gloom again. "It was rather premature, because I hadn't talked to Nita, but I told her father I wanted to marry her, and I loved her and all that."

"And her father," suggested Gerrod, "asked what your prospects were, and the rest of it. It takes a millionaire to be really middle class."

"That's what he did," admitted Davis miserably. "I told him my pay amounted to something, and I had about two or three thousand a year income from stocks and bonds and such things, and he laughed at me. Told me how

much Nita cost him. Damn it, I don't care about how much Nita pays for dresses!"

"We men are deuced impractical," said Gerrod with a smile. "But what was her father's next move?"

"Oh"—Davis looked as if he could weep—"he was polite and all that, and said how much he liked me and such rot. Then he asked me not to see Nita again until I was in a position to offer her the things she had been raised to expect. You see the idea. He put it that he didn't want Nita to learn to care for me unless it were possible for me to make her happy and so on. It made me sick."

"I know." Gerrod nodded again. "He practically put you on honor to preserve Nita's happiness at the cost of your own."

"Damn him, yes!" Davis clenched his fists. "But Nita does care something about me. I know she does!"

Gerrod watched Davis with eyes from which he had banished every trace of a twinkle, until Davis had calmed down a little. Then he said cheerfully:

"Let's go ask Evelyn about it. His late majesty, King Solomon, once remarked that women should have the wisdom of the serpent, among other qualifications. We'll see if Evelyn comes up to Solomon's specifications."

He led the morose Davis out of the room.

The great American public became alarmed and rather resentful when its harbors were blocked by the silvery jelly. It felt, though, that the Silver Menace was more of an imposition on the part of mother nature than anything else.

Passenger traffic with Europe could be maintained by air, and freight could probably be routed through the far Northern seas to which the Silver Menace had not yet penetrated. The public considered it an annoyance, and those who were accustomed to go to the seashore for their vacations were disgusted that the mountains would receive them that summer.

They were quite sure they did not want to go down where that slimy, disgusting, musklike odor from the stilly, silent silver sea would make their days unpleasant and the nights unendurable. Fresh fish, too, became almost prohibitive in price, as the fishing fleets were immured in the harbors that had now become mirrorlike masses of the disgusting jelly.

The public resented those things, but was not really afraid. It was not until nearly a week, after the closing of the harbors had passed that the world was informed of the Silver Menace's real threat to the human race, and began to feel little shivers of horror-stricken apprehension when it looked at the morning papers.

The news was at first passed about in swift, furtive rumors, but half believed as something too horrible to be credited. The rumors grew, however, and became more circumstantial, but the newspapers remained silent.

It is known now that the government had ordered that no hint of the new danger be allowed to become public, while its scientists worked night and day to discover a means of combating this silent, relentless threat that menaced our whole existence. Whispers flew about and became magnified, but the facts themselves could not be magnified.

At last the government could keep silence no longer, and the world was informed of the true malignity of the Silver Menace. The silvery jelly had reached the American coasts, invaded and conquered the harbors, and was even then rapidly solidifying the rivers, but its threat did not end there.

Just as it had crept up the sides of Gerrod's test tubes, and as it had overwhelmed the yacht, now it crept up the beaches. Slowly and inexorably the slimy masses of jelly crept above the water line. The beaches were buried below thick blankets of sticky, shimmering animalcules and still the menace grew.

They overwhelmed all obstacles placed in their path. The whole green, fertile earth was threatened with burial beneath a mantle of slimy, silvery, glistening horror!

TO BE CONCLUDED

in the September 15th number of THE THRILL BOOK. Order a copy from your news dealer at once so you will not miss the end of this amazing yarn.

THE PICK-UP
By Charlotte Mish

SHE was standing on the corner, watching the passers-by wistfully. She shivered a little in the chill breeze that was blowing around the corner.

As I came nearer, and her gaze fell upon me, her brown eyes seemed to plead with me. I hesitated for a moment—and passed on. When I reached the next corner I turned. I saw her still standing in the same place, and I retraced my steps until I stood close beside her again. I noticed that she was very thin and her eyes looked hungry. She shivered again pitifully, and her eyes smiled a wan invitation.

Well, I took her to a restaurant and got her something to eat. She ate ravenously, probably her first good meal for days.

Then I called a cab and we climbed inside. As she sat beside me on the seat I cautiously put my arm around her. She did not resist, but snuggled closer. I took her home.

Yes, she is an Airedale, and will make an excellent watchdog.

Cobra Girl
Rothvin Wallace

CHAPTER I.

THE BREATH OF ADVENTURE.

TO begin, it is well to tell you that the adventure opened in San Francisco, on the day that I met Chilling Manners at the golf club.

I had known Manners for all of ten years—since I was a harum-scarum lad of twenty—but I never had known much about him, except that he always had plenty of money, and, at the times when he appeared in Frisco, as if he had been dropped from the clouds, mingled freely with the best social circles.

About thirty-five, a six-footer, fat, jolly, educated, cultured, elegant, widely-traveled—a most agreeable companion was Manners. A mystery, though, he always had been to me.

Even his name suggested mystery. I suspected that it was assumed, but for no tangible reason, except that it fitted him so illy. He had anything but chilling manners. In fact, there was a no more warm-hearted, warm-blooded, approachable fellow of my acquaintance.

Manners had a habit, however, that had puzzled me on more than one occasion. It was a habit of disappearing. To-day, one would be chatting pleasantly with the fellow over a highball; and to-morrow he would be gone—none of his acquaintances knew where.

Three months, maybe six months, later, he would drop in on us as casually as though he had left us only on the day before.

The day to which I referred in the beginning came after one of Manners' usual disappearances. As I said, I was at the golf club, sitting on the broad veranda, hating myself and the world in general, and giving desultory attention to both the blue, heaving Pacific, and to a game in progress on the links.

"Hello, Farnworth," greeted a cheerful voice at my elbow.

Not recognizing the voice, and fearing another club bore, I was not keen to respond. My feelings changed, though, when I glanced up and saw Manners. There he was, smiling, fastidiously groomed, looking not a day older than when I had seen him last

"Hello yourself," I said casually.

I knew Manners well enough not to

make a fuss over him, though I confess I was glad to see him. I arose and extended my hand, which he clasped eagerly.

"Quite as well as I look," he returned easily. "And you?"

"Splendid. Sit down and have something?"

"Thanks." Manners dropped into a chair beside mine, while I motioned to a waiter. "We were talking about your try at the thousand-yard butts," he added, "when Thompson broke in with that rave about his new motor. How did you make out?"

I looked at the man in amazement, and it took me several seconds to get the drift of his conversation. He was taking up a talk that we had had five months before, just where we had been interrupted. He had remembered, while I, having nothing to do but to lounge about and laze my time away, had all but forgotten.

"Oh," I said, "I won the trophy."

"Good. Wish I could shoot like you."

"Practice," I said laconically. I was just vain enough to be pleased by his commendation, because marksmanship was my pet hobby.

"I haven't the patience, even if I had the eye," replied Manners. "How are you with a pistol?"

"Rather good," I boasted smugly. "Only yesterday I split a penny at thirty paces."

"Some shooting, that," he lauded. "Ever get you anything?"

"Only a few tin cups and brass medals, and the satisfaction of shooting a little straighter than the other fellow."

We entered, then, into a casual conversation. Finally, after I told him that I was somewhat bored by the life I was leading, he asked if I would like to join the Mystery Club.

"The Mystery Club!" I repeated. "What, pray, is the Mystery Club?"

"Come and find out," he replied. "We're having a dinner to-night at the Renaissance, and I should be glad to have you. Of course, you won't be expected to scuttle a ship or rob a train right away." Manners paused and laughed sincerely—one of his old-time, well modulated outbursts. "And you will have the compensation of a good dinner, in the company of a bunch of real men."

I was sure, now, that Manners had been having a bit of fun at my expense, and the thought caused me a flash of anger. Well, I decided to make him pay for it. I would take him at his word, and let him stand the cost of dinner.

And it wouldn't be a cheap dinner, either, at the Renaissance, one of the newest and most expensive cafés in the city. Besides, I was sure that I would be quite safe there, whether dining with the Mystery Club or a delegation from the Mothers' Union.

"You're on," I said simply.

"You mean that you will join?" There was a note of eagerness in his voice that was not lost on me.

"I mean that I'll have dinner with you," I hedged.

"Good!" He slapped me jovially on the back. "You'll have the time of your life."

In the weeks to come, I remembered that remark, and agreed with him—that I was to have the time of my life. I did not know then, of course, that the simple fact of accepting a dinner invitation was destined nearly to cost me my life; I could not dream of the strange and far-reaching consequences that were to ensue.

Promptly at eight o'clock, having, in the meantime, togged myself in evening clothes, I presented myself at the Renaissance. Manners, similarly attired, was there ahead of me.

"We're a little early," he said. "The chief is not here yet."

"The chief?" I interrogated.

"Old Snakes."

"Eh?" Manners, I feared, had suddenly taken leave of his senses.

"I beg your pardon," he laughed. "I was referring to Runyon—Professor John Wagamore Runyon, to be exact."

"Why the snakes, then?" I demanded.

"He eats 'em alive."

"What?" My amazement was growing apace.

"The snakes." Then, catching sight of my puzzled expression: "Oh, no, not literally; he's just a snake man—an ophiologist."

"A—what?"

"An ophiologist—that is, a person who is a student of the science of serpents—is up on their habits and modes of life. It's a branch of herpetology, you know."

"No, I didn't know," I confessed frankly, "but I'll take your word for it. What's he the chief of?"

"The Mystery Club. Ah! Here he is now."

Before I had time to question further, I was being presented to Professor John Wagamore Runyon. And as I looked at him, an involuntary shudder passed through me.

He seemed to me quite to fit his strange calling, for the touch of his hand was cold and clammy, like the touch of a snake, and his close-set, bead-like black eyes gleamed with the sinister cunning of a serpent.

And yet he was a man of striking appearance—such a man as would attract attention in any crowd. Tall and straight and spare he was, with a sharp, bony, leathery face, as yellow as old parchment, and topped by the most wonderful suite of hair that I ever have seen on a man. It was as white as new snow, and tumbled about his collar in thick ringlets.

"Mr. Farnworth," he repeated, acknowledging the introduction with a most courtly, old-world bow. And then, turning to Manners: "Another?"

Manners shook his head, and left me puzzled at the by-play.

"Well, in any event, I am more than glad to know Mr. Farnworth," said Runyon.

His voice, soft and silken and insidious as the soughing of a gentle night wind, got on my nerves. Instinctively, I did not like him; but I put this down as a silly notion, perhaps due to my aversion to the crawling things that, according to Manners, were his stock in trade.

I could see that he was appraising me through those piercing pin points of pupils that seemed to swim in ink, and, in turn, I tried to sum up his character.

He had the nose and chin of determination, yet his mouth was weak; there was strength written in his face, as against a certain furtive fear; he had, too, cunning and stealth and ability and intelligence.

As to his age, though, I could not have hazarded a guess. He certainly was forty, yet he might have been eighty. I remember how my thoughts ran then:

"So, this is an ophiologist. Henceforth, I shall think of an ophiologist as a man who looks like a snake."

"Suppose we go in," interposed Manners. "The boys are waiting."

Runyon bowed his acquiescence, and signified for me to precede him. It impressed me then that even his movements were soft and sinuous, like those of a snake.

Manners nodded to an obsequious flunkey, who conducted us to a floor above that on which the main café was situated, and to the door of a private suite. We entered, then, a reception room, where we were hailed vociferously by upwards of a dozen men.

They were mostly young men, but a few grayheads were represented. And a more heterogeneous assemblage I never had seen forgather for a dinner.

At once I tried to identify them by nationality.

There were an Irishman, two Spaniards, a large, fat Chinese, a German.

They were unlike any men I ever had known—like a horde of buccaneers, attired in hired evening clothes.

While I was still appraising them, and wondering how I might get away without offending them, the door of an adjoining room opened, and a servitor announced that dinner was served. And I was mighty glad to see that waiter. He seemed at least a link between me and the safeguards of civilization that I had left on the floor below.

While oysters were being served, I morbidly counted the diners, only to receive a shock of superstitious dread.

There were thirteen of them:

"Yes," murmured Runyon, with a queer, snakelike movement of his hands, "you are the thirteenth man!"

With what devilish form of conscience had he interpreted my thoughts, I wondered. That fact gave me a thrill of horror. The others, however, seemed not to mind, if I might be permitted to judge from the babel of merry voices about me.

And such a conversation, or conversations, I should say, that were going on! Across the table from me, the Irishman was telling how he had scuttled a junk in the China Sea; one of the Spaniards was boasting of the assassination, by himself, of a Polynesian king; the German and Chinaman were comparing notes on the massacre of a band of natives on the Gold Coast.

What sort of men were these that Manners had brought me among? I wondered. Surely, they were the worst type of murderers, judging them by their own admissions. But were they actually murderers, as they said?

For a moment, I suspected Manners of hoaxing me. I looked at him from the side of my eye. He was smiling.

I was sure, then, that he was playing a scurvy trick on me.

He had framed this thing up, for my especial benefit, just to give me a scare. Well, in that case, I should play my part differently. I could assume quite as much bravado as any of the crew about me.

"Mr. Farnworth, professor," said Manners presently, "has a hobby for guns and pistols. He's one of the best shots in the country."

"The best," I boasted, keeping my face straight.

By and by, after I had had several glasses of wine, I began to feel more at ease with my unusual companions. In fact, I was rather enjoying the experience. This state of equanimity, however, was not to last long.

I had been noticing, from time to time, an unaccountable movement inside Runyon's coat, on the side next me. And now there was a more violent agitation.

Marveling, I watched with fascinated eyes, until, to my horror, I saw a forked tongue dart across the edge of the black table cloth, followed by a flat, hideous head. I cried out in horror and sprang from the table, knocking my chair over with a crash.

"What is it?" Runyon asked the question, while I again was the object of general attention. "Oh! I see," he added, and laughed. "My little pet tired of her nest, and was taking a bit of exercise. She wouldn't hurt you, Mr. Farnworth."

And then Runyon gathered the slimy thing up and laid its nasty head caressingly against his cheek. It was a rattler, I noted, all of four feet long.

The men about the table laughed at the incident, but I remained standing until the professor had returned the snake to his pocket. I sat down, then, not wishing to be accounted altogether a coward.

Several times my glass was refilled,

and I went on with my dinner. When I again looked about the board I saw that the men were leaving noiselessly, one by one. Only Manners, Runyon, myself and the Irishman remained, and he, in a moment, went the way of the others.

And then, for the first time, I felt a strange dizziness. I was ill at the stomach, too, and I wanted air. I was not drunk, I knew, but I could not account otherwise for my condition.

"Fill up your glass," said Manners, "and drink to the success of the Mystery Club."

His voice seemed hollow and far away. I tried to speak, but I had no command of words. I attempted to wave him away, but my efforts were vain. I saw the amber wine flow into my glass; and then I was conscious of the evil eyes of Runyon burning me with their very blackness.

"Drink, Mr. Farnworth, to the success of the Mystery Club," I heard him say.

Feebly, unsteadily, I raised my glass —that is, I tried to raise it. At the same time, I was conscious that Manners was leaving the room—leaving me alone with the awful Runyon.

I tried to call to him, to implore him not to leave me; but he was gone, before I could utter a word. The glass fell from my fingers, and I felt a chill, as the wine wet me to the skin. Then came oblivion.

CHAPTER II.

THE MORNING AFTER.

IF you ever have had a hard night with the boys, you will understand how I felt when the spark of consciousness again quickened my mind. My mouth and throat were parched, my head aching, my eyes smarting, my body sore and tired. I pressed my hot, heavy hands to my throbbing temples, and made the usual vow: "Never again!"

I tried to think, then, of where I had been and what had happened to me. I remembered the golf club, and my meeting with Manners. Those incidents were quite clear. I had a vague recollection of meeting a strange man at the Renaissance Café, and of dining with a ferocious band of cutthroat adventurers.

It was all very puzzling, and I sat up to think it over. I became conscious, then, of a feeling of nausea. Also, I discovered that I was in bed. And then I became aware that my bed was moving—undulating from end to end, with an occasional lurch sidewise. Or was it the condition of my head that made me fancy this?

I stepped painfully to the floor—and shrank backward, as the wall seemed to lurch forward to strike me. Or perhaps I lurched toward the wall. I was not quite sure.

I was determined, however, to glimpse the outlook from the small, round window at the head of my bunk —the only window with which the room was provided. Four staggering steps carried me thither, and I gasped with amazement at what I saw.

Below, beyond, all about me spread the billowing, sunkissed reaches of the Pacific! I was at sea!

This, then, accounted for the antics of my berth and room. I was in a tiny stateroom, and, judging by its mean equipment, the ship that was bearing me away was not by any means of the first rating.

Suddenly, the vessel lurched, and hurled me violently against the wall. A great shadow swept out across the water. When I got my legs again, it dawned on me that I was on a sailing vessel. The lean of the ship, as it went about on a new tack, and the shadow cast by the mainsail, told me that.

It is difficult to describe the emotions that surged through me at that moment. Fright, wonderment, anger, commingled, and threw me into a panic. I had no recollection of coming aboard this ship. I did not want to go to sea.

I wanted to be back in San Francisco —not because I had anything in particular to do, other than to lounge about the clubs and pay court to Elsie Vandman, but because such a life suited my sybaritic taste much better than the annoyances of ocean travel.

Yes, it was rather important that I should press my suit with Elsie—not because I bore any great love for her, but because it was high time that I had married and settled down, and, as her family and mine had been friends for years, it was quite safe and sane for us to form a matrimonial union.

Elsie, who was near my own age and had a fortune in her own right, felt much the same way about it. So, you see, we had arrived at that time when marriage becomes a convenience rather than a pleasure.

But now—well, I could not figure why I was on this ship, nor where I was going. In any event, though, whether I had come aboard in a moment of mental aberration, or had been brought at the will of another, a substantial check might induce the captain to put about and return me to San Francisco.

That was the most sensible thought that had entered my distressed mind. I decided to put it into execution at once. But I was in my underclothes! My outer garments had disappeared, and I had a hesitancy about venturing on deck in my present attire.

Can you fancy my mental state, standing there on a strange vessel in my underclothes, going I knew not where?

In the midst of my cogitations, I heard a rusty key scrape in the lock, and the next moment the door was flung open. Need I tell you that I was filled with delight, when I saw that the huge figure of Chilling Manners filled the aperture?

"What, ho!" he cried gayly.

I noticed that he was clad roughly in coarse trousers and a gray flannel shirt, open at the throat.

"What was the idea of locking me in, and making it necessary for me to yell at all?" I demanded. Now that I had to deal with Manners, I was afraid no longer. I could afford to assert myself, I thought.

"Well, say, Farnworth," he drawled, and treated me to a queer smile; "if you could have seen yourself when you came in here, you would be wondering why we did not put you in irons and a straightjacket."

"What do you mean?"

"Why, my boy, you were a bit—er —violent, I may say. If I might venture an opinion, you had been drinking a little too much."

Manners' tone seemed patronizing, and I did not particularly like it. His full, round, good-natured face, however, was beaming with kindly humor.

"How, then, did I manage to get aboard this ship?"

"Don't you remember? But of course you don't. Well, naturally, your friends—Professor Runyon and I— carried you aboard. You remember, of course, joining the Mystery Club, and after——"

"Joining the Mystery Club!" I cried indignantly. "I remember nothing of the sort, Manners."

"But you did, old man, before you went under. Let me show you."

Manners drew a wallet from his back pocket, and extracted a sheet of paper therefrom, which he handed to me. You may fancy my horrified amazement when I read these lines:

Agreement entered into this day between John Wagamore Runyon, party of the first part, and Douglas Farnworth, party of the second part: The said party of the second part hereby becomes a voluntary member of the Mystery Club, and, for a period of six months from date, places his services absolutely at the command of the said party of the first part, in consideration whereof he shall receive food and lodging, and, if it be his good fortune to return to San Francisco, the sum of one thousand dollars in cash. This money has been deposited in trust in his name, and, should he fail to return for any reason, it will revert to Chilling Manners.

This strange agreement was dated in San Francisco, on the day before, and bore the signatures of Runyon and myself, with that of Manners as a witness.

With the document still in my hand, I sank weakly on the side of my bunk, and stared stupidly at Manners.

CHAPTER III.

INTO THE EASTERN SEAS.

TO state my situation briefly, I was virtually a prisoner on the schooner *Bonaventure,* in company with these men whom I had met at the Mystery Club dinner.

I scarcely need describe the succeeding six weeks, except to say that the interval enabled me to establish friendships with several members of the crew. We passed to the south of the Hawaiian group, but did not sight land. Indeed, though, I had become almost reconciled to my lot.

At the end of six weeks, I was as brown as any white man aboard the ship, due to exposure to the tropical sun, and my muscles were as hard as steel, for which fact I had to thank my voluntary descent to plebeian labor.

In truth, I had come to enjoy the novelty of my experience, just as Manners had said I might, and I thought no more of taking a bucket and mop and swabbing the deck than I had about a game of golf or billiards, two months previously.

Also, I had taken example from the other men—went barefoot, and allowed my beard to grow. I smiled more than once when I glanced into the small mirror that adorned my cabin, and wondered, should a vote be taken, if I would not be adjudged as desperate a looking

adventurer as there was on the *Bonaventure.*

During these days, too, I managed to filch an automatic pistol from the master's cabin, and acquired a certain tolerance for Runyon, though I still disliked him heartily. Also, I made at least one firm friendship.

This was with a Chinaman, who called himself Ling Wah. A splendid, stalwart fellow was Ling, who, despite the usual Oriental inscrutability and reserve, had traveled the world over, possessed a fund of information, an excellent education and spoke English quite well. I was considerably puzzled about Ling. He did not take me fully into his confidence, but, from casual remarks that he made, I surmised that he had descended from the nobility of China, but, for some reason, was an exile from his native land.

Try as I might, I could not even guess the potential purposes of the Mystery Club. If Manners knew, he would not tell me; but always was he agreeable, and tolerant regarding my frequent questioning.

Well, I reasoned at length, I would know some time the real object of the Mystery Club, and the purpose of the *Bonaventure's* cruise into far eastern waters. And really, I had grown keen for the adventure, even though, at times, my mind did stray to far-off Frisco.

I was worried, particularly, about Elsie Vandman, and what she must think of me. The day that we had fixed tentatively for our wedding had passed, and I had been unable even to get word to her.

Would she think that I was dead, or would she believe that I had willfully deserted, at the brink of the altar? These thoughts gave me many moments of mental disease. However, I was helpless, and worry would avail me nothing.

Time passed monotonously, and,

from the distance that we had covered, without seeming to be any nearer our destination, it began to look to me as if the strange old ophiologist who was directing our destinies intended to circumnavigate the globe.

Day piled on day, while we plowed through the South China Sea, skirted the Philippines and made for the Strait of Malacca. Past Singapore and the peaks of Sumatra we raced, and on into the Bay of Bengal.

One morning I awoke to find India, where the Eastern Ghats frame the shore, looming before us. Northward we continued, until we reached Yanaon and the mouth of the Godavari. And when the *Bonaventure* swept into the river, I felt that we were approaching the end of our long cruise.

CHAPTER IV.

A GIRL AND A FIGHT.

WE progressed slowly up the Godavari, and, as the river narrowed, I sensed an atmosphere of suppressed excitement aboard the *Bonaventure*. It seemed to pervade the entire company, and even I, though unable to attribute any real cause, suffered from the tense strain.

I thought, perhaps, that it might be due to overstrained nerves, the result of the long, trying voyage, and the uncertainty of the outcome.

For the first time since we had left San Francisco, Old Snakes frequented the deck and made himself agreeable to the men. He ordered liberal portions of whisky for their consumption, and, almost at any hour of the day or night, he might be found nervously pacing from the forecastle to after deck, eagerly scanning the shore line.

By the time we had traversed two hundred miles of the stream, I felt that I was quite well versed in jungle lore.

Late one afternoon I was puzzled by the actions of Runyon and Manners.

They had been standing in the peak for an hour, conversing more or less excitedly, and in low tones, while they bent, from time to time, over a sheet of paper that the professor held. Was this the treasure map, I wondered.

"There it is!" I heard Manners cry excitedly, pointing shoreward.

The *Bonaventure,* now under her auxiliary power, swung around in a half circle, and headed directly for what appeared to be an abandoned temple on the bank. And then, to my surprise, I noticed a small wharf, its timers rotted with age. To this we made the ship fast.

Came the swift, tropical night, and a huge, brilliantly luminous moon transmuted the yellow stream into molten silver. Runyon had served whisky in plenty among the men, and several already had become maudlin, while others engaged in bickerings and minor quarrels over their cards.

To me, this seemed almost a desecration of the heavenly night—a foul blot on the tranquil scene, wherein the spice-laden breezes bore to our ears a weird medley from the throats of the jungle creatures.

For this reason, perhaps, I was strangely ill at ease. Or was it a premonition of something that was about to happen? I did not know. I was conscious only of a sense of apprehension and lonesomeness.

I strolled off alone, and, leaning against the rail, tried to penetrate the jungle tangle, wondering, the while, what lay beyond that had brought the *Bonaventure* and her men to this far distance.

What was that? Was I suffering from delusion? Had I seen a ghost, or had my strained nerves merely caused my fancy to conjure a human form up there, peering over one of the balconies of the temple?

As surely as I was standing there, on the deck of the *Bonaventure,* I had seen the face and shoulders of a woman! It was but a momentary glance that I had had of her, but the impression had been vivid, the image lingered.

She was clothed in white, and a mass of black hair tumbled over one of the most radiantly beautiful faces that it ever had been my good fortune to behold. Her eyes, black as midnight, seemed to have caught the starlight, and to match even the low-hanging moon for brilliance.

My impulse was to explore the temple—to find the girl who had looked at me. She was not a native, I knew; and perhaps she needed help. I don't remember, ever before, of having set out deliberately to befriend strange women; but there was something so appealing in this face that I had seen—an element of pathos that stirred me to the depths.

At home, I know, I should not have bothered; but here, out in the jungle wilds, a certain spirit of romance seemed to possess me. I was quite mad, I know. However, I recked not of consequences when I leaped from the rail of the *Bonaventure* to the little wharf by the side of the temple.

First, I went to the end of the small dock, and skirted the temple, hoping that I might find an entrance on the land side. There was a door, but it was locked.

A window, higher up, attracted my attention. It was paneless, and, by a flying leap, I thought that I might be able to reach the sill. I stepped back a few paces, ran and jumped. My fingers closed on the window sill above, and it was an easy matter to draw my body through the aperture.

I found myself in a square, empty room, on the floor of which reposed the dust of ages. I could feel the dust, soft under my feet, and could see it in the moonlight, which poured through a window opposite.

The light of the moon also disclosed a flight of steep, narrow stairs, in one corner. I listened intently. There was no sound, save the boisterous laughter of the men on the *Bonaventure,* and the cries of the jungle habitants.

I confess, now, that I was possessed of a strange, creepy sensation, and that cold fear clutched at my stomach—a fear of the unknown and the intangible. However, I was determined to see again the girl who had peered at me on the deck of the schooner.

There was some sense of safety in the automatic that I carried—the pistol that I had filched from the gun room of the *Bonaventure.* I drew it reverently from my pocket, examined it, and found that it was ready for service. With the weapon in my hand, then, I mounted the stairs.

I crept up cautiously, and found myself in another room, the exact counterpart of the one below, except that it was smaller. It, also, was empty. I went to the window on the river side, and looked down on the schooner; but this was not the level from which the girl had gazed down at us.

It required another urge to my courage to mount the next flight of stairs, but I accomplished it. Both relief and disappointment mingled when I saw that the third room also was deserted. It was from the balcony outside the window of this room, however, that she had looked down. But she was gone! Gone where? I wondered.

I made an examination of the dusty floor, and I was rewarded by the sight of tiny footprints. I followed them, down to the floor on which I had entered. There they marked a course to a staircase that led downward.

I took the stairs, which brought me to the water level. And there the trail ended. The moisture of the river had dispelled the dust, and there was no evidence of the girl's passage, nor was there anything to indicate her presence.

I went to the door—the one that I had found locked on the outside—and thought that it might have a spring lock, which would enable her to have gained egress; but it was bolted on the inside!

This puzzled me sorely. How had the girl escaped from the place? Had she leaped from the window by which I had entered? That must be it, I reasoned. Well, I should have to leave by the same means.

I returned to the first room. A small, glittering object, that had escaped my notice before, now attracted my attention. I seized it eagerly from the floor.

It was a gold heart, such as one gives to a baby, and there was a little ring at the top, through which to pass a chain. But more than the heart itself was the name that was engraved thereon. I read it by the light of the moon—Zadra!

What a strange name, I thought. Was it the name of the girl whom I had been seeking in the temple? Had she lost this bauble? In any event, the name interested me. I felt that I should like to know the one who was called Zadra.

As I had entered the temple, so I departed. I turned toward the jungle, and, to my amazement, discovered a road that led inland. It had become weed-grown through disuse, but there remained the clearly defined trail of a corduroy highway.

Curiosity impelled me to follow this road into the dark depths of the jungle. And for some reason I had ceased to be afraid. I had a notion that the girl had traversed this same road only a few minutes before, and, if it were safe for her, it also held no terrors for me.

Then, too, a woman could not proceed very far through the jungle at night. Her home must be near, and, without doubt, I should find it after a short walk.

For half an hour I continued onward, pausing now and then in the hope of hearing fleeing footsteps ahead of me. I was mad, of course, but I did not realize it at the time.

My reward came, presently, when I arrived at a pretentious clearing, in the center of which a gleaming white palace reared its stately domes and minarets. I paused, in a maze of bewilderment.

My first thought was that I was looking upon a mirage. I could not conceive that so magnificent a structure could actually exist here in the midst of the jungle. A light, though, flared suddenly from one of the many windows, and convinced me that the mansion before me was real.

And then I saw a white apparition, with a mass of black hair that fell about her shoulders, emerge from a smaller structure, at the left, and stand silhouetted in the moonlight.

"Zadra!"

The name leaped to my lips unbidden, and, intuitively, I started forward. But at the same moment, I heard a slight commotion in the undergrowth at my side. I turned, just in time to avoid the full force of a blow that had been aimed at my head with a club.

It struck me glancingly, and I reeled, in a daze. I raised my pistol swiftly and fired at my assailant; but the same instant, I became conscious that other dark forms were emerging from the shadows and pressing close around me.

I realized that I was in for a fight; but I had not rallied from the effect of the first blow, when a cloth was thrown over my head, and I felt the pressure of many hands. I was helpless, and did not know, even, if my first and only shot had taken effect.

Incidents, however, were crowding each other in rapid succession. Scarcely had I been made prisoner, when I heard a woman's voice. She spoke in a strange tongue, but I fancied, from her tone, that she was giving a sharp command to my captors.

And somehow, I caught the impression that it was a friendly voice. In any event, the hands of my captors fell away, and the cloth with which I had been so deftly bound was snatched from my head. I grasped my pistol, which lay undisturbed on the ground, and scrambled to my feet.

"Come," commanded a sweet voice at my side.

It was she—the girl whom I had seen in the temple on the Godavari.

CHAPTER V.

THE GARDEN OF THE SNAKES.

STILL in a daze, I stood frozen to the spot. All had happened so swiftly that I scarcely could believe that it was real, and that I, prosaic clubman, was the center of such an adventure. I half expected Ling to come to my bunk and give me a shaking, and tell me that it was time for me to take the watch.

The revolver that I still held in my hand was genuine enough, however, and they were no dream men—those dark objects that were scampering to cover in the underbrush.

Nor was the girl at my side a mere figment of morbid imagination. I looked across the moonlit space toward the palace. Still it stood there, in stately grandeur. No, I was not dreaming.

"Come," repeated the girl.

She blessed me with a radiant smile, and I took a step toward her, mechanically slipping the pistol into my pocket as I did.

"Anywhere—with you," I replied gallantly.

To an observer, I fancy that I must have appeared foolish. But to me, at that moment, things seemed to be just as they should be. I did not know that it was moon madness or the Spirit of Romance that had taken possession of me.

And then she stretched out a white, slender hand, and took hold of mine. I confess I was thrilled by the soft pressure of her fingers—that my heart began to pound madly at the contact with her. Friend or foe, I was prepared to go wherever she might lead me.

Was she friend or foe, I asked myself. She had performed one friendly act—and yet, might she not have dispersed my enemies, only to find an easier way of disposing of me? Who was she? I wondered. What was she doing here? What was the secret of her power over the natives who had attacked me? What, indeed, was the secret of her power over me? For she did exercise a strange, compelling power that I could not fathom.

At the moment, I would have done anything that she had commanded. I would have fought for her, died for her. I had an insane desire to fall at her small, sandaled feet, and kiss the hem of her flowing white robe.

Like a goddess she stood there in the moonlight, head upflung, eyes gleaming, lips parted, hair flowing in a mass of ringlets over her perfect shoulders.

"Come," she said again; and again she pressed my fingers, and started in the direction of the palace.

I followed by her side, without protest. I knew not where she was taking me, nor for what purpose; but I enjoyed a thrill of gladness, just to be there with her.

She was tall—only a head shorter than I—and young. I guessed her age at twenty, and, in a quick appraisement, took her to be an American.

"Where are we going?" I ventured to ask presently.

"To the temple," she responded; and the voice of her filled my ears as with sweet music.

"To the temple!" I gasped. "But this is not the direction. I just left there, and——"

"You do not know the temple to

which I am taking you," she interrupted.

"Why do you wish to take me there?" I inquired.

"Because I like you," was her frank avowal.

"Because you like me?" Her ingenuousness rather startled me; and I wondered, indeed, what she could find in me to admire—a bronzed, disheveled, half-dressed specimen of humanity, who might have been a buccaneer, from his appearance—or worse.

"Because I do not wish you to be killed," she supplemented.

"Who—who wants to kill me?" I gasped.

"Evidently, the Naib of Nagpur. His men were the ones who attacked you."

"Why? I had done nothing to them."

"They thought you might, I suppose. You had trespassed on the Naib's territory, and—well, they probably fancied that you might be of some service to me."

"I wish that I might be of service to you," I hastened. "Please tell me how I may serve you."

"I shall; but hurry, now."

I had seen nothing alarming, heard nothing; but she seemed to have sensed a lurking danger, and began to cast apprehensive glances over one shoulder.

I grasped my pistol tightly, and determined not to be taken again by surprise. There were ten shots there—nine, now, since I had discharged one—and, with my skill as a marksman, I felt able to cope with half a dozen men, at least—provided I saw them coming.

"We shall be quite safe in the temple," she panted. She had quickened her pace almost to a run, and was breathing heavily.

"Let us go back to my ship," I suggested. "We would be safe there."

"Oh, no, no! Not now. They would be lying in wait for us in the jungle."

We had been skirting the edge of the clearing, and now were passing the palace. But the girl went on, until, before us, rose a small pagoda on the edge of the jungle. She slackened her pace, then, and gave a sigh of relief.

"The temple," she said. "We are safe now."

The building, I noticed, was surrounded by a small garden. She bade me pause at the outer gate. I followed her instructions, of course, but I was puzzled by the appearance of half a dozen dark objects that lay in the path to the pagoda. In the deceptive light of the moon, they looked like rope ends; but a creepy, intuitive sensation told me that they were not.

"What are those things in the walk?" I asked.

"Snakes—cobras," she replied unconcernedly. "You wait here for a moment."

I shrank back in alarm. Since childhood I had heard and read stories of the deadliness of the cobra-di-capello, the sacred snake of India. I knew that thousands every year paid toll with their lives to the venom of the reptile's bite.

Even though I stood twenty feet from the sluggish, crawling monsters, and held a pistol in my hand. I was seized with a thrill of horror. The girl stepped into the garden, but I seized her roughly by the shoulders and drew her back.

"Where are you going?" I gasped. "Don't you know it is certain death to enter there?"

She laughed lightly, and looked at me with level, luminous eyes.

"And don't you know that it is more certain death not to go?" she retorted. "Look behind you."

I turned quickly, and, to my further alarm, saw several skulking forms making their way in our direction. They were not more than two hundred yards distant. We were between two fires, but I preferred to risk a battle with the men than with the snakes.

Just then a noise in the garden drew my attention in that direction.

"You vixen!" cried the girl.

"My God!" I cried, and started forward.

The blood seemed to congeal in my veins, for there, in the middle of the path, stood the girl. She was holding one of the cobras in her hands, by neck and tail, shaking it as she might have shaken a mischievous puppy. And then she raised the thing above her head and flung it from her into the bushes.

All the other snakes but one had disappeared, and, before I could reach her, she had darted at this one with her bare hands, seized it back of the head and thrown it from the path.

"Good God!" I gasped. "Why did you do that?"

"So that you might enter in safety," she replied simply.

"So that I might enter in safety!" I repeated in amazement. "It was wonderful of you to take such a desperate chance for me. Why should you?"

"I took no chance."

"But suppose you had been bitten?" I insisted. "You would have been dead——"

"I was bitten," she interrupted: "but I am not going to die, my dear friend. See?"

To my horror, she held up for my inspection a slender, white hand, on the back of which appeared two drops of blood. I was dazed, stupefied. I had no idea of an antidote, and felt that this fair creature had sacrificed her life to do me a service.

"But—but," I stammered stupidly, "the bite of a cobra is certain death, and——"

"To you, of course; but not to me," she interposed. "Look!" She put her dainty mouth over the punctures that that snake had made, then brushed her other hand lightly across the slight wound. "Now it is all over," she smiled.

"All over?" I repeated.

"Quite all over. I have been bitten many times, but this is the first in a long while. That fellow was savage, and didn't seem to like being disturbed. But the snakes, you see, are my friends—the best friends I ever have known in the world."

As she ceased speaking, a dreamy, far-away look came into her eyes, and I fancied that a great tear dropped to her cheek.

"One must have some friends," she went on in a melodious monotone, "and the snakes have been my friends—my preservers."

It seemed uncanny to me that a woman thus should be bitten by the most venomous snake that lives, and suffer no ill effect from it.

"Are you a woman of the flesh or a goddess?" I demanded.

"They call me the Daughter of Siva," she laughed. "But come; let us go inside. Do you not see that our enemies are approaching?"

I followed the graceful sweep of her arm, and noted that half a dozen crouching forms were lurking on the edge of the jungle only a few yards distant.

"Let me lead the way," she suggested, "to be sure that none of my friends gets his fangs into you."

I permitted her to go ahead. For myself, I preferred to guard our retreat against a rush from the natives. None was attempted, however, and, a moment later, we entered the temple.

CHAPTER VI.

"THE DAUGHTER OF SIVA."

I SCARCELY can describe my first impression of the temple. As the door opened, I was struck by the strong odor of burning sandalwood. It was being offered as incense, no doubt, but, in the gloom of the ante-chamber in which I found myself, I could not see where it was being used, nor who was burning it.

From a door on the far side of the room, however, came a faint, red glow, and I fancied that the smoke was coming from within.

"Be quiet," admonished my charming guide; "Nana may be at prayer."

"Nana?" I interrogated.

"My faithful old servant—God bless her," she explained.

In this heathen temple, I was surprised to hear the girl mention the name of God, but I ventured no comment on the anomaly.

"You left the door open," I reminded her apprehensively.

"Yes, of course. The moonlight will enable us to see better."

"But those fellows will follow us," I said.

"Not in here." She laughed softly. "They fear me, they respect their gods —and they both fear and respect the cobras."

I shuddered at her reference to the cobras. I, too, feared them, though I did not respect them.

"Let us see if Nana is within," she said.

She walked softly toward the interior door, while I stalked closely at her heels. And what I saw, looking over her shoulder, contributed still further to the uncanny dread that had obsessed me ever since I had seen what the girl was pleased to call her "friends" in the garden.

Before me, on a low altar, were three hideous idols—a large one in the center, and a smaller one on each side. A huge vessel, at the base of the altar, belched forth clouds of aromatic smoke, while, from the ceiling, hung a massive lamp, that shed a spectral, red glow over the place. On the floor, with head pressed to a small mat, was the form of a thin, old woman.

"Nana," said the girl softly. "As I thought, she is at prayer."

"Praying to those horrible images?" I remarked scornfully.

"No, she prays only to Vishnu, the preserver, on the left. But the Naib, you see, is a reformed Brahman; he worships the trinity. So in his private temple he has Brahma in the center, with Vishnu on one side and Siva, the destroyer, on the other."

"And you are the daughter of Siva," I mused.

"I said that that was what they called me." She turned away, that Nana's worship might not be interrupted, and laughed softly. "It is well, too, that the natives so have dubbed me."

"Why?" I asked vacuously.

"Because their superstition has been my preservation. You see, they are amazed by the way I handle the snakes."

"Ugh! The snakes!" I interrupted, with an involuntary shudder, and looked apprehensively about, to see that none was crawling at my feet.

The girl paused, while I waited for her to go on with her story.

"Please continue—Zadra," I begged at length.

"Zadra!" she flashed, and gave me a queer look.

"Pardon me," I hastened. "The name slipped from my lips inadvertently. I should have said Miss Zadra."

"No, that is not it," she returned. "I should like you to call me just Zadra. But I am curious to know how you learned my name."

"I found a locket in the temple by the river, after you were there to-night, and the name was engraved on it."

"Oh!" A look of infinite relief spread over her face, while she thanked me profusely for its return. "My father gave it to me when I was a child," she explained. "And so," she added, "you were in the old house, too. How did you get in?"

"Leaped through a window."

"And why?"

"To find you."

"Why did you wish to find me?"

"Because I—oh, I don't know why," I faltered. "I saw you looking over the balcony, and I was lonesome, I guess—and perhaps a bit curious. Why were you there?"

"I?" She seemed startled by my question. "Why, I go there often—always in the hope that I might find a ship with a kindly master, who will take me away from this terrible place. But always they are afraid of the Naib of Nagpur."

"I'm sure the master of the *Bonaventure* will not be afraid of him," I assured her.

"You think not? Oh, I hope that you are right." There was eagerness in her voice, and she touched me with one of her slender hands. I noticed, then, that she was trembling.

"How did you get in and out of the old house by the river?" I inquired irrelevantly.

"I suppose that is a secret," she replied. "However, I don't mind telling you. There is an underground passage from the palace. It was designed to give the Naib a means of escape to the river in case of attack. But it has fallen into decay, and the ground has caved in just beyond the far side of the clearing. So, you see, it is easy for me to reach the river without being observed."

"That's splendid!" I cried. "We'll hike right back there and be safely aboard the *Bonaventure* within half an hour."

"Not to-night," she said quietly. "Come here and look."

She led me to the door, being careful to keep out of the stream of moonshine that was pouring in, and swung her arm significantly in a graceful semicircle. A dozen skulking forms, only half concealed by the shadows of tree and building, told me that my foes were closing in.

"But you said they were afraid of you," I reminded her; "and I can take care of myself."

"It's of no use to be foolhardy," she protested; and, on second thought, I agreed with her.

"What shall we do, then?" I asked.

"Wait until morning, and, in the meantime, get some sleep."

That, indeed, was a sensible suggestion, though I did not fancy that I should do much sleeping. My nerves were too much on edge, my surroundings too strange, my apprehension too great.

The self-assurance of Zadra, however, gave me confidence and courage. And, queerly enough, I had no feeling of fear, despite the enemies who lurked in the shadows outside.

We strolled back toward the inner door, Zadra and I, and again I peered into the weird dimness of the cella. The old woman was rising from her prayers, and delivering herself of a final incarnation.

The huge censer was emitting, now, only a thin spiral of smoke. The red light that swung above had grown more dim, but, in the uncertain glow, I now discerned a double row of squat, round baskets, ranged alongside one of the walls.

"What are they?" I asked.

"Takra."

"Takra?" I repeated. "I don't understand——"

"Baskets for the snakes," she informed me.

Again I shuddered at mention of those deadly cobras. I was not afraid of human foes, but even a thought of the snakes filled me with dread. I wondered if the baskets were filled with the filthy reptiles, but did not question further.

The old woman now was coming forward, and at sight of me stopped in alarm. Zadra said something to her in her native tongue, however, then turned to me.

"You did not tell me your name," she said.

"Pardon me—Douglas Farnworth," I hastened.

Again she spoke to Nana, and the emaciated old hag bent me a grave curtsy. Then, in a strange jargon, she addressed Zadra.

"She says," Zadra informed me, "that she can make you comfortable for the night in one of the upper rooms. She is a dear, kindly old soul, is Nana —fetches my food from the palace, and always seems to anticipate my wishes."

"Fetches your food from the palace?" I repeated, in amazement. "I thought that you and the Naib were enemies——"

"Ah, no, not exactly enemies," she interrupted. "He would like to have me in the palace, but he is afraid of me, and it is well. He, like the others, has the superstitious belief that I am the daughter of Siva. But come; Nana is ready to conduct you. Good night and pleasant dreams—Douglas."

She hesitated but the fraction of a second over the use of my given name; and I confess that the way she said it, the dainty little twist of pronunciation that was distinctly her own, not only surprised but delighted me. And then her starlike eyes, her full red lips joined in a smile of rare witchery, while her hand went out to meet mine.

"Good night, Zadra," I said simply, then turned to follow my aged conductor.

As I made my way up the dark, winding stairs that occupied one corner of the outer room, I could see Zadra, still standing in the moonlight, following me with her eyes. And the heart of me seemed to swell and beat faster, and I was filled with a strange, intangible tenderness for the lonely girl below. Then I lay down and slept.

CHAPTER VII.

THE NAIB MAKES AN ATTACK.

I HEARD the pounding on my door. I leaped from my couch, to find the sun high in the heavens, and the welcome light of day pouring in at my open window My visitor was Nana, with a tray of steaming, native viands, which she proffered for my breakfast.

Before I had finished eating, there came another knock at my door, and, to my delight, the one who sought admission was Zadra.

"I hope you spent a comfortable night," was her greeting.

I assured her that I had.

"To-day, I hope, we may be able to reach your ship," she said abruptly.

"To-day we *shall* reach my ship," I assured her emphatically.

"I don't know—Douglas; I fear that they are on the watch."

"Suppose they are?" I demanded boldly. "You say that they will not disturb you, and I am quite sure that I can fight my way to the river."

"Ah, no; I would not permit you to do that. You do not know the Naib of Nagpur."

"Why are you here, apparently so much in his power?" I ventured to ask.

"He took me."

"Took you? How?"

"I was with my father on a scientific expedition in India, when the Naib saw and seemed to admire me. His men abducted me, one night, and brought me to this place. The Naib wanted me, he said, for his wife; but I loathed the creature, of course.

"And one day in the palace, when he attempted to put his hands on me, I seized a cobra with which a faker was amusing the household, and flung it in the Naib's face. It did not bite him, but the commotion that I caused enabled me to escape.

"As I left the palace, I conceived an idea, and grabbed a tubri that was lying in one of the halls, doubtless the property of the faker. I——"

"A tubri?" I inquired.

"An instrument that they use for charming the snakes," she explained. "With this, I went into the jungle and played to the snakes; and they came to me, Douglas—several of them. I knew that they could not injure me—that I was immune from their bite—and they were my only defense, my only protection. For the Hindu, you know, has a reverence for the cobra, and a wholesome fear of its bite.

"With three of the snakes in my hand, I came here into the little private temple of the Naib. Of course, his henchmen sought me, with the intent to take me back to the palace; but I threatened them with the snakes, and they retreated. And then, much to my advantage, one of the superstitious natives conceived the notion that I was the daughter of their god, Siva, because of my ability to handle their sacred cobras without injury to myself. I suppose it did startle them." She paused and laughed.

"But, really there is nothing at all supernatural about it. Fortunately for me, though, the Naib became convinced that there was, and provided me with Nana and permitted me to dwell here in his temple. But I have waited—oh, how I have waited for my deliverance!"

"And it has come at last," I assured her.

I know that my heart must have been in my eyes as I looked across the table at her, and the glance that she gave me back caused me a strange, palpitating thrill, such as I never had known before.

"But tell me," I urged, "how it is that you are able to handle those reptiles, and why their venom has no effect on you."

Zadra's musical laugh rang out and charmed me, even as the shrill music of her tubri must have charmed the

crawling creatures that had been her protectors. There was a strange fascination about the girl that I could not define. She was so sweet, so innocent, and yet so sophisticated.

I confess, to my shame, that I had forgotten Elsie Vandman and my promise to wed her. Zadra had made me forget all else, in the short space of a dozen brief hours; but the moon madness, maybe, still had hold of me.

No, I don't mean that I was exactly in love with Zadra. I had not defined my feeling for her as such; but—well, I did not know. I was in too great a turmoil to know exactly how I did feel. The soft voice of the girl across the table from me interrupted my thoughts.

"I suppose it does seem spooky to you, how I manage to handle the cobras," she was saying; "but, indeed, it is very simple. You see, my father— listen!"

Stopping her speech abruptly, she arose excitedly and sprang to the window. I turned and watched her, and, to my ears, came the shrill tones of a strange musical instrument. I got up, and followed her to the window, to find her staring, wide-eyed, at something that was happening in the direction of the palace. And then my gaze focused on an amazing sight.

At the entrance to the small garden that surrounded the temple, three men were sitting, tailor fashion, on the ground. One was playing an elongated fife, that, from Zadra's description, I took to be a tubri; a second was beating with his hands on a kind of drum, and a third was attending to half a dozen low, round baskets, that, the night before in the cella, Zadra had designated as takra.

Nor was this all that I saw. One by one, a trail of brown-backed cobras was wriggling in the direction of the music; one by one, the man who had charge of the baskets was making them captive. I could not understand the strange scene, until I heard Zadra's amazed expression.

"They are stealing my snakes!" she cried.

"Sealing your snakes?" I repeated stupidly.

"Don't you see what they are doing? The Naib has got some snake charmers to imprison my snakes—my weapons of defense. Oh, if he gets those snakes we are lost! Maybe he has awakened from his belief that I am the daughter of Siva; maybe, now, he is afraid only of the snakes, and he is taking them away from me, so that his men may storm the temple and make captives of me and you."

"He won't!" I said determinedly.

I had made a sudden resolve. It would be quite easy for me to pick the snake charmers off with my automatic, and preserve all the weapons that would avail in our prospective fight to gain our liberty. With this intention in view, I drew my pistol.

"What are you going to do?" cried Zadra.

"Shoot 'em," I said briefly.

"Oh! Can you?"

I caught eagerly at the note of pleasure in her voice, and was encouraged. I had thought, at first, that she might not approve of this manner of ridding ourselves of the snake charmers. I raised my pistol quickly, and aimed at the man with the tubri; but I dropped it just as quickly, as two scores of other actors appeared on the scene.

Suddenly, from the far edge of the clearing, a volley of shots rang out. A body of natives, armed with long, old-fashioned guns, came into view, pursued by a band of white men.

They came from the jungle, along the corduroy road that I had traversed the night before, and, evidently, the fight had been a running one, with the natives in retreat, but battling stubbornly over every inch of ground.

Even at the distance that separated us, I recognized the pursuers.

"The men from the *Bonaventure!*" I gasped.

"Your friends?" breathed Zadra.

"Yes, thank God!" I said fervently. "And I must get out there and help them."

"No!"

Her tone was commanding, and, as I attempted to turn from the window, she laid a firm had on my arm. But the look in her eyes, more than her weak physical restraint, caused me to pause.

"I must, Zadra," I said quietly.

"But I—I need you," she trembled.

Another volley, followed by scattered shots, came from the warring factions. I hesitated, not quite determined wherein lay my duty. And my thoughts raced quickly. Here was a girl, alone, defenseless. Outside were my comrades; and in my hand was an automatic pistol, that contained nine shots. With my skill as a marksman, those nine shots might turn the tide of battle for them.

As I was thinking thus, Zadra turned to the window. Suddenly I saw her face go white, and her arms, with an impulsive, involuntary movement, went out.

"Praise God, it is—it is he!" she cried.

CHAPTER VIII.
THE BATTLE OF THE COBRAS.

I ADMIT that I was excited and eager to be down there in the clearing, in the midst of the fray. For here, I reasoned, must be the treasure that Runyon brought his strange crew across the long reaches of the Pacific to find.

The Naib of Nagpur, no doubt, was the keeper of that treasure; and the Naib of Nagpur had been the oppressor of the girl who stood by my side. Thus, if only I could take part in the fight, I might serve a double purpose. But the secondary purpose, I realized, had become the first. I wanted to avenge the wrongs that had been done to Zadra.

I had not heard all of her story, but I knew enough to make me ache to have the Naib by the throat, or, preferably, to plant a bullet in his yellow body.

"It is—it is!" repeated Zadra excitedly.

"Is what?" I demanded.

"My father!" she breathed.

"Your father—who?" I gasped.

"The man there with the white hair. Oh, some one must have told him! He has come to rescue me! And last night I did not know that he was on that vessel at the dock!"

"Whom do you mean—Professor Runyon?" I questioned amazedly.

"Yes—Professor Runyon—he is my father!"

The girl's breath was coming in gasps; her face was pale; her small fists were clenched. And I confess that I was in a maze of bewilderment. So, Zadra was his daughter.

My first realization of the fact left me rather sick at heart, because I had no great regard for Runyon. I thought that he was not trustworthy, and I was quite convinced that he had done me a great injustice in bringing me to this far clime in the condition that I was in that last night in San Francisco.

However, if Zadra were his daughter, I must reconstruct my opinion of him; for Zadra, I was forced to admit to myself, was a superlative woman.

And then, there was another point to consider. Doubtless, it was due to the training of the queer old ophiologist that she was able to handle the deadly cobras as she did; and the cobras not only had saved her honor, but perhaps her life, as well. That, indeed, was something for which to thank the old man.

Another thought struck me with the force of a great revelation. Runyon had told us that there would be no treasure to divide. Was the treasure

he had in mind this beautiful daughter? Was it to rescue her that he had brought us across the seas? If so, I decided, the prize was well worth all the trouble.

"Look!" cried Zadra. "The natives have taken shelter behind a corner of the palace. Our men are at a disadvantage."

I saw, at a glance, the truth of her words. The natives now were strongly entrenched behind a wing of the building, in such a manner that they could command the further approach of the enemy, without exposing themselves to fire.

And my comrades, I noted, were in a quandary. I saw Runyon and Manners hold a brief consultation, then lead their men in a hasty retreat to the jungle. Doubtless, they had a flank movement in mind, but they were concealed by the undergrowth, and I could not observe their further progress.

I had intended, just at that moment, to open fire on the natives from my position, in the hope of driving them from cover; but the fear that my comrades were leaving, and would not back up my attack, in which event the natives might storm and take the temple, deterred me. I was thinking, too, of the protection of Zadra.

While I was wondering what next would happen, a side door of the palace opened, and there isued forth a tall, richly-attired native, at the head of a dozen followers. They went to join the others, who had repulsed the men from the *Bonaventure*.

"That's the Naib!" informed Zadra.

As I looked at the fellow, I thought how easy it would be to plant a bullet in his heart; but I refrained, for the reason that had deterred me before. I noticed, however, that the snake charmers had deserted their baskets, and had run to join the native forces at the palace.

"I can help!" cried Zadra suddenly.

"How?" I demanded eagerly.

"Wait—watch!" she replied.

She was gone in a moment, hastening down the spiral staircase to the floor below. I cast a final glance from the window, saw that the natives still held their position, found no trace of the men from the *Bonaventure,* and followed Zadra.

When I reached the lower level, I found Nana carrying the takra from the cella into the front room, while Zadra, squatting in the doorway, was making weird music on a tubri.

While I sensed her purpose, I gained ocular proof of it when I saw, to my horror, a procession of cobras start from the bushes in the garden and circle about her, with heads erect, hoods flattened, bodies swaying to the rythmical beat of the music.

I drew back with instinctive dread, and stood, shivering, like a rat in a corner, while Zadra grasped the snakes, one by one, and thrust them into the baskets. And when a basket was full of its wriggling contents, Zadra would clamp the lid down and Nana carry it to the far end of the room.

I was amazed, fascinated, by the number of snakes that came in answer to the call, and the manner in which they were made captive. It was all so startlingly weird, so unusual, so appallingly uncanny, that I stood like one in a trance until it had been finished. Indeed, I, like the hundred or more snakes that had been imprisoned, had been charmed by the shrill incantation of Zadra's tubri.

She arose, finally, flushed, radiant, smiling. And I stood there still, like a stupid fool, looking at her with open-mouthed wonderment.

"Now I am prepared for them," she said lightly.

"You are a witch," I murmured.

"Oh, no, Douglas," she laughed. "Only I am a very practical person."

"And how," I inquired, "are you prepared for them?"

"I am, to them, the daughter of Siva," she replied enigmatically. "They are afraid of me, and they have a certain reverence for the cobra; and you shall see. Wait!"

It was a comfort to my overwrought nerves that we did not have long to wait, for, a few minutes later, the shooting was resumed in a desultory way. I could see nothing from the lower door, so hastened to the window above, accompanied by Zadra.

Then I saw that the men from the schooner had planted at least one telling shot. The natives, at the direction of the Naib, were removing an inert member of their force from the field of battle, while the others were covering the operation with an attack on a point in the jungle to the left of the temple.

I could see nothing of my comrades, however, though an occasional report of a rifle told me that they were attempting sniping from the concealment of a grove of blackwood. The natives, however, merely shifted their position slightly, so that they were protected by another angle of the wall.

To me, though, they were in plain view, and open to my fire.

I did not acquaint Zadra with my intention, but raised my pistol quickly and took a snapshot at a big native who was looking for an opening to fire at my comrades in the jungle. To my satisfaction, I saw him crumple up like a limp rag and fall at the feet of his amazed companions.

"Fine shot," commented Zadra nonchalantly.

I was both pleased and gratified at her attitude. I had feared that she might be startled and protest against my participation in the battle. But as she took the matter so philosophically, I prepared to repeat my performance. The natives, however, were not intending that I should.

After their first surprise at being attacked from this new quarter had passed, they took cognizance of my presence in the temple, and a rain of bullets came hurtling through the window and buried themselves in the ceiling. I had just time to drag Zadra to the floor, and to take refuge myself behind the casement.

When I ventured again to peer forth, I found the natives streaking across the intervening space, in the direction of the temple. Only half a dozen still were within the range of my pistol, and, by the time I had got two of them, the others were safe.

And the men from the *Bonaventure*, so far as I could see, had not attempted to come to my rescue. Had they not heard my shot? But of course, they could not know that it was I. It seemed, indeed, that I was doomed, for the aroused natives, within two minutes, would be pouring into the temple, and overpower me by sheer force of numbers. I had not reckoned, however, on the courage and resourcefulness of Zadra.

"Wait here!" she cried. "Let me take care of them."

Though I was in no mood to allow the girl to fight my battle, she beat me in a race for the door, thrust me aside, and bounded down the steps. I was close at her heels, though, and just in time to see her halt the first native as he was about to put foot in the temple.

She pushed him violently, and, as he toppled over backward, the others of the party hesitated. I could see that they were in a quandary, and one of the leaders turned to the Naib, who was in the rear.

It must have been that he ordered them to advance, as they began to move forward slowly, but with seeming reluctance. Zadra, now, was berating them excitedly in their own tongue, which, of course, I could not understand. Again they came to a halt, and engaged in a brief colloquy.

"Shall I shoot?" I asked Zadra breathlessly.

"No, no, no!" she cried.

Then she said something to Nana, who stood in the background, and the old woman began bringing the baskets of snakes forward. I had an inkling, now, of Zadra's plan of defense, but, if my suspicions were correct, I wanted to be out of the way when she put it into effect. To my own surprise, I found that I had no fear of bullets, but I had a horror of being bitten by one of those terrible cobras.

While I was speculating thus, the Naib of Nagpur drew his forces about him, and began to harangue them in a loud voice, pointing, in the meantime, in our direction.

I could fancy that he was exhorting them to make a dash for us, irrespective of the awe in which the ignorant natives held the girl who guarded the doorway. And, in the end, he doubtless persuaded them to do his bidding, for they turned again toward the temple, and began to advance, though with not any great alacrity.

We were in for it now, I thought, and despite Zadra's caution not to shoot, I was prepared to empty the contents of my automatic into the horde.

But there came a sudden diversion that, at the moment, made it unnecessary for me to risk our position by driving the natives to further fury. It was an attack from the rear by the *Bonaventure's* men, and several of the natives went down at the first fire.

I saw them come pouring out of the jungle, shooting as they ran. It was a surprise to the Naib's force, and, instead of returning the fire in the open, they wheeled, in a disorganized mass, and started for the protection of the temple.

It was my cue, then, to inject myself into the fighting, which I did, to the best of my ability. And I had the satisfaction of seeing that many of my shots went home, and that the natives halted, for a moment undecided what to do. Then, at command of the Naib, they made a stand, and fired a volley at their foes.

It was at this moment that Zadra took a hand in the game, but in a manner that was quite unexpected. I would not have been surprised at her method, had she stood in the door and repulsed the natives when they tried to enter; but to rush forth to engage them was a move that took me quite off my guard.

I was reloading my pistol, when Zadra, seizing one of the baskets of snakes, leaped down the garden path and sprang into the mêlée. I shouted to her, fearing that she might stop a stray bullet, but she gave no heed.

And though I raced after, before I could catch up, she had thrown the cover from her basket, and was hurling live snakes into the midst of the natives, at the same time screaming at them in their own jargon.

Before this onslaught, the men were dumfounded. Many threw down their arms and ran, howling like frightened children. The Naib, too, took to his heels, after one of the snakes writhed past his ugly face. Only one—a big, sour-visaged fellow—ventured to meet the attack. He raised his gun, as if to shoot the girl; but a bullet from my own weapon suddenly altered his plan.

It was incredible, indeed, the rapidity with which they vanished, and, within the space of a minute, we were in undisputed possession of the field. And then, in another moment, we were surrounded by the men from the *Bonaventure*. I found myself the center of my comrades, and the target for a hundred questions, while, at one side, stood Zadra, in the arms of her father, Professor Runyon.

It was at my suggestion that we retired to the protection of the temple; for I had an idea that the Naib might rally his forces, and begin shooting at us from the protection of the palace.

Zadra, evidently, had sung my praises without stint to her father, for the old snake man really abashed me by the thanks he showered on me for the service that I had been to his daughter. And I must say that, then, I liked him better than I had before. Perhaps this, though, was because he was Zadra's father.

The men, generally, were curious about the girl, and Manners, much to my annoyance, assumed an air of proprietorship over her. I suppose I was jealous, but, at that time, I did not analyze my feeling as jealousy.

I warned the men to give a wide berth to the takra, in which Zadra had imprisoned the snakes; but old Runyon, when he learned of the contents, went wild with delight.

"Fine, fine!" he gloated, rubbing his hands. And, to my disgust, he took one of the filthy snakes from a basket, and fondled it as though it were a purring kitten.

"We'll take these beauties with us," he said to Manners.

To Manners' protest, the old fellow reminded him that, aside from their value for experimental purposes, the snakes would bring a goodly sum from zoological societies and museums in the United States. Some of the men, finally, volunteered to carry the baskets when assured that they would be in no danger from their venomous contents.

"And now back to the ship," Runyon shouted gleefully. "Ah!" he added, in a lower voice. "I had forgotten." He came over to Zadra, who was standing by my side. "My dear, my dear," he palpitated, "have you got it? Have you got it? I was so elated at finding you that, for the moment, it slipped my mind."

"It is here, father," she answered; "and here, also, is your first analysis."

As a matter of courtesy, I turned away, but, meanwhile, kept a curious eye on father and daughter. And I confess I was surprised when I saw Zadra reach into her bosom and withdraw a small vial, half filled with a colorless liquid, a hypodermic syringe, and a slip of paper, all of which she handed to her father.

"Thank God! My treasure! My treasure!" breathed the old man. And in an excess of joy, he pressed the paper and the vial to his lips.

So, this was the treasure, at last. But what a curious sort of treasure, I thought. And what could it be that was so valuable? Did the paper contain a map that would lead to a buried hoard of gold or jewels?

My cogitations were interrupted by a command from Manners, who was marshaling the men for the return to the Bonaventure.

CHAPTER IX.

MYSTERY.

WE observed extreme caution in leaving the temple, lest the Naib and his men strike at us from an ambuscade, and made a quick dash for the concealment of the jungle that fringed the clearing. Our care seemed unnecessary, however, as we saw nothing of our enemies.

Zadra, when we reached the head of the corduroy road that ran to the river, suggested that we take the subterranean passage, to avoid a possible clash in the forest beyond; but several of the men, whose love of a fight had not been satisfied, protested. They were eager to force the conflict, and make an end to the natives. The professor, however, ended the disagreement.

"We've got what we came for, boys," he said firmly, "and there's no use in putting our necks in a halter. My chief object now is to get back to the ship and away as soon as possible."

Those who would have continued the fighting yielded, of course, and, under the direction of Zadra, we took to the tunnel. It was a dark, dank place, and at every step I was in fear of treading on a snake. I wanted to walk beside Zadra, too, and I was raging when Manners took hold of her arm and elbowed me out of the way.

Finally, we saw daylight ahead, and in a few minutes arrived at the river. And it was with a great deal of satisfaction that I saw Zadra safely aboard the Bonaventure, and her baskets of snakes stowed away in the hold.

I was thankful, indeed, that we had escaped so luckily from our adventure, and I looked forward with infinite joy to the long voyage back home, during which I should have the close companionship of the girl I had found in the temple.

For the first few hours of our embarkation, I was too busy in assisting to warp the ship out into the channel to give Zadra any of my attention. But after our evening meal, when the full, round moon flamed forth to guide us as we slipped down the river, I saw her standing by the rail, a dark, statuesque silhouette, gazing pensively into the jungle that lined our course.

I watched her from afar, content to stand there and admire her, fearful to disturb the privacy of her mind. She was a mystery to me—but there are some mysteries that one does not like to fathom. They possess greater charm while they still are mysteries.

I wondered if I should find Zadra so. She seemed, now, to embody all the witchery of untrammeled wilds—a primitive woman—yet with the grace and finish and education of one who had been intimate with the fine things of man's hewing.

She was a distinct paradox—clinging, yet self-reliant, as she had proved to me: womanly to the highest degree, yet with a man's resourcefulness in time of stress; unrestrained as any jungle creature, yet, in turn, reserved, dignified, cultured.

A strange spell seemed to come over me as I watched her, admired the haughty poise of her superb head, the curve of her fine shoulders, the contour of the rounded arm that rested on the rail. Indeed, the body of her was perfect. But the mind of her was the great problem.

I confess a curiosity concerning her uncanny power over the cobras, her immunity to the bite of the serpents. I was puzzled by the little vial and the slip of paper that she had handed to her father in the temple.

But as I have inferred before, to know these things might destroy the halo of illusion with which I had invested her—for knowledge oft is a bitter iconoclast, that tears down and smashes one's apotheosization of an idol.

I was content, then, just to stand and watch her at her thoughts. But, suddenly, I was seized with a revulsion for my own act. I seemed to be doing something that was mean and sneaking. I was prying, with vulgar eyes, into a privacy that I had no honest right to violate.

And then, even as I thought of turning away, I became obsessed with a mad desire to rush forward and clasp the graceful body in my rough, bronzed arms. What was it, this crazy impulse?

It came to me with a start—the realization of the emotion that I had been trying to analyze. I loved the girl! Yes, I loved her. That was it. And I wanted to go to her at once and tell her so. But, then, with bitter revulsion, I hated myself. I was the betrothed of Elsie Vandman, back in San Francisco!

With what poignant heartache did I comprehend the barrier that lay between Zadra and me! It was an insuperable barrier, it seemed. The spirit of romance that had been awakened within

me must die as it came, silently, without expression. I turned, intending to attempt to divert myself by a game of cards with the men.

"Douglas! Oh, Douglas!"

She saw me—was calling to me, and the call was a command that took me swiftly to her side.

"Am I to understand that you were passing me, without even so much as saying good evening?" she demanded, with affected indignation. "And on such a night as this!"

I was abashed, but the smile that she gave me, the frank hand with which she gripped mine, told me that she was not actually offended.

"I—I was passing hurriedly, and did not see you," I lied apologetically.

"What! Am I so insignificant?" She made a pretty *moue*, and transfixed me with those wonderful eyes of hers.

"N—no—not that," I stammered; and I could feel my face flame beneath the tan.

"All right, then, I'll forgive you," she laughed. "So, you may tell me all about the interesting men on the *Bonaventure*. If I weren't reassured by the presence of you and father, I should think I was coursing the old Spanish Main, with a crew bent on piracy."

Her conceit amused me, and I lapsed into biographical recital, going as far as my knowledge of the men would permit, and, sometimes, I fear, a little further.

We had stood there for half an hour, perhaps, charmed with the beauty of the night, enjoying the wilderness of nature spread about us, interested only in ourselves and the subject of our conversation, when Manners came along. He greeted Zadra with unctuous politeness, and then turned brusquely to me.

"I think the captain has some work for you, Farnworth—up front there," he said.

"I don't believe the captain has any

work for me that I care to do," I replied just as brusquely.

I did not like Manners' tone, nor did I relish his intrusion.

"I think I would go see, if I were you." His voice was icy, and his usually soft, jovial face flamed with anger.

"I prefer to think that I am not on this ship in the capacity of a seaman," I flashed. "And, besides, I am having a very pleasant conversation with Miss Runyon."

"I should like, also, to say something to Miss Runyon," began Manners, but, before he could go further, she interrupted.

"Indeed, Mr. Manners," she said freezingly, "Mr. Farnworth and I were having a very enjoyable talk when you interrupted."

"I beg your pardon," clipped Manners, and, swinging on one heel, he went aft.

I was at a loss to understand Manners in such a mood. Usually he was too urbane, too suave, too diplomatic to give the slightest offense.

I had noticed, however, that he had been extremely cool with me since the afternoon, when we met in the temple. Why, I wondered. What had I done to offend him? I could think of nothing. However, I was not worrying. I had become quite hardened by contact with conditions more or less primitive, and felt perfectly well able to take care of myself, under all circumstances.

The intrusion of Manners, however, had cast a damper over both Zadra and me, and, after the conversation had dragged in a desultory fashion for a few minutes, she bade me good night. I accompanied her to the door of her stateroom—if the small quarters that she occupied might be dignified by such a name—then filled my pipe and began to stroll back along the deck. About midship I met Ling. He pressed a finger to his lips, to enjoin silence, and grasped me by the arm.

"Come see what old man do," he whispered.

"Runyon?"

"So be. Say nothing."

I had noticed that a light was streaming through a porthole in the professor's cabin, but it had not occurred to me to spy on him. Now, however, my curiosity having been aroused by Ling, I crept up and peered inside.

"Look!" sibilated the Chinaman. "Girl, she come, too."

Yes, Zadra had just stepped through the door that separated her quarters from those of her father. And moreover, I noticed, on the floor, half a dozen of the snake baskets that we had brought from the temple. The old man had taken these from the hold, where we had stowed them on our arrival.

"But what was he doing, that caused you to bring me here?" I asked Ling.

"He choke snake when I see him first."

"Choking a snake?" I repeated. "Why?"

"Don't know; maybe we see."

I saw Zadra, now, go to one of the baskets, lift the lid boldly, and thrust a delicate hand inside. She brought forth a huge, six-foot cobra, and straightened it out on the table that her father used for his laboratory work.

The old man, in the meantime, had provided himself with a goblet, and advanced to the end of the table toward which the snake's head lay. I watched them, fascinated, wondering what they intended doing now. My curiosity had not long to wait.

Zadra, then, began to prod the serpent, driving it into a frenzy of anger, in which it writhed and struggled in a vain effort to turn on her. But her slender hands were firm, and she was quite the master of the situation.

Suddenly Professor Runyon's hand shot forward, and with the mouth of the goblet he struck the snake a sharp blow on the nose. Zadra, at the same instant, allowed the cobra to raise its head under the guidance of her hand. Swiftly, unerringly, it struck the goblet with which the old ophiologist was tormenting it; and into the glass spurted a small portion of a viscid, amberish liquid—the venom of the cobra.

"They're taking the snake's poison," I whispered.

"So be," agreed my companion. "Ling no like."

"Nor do I," I said. "Come away."

We turned, and I saw a dark shadow flit around a corner of the deck house. I could not make out who it was; but he, too, doubtless had been watching the operation within.

I said good night to Ling and went to my berth; and I lay for a long while before sleep came to me, wondering why Zadra and her father had extracted the venom of a cobra; wondering who was the man who, over our shoulders, also had watched them at work; wondering why Manners had attempted to pick a quarrel with me.

Ah, there were many things that puzzled me, but, at that time, I could not know that I was to face a greater, graver problem before matters were to be explained. It was well that I did not know, and that benign Nature elected to lull me into tranquil sleep.

CHAPTER X.

A SNAKE'S VENOM.

A WEEK passed, during which I enjoyed thoroughly the companionship of Zadra, even while I gained the further scorn of Manners. For several days he had not spoken to me, nor did I inquire into his coolness.

At first, his attitude had vexed me sorely; but I had come to the conclusion that it was caused by jealousy—resentment of the close friendship that existed between Zadra and me.

It seemed strange, too, for him to feel that way about a woman, for I never had known him to show interest in any member of the sex. However, that was the only explanation that I could make to myself.

I was pained, too, by the uncontrollable, ever-growing love that I had for Zadra. Something about her seemed verily to hypnotize me. I was quite her slave; yet I dared not breathe a word of love to her, for back in San Francisco there was another waiting.

It was hard, too—terribly hard to walk with Zadra about the deck, to linger at the rail, under the light of the moon, to exchange sweet little confidences with her, and not to tell her of the great, consuming passion that surged within me. And I had reason to believe that Zadra would have welcomed a declaration of love from me.

I am not necessarily conceited, but a woman, however modest, may tell a man of her heart in a thousand little ways, and, without a spoken word, make him understand that he is *the* man. It was thus that I learned that Zadra held for me something more than a feeling of conventional friendship.

One evening, as usual after the evening meal, we went for our stroll about the deck. As was my custom, I extended an arm to Zadra, but to my surprise she pretended not to see it. I put her action down as a little whimsicality, made no comment, and lighted my pipe, puffing silently as we made our rounds. Twice I saw Manners watching us, but presently he joined Runyon in the latter's improvised laboratory.

A pale, lopsided moon came presently out of the horizon, and Zadra and I took our accustomed place by the starboard rail. She still was silent, and in her great, luminous eyes there was a look of plaintive sadness that I could not fathom. Finally, when I could stand it no longer, I spoke.

"Has something gone wrong, Zadra?" I asked softly.

She made no immediate answer, but

turned her head slowly, and pierced me with those pained eyes of hers. She was breathing heavily, as though under the stress of some great emotion. Then:

"I love you, Douglas!" she cried passionately. "I—oh!"

She seized me suddenly by the hands, and buried her face against my shoulder.

She was sobbing now, and I could feel her body tremble. My first feeling of surprised elation at her voluntary, impulsive admission gave way quickly to a dull, throbbing ache, and a painful tightening of the heartstrings for the pity of it all. It was enough for me to suffer; but for her—oh, it was horrible!

"And I love you, too, Zadra, dear," I whispered, putting a tender arm around her shoulder. "But——"

"Yes, Douglas, I know," she said gently. "I shouldn't have spoken, because—because it was unfair to—to the other woman."

"Yes, there is another woman," I admitted dumbly. "God help us!"

I knew who had told her about the other woman. It was Manners. There was no one else aboard the *Bonaventure* who knew of my betrothal to Miss Vandman.

"Forgive me, Douglas." She straightened up suddenly, and tried to smile through the tears that filled her eyes. "I am bold, unwomanly, too impulsive. You should hate me."

"You are nothing that you have called yourself," I protested. "And I never could hate you—because I love you."

"And we have made misery for each other," she said: "but we are brave people, you and I."

"Yes, we are brave people," I agreed. But at the same time I wondered just how brave we were. There are those whom chains cannot bind, yet who may be imprisoned by the slender strands of Love's weaving.

"I'll go to bed now," she said abruptly. "Good night."

"So soon?" I took her hand gently, and would have detained her.

"Good night, Douglas," she repeated.

She was gone. I watched her flit up the deck, like a gracile moonbeam. And then I saw another, darker figure steal from the shadows of the deck house and enter the laboratory.

Was it Runyon or Manners? I could not tell. Whichever it was, however, his object undoubtedly had been to eavesdrop on Zadra and me. Well, it was of no consequence. With a heavy heart, I leaned far over the rail, and watched the harbor lights of Singapore winking in the distance.

I was in a curious, fanciful mood—awake, yet dreaming; for in every dancing, moon-splashed billow I saw the face of Zadra; and in the soft soughing of the breeze through the rigging, I could hear her words: "I love you, Douglas!"

Presently, I grew weary of my lonesome occupation, and decided to turn in. I was not particularly sleepy, but, once down, I thought that the motion of the ship might lull me into slumber. In any event, I should try it.

I knocked the ashes from my pipe, and hastened to my cabin. I still was uneasy about the propinquity of the professor's snakes, but, as they had not injured me so far, I did my best to make myself believe there was no danger. However, I never failed to look carefully under my bunk and into the corners before retiring.

Having assured myself that there were no snakes in my room, I laughed at my fears and flung myself down on my bunk. An hour, probably, passed, while I tossed from side to side, unable to sleep.

My mind was too keenly active in attempting to digest the mysteries that beset me, in worrying over the condition that had engulfed Zadra and me, in wondering what the outcome of it all might be.

And then, suddenly, I was startled by a light tap on my door. I sprang from bed and responded. The visitor was my friend, Ling.

"Me heap sick," he announced plaintively, pressing both hands to the pit of his stomach. "Maybe have a cramp. And, besides, me think one damn snake come in my room."

"A snake?" I cried. "Are you sure?"

"So be; me see him crawl. And then me——"

Ling doubled up in another spasm of pain, and I hastened to fix him up a strong dose of ginger. Then I led him to my bunk and told him to sleep there, if he could. It was more comfortable than the one he occupied, and, from the way I felt, I didn't imagine that it would be of any service to me. In any event, I could crawl into the upper bunk if I should become sleepy.

My simple remedy helped the patient, and, leaving him resting easily, I went up to the deck. I had no notion of going to Ling's quarters to look for snakes. That was a daylight job, and better suited, any way, to some one other than myself.

So I gave Ling's quarters a wide berth, and went as far into the peak as I could. It was cool there, and I would not be disturbed. I made myself comfortable on a coil of rope, with my back propped against the capstan, and lighted my pipe.

I will not attempt to conjecture how long I sat there, brooding. The fact remains that, lulled by the cool breeze and the solitude of boundless, moonlit waters, I went to sleep. Nor do I know how long I slept.

I was startled into awaking by an untoward commotion among the men. I saw at once that it wasn't a storm that had aroused them. Perhaps the ship was afire!

I sprang to my feet, and hastened aft, to where a group was standing, chattering loudly in half a dozen languages. On my approach, a strange cry went up, and I noticed that several of them shrank away from me, as though I were plague-stricken, or a ghost.

"What's the matter?" I demanded.

A man we called The Don, a wiry, dapper little Spaniard, began to laugh.

"Olsen, here," he said, indicating a giant Norwegian, "just woke us all up, with the story that he had found you dead in your bunk, when he went to call you for your trick on the watch. What kind of liquor you been drinking?" he added, turning to the puzzled Scandinavian.

He laughed again, uproariously, and was joined by many of the others.

"Perhaps he did find a dead man in my bunk," I said quietly. "Naturally, he thought it was I."

"What?" cried The Don. "Who?"

"Poor Ling: he came to me ill a few hours ago, and I put him in my bunk. I wasn't sleepy then, but while sitting up in the bow on a coil of rope I dropped off unexpectedly."

"What's the row here?" suddenly demanded the querulous voice of Professor Runyon.

He was wearing pajamas, and elbowed his way through the group, making directly for me. His white hair, disheveled, made him appear almost ghastly in the moonlight; his black, snapping, snakelike eyes made him seem almost a fearsome thing, and, intuitively, I shrank backward. I should have felt the same had I been approached by one of the cobras which were his playmates.

"What is it?" he repeated authoritatively, piercing me with those awful eyes of his.

I explained the situation to him in as few words as possible.

"Well," he snarled, "what are you standing here for? Maybe the man isn't dead. Let's have a look at him."

I led the way eagerly, but, at the door of my room, I was inclined to hesitate. Dumb, nameless fear seized me, and I had to conquer it by sheer force of will. I could not afford to let the others see that I was afraid, so, as bravely as I was able to pretend, I scratched a match and lighted the lamp on the wall.

No second glance was needed to assure one that Ling had gone to his last sleep. His body was contorted, swollen, and his skin of a queer, purplish hue.

"Snake bite?" I cried in horror.

Runyon nodded his head silently, and stepped to the side of the bunk.

"There's one of those damned cobras in the room! Look out!" I warned.

The men scampered, but Runyon turned on me with a snarl.

"Don't be a fool!" he snapped. "Come here."

Reluctantly, I stepped to his side.

"Look?" he commanded. "The poor fellow got it in the neck—right in the jugular; but while it was a cobra's venom that did the job, it was not a cobra that did the striking."

"What?" I gasped. "What do you mean?"

"That if a cobra did strike the beggar, he had only one fang, and that one smaller than any I ever have seen in a snake's mouth! My dear fellow, this was done with a hypodermic syringe! What do you know about it?"

"What do I know about it?" I gasped. "My God! You don't think——"

"I'm not thinking," was the curt rejoinder. "I am asking you a question."

I was staggered at the man's imputation, horrified at the terrible fate that had overtaken Ling, almost speechless from the shock of the tragedy, for Ling I had accounted my best friend aboard the ship. However, I collected my wits, and, simultaneously, I was obsessed with a suspicion of the truth.

"Well," demanded Runyon impatiently, "why don't you answer?"

"You remarked a moment ago," I replied icily, "that you were not thinking. Permit me to say that I am. I think that Ling's colic saved my life; I think that the poison that killed him was intended for me!"

I, quite naturally, was the center of interest, and many questions were put to me. But I was careful not to let my exact suspicions be known. The men, however, became morose and fearful of the snakes. Then a delegation demanded that they be cast overboard; but Runyon refused.

The consternation of the crew may be well imagined when, one morning, Olsen, the big Norwegian, was found dead in his bunk, just as Ling had been found. In this instance, however, there were two incisions in his throat, and it was agreed that he actually had been bitten by a cobra.

The same day, one of the snakes was found lying in the sun, on the forecastle hatch. This gave further credence to the belief that Olsen had been attacked by a snake, while he slept, and, in retaliation, one of the men dispatched the reptile with a club.

This act drove the professor into a frenzy of rage, and, had it not been for his fear of arousing his discontented crew to some deed of violence, he would have punished the man severely.

If the ship's company were distrait after the death of Olsen, it became mad with fear and anger when The Don, a popular Spaniard, a few days later, went the same way. As Ling and Olsen had died, so died The Don. His bloated, blackened body was found in his berth in the morning, with those two deadly pin points of scars in his neck, to show where the venom of a snake had entered his veins.

But an immediate search for the serpent that had struck the deathblow failed to reveal one that was not confined in the hold, or in the professor's laboratory.

As a result of The Don's death, the men held a conference in the forecastle, and a committee, of which I was chosen the head, was named to wait on the professor once more and ask that all of the snakes on the ship be thrown overboard. But Runyon, as I had expected, would not countenance the proposition. All of my arguments—the disease of the men, the possibility of a mutiny, the saving of other lives—were in vain.

"Tell them to go to the devil, Farnworth," was his parting declaration, and I delivered his message literally.

There were threats, you may be sure, on all sides, but I managed to stay the rising storm.

Thus we found ourselves in the mid-Pacific, when, one morning, De Cosmos, another Spaniard, and Heisler, a brawny German, were found dead in their berths—killed in the same way as had been their comrades who had gone before.

The circumstances were the same—two tiny holes in their necks, and no evidence on the ship, though thorough search was made. that a cobra had gained its liberty.

I admit that, then, I had a horrible suspicion. I remembered a hypodermic syringe that Zadra had handed to her father in the temple, in addition to a vial, half filled with a colorless liquid, and a slip of paper; and I remembered the night when Ling had called my attention to proceedings in the professor's laboratory, and I had seen him, with the assistance of Zadra, extracting the venom of a cobra.

And the men had blamed the professor for the previous deaths! But why—why? Ah, no; the thing was too horrible, too inhuman to contemplate! For what could be his object?

There is no doubt in my mind that the men would have mutinied then had it not been for a sudden interruption imposed by nature—one of those quick, violent, brief storms that come from nowhere, but sweep the Pacific with demoniacal fury while they last. It left us a battered hulk, our mainmast gone, limping lamely through a white smother of water.

Standing at the head of the companionway, I noticed that, in falling, the mainmast had knocked the deck house, in which the professor's quarters were located, askew. I heard a scream from that direction. It was a man's cry—a cry of terror.

The deck was slippery and the ship still pitching dangerously. Nevertheless, I determined to investigate. Some one in the professor's laboratory needed assistance. Gauging well the slant of the vessel, I made a quick dash along the port rail, and gained the laboratory in safety. I turned the knob of the door. It was locked.

"Help, for God's sake!" came a faint call from within.

I could not recognize the voice, but I thought that it might be Runyon, injured, perhaps, by the crashing of the mast. The door was frail, and with one heave of my shoulder I burst the lock. I would have rushed in at once, but a warning from the dim interior deterred me.

"Careful, there," cautioned a man whom I could not see.

No need to tell me to be careful, for, at that moment, I saw only too plainly what had happened. The tossing of the storm-swept vessel had broken open the cages in which the professor had kept his cobras, and the floor was alive with the venomous creatures.

I shrank back intuitively, but, at the same time, whipped out my pistol and began shooting. One after the other I spattered the hideous heads of the snakes over the floor, until I had emptied my weapon.

"That you, Douglas?" came the voice from within.

"Yes. Is that Manners?"

"Yes, old man."

Manners! I hesitated in the process of reloading, half inclined to leave him to his fate.

But my spirit of humanity prevailed, and, with my pistol again charged, I began anew to pot snakes from my position in the doorway. In the midst of my fusillade, however, I was startled by an hysterical shriek.

"Manners!" I cried. "Manners!"

"One of them got me at last," came faintly from within.

"What is it, Douglas?"

I turned, to find Zadra at my elbow.

"See," I explained; "the snakes have escaped! One has bitten Manners!"

She commanded me to stand aside, and, in a flash, she was in the room. The next moment I saw a snake go hurtling over the side of the ship and into the water, to be followed by others in quick succession, until fully a dozen must have been cast into the sea. Zadra certainly was clearing the laboratory of its dangerous occupants in short order.

"All right, Douglas," she called presently.

Though still apprehensive, I ventured to enter. I found Zadra bending over her father, who was lying on his table, while Manners, sitting beside him, was making a tourniquet around one of his own legs.

As I approached, he whipped out a knife and made a cross cut in the snake bite, that the poisoned blood might escape more freely. But I could see that he was pale and weak already, and that the leg had begun to swell and discolor. Such is the deadliness of the cobra's bite, and the speed with which its venom courses through the body.

The professor, too, had been bitten; and it puzzled me to know why the poison did not seem to have the same effect on him as it had on Manners. His ankle was only slightly swollen where the snake's fangs had entered, and he lay placidly, in a semi-comatose condition, while Zadra began filling him with antidotes.

I, of course, performed the same service for Manners, but within fifteen minutes he was in the throes of a convulsion.

It passed, presently. Then he opened his eyes, over which a glassy film was drawing rapidly, and recognized me. He stretched out one hand imploringly, and I grasped it.

"Douglas," he murmured, "I'm going. I am not sorry; but—but before I go, there's something I must say to you. Don't—don't let me die till then; will you?"

CHAPTER XI.
THE SECRET REVEALED.

ONCE, you will remember, I had liked Manners, and had regarded him as a friend; and now his pitiable plight awakened within me all of the old feeling of attachment, even as it obliterated the rancor that had been engendered by his strange treatment of the last few weeks.

Already, in my mind, I was finding excuses for him. Perhaps his brain had been turned by something of which I knew nothing. So, with tender hands, I gave him a large drink of whisky.

"Thanks, old man," he murmured. "That's better." And then, it seemed, Manners divined what was passing in my thoughts. "No, Douglas," he continued weakly, "there's no excuse for me; but you—you are a kind-hearted chap, and maybe you can forgive me. I'm bad, old man—bad. Understand?"

"There, there," I soothed. "Don't exert yourself. Save your strength."

"It's no use." He smiled wanly. "No, it's no use in saving my strength. I want to use it in telling you how wicked I have been—how I have hurt you. You remember that agreement I showed you, after we left Frisco? Well, that was a forgery.

"You never knew what a clever forger I was. I drugged you at that dinner at the Renaissance, and shanghaied you. You didn't know that—and you have no idea why I did it. I'll tell you. You see, Miss Vandman——"

Manners stopped, and his eyes went shut.

"Miss Vandman!" I cried. "What of Miss Vandman?"

But Manners made me no answer. He was in the throes of another convulsion. Again I poured a large dose of· whisky down his throat, and, presently, he revived. He was weaker now, though, than he had been before. The poison was telling on him rapidly.

"Where was I?" he said suddenly, opening his glassy eyes. I marveled at the man's great vitality.

"Oh, yes; I was telling you about Miss Vandman. I knew, of course, that you and she were to be married; and I knew just why. You were old friends, but you didn't love each other. And—and then you remember Count Lornville, who came to Frisco six months ago. He really fell in love with Miss Vandman.

"I think he loved her money, too. Anyway, he made me a proposition: If I could get you out of the way, so that he might marry Miss Vandman, he would give me twenty-five thousand dollars. And I got you out of the way, old man.

"But I did more. I wrote Miss Vandman a letter, purporting to come from you, to the effect that you did not care to marry her, and were leaving with another woman. The writing was like yours, because—well, I told you that I was a clever forger."

I was fairly staggered by the man's story, and the thought that such a villain had deceived me all these years. But can you blame me, loving Zadra as

I did, when I say that I held no resentment toward the dying man—in fact, was rather glad that he had done as he did?

"And then I tried to hurt you with Zadra—Miss Runyon," he went on weakly. "I loved her myself, Douglas —at sight. I was furiously jealous of her preference for you. So I told her that you were engaged to marry Miss Vandman, and then—then I tried to kill you.

"I am glad that Ling was in your berth that night. I got the snake's venom and the hypodermic from the old man's laboratory, and I—killed all the others, too. You don't laugh. Well, I had arranged with all of these adventurers, when I engaged them for Runyon's expedition, that, if they should not return, the money they were to receive should revert to me.

"So I killed them for that little bit of money, old man. You see, now, what a desperate person I have been. And that is how I have lived these many years—by blood. And at intervals I would go to Frisco, to spend my gains and to mingle with my intellectual equals. Tell me, what do you think, now that——"

The poor devil never finished. His body stiffened, and his voice trailed away in a throaty gurgle. I stood there, appalled by his confession, scarcely realizing that he would speak no more, hardly knowing what to think. And then Zadra came and laid a hand on my arm.

"Has he gone?" she whispered.

I nodded my head and turned away.

"And your father?" I questioned.

"I think—I hope he will recover."

With my assistance, she made him as comfortable as possible in his berth, and then I strolled forth on the deck. The men, in the meantime, had cleared away the débris that the storm had left, but it was determined not to attempt to step the broken mainmast. Nor was it at all necessary, as we were bowling along merrily under the propulsion of our single screw.

I made no mention to any one, except Zadra, of the confession that Manners had made to me, but, somehow, the men seemed to divine that it had been he who had caused the deaths of their comrades.

This belief was strengthened, of course, by the fact that there was no more trouble aboard, and that the remainder of our voyage was as tranquil as any that ever had been made by a liner.

Immediately on our return to San Francisco, I telephoned to Elsie Vandman, and was informed that she was on a honeymoon tour around the world with her husband, Count Lornville.

If I had any regrets, I found quick solace in the arms of Zadra; and I may remark that she was pleased by the news that I brought her.

"There's one thing that I am aching to know," I said one afternoon to the most wonderful wife that a man ever had; "no, there are several things, dear. I want to know what was the treasure that we sought in far-off India—you, or the slip of paper and the vial of colorless liquid that you gave to your father that day in the temple."

She laughed adorably, and then she bantered:

"What do you think?"

"That you were the treasure—at least, *my* treasure."

"Your treasure, of course; but I don't know." She gazed pensively from our window, out over the bay. "The real treasure of intrinsic worth was in the vial and on the slip of paper. The first contained a serum that immunizes one against the bite of a cobra—or any other snake, for that matter; and the other held the formula for its composition.

"Father got them from an old East Indian mystic, and thought that a fortune lay in the manufacture and sale of the serum. Then, while we were at Madras, he was compelled to go to Calcutta on business. I went out into the country on a visit to some English friends, and it was there that I met the Naib of Nagpur.

"He abducted me, as I told you; but, previously, I had been immunizing myself, hypodermically, against snake bite. And the Naib had his servants pack up all of my belongings and bring them with us. So, I still had what was left of the serum, as well as the formula.

"I was lost to father entirely, until Mr. Manners told him one day a story of an American girl who was held by the Naib of Nagpur, and who could handle the cobras without danger. He had not seen me, of course, but it seems that the story spread through the country.

"And father was afraid to call the attention of the authorities to my condition, fearing that the Naib was powerful enough to make away with me, and cause them to believe that the story was a mere fiction. So he organized what Mr. Manners picturesquely called the Mystery Club—a band of fearless adventurers, and set out to find me."

"And thank God we did!" I interposed heartily. "But tell me," I added, "how it was that, with this wonderful serum, your father was affected at all by the bite of the cobra."

"He had not taken enough of it to make him entirely immune. That is why he became so ill."

"Why, then, did he venture to handle a cobra? Why did he bring those nasty snakes on board the *Bonaventure?*"

"He needed them, because their venom is one of the ingredients of the serum."

So, now, it all was clear. I prefer to call this a treasure story, for I found my treasure, and Professor Runyon gained his. Ergo, both of us are happy.

When Wires are Down

Lillian Beynon Thomas

"SPEAKIN' of spirits and the angels at Mons, and all them kind of things, I don't believe in none of it," the mail carrier said.

No one had mentioned spirits or the angels at Mons, and I sat up suddenly, for I was at that minute trying to read by the flickering light of the one lamp in the station waiting room, an article on the great revival of interest in spiritualism that the war has occasioned.

"Strange that you mentioned that now," the agent said in a husky, disgruntled voice, for he was suffering from la grippe, that had settled in his throat and his mental outlook on life.

He was half lying on his desk in the inner office, and without raising his head from his arms, he mumbled: "One of the fellows was telling me to-day that Simpson left because this station is haunted."

"I've heard that yarn," the mail carrier replied with evident disgust, and he projected a great wad of tobacco toward a cuspidor that stood to the right of the stove, surrounded by the well intentioned, but overreaching or too weak efforts of a careless public; "but if it had been haunted I'd have

seen something of it, for I've been here every night for five years. There may be spirits in the world, I don't say there ain't; but when a fellow begins to tell me he has been seein' signs, and gettin' messages, I asks him what he's been eatin' and drinkin'. It's what's inside, I says, not outside that is makin' the trouble."

"Simpson didn't drink too much," the agent mumbled.

"Naw!" the mail carrier agreed as he pushed the mail bags out of his way with the toe of his boot and tilted his chair back until he could raise his feet to the ledge around the center of the stove. "Simpson was city bred, that was what was the matter with him; he got lonesome. He imagined the wind in the telegraph wires was voices, and just ordinary silence was to him a terrible hush. When there was a blizzard ragin' on the prairie the way there is to-night, and the wires got down both goin' and comin', he began to think how far he was from home and friends and got panicky; and when you get that way, you can see and hear things as never was."

The agent shoved back his chair, and

it made a screeching sound on the floor of the inner office. He buttoned his gray sweater around him, put on his coat and fastened it up close to his throat, put on his cap and pulled it down over his ears, and came out into the general waiting room.

He stopped a minute at the stove, that looked like a tippler who is so far gone he does not care for his personal appearance. It was dribbled with ashes all the way down its neglected front; its top and bottom showed some signs of having once been black, but its belly was a faded gray, with a faint reddish glow in one spot in the back that showed there was some life within.

The agent extended his hands over the stove and shivered slightly as those do affected with la grippe. Then he reached for the coal scuttle that was half full of coal. It had a small shovel in it, and with the shovel he opened the stove door, then stooped down to the scuttle and made a great rattling among the coal, trying to fill the shovel and carry it full to the stove; but much of it fell back, and much dribbled on to the floor, and scattered in all directions. I noticed two pieces that rolled until they hit a door back of the stove, a door that gave back a hollow sound.

The agent was too ill to gather them up. He slammed the stove door shut with the shovel and when it did not catch, being clogged with ashes, he kicked it with the sole of his boot until it did. Then he went to the door leading to the platform and opened it carefully, but the storm that was raging outside came through with such force that it knocked him back and took away his breath.

He tugged at the door to get it closed after him, but it was not until the mail carrier got up and put his shoulder to it that the catch finally caught and stayed.

I was sitting on a bench beside the wall on the same side as the station platform door, and I noticed how the tables and calendars and exhibition announcements on the walls rattled and swung backward and forward.

A big calendar of a harvester company on the back of the door on the opposite side of the room from me blew down and I got up and picked it up and hung it back on the door.

I noticed as I did so, that stripping had at some time been nailed around the door to keep out the wind, but it looked dusty and settled, like a door that is not used.

After hanging the calendar back on its nail, I returned to my seat; the agent came in and, after another fight with the wind, succeeded in shutting the door with a bang that sent such a gust of air through the room that again the calendars and time-tables rattled, and the light in the one lamp that was in a bracket near the ticket wicket, bounded out of the top of the chimney and went out in a burst of smoke.

We were not in complete darkness, for there was a slight glow from the stove; and the ticket wicket and the door into the inner office were both open, and the light in there, while it danced and flickered, did not go out.

The mail carrier got up and reached for the lamp in the bracket, while with his other hand he struck a match on the seat of his trousers. The agent went on into the inner office.

"Any sign of her?" I asked him. The train was already three hours late and it was almost midnight.

"Not a sign," he said, "and it's a terrible night—like hell let loose—I pity any one who is out to-night."

"It was just such a night as this that a woman out in the country was frozen to death." the mail carrier said.

Not desiring to hear any tales of horror, such as are popular among the people who do the waiting work of the world, I got up and went to the wicket and asked: "Can you find out where she is? Has she left Brandon yet?"

"Can't tell you a thing about her," he said. "The wires are down. She may be canceled."

"It's a bad time of year to be traveling," the mail carrier continued. "Last week Simpson and a traveler like yourself, sir, and I waited here until four o'clock in the morning, and then the traveler gave up and went back to the hotel, and didn't she come through at four-thirty, and it was important for him to get to Winnipeg that night, too."

He waited for me to ask a question, but when I didn't, he continued: "He was a detective, working on the Morrison case—that was the one I mentioned—it was Mrs. Morrison who was frozen to death."

"Oh," I said. "How was that?" I found myself sitting up rather straight.

"I guess you saw it in the papers— you did if you belong in these parts." He waited for me to enlighten him, but when I didn't he asked: "You don't belong here do you?"

"No!" I answered.

"Just came in at noon, didn't you?" he continued with the curiosity of one whose chief interest in life is the casual traveler, who is rather rare at such little stations as Oakhom, in the middle of a Northern winter.

"Yes," I said.

"Ever been here before?" he asked with frank curiosity.

"No," I said. "Never before."

"Morrison was a farmer," he continued, returning to his story. "I lived on his homestead about ten miles from here. I didn't know him—nobody knew much about him—he lived pretty much to himself. Some people said Morrison wasn't his name, he was hidin', I don't know. But he disappeared three weeks ago and nothin' has been seen or heard of him since."

"He has likely gone to visit friends or to see the world," I said. "No doubt he'll turn up before spring."

"I'd say that, too, if there hadn't been somethin' mysterious about his disappearance," he explained.

He was still holding the lamp in his hand, but he turned to put it up in the bracket, and as I watched him, I was conscious of something moving behind him.

I peered into the shadows with some surprise, for I thought there were only the three of us in the station waiting room; and I had not seen a cat or dog or anything else alive, and no one could come in from outside without an accompaniment of wind and snow.

The mail carrier returned to his seat, and I saw that it was the calendar I had hung on the door opposite that I had seen moving. It was swaying forward as if impelled by a gentle, but constant wind.

I recalled that as I had felt up and down the door to find the nail on which to hang the calendar I had thought it seemed more solid than the usual soft-wood doors in such places.

"What is there mysterious about a man going away for a few weeks in the middle of the winter?" I asked absently, my eyes still on the calendar.

"Morrison did his business and got his mail at a small town on the other line," the mail carrier continued," but six weeks ago he came over here and left a sealed envelope with the lawyer. He would not explain anything but he told the lawyer that he would report to him every Monday, and if he missed a Monday the lawyer was to open the envelope and follow the instructions given inside. The lawyer thought him a bit queer, but promised to do as he wished."

"Sounds mysterious!" I said when he paused for effect.

He paused so long that I noticed how the elements were tearing at the little station house. It was like some wild beast worrying it until it creaked and groaned in protest—and all the while the wind was playing some wild dirge on the frosty wires—something that did not seem of earth or things human.

"A bad night," the mail carrier said, as the wind beat against the window. "But that night was worse, the night she was frozen to death. But I was speaking about Morrison. He called to see the lawyer for three Mondays, then he missed. The lawyer opened the envelope."

The agent got up and came into the general waiting room and stood beside the stove. He was a newcomer and he had evidently not heard the story.

"Morrison stated that his life was in danger, and that a search was to be started for him at once. He said they were to look for him and a man who wore a gold ring with a peculiar crest on it. He gave a rough sketch of the crest. It was heart-shaped, with two crossed keys in the center."

"Was there no clew to his disappearance?"

"No and yes," the mail carrier answered ponderously. "When Morrison came to the farm his wife was with him —a young bit of a girl who didn't know any more about a farm than I do about a machine gun, and not as much I guess. The neighbors said she was much above him—educated and accomplished and all that—and he was ignorant and coarse. I don't know why, no one does, but he and his wife did not seem to get along from the first, and it was on a night like this that she started for a neighbor's in her night clothes. She was frozen to death of course. He said she walked in her sleep —no one will ever know."

I felt my hands twitching—closing and unclosing spasmodically—it was such a terrible night for a young bit of a girl, all alone on the prairie.

"A strange story!" I said.

"Yes," he agreed, and paused again

like one who has yet more startling things to tell.

"Yes, and the neighbors say his wife had a gold ring with a heart-shaped crest, with two crossed keys in the center."

"What is their explanation?"

"Some say they belonged to a secret society, maybe spies hidin'; some say she belonged to a titled family and ran away with him; and some say she wasn't his wife, that she was married to another man, but"—he paused—"it's all gossip; nobody knows."

I pulled my cap down over my eyes and picked up my gloves that were on the seat beside me and put the one on my left hand—then I glanced around in a casual way to see if the others were watching me.

I suddenly sat bolt upright, my eyes almost popping out of my head, for on the bench, on the opposite side of the room, a man, evidently a farmer, sat huddled up, his legs drawn in under the seat, his arms hanging stiffly down at his side, his whole appearance that of a man too ill to care for anything.

He wore a sheepskin coat, a nondescript cap of some kind, and a muffler around the upturned collar of his coat. His cap was drawn down over his ears and forehead until only his eyes were visible—and there was something grotesque in his appearance—caused I decided by a projecting end of his muffler that stuck up back of his head like a cord to hang a picture or a statue.

The mail carrier was still talking to me and when I did not answer, he looked at me, and then his eyes followed the direction of mine. His feet and his chair came to the floor suddenly with a bang.

"By gosh! how did you get in? I didn't hear you."

The stranger did not answer, but seemed to sag down like one too utterly weary to bother.

"La grippe?" the mail carrier asked

sympathetically, after a pause, when the stranger did not move or speak.

The agent beckoned me to go into the inner office.

"When did he come in?" he asked in a low voice when we were beside his desk.

"I don't know," I said. "I had no idea any one had come in until I saw him sitting there."

"He didn't come through that door," he said, and nodded toward the door leading to the station platform. "No one can come in that way to-night without creating a commotion."

"He must have come through that door," I said, and nodded toward a door in the inner office.

"No he didn't," the agent said decidedly. "I locked that door when I brought in the coal. Tramps might get in and set fire to the place."

He evidently wanted me to believe that it was not fear that made him lock the door.

"There is another door into the waiting room," I said, and looked toward the door on which I had hung the calendar.

"He must have come in that way," the agent agreed. "I'll see that it is locked. No one else will come through there while I'm here!"

He went out and tried the door.

It resisted.

There was a key in the lock and he tried to turn it. He looked over at em and said: "It is locked."

He came back into the inner office. "He must have locked it when he came in, but he'll get out before I leave to-night. This is not going to be a hotel for tramps."

I could see that the stranger was getting on his nerves, for no one would turn a man out on such a night.

The mail carrier had been watching us, but when I returned to my seat in the outer office, he turned to the stranger again and said, "La grippe?"

The man appeared to nod in affirmation, but the mail carrier had not fitted the lamp properly into the bracket, and the flame was turned against the side of the chimney, which was already black and smoked, and I could not be sure that the stranger had moved.

"I know what la grippe is," the mail carrier continued, and then paused.

Everything was suddenly as still as on the calmest summer day. Prairie dwellers all know those pauses that come in even the worst storms, when the elements seem to take a second or two to get their breath, only to come back in renewed fury.

We waited to hear again the whistle and scream of the wind, but instead we heard the soft distant tones of a pipe organ. It was on the other side of the door opposite me—the door on which I had hung the calendar—at first low, then gaining in power and volume as it seemed to approach, until it seemed that we were beside it; and we recognized the grand but solemn music of the dead march.

The agent, who was still in the inner office, came to the wicket and looked out at us; the mail carrier sat up very straight, with a plug of black tobacco from which he had been taking chews all night halfway to his mouth; and I rose to my feet, but the man in the corner did not move. I looked to see if he had noticed it, and I felt suddenly that there was something familiar about him.

"By gosh, it sounded like an organ!" the mail carrier said, when the wind came again in a rush and tore at the building, snarling as a dog snarls, when it shakes a rat.

"It sounded like the dead march to me," the agent said, and returned to his chair.

"There isn't a pipe organ within two hundred miles, and not an organ of any kind nearer than the village, and that's half a mile away, and you couldn't hear it fifty yards," the mail carrier declared.

Something made me look again toward the calendar I had hung on the door opposite. It was doubtless the fact that it was still blowing forward.

"What is on the other side of that door?" I asked the mail carrier.

"That is a freight shed, but it has never been used. It has never been needed, so it was nailed up."

"It must be a drafty place," I said. "Look at the way that calendar is blowing."

He looked at it for a few seconds steadily—then looked away—like one who distrusts his eyes, then back again.

I noticed that the calendar made a still greater angle with the door.

The mail carrier got up deliberately and went to the door opposite and felt under and around the calendar. He felt up and down the cracks where the stripping had been nailed and then he shook his head.

He pushed the calendar back against the door with his hand, but when he released it, it returned to its former position.

"By gosh!" he said, and he stood back and looked at it.

Something in his tone brought the agent to his feet. He came to the door of his office, which was quite near the door on which the calendar hung.

"What is it?" he asked.

"Look at that calendar."

"There must be a terrific wind through that place," the agent said, after looking at it.

"Come and feel!" the mail carrier suggested.

The agent reached out and felt under the calendar and up and down and around it—then he looked at the mail carrier—and then they both turned and looked at me.

I went over and felt around the door as they had done, but, as I expected,

I could not feel the slightest draft; the door seemed singularly solid.

"I swan!" the agent ejaculated.

"By gosh!" the mail carrier said again.

I did not say anything, but nodded toward the calendar, that had again defied all laws of gravity—and was hanging in a horizontal position, making two right angles with the door.

I went to it, put my two hands on it, and pushed it down.

It yielded as a feather bed yields, but returned to its horizontal position when I removed my hands.

"The place is haunted!" the agent said, and glanced toward the huddled figure in the corner, but the man appeared to be too ill to care even for ghosts.

I could see his eyes and they were fixed and starey, like the eyes of one who is very ill or asleep with but half-shut eyes. I wondered what it was about him that made him seem vaguely familiar.

"I've been here every night for five years," the mail carrier said skeptically, "and if this place is haunted I'd know something about it."

He went to the door, took the calendar from the nail and put it on the floor. It lay where it was put like an ordinary calendar.

The agent took a calendar from the door leading into his office and hung it on the door of the freight shed. It remained still a second, then began to rise.

"It's electricity," the mail carrier said. "It's electricity and there is——"

He stopped suddenly for again there was the peculiar hush that had preceded the organ music. It may have been that our nerves were unstrung, but it seemed to me to be a more intense hush than the usual lull in a storm and also that there was something expectant and ominous about it.

Instinctively I stepped forward and

stood between the agent and the mail carrier and closer to them.

We stood facing the door leading into the freight shed, and I shivered when I saw the calendar sink slowly back into a normal position; and icy fingers seemed to play up and down my spine.

Again it began at a distance, on the other side of the door, on the far side of the unused freight shed.

It sounded at first like some one shoveling coal, but the coal scuttle was still beside the stove with the shovel in it.

Soon it seemed that some one was dumping a whole load of coal on the other side of the door—and we could hear the odd pieces rolling quite up to the other side of the door, until it seemed that the ones the agent had dropped on our side, had just come through.

Then there was a great crash, as if a whole carload of coal had suddenly been backed up against the shed and was all being dumped at once on the other side of the door.

We shrank back at the onrush of the great mass that we knew the door could not withstand. On it came like thunder and hurled itself against the freight-shed door.

The door did not yield—the calendar did not even tremble—we felt no physical shock from the impact; and the wind was again whistling and sighing and tearing at the desolate little station house.

"My God, what is it?" I asked. I am not a coward, but it was getting on my nerves. I could see that the other two men were also badly shaken up.

The huddled figure in the corner had not moved, but instead of being a comfort to us, for there is always comfort in numbers at such a time, the man with the grotesque handle at the back of his neck, his queer starey eyes, and general air of illness and remoteness, added to our discomfort.

"They say these things go in threes," the agent said, and I could see even in the wavering light that he was very pale.

"I don't believe it," the mail carrier said, but his tone did not carry conviction.

"It is the third day, of the third month, of the third year of the war," I said, thinking out all the threes I could as I went along.

"It is the third day of this storm; the third train that has been so late; and the third time three of us have waited here nearly all night," the mail carrier said, then added with a zest for the gruesome, "the third month since Morrison's wife was frozen to death, and the third week since he disappeared."

I glanced toward the huddled figure in the corner, when he spoke of three of us waiting for the train.

"He might as well not be there for all the good he is," he said in an undertone. "He seems half asleep all the time."

We stood around the stove a few minutes in silence. It was the mail carrier who spoke.

"I am going to open that door," he said. "Some one has been dumping a carload of coal."

"But there is no coal here," the agent said. "I would know if there was any coal at this station."

"It must have been here before you came, or just came in to-night, or something," the mail carrier insisted, and went toward the door.

I instinctively put out my hand to stop him, and I saw the agent do the same; but we did not care to be thought cowards, so we said nothing.

He went to the door.

It seemed to me that he stepped more firmly and heavily than necessary.

He did not hesitate, but turned the knob, and pulled.

I confess that every separate hair on

my head and body seemed to have come to life, and was standing at attention; and I was not sorry when the door resisted.

The key was in the lock and the mail carrier turned it. The lock went back with a dull thud. I shivered and I noticed that the agent was standing very tense.

The mail carrier pulled on the door again—he jerked it—but it still resisted.

"It is nailed up on the other side," he said, and looked back over his shoulder at us.

There was a queer hollow chuckle—not human—not like anything we had ever heard—we all looked toward the man in the corner, but he had not moved. Again I felt the irritation of something familiar about him that I could not account for.

"What are you chuckling about?" the mail carrier demanded, and advanced toward him. "Why don't you get up and help find out what is making the trouble if you know so much about it?"

The mail carrier's nerves were beginning to feel the strain.

I do not know what he would have done to the huddled figure in the corner, if at that second the terrible hush had not come upon us a third time.

If you have ever waited at a deathbed in the stillness of the night—alone with the soul that is getting ready for flight—you know something of how we felt. Our bodies were tense, our faces white and strained, and I recalled afterward how the eyes of the mail carrier and the agent stood almost out of their sockets.

The silence lasted so long that I thought I would scream—that I must do something to break the spell—when on the far side of the shed, on the other side of the door, we heard footsteps.

There could be no doubt about it—they were stealthy, stealing, menacing steps, and they were coming toward the door behind which we stood.

We were held like people in a nightmare, who feel the approach of something more than human intelligence can bear.

The steps stopped—we listened—they came stealing on again, nearer and nearer.

Across the big freight shed we heard them approaching closer and closer, until they were just on the other side of the door—and then they stopped.

The hush continued; and then I saw the knob of the door turn. I made a queer sound in my throat.

The door began to open as stealthily as the knob had been turned—slowly and silently.

I sprang toward it.

"Hold it! Hold it!" I screamed, or I think I screamed. The others said I made no sound, but they sprang with me.

We put all our strength against it. We pushed and strained.

It opened as resistlessly as the raging storm outside; we were shoved back slowly, steadily, silently.

Inch by inch the door opened, and inch by inch we yielded.

At last it was open, and we saw thick dust undisturbed on the floor—cobwebs hanging from rafters and walls; nothing human had crossed the threshold of that door for months, possibly years.

It was the mail carrier who went into the inner office and brought out a trainman's lantern, one with a strong reflector that threw a clear light ahead.

I stood at his right, the agent at his left, as he turned the light of the lantern into the freight shed.

I do not know who made a queer gurgling sound, or groaned, or gasped; but all those sounds were made, as the light of the lantern fell on a queer, huddled-up figure in a sheepskin coat, with its legs bent under it; its arms hanging down stiffly at its sides; its cap drawn down over its ears and forehead until only its eyes, starey and fixed, were visible; and the projecting end of something stuck up back of its head, like a cord to hang a picture or statue.

My eyes followed the projecting end of the cord up and up, and from the low rafter above there dangled the other end of a cord.

As one man we turned and looked into the corner where the stranger was sitting.

He was not there.

We looked around the room. There was no one in the waiting room, but the mail carrier, the station agent, and myself.

It was the agent who, with a panting sound, caught the door and slammed it shut.

It was the mail carrier who fumbled at the key until he turned it, and the lock went back into place with a dull thud.

I saw that their faces looked like the faces of men who have seen things for which men have no words.

I do not know how long we stood there, the wind tearing at the building, the snow beating against the windows, the telegraph wires shrieking and moaning and groaning in protest against something they did not understand—it seemed an eternity; but it was not yet one o'clock when there was a shuffling sound on the station platform, the door was opened, and a man in a long coon-skin coat entered.

He struggled with the door and finally succeeded in getting it shut; then he looked at us.

"Why, what's the matter? Has anything happened?" he asked

No one answered him.

"You all look as if you had seen a ghost," he said.

"We have. We've been spending the night with one," the mail carrier said.

"You talking about ghosts," the man laughed. "We'll begin to think the place is haunted if you talk like that."

"Don't laugh, doctor," the mail carrier said solemnly, "it's in there." He nodded toward the shed. "But it spent the night on that bench," and he pointed to the corner where it had been.

"What are you talking about?" the man called the doctor asked.

"Look in there and see," the mail carrier answered, and handed him the lantern.

We all stood back of him—we did not wish to look in again—but we knew we would.

The doctor took the lantern and opened the door which yielded readily to him, and looked into the freight shed.

"My God!" he gasped when his eyes fell on the thing. "It's a man!"

He looked intently at it without stepping over the threshold of the door, for a long time, then he turned toward us and said: "It's Morrison! That's who it is! It's Morrison!"

He looked again, still without stepping over the threshold of the door, and twisted the lantern to get different views. He turned toward us again.

"Yes, it's Morrison! Looks like a case of suicide! I guess the poor devil was a bit off his balance; the loss of his wife and all that. That letter about being threatened by a person with a peculiar ring sounded queer. No one with a crest has been in these parts."

He closed the door carefully, locked it and put the key in his pocket. "I'll get the coroner in the morning."

"That doesn't explain how he came to be sitting in that corner all night," the mail carrier said, and pointed toward the corner.

"You've been eating something that disagreed with you," the doctor answered good-naturedly.

"We haven't all been eatin' somethin' that disagreed with us," the mail carrier insisted, "and we all saw it, didn't we?"

We corroborated his statement; but the agent was new to the place, and I was a stranger, just there for a day.

"Then I guess you've all been drinking the same thing," the doctor said skeptically. He looked at me sharply and asked: "You were asking for Morrison to-day?"

"Yes, I came out to see him on business," I replied.

"Didn't you recognize him to-night?" he asked.

"No, it is some years since I saw him, and he had changed."

"Yes, he had," the doctor said reminiscently. "I remember him when he came. He looked a lot younger. Did he owe you anything?"

"No, I owed him something, but I find he has canceled the debt."

At that minute we heard the long-delayed train.

I took my grip and got on board.

Fortunately I had reserved a berth in the Pullman—but I got on the day coach, and sat there until the train started.

Then I took my grips and started back through the train; but when I reached the platform of the day coach, I put down my grips and removed my gloves.

From the little finger of my left hand I drew a ring, which I took between the finger and thumb of my right hand, and threw as far as I could out into the ice and snow—somewhere between Oakhom and Winnipeg.

It was a gold ring, with a heart-shaped crest, and crossed keys in the center.

I went into the Pullman and put my grips in my berth, but I did not feel like sleep, so I went to the smoking room; to my surprise I found it occupied by a soldier.

He told me that he had been at the front for two years.

"What do you think of that story about the angels at Mons?" I asked.

"I can't exactly say," he replied with a tightening up of reserve, "although I was in that battle."

"Were there angels there?"

"I didn't see any."

"I am particularly interested," I explained, "because I had a peculiar experience to-day. I went out to Oakhom to find a man who did me a great injury. When I got there I heard he had disappeared in a mysterious way. I did not pay any attention to the mysterious part of it, for I thought he had heard I was on the way, and knew it was safer for him to get out. I felt certain that he would not return until I was at a safe distance, so after making arrangements with the lawyer to let me know if they heard anything about him, I went to the station to wait for the train."

I paused, and the soldier said, "Well!"

I told him what had happened. He listened without comment.

When I finished, we sat in silence for a while. The train had stopped, the light flickered in the one lamp in the smoking room, and we could hear the storm beating and tearing at the train.

"I have lived on these prairies twenty years," he said, "and things I couldn't explain have happened, "but I don't think there is any mystery about what happened to you to-night."

"How would you explain it?" I asked.

"Farmers all look pretty much alike when wearing those sheepskin coats with their caps pulled down over their eyes. There is an epidemic of la grippe in the district, and I think that was a farmer who was too sick to be bothered talking."

"How did he get in?"

"He could have come in during a pause in the storm—you know it is perfectly calm at such times—and your attention was concentrated on the mail carrier's story; and doubtless he went out in disgust while you were watching that door."

"But the music, the coal, and the stealthy steps?"

"Listen!" he said.

I listened.

It seemed that I could hear queer sounds, almost like human moans around the train.

"A fellow imagines a lot," the soldier said.

"Yes," I agreed, "perhaps you are right."

"What is your explanation?" he asked.

"I haven't any," I said.

HE GOT AWAY WITH IT

By E. B. Whiting

FOR years he had been doing it.

For years he had been bringing home rocks and stones in his pockets.

He could not afford an auto. "How else can I get them home?" he always answered when chaffed or chided by his wife for his self-styled hypochondriacal hobby.

"The sea is washing away my land. Why should I not do what lies in my power to stop the sea?"

His wife tried every means to reason him out of his, to her, ridiculous hobby. Yet with the passing of the years it had become a fixed habit of his to search eagerly along the path or even along the sidewalk or street for "silicon dioxide" as he persisted in calling the pebbles of any size up to the limit of his pockets. Furtively he stooped to pick them up, and furtively he slipped them into the pocket where they would attract the least attention.

Night after night he would greet his wife with a kiss and the inevitable remark, "See what lovely quartz I have brought you," and once in a long while he would add, "It will last long years after we are both gone and forgotten." In his own mind he was satisfied that he was doing his bit, however puny and ineffective, to hold the sea at bay.

Years passed. The age-long conflict became for this man a draw. The erosion and the rebuilding of the land just about kept pace with each other. Pebbles persistently purloined from the city's streets came in handy as filling among the larger rocks the man could bring by boat now and then of a calm summer Sunday afternoon.

But the sea was patient.

The wife often shuddered in secret. "Better let the sea wash the land all away than to become a confirmed hypochondriac for the sake of a few miserable pebbles." And then came the night when she waited in vain.

A crowded trolley car. A broken brake bar. An open drawbridge. A waiting wife. A few escaped through broken windows and swam the icy waters to safety. Her husband was a good strong swimmer, but the pebbles, the heavy pebbles in his pockets. For the moment she forgot them——

The sea had won.

Fragments

By Tod Robbins

I AM sitting before the window. Summer is dead; and Nature has buried her with leaves. The trees stretch out their naked limbs, like beggar children asking alms. The pale moon, surrounded by clouds, resembles the face of a man who has perished in the snow. Now a cold breeze comes moaning through the forest. There is no warmth left in the bosom of the sea.

The white silence of frost rests over the face of the sleeping earth. Except for the melancholy murmur of the wind, there is nothing to be heard. The moonlight is flowing steadily, like a pale silver river, through a rift in the clouds. Beneath the trees fantastic shadows move about, keeping time to the solemn swaying of the branches overhead.

There is a little clearing in the center of the forest; and, in the middle of this clearing, stands a house. For many years it has been deserted. Now it is crumbling into decay. It is aging fast, like an old man who has no one left to love. The country people fear to pass it after nightfall. They think it is haunted by the ghost of a man who was murdered there years ago.

Once two brothers lived in this house. One winter night, they quarreled. A week later, when some of their neighbors broke down the door, a headless corpse was found lying near the fireplace. . . . The murderer was never found.

I think that I shall visit the house by moonlight. There is something about this deserted ruin which attracts me. Even in the broad daylight, its broken windows have what might be called a strange expression. There is something odd about its thatched roof. Yes, I must certainly see it by moonlight.

Last night I visited the haunted house. Rising, I dressed quietly, so as not to disturb my host, and walked out into the night.

Stealing across the lawn, where the frost lay like a fine, white veil, I soon found myself in the shadowy forest. Above my head, through interlacing branches, the moon peered at me from the corner of a cloud; beneath my feet, the fallen leaves were wet and sparkling with tiny drops of water.

Following a winding path, I soon reached the outskirts of a little clearing. *There* stood the deserted house, like a creature at bay, surrounded by an army of dark, silent tree trunks. As I stepped out of the wood, the moon shook off her veil of clouds and appeared in all her wonted brilliancy.

The haunted house looked even more dilapidated than when I had seen it last. The roof had partly fallen in, as though beneath the weight of a heavy blow; the door stood ajar, resembling a sagging lower lip; and the windows were like black, empty eye sockets.

As I stood in the clearing, looking at the haunted house, suddenly a light flashed up in one of the deserted rooms; a light which made the hovel resemble a gigantic, moldy pumpkin, cut in the likeness of a human head. It was as though a skull had suddenly regained its eyes.

Mustering up all my courage, I approached the house cautiously. The dying grass made no sound beneath my feet; the wind from the sea had died away; and the moon, as though in fright, had darted behind a cloud. Soon I reached one of the windows. I peered in, and this is what I saw:

The room was small and bare. Faded paper, like strips of dead, discolored skin, hung from the walls. In one place, a large piece of plaster had fallen to the floor. There was a small wooden table in the center of the room. Sitting in a dilapidated chair before this table was an old man. His head rested on his arms; his arms rested on the table. Near him, two candles flickered in their sockets. They threw their light over the white hair, the bent back, the wrinkled hands. The shoulders of the old man shook convulsively; bright drops glistened on his beard, like hail on frozen snow. He was weeping bitterly.

LIFE'S LAST SONG
By Arnold Tyson

WHAT would you do if I made love to you?
 Would you make me a slave to bow before
The shadow that I found beyond the door
Where each love stood a while and then passed
  through?
Would you be weary when at last you knew
 That all loves have their day and not one more?
 Would you beat at my window when the roar
Of love's flame settled to a sickly hue?

Would we find in the sunshine food for tears
 And in the sunset of that splendid day
Build up a sorrow that would haunt the years
 Till life's last song forever passed away?
And have you strength to know how life appears
 When love's cup, emptied, must be thrown away?

The Heads of Cerberus

Francis Stevens

SYNOPSIS OF PRECEDING CHAPTERS.

Robert Drayton, a young lawyer, reduced to poverty by the persecution of a dishonest corporation, arrives penniless in Philadelphia, where, at the end of all honest resources, he determines to turn criminal. He breaks into a house with the purpose of robbery, and is attacked by a cracksman who is pilfering a safe. Drayton regains consciousness the next morning. Then he finds that the occupant of the house is his friend, Trenmore, a rich Irishman and soldier of fortune, whom he has not seen in several years. Trenmore, a huge, powerful fellow, is still very fond of Drayton. Trenmore tells him that the cracksman had broken into the safe, looking for a mysterious antique which Trenmore has recently bought at an auction. This is a silver phial carved in the likeness of three snarling dogs' heads—the legendary "HEADS OF CEREBUS." Since Trenmore has owned it, several unsuccessful attempts have been made to rob him of it, but he has hidden it securely. An unknown who claims to know the power of the phial makes these attempted thefts. The phial is said to have been carved by Benvenuto Cellini for the Duke of Florence, and its contents have never been examined. The legend runs that the gray dust which can be seen through the glass of the phial is the dust gathered by the poet Dante at the gates of Purgatory. Trenmore and Drayton pry the top from the phial and pour out the dust. Trenmore stirs the dust with his fingers, and from it arises a puff of thin smoke. Then Trenmore vanishes from view. A few minutes later Viola, Trenmore's sister, comes to the house to see him. She grasps up some of the dust; then she, too, vanishes. Drayton next takes the fateful step. Trenmore's house is now empty. A thief enters and steals the now powerless phial, leaving the precious dust unnoticed. Trenmore's servant comes in to straighten up the library, and wraps up the dust to save it for his master. Meanwhile, without any sense of time, place, or transition, Drayton finds himself on a wide green plain. It is a strange, silent, desolate world. He sees the ruins of a medieval castle on a hill. He goes toward it, and comes to a mound overgrown with grass. A premonition moves him to tear away the grass, and under it he finds the still living body of Viola Trenmore. Going to the other side of the wall, he is face to face with Trenmore. The men and the girl wander on through this strange world, encountering many fantastic beings. They see phantoms dancing, and Drayton goes forward too near them, but the Voice of Illusion warns him that there are strange things in this land of Ulithia. The three chance upon the White Weaver, spinning the web of years. She tells them Ulithia is the phantom borderland of life, and to go onward, deeper into the unknown. Drayton's feet are tangled now in the silver web the Weaver has spun around them. "Go forward—go deeper," says the Weaver, and Drayton is borne outward upon a wide white sea.

CHAPTER VI.

A MATTER OF BUTTONS.

WHEN Drayton and his friends walked through the Ulithian "moon," they were none of them either quite unconscious nor entirely devoid of sense. Drayton, for instance, knew that Viola extended her hand to him; that he took it and that her other hand was held by some one else, an indistinct personality whose identity was of not the slightest interest or importance.

They all knew that with the dizzying fragrance of a million blossoms in their nostrils; with blinding radiance before them; with behind them only silence and the silver plain, they three joined hands and so passed beneath the black arch which had seemed a moon.

This dim apprehension, however, was wholly dreamlike, and unmingled with thought or foreboding. They possessed no faint curiosity, even, as to what might lie beyond that normally incredible archway.

Active consciousness returned like the shock of a thunderbolt.

They had emerged upon the sidewalk of a wide, paved street. They were but three of a jostling, hurrying throng of very ordinary and solid-looking mortals.

For several moments they experienced a bewilderment even greater than had come upon them in passing from a prosaic house on Walnut Street into the uncanny romance land which they knew as "Ulithia." The roar and rattle which now assailed their ears deafened and dazed them. Ulithia had been so silent, so unhuman and divorced from all familiar associations, that in this abrupt escape from it they felt helpless; unpoised as countryfolk who have never seen a city, and to whom its crowds are confusing and vaguely hostile.

In this new place there was none of that bright, dazzling mist which had filled the archway. Instead, it was well and more satisfactorily illuminated by numerous arc lamps. With a thundering clatter an electric train rushed past almost directly overhead.

Before them, the street was a tangle of dodging pedestrians, heavy motor trucks loaded with freight and baggage, arriving and departing autos, and desperately clanging street cars. Above, iron pillars and girders supported an elevated railway system. Close to where they stood a narrow moving stairway carried upward its perpetual stream of passengers, bound for that upper level of traffic where the electric train had passed.

Turning, the dazed wanderers saw behind them, not any vast expanse of silver light, but the wall of a long, low building, pierced with many windows and several doors. From one of those doors they had apparently just emerged.

With some difficulty the three extricated themselves from the throng of hurrying foot passengers. Finding a comparatively quiet spot by the wall of the building they stood there, very close together.

Suddenly Viola gave a sharp exclamation.

"But this—this is *Philadelphia! This is the entrance to the Market Street Ferry in Philadelphia!*"

Her brother slapped his thigh.

"And to think I did not recognize a place I've been at myself at least three times! But who would have thought we'd get home so easy—or at the other end of the city from where we started?"

Suddenly the melancholy ex-lawyer chuckled aloud.

"I never thought," he said "that Philadelphia, city of homes or not, would seem homelike to me. By George, I realize now what a charming old place it is! Terry, couldn't you resign wandering and settle down here for the rest of your life—right on this spot, if necessary?"

The Irishman grinned cheerfully.

"I could that, so be there were not a few better spots to be got at. Viola, I'm fair dead of hunger and so must you both be. Is there a café in this elegant station building? Or shall we go home and trust Martin? Heaven bless the boy! I never thought to see him again—trust Martin to throw us together some sort of sustaining meal?"

"I'm hungry," confessed Viola frankly, "but it seems to me we should go straight to Cousin Jim's house, rather than to a restaurant. You know that gray powder was left there——"

Trenmore gave a great start and his smile faded.

"That devil dust!" he burst forth. "And all this time it's been laying open and unguarded! Faith, after all we may not find poor Martin to welcome us home!"

"My fault again," said Drayton grimly. "If anything has happened to Martin, I am entirely to blame. In common justice I shall have to follow him——"

Trenmore turned with a growl. "You will *not* follow him! Is it an endless chain you would establish between this world and that heathenish outland we've escaped from? You after Martin, and myself after you, and Viola after me, I suppose—and there we'll all be again, with nothing to eat and no one but spooks to converse with! No; if Martin is in Ulithia this minute, may his wits and his luck bring him out of it. At least, he's the same chance we had."

"Call a taxi," suggested Viola practically. "It's just possible that Martin hasn't yet fallen into the trap."

"A very sensible suggestion, my dear," commended her brother.

By the curb stood an empty motor cab, its driver loafing near by. The latter was a thin, underfed-looking fellow, clad in a rather startlingly brilliant livery of pale blue and lemon yellow, with a small gilt insignia on the sleeve. A languid cigarette drooped from his lips. Beside his gaudy attire he wore that air of infinite leisure, combined with an eye scornfully alert, which all true taxi drivers are born with.

"Seventeen Walnut Street, my man," directed Trenmore, "and get up what speed you're able."

Drayton had made to open the cab door, since the chauffeur made no move to do so. To his surprise, however, the latter sprang forward and pushed his hand aside.

"You wait a minute, gentlemen!"

"Is this cab engaged? You have the 'Empty' sign out."

"No, we ain't engaged; but wait a minute!"

The fellow was eying them with a curiosity oddly like suspicion. Surely, aside from the fact that Trenmore and Drayton were hatless, there was little out of the way in their appearance. Viola's attire was the picture of modern propriety. In crossing that ghostly plain nothing had occurred to destroy the respectable appearance with which they had all begun the journey.

"Wait!" ejaculated Trenmore. "And what for? Isn't this a public cab?"

"Yes; it's a public cab, right enough. There ain't nothing the matter with me ner my cab either. The trouble's with you. Why ain't you wearin' your buttons?"

"Wearing—our buttons?"

Terence glanced frantically down over himself. Had the rapid transition from one world to another actually removed those necessary adornments from his garments? Everything looked in order. He glanced up angrily.

"Not wearing our buttons, is it? And what in the devil do you mean by that, you fool? Is it fuddled with drink you are?"

The chauffeur's alert eye measured the Irishman. It's owner shrank back against the cab.

"Don't you!" he cried. "Don't you hit me! I don't care who you are, you haven't any right to go about that way. You hit me, and you'll go to the pit for it! I've drove more than one of the Service itself, and they won't stand fer nobody beatin' me up!"

Drayton caught the half-raised arm of his friend.

"Don't, Terry," he cautioned softly. "Why start a row with a lunatic?"

Trenmore shook him off. He was

doubly annoyed by Drayton's assumption that he would attack a man of less than half his weight. For an instant he felt inclined to quarrel with his friend on the spot. Then the petty childishness of his irritation struck him, and catching Viola's appealing and astonished glance, he laughed shamefacedly.

"I left my temper behind the moon, Bobby," he grinned, as the three started off down the sidewalk in search of another vehicle. "Somewhere along here there's a bit of an office booth of the taxicab company's. Isn't that it, beyond the escalator?"

"Yes," contributed Viola. "I remember there's a sign over it. 'Quaker City'—— Why, but they've changed it to 'Penn Service!' Last week it was the Quaker City Company."

Whether "Penn Service," however, meant taxi service or something different they were not to learn just then. Ere ever, they reached the wooden booth beneath that white-lettered signboard, a heavy hand had grasped Drayton's arm from behind, whirling him about. The two others also turned and found themselves confronted by a police officer. At a safe distance in the rear their eccentric acquaintance, the chauffeur, looked on with a satisfied grin.

"And what is this?" demanded Trenmore sternly.

Drayton said nothing at all. With the policeman's hand clutching his arm, fear had him in a yet firmer grip. Was this another phase of the persecution to which he had been recently subjected? Was he about to suffer arrest, here in the presence of Viola Trenmore, upon some such trumped-up charge as had sent his partner to prison and death?

In the bitter grasp of this thought, it was a moment before he comprehended what the officer was replying to Trenmore's question.

"——and if you've lost your buttons, for why have you not reported your-

selves at the proper quarters? Sure, 'tis me duty to run ye in without further argument; but 'tis a fair-spoken, soft-hearted man I am. If you've a raison, give it me quick, now!"

Drayton grasped the fact that it was not himself alone who was involved. Equally, it seemed, Trenmore and his sister were objects of the man's absurd though apparently official attention. The lawyer in him leaped to the fore. Here might be some curious local civic ruling of which he, a stranger to the city, had heard nothing.

"What about the buttons, officer?" he queried. "Do you mean that we should be wearing some sort of button as an insignia?"

"Is it crazy ye are all after being? *What* buttons, d'ye say? Why, what should I be meaning, savin' yer identification buttons? What are yer numbers now? At least ye can tell me that! Or are ye the connictions of a family?"

There was a moment's silence. Then Trenmore said heavily, as if in some deep discouragement: "Faith, I myself was born in County Kerry, but till this living minute I never knew the meaning of the words 'a crazy Irishman!' Micky, or Pat, or whatever your name may be, we are connected with families so good that your ignorance never heard tell of them!

"And as for numbers, I do not doubt that you yourself have a number! I do not doubt that the driver of the poor little jitney bus yonder has a number! In jails men have numbers, and perhaps in the lunatic asylum you both came from they have numbers, and wear buttons with those same numbers on them; but myself and my friend here and my sister, we have *no* numbers!

"We have names, my lad, names. And 'tis my own name I'll send in to the poor, unfortunate chief that has charge of you, and you'll find that it is not needful for Terence Trenmore to be given a number in order to have such as you discharged from the force your low intelligence is now disgracing!"

As Trenmore delivered this harangue his voice gradually grew in volume as his sentences grew longer, until it boomed out like the blast of a foghorn. The two or three idlers who had already gathered were reinforced by a rapidly increasing crowd. His last words were delivered to an exceedingly curious and numerous audience.

The policeman, a man of no very powerful physique, quailed before Trenmore's just wrath much as had the taxi driver. He, too, however, had another resource than his unaided strength. His only reply to the threat was a sharp blast on his whistle.

"You've done it now, Terry," groaned Drayton. "Never mind me. Get your sister away from here, if you can—quick!"

The young lady mentioned set her lips.

"Terry shall do not such thing, Mr. Drayton. Officer, surely you won't arrest three harmless people because of some foolish little misunderstanding that could be set right in the twinkle of an eye?"

The policeman eyed her admiringly—too admiringly, in Drayton's estimation.

"Sure, miss," he declared, " 'tis myself is most reluctant to place inconvenience on so pretty a lass; but what can I do? Ye know the regulations."

"But indeed we do not," protested the girl truthfully.

Before more could be said on either side, there came an eddy and swirl in the crowd, and two more policemen burst into view. One of them, a sergeant by the stripes on his sleeve, came bustling forward with an air of petty arrogance which Drayton prayed might not collide with his huge friend's rising temper.

"What's this? What's all this, Forty-seven? What have these people been up to? What? No buttons? What do you mean by going about without your buttons? This is a very serious and peculiar offense. Forty-seven! The first I've ever met in this ward, I am glad to say. Under arrest? Certainly you are under arrest! The wagon will be here directly. What did you expect? What are your numbers? What have you done with your buttons, anyway?"

How long the sergeant could have continued this interlocutory monologue, which he delivered at extraordinary speed and without pause for answer or comment, it is impossible to say. He was interrupted by a clanging gong and again the crowd swirled and broke. A motor patrol drew up. Three more officers leaped down and stood at attention.

The accession of numbers drove from Drayton's brain any lingering hope that Trenmore might pick his sister up under his arm and bear her bodily from the shadow of this open disgrace.

That the exasperated Irishman had not acted was due partly to reluctance to leave his friend in the clutches of the law; partly to a rapidly increasing bewilderment. He could now observe that every person in the front ranks of the staring crowd did indeed wear a large yellow button, pinned below the left shoulder, and each bearing a perfectly legible number in black.

He could also see that these numbers ran mostly into five, six and even seven figures; but what those figures represented, or why the wearers should be so adorned, or what bearing the ornamentation might have upon their own liberty, was a puzzle before which the recent mysteries of Ulithia faded.

"Button, button, who's got the button?" he muttered. 'Faith, 'tis a wild and barbarous land, this Philadelphia! Sergeant, are you really going to run us in, just for not knowing what you and the rest are talking of?"

The sergeant looked him up and down appreciatively.

"You know very well that I must. But Lord, man, you've nothing to worry over with the contests coming off in a couple of days. Or haven't you any muscle back of that size of yours?"

Distractedly, Trenmore clutched at his black, wild hair.

"Take us to the station, man!" he snarled. "And be quick, as you value your poor, worthless life! Muscle? I've the muscle to pull you to bits, and by all the powers I'll be driven to that act if you do not take me to speak with some sane man this living minute!"

CHAPTER VII.

A FEW SMALL CHANGES.

THE ensuing patrol ride, while commonplace and uneventful from the viewpoint of one accustomed to such jaunts, produced in the bosom of at least one of the prisoners emotions of the most painful and poignant nature. It was not for himself that Drayton suffered.

In the recent past he had been too thoroughly seared by the fires of undeserved disgrace to be hurt by so trifling a touch of the flame as this. But that Viola Trenmore—Viola of the clear blue eyes and innocent white brow— that she should be forced to enter a common patrol wagon and be carried openly, like any pickpocket, through the city streets, was an intolerable agony in whose endurance he alternately flushed red with shame and paled with ineffective rage.

Trenmore the mighty also sat quiescent; but his was the quiescence of a white-hot anger, held in check for a worthy occasion and object. A pity to waste all that on mere underlings!

Having slowly ascended the short, steep incline where Market Street descended to the ferry, the patrol drove on with increased speed. A mile

ahead, at the end of a long, straight, brilliantly lighted perspective, reared the huge bulk of City Hall. The immense building's lower part was sketched in lines of light; its tower gleamed gray and pale against the black sky.

High upon that uttermost pinnacle there brooded a ghostly figure. It was the enormous statue of William Penn, set there to bless the children of his city, with outstretched, benevolent hand.

"Are you taking us to City Hall?" queried Drayton, turning to the officer on his left.

The man nodded. "Your offense is too serious, of course, for a branch temple."

"A—what?"

"A branch," said the man impatiently. "Headquarters will want to handle this; eh, sergeant?"

"They will, but no more conversation, please. Everything you say, my man, will be used against you."

"One would think we were murderers," reflected Drayton bitterly. Of what real offense could they have been guilty? Beneath surface absurdity he had begun to sense something secret and dangerous; something upon which his mind could as yet lay no hold, but which might be revealed to them at City Hall.

The night was fine; the hour eight-thirty by the clock in City Hall tower; the streets well filled. Most of the stores seemed to be open, and innumerable "movie" theaters, saloons and shooting galleries each drew in and expelled its quota of people, like so many lungs breathing prosperity for the owners.

There was a New York Bowery touch to the amusements and the crowds which Drayton did not remember as characteristic of Market Street. The thought, however, was passing and only half-formed.

The patrol clanged its way over the

smooth pavement, attracting the usual number of stares and fortunately unheard comments, and presently swung off Market Street into Juniper. They had approached City Hall from the east. The patrol entrance, being on the western side, it was necessary for them to pass half around the great building to reach it.

As they passed the Broad Street entrance, Drayton chanced to glance upward. Above the arch hung an emblem done in colored lights. It seemed to be a sword crossing a bell. Above the emblem itself glowed a number, consisting of four figures done in red, white and blue electric bulbs—2118.

The bell, thought Drayton, might represent the old Liberty Bell, Philadelphia's most cherished possession; the numerals, however, conveyed to him no more significance than had those on the yellow buttons these police so harped on.

Again turning, the patrol reached Market Street on the western side. Shortly afterward it was rolling slowly beneath the portico of City Hall.

The Public Buildings, to use the more ancient name for Philadelphia's proud edifice of administration and justice, are built in the form of an irregular hollow square. The large inner court may be entered by means of any one of four short tunnels, placed at the four cardinal points of the compass, and passing beneath the walls of the building proper.

As the three prisoners recalled it, that inner court was squarish in shape, paved with gray cement, and of no very beautiful or imposing appearance. Several old cannon, relics of past wars, adorned the corners and stood at either side of the northward entrance. In the northeast corner there was a sort of pavilion, where various free civic exhibits were perennially on view.

A patrol wagon, or a "Black Maria," generally waited near the southern side of this court. As the center of the place was actually the intersection of those two main arteries of the city, Broad Street and Market, two continuous streams of pedestrians passed through there all day long.

Such was the interior of City Hall as the three prisoners remembered it and into which they now expected to be carried.

While yet in the short, dark entrance tunnel, however, the patrol halted. Rising from their seats, the officers hustled their prisoners from the wagon. A moment later and they all stood together, halted just within the rim of the inner arch.

And there the three received another of those wildly disturbing shocks, of which they had suffered so many in the past few hours.

Instead of a bare gray courtyard, open to the sky, there stood revealed an interior which might have been lifted bodily from an Arabian Nights entertainment.

Above, rounding to a level with the roofs of the fourth story, curved the golden hollow of a shallow but glorious dome. It seemed to have been carved solid from the yellow metal itself. The entire under surface was without a seam or trace of ornament, and was polished to almost blinding brilliance.

Striking upward upon it from invisible sources at the sides, light was reflected downward in a diffused glow, yellow as sunshine and giving a curious, almost shadowless appearance to the great chamber below. From the center of the dome, swung at the end of a twenty-foot chain, depended a huge bell. This bell had either been enameled smoothly, or was cast of some strange metal.

The color of it was a brilliant scarlet, so that it hung like an enormous exotic blossom. Some change or repairs to the thing seemed to be in progress for out to it from the southern wall extended a narrow suspension bridge of rough planking, that terminated in a partial scaffolding about one side of the bell. No tongue or clapper was within the bell, nor was there any visible means of ringing it.

As for the floor beneath, it was of common gray cement no longer. An exquisite pavement gleamed there, made of white porcelain or some similar substance, seamless and polished. In it the blood-red bell and certain colored panels of the golden walls were reflected as in a pool of milk. Near the northern wall a design appeared in this floor, set in as a mosaic of varicolored marbles.

Where had been the southern and eastern entrances, short flights of green marble stairs led up to carved golden doors, gothic in style and all closed. The windowless walls, also of gold, were carved in heavy bas-relief. At regular intervals appeared panels, done in bright enamels, representing various weird figures resembling Chinese gods and heroes. The entire color scheme of red, gold, green and white had a peculiarly barbaric effect, itself entirely out of keeping with the formerly staid and dignified old Public Buildings.

Trenmore, as he gazed, forgot even his anger, and stared open-mouthed. They all had time to stare, for the sergeant, having pressed an electric buzzer near the door, stood at ease, obviously waiting for something or some one to answer the summons.

"And is this the place they have for a courthouse?" Trenmore murmured. "I've seen the Taj Mahal, and I've seen the inside of Westminster Abbey and St. Pauls, but never, never——"

"I can't understand it!" broke in Drayton desperately. Amazement had given place to distress, as the enormity of the change came home to him. "Why, but this is incredible; it's preposterous! I——"

"Here, here!" broke in the sergeant's brusque voice. "None of that. What were you muttering there? Never mind. Be silent. Here comes a gentleman who will dispose of your case in quick order."

At the south, a golden door had opened and a man was seen descending the short flight of green marble steps before it. Even at a distance, he seemed an impressive figure. Over a largely checked vest he wore an exquisitely cut frock coat. His trousers were of a delicate pearl-gray hue, and a pair of white spats surmounted immaculate patent-leather pumps. On his head gleamed a shining silk hat.

Had the gentleman but carried a flag, gasoline torch, or Roman candle, he might have creditably adorned a political parade. A large bouquet would have passed him well at a Bowery wedding. Amid the barbaric splendor which actually surrounded him, he seemed out of place, but happily unconscious of that fact.

Slowly and with dignity he advanced, while in the gleaming porcelain beneath an inverted, silk-hatted replica of him followed every step. At last his majestic progress ceased. He had halted some six paces from the group of prisoners and policemen. Without speaking, he surveyed them with a slow, long, insolent gaze.

He was a small man, handsome in a weak, dissipated way; old with the age of self-indulgence rather than years. His greenish-hazel eyes were close-set and cunning. He possessed a little, pointed mustache, and, in the opinion of the prisoners, an unjustifiably impertinent manner.

Out of the tail of his eye Drayton saw that his Irish friend was bristling anew. Well, if the outbreak had to come, he wished it would burst now and annihilate this silk-hatted monstrosity. No man could eye Viola in just the manner of this stranger and deserve continued life!

The high-hatted one deigned to speak.

"Well, Fifty-three," he drawled languidly, addressing the sergeant, "and why have you brought them here? The chief is in attendance on His Supremity, and there's no one else about who cares to be bothered. I myself came over to warn you that Penn Service is tired of having these trivial cases brought to the Temple. Lately you police chaps seem to consider the Temple a sort of petty court for pickpockets!"

Trenmore passed the sergeant in one stride.

"You miserable, insolent, little whippersnapper!" he thundered in a voice that was amazingly reëchoed from the golden dome above.

Instantly, as if sprung by a single trigger, the six policemen had hurled themselves upon him. High-hat skipped back nimbly out of the way. Drayton, seeing no alternative with honor, flung himself into the combat, and was promptly knocked out by the blow of a policeman's billy.

CHAPTER VIII.

LEGAL PROCEDURE EXPEDITED.

WHEN his senses returned, Drayton found himself sitting on the polished white floor, his back propped against a golden pillar. He became aware that his head ached horribly; that his wrists were handcuffed behind him; and that his tempestuous Irish ally was no better off than himself. Trenmore, in fact, lay stretched at full length close by. Tears streaming down her face, Viola was wiping ineffectively at his bloody countenance with her pathetic mite of a handkerchief.

Two of the six policemen stood looking on with no evident sympathy. The other four lay or sat about in attitudes of either profound repose or extreme discomfort. Though Terence Trenmore had gone down, he had taken his wounded with him.

"Get an ambulance, one of you chaps!" It was the voice of silk-hatted authority. "You think we want the Temple cluttered up like an accident ward? And bring those crazy prisoners of yours to the Court of Common Pleas. Mr. Virtue is there now, and one court will do as well as another for this sort. Look sharp, now!"

Saluting reverently, the two uninjured officers proceeded to execute high hat's various behests as best they could. They were forced, however, to leave the wounded while they bore Trenmore across to the southern door. Viola started to follow, then looked back anxiously toward Drayton. High hat, following her glance, beckoned imperatively.

With some difficulty, Drayton gained his feet and staggered toward the girl. He felt anything but fit, and he was keenly disappointed. All that shindy had been wasted! The insufferable one yet lived—had not even suffered the knocking off of his intolerable hat!

"Lean on me, Mr. Drayton," he heard Viola's voice, curiously far away and indistinct. The absurdity of such a request moved him even to laughter; but he certainly did lean on some one, or he could never have crossed that heaving, rocking, slippery floor without falling a dozen times.

Presently blackness descended again, and he knew no more till the strong taste and odor of brandy half-strangled and thoroughly aroused him.

A policeman was holding a tumbler to Drayton's lips, and seemed bent on pouring the entire contents down his throat. Twisting his head away the prisoner sat up. The officer eyed him wonderingly, then drained the glass himself and set it down.

"Feel better?" he queried.

"A little," muttered Drayton. He was seated on a leather-covered couch in a small room, and his only companion was the policeman. "I suppose," he added disconsolately, "that Trenmore was badly hurt. Where are they now?"

The officer laughed. "If Trenmore is your big friend, he came around sooner than you did. Lord, I wish't we had that guy on the force! Can you walk yet?"

Drayton rose unsteadily. "I guess so. Have you put the others in cells?"

"Hardly!" The officer stared at him. "They don't keep a case like this waiting. Your friend won't go in no cell, nor you either. And as for the girl ——" He broke off, with a shrug.

"And the girl?" Drayton repeated sharply.

"I dunno. Mr. Mercy was looking her over. I doubt he'll let that beauty go to the Pit. But come along, or we'll keep Mr. Virtue waiting."

"Mr. Virtue!" What a very odd name, thought Drayton, as he walked to the door, leaning heavily on his jailor. And Mr. Mercy, too. Had he fallen into a chapter of Pilgrim's Progdess? What had they fallen into, anyway? Had the whole world gone mad while they wandered in Ulithia? And what of this amazing "Temple" that had usurped the interior of City Hall?

On the streets outside, everything had appeared normal—except for those infernal buttons. Surely this *was* Philadelphia that they had returned to. Who that had ever visited the city could doubt its identity? It was distinctive as New York, though in a different way. And all the familiar details—the Market Street Ferry, the outer architecture of City Hall, Broad Street—oh, and above all that benevolent, unforgettable statue of William Penn——

The door opened upon a long, low-ceilinged, windowless room, illuminated by hidden lights behind the cornice. The ceiling was a delicate rose-pink,

and, like the golden dome, shed its color downward upon a scene of Oriental splendor. Unlike the white-paved court, however, this chamber was far from bare.

The dark, polished floor was strewn with silken rugs of extravagant value and beauty. The many chairs and small tables scattered here and there were of ebony carved in the Chinese fashion, their cushions and covers of rose-pink velvet and silks gleaming richly against the dark austerity of black wood.

Here and there the prevailing rosy tinge was relieved by a touch of dull blue, or by a bit of yellow ivory carved work. Several excellent paintings, uniformly framed in dull black, showed well against the unpatterned matt-gold of the walls.

Rather than a courtroom, indeed, this might have been the drawing-room of some wealthy woman with a penchant for the outre in decorative effects. At the chamber's upper end, however, was a sort of dais or platform. There, enthroned on a wonderfully carved ivory chair, a man was seated.

He wore a black gown and a huge white wig, like that of an English justice. He was hawknosed, fat-jowled, coarse-featured and repellant. If this was—and Drayton assumed it must be —Mr. Virtue, then his appearance singularly belied his name.

Before the dais were gathered a group consisting of Drayton's fellow-prisoners, a single policeman, and also the little man in the silk hat and frock coat. From above them, Mr. Virtue stared down with an insolent disdain beside which the high-hatted one's languid contempt seemed almost courtesy.

"Come!" whispered Drayton's guardian. "Walk up there and bow to his honor. They've begun the trial."

"The trial!" thought Drayton. There were present neither witnesses, jury nor counsel.

Having no alternative, however, he obeyed, ranging himself beside Viola and bowing as gracefully as his manacled condition would permit. As a lawyer, though disbarred, he still respected the forms of law, however strangely administered. His own demeanor should be beyond reproach.

Glancing at Trenmore, he saw that the Irishman had suffered no great damage in the recent unpleasantness, and also that he was eying the enthroned judge in anything but a penitent spirit.

As for Viola, she stood with hands folded, eyes meekly downcast, an ideal picture of maidenhood in distress. Drayton, however, caught a sidelong blue flash from beneath her long lashes which hinted that the Trenmores were yet one in spirit.

There was a further moment of awe-inspiring silence. Then the judge, or magistrate, or whatever he might be, cleared his throat portentously.

"Mr. Mercy," he said, "I believe there need be no delay here. From your account and that of Sergeant Fifty-three—by the way, where is Fifty-three?"

"In the hospital, your honor, having his wrist set."

"I see. He should have waited until conclusion of trial. His presence, however, is not essential. As I was saying, from his account and yours there can be no question of either verdict or sentence. In view of the prisoners' conduct within these sacred precincts, there will be no need to appoint counsel or investigate the case further.

"To conform, however, to the letter as well as spirit of the law, and in the interests of purely abstract justice, I now ask you, Mr. Mercy, as sole responsible witness of the worser outrage, if you can bring forward any extenuating circumstances tending to mitigate their obvious culpability and modify the severity of their sentence?"

Drayton wondered if the policeman's billy had addled what sense Ulithia had left him. Had he really understood that speech? He seemed to catch a phrase here and there, stamped with the true legal verbosity. As a whole, the speech was incomprehensible. And now Mr. Mercy was replying.

"Your Honor, in the case of the male prisoners, I know of no excuse. Not only have they appeared in public buttonless, but beneath the very Dome of Justice, with their eyes, so to speak, fixed on the scarlet Threat of Penn, they have assaulted and wounded the emissaries of sacred Penn Service. For the third criminal, however—for this mere girl-child—I do desire the mercy for which I am named! Separate her from her evil companions, and who knows? She may become as innocent in fact as in appearance?"

Mr. Mercy uttered this plea solemnly enough; but at the conclusion he deliberately and languidly winked at the judge, and smiled upon the girl prisoner in a way which made Drayton's blood surge to his wounded head.

Were these proceedings in any degree serious? Or was this all part of some elaborate and vicious joke? One hypothesis seemed as impossible as the other. Once more Drayton bowed.

"Your Honor," he said, "surely, even at this preliminary hearing you will permit us——"

But the judge interrupted him. "Preliminary hearing?" he repeated scornfully. "No man within the jurisdiction of Penn Service can be so ignorant of law as your words would indicate. Were there any shadow of doubt as to your guilt, we, in our perfect justice, might grant you a public trial. We might even permit you an appeal to Mr. Justice Supreme himself. But in so obvious and flagrant a case of law-breaking as yours, the Servants of Penn must decline to be further troubled!

"I now, therefore, condemn you, sir, and you, the big fellow there—my soul, Mercy, did you ever see such an enormous brute?—I condemn you both to be immediately dropped into the Pit of the Past. And may Penn have mercy on your probably worthless souls!"

Having delivered himself of this remarkable and abrupt sentence his honor arose with a yawn, tossed aside the black robe and removed his wig. Beneath the robe he was dressed in a costume similar to that of their earlier acquaintance, Mr. Mercy. Descending from the dais, Virtue paused to wave an insolent hand toward Viola Trenmore.

"You saw the girl first, Mercy," he addressed his silk-hatted associate. "So I suppose she's yours. You always were a devilish lucky dog!"

CHAPTER IX.

THE PIT OF THE PAST.

BENEATH the golden Dome of Justice, directly under the blood-red bell, where looking downward they saw the latter's crimson reflection as in a pool of milk, stood the three prisoners. That Viola was there had been the result of pleadings so passionate that even Mercy the pitiless and Virtue the gross were moved to grant them.

As to why any of them were there, however, or what the queer sentence of that still queerer judge might actually imply, they were yet ignorant.

This was their own world to which the white moon gate of Ulithia had returned them; and yet in some dreadful manner they had been betrayed. Some mighty change had taken place during their brief absence. *How brief had that absence been?*

Beneath the bell, Drayton and his companions had at least a few moments alone together. Their isolation offered no chance of escape. The three doors of the great chamber were shut and locked, while across the old patrol entrance at the west a grate of heavy golden bars had been lowered.

"Viola, my dear," said Trenmore, "my heart aches for you! Whatever this 'Pit' of theirs may be, they've not condemned you to it along with us. I fear 'tis for an ill reason that they have spared you. My own folly and violence have brought me where I can no longer protect you, little sister; but for all you're so young and—and little—you're a Trenmore, Viola. You know what to do when I'm gone? Oh, must I tear out my very heart to be telling you?"

Viola shook her head, smiling bravely.

"I'll never shame you, Terry. When you go, dear, life will be a small thing, that I'll not mind to be losing. And, Terry, I've a thought that this world we've come back to is our world no longer. We've no more place here than we had in Ulithia."

Drayton started slightly.

"Then you believe——"

"You must end this now," broke in a languid voice. Mr. Mercy had come up behind them unawares. Back of him appeared the figures of four other men, apparently convicts. They were dressed in loose, ill-fitting costumes, yellow in color and barred with broad black stripes. Their ugly heads were close cropped; their faces stupid and bestially cruel.

"Awfully sorry to interrupt," continued Mercy, fanning himself lazily with a folded newspaper he carried. "But we can't keep the Pit Guard waiting forever, you know. Don't cry, little one! I'll look after you."

Viola turned upon him with flashing, tearless eyes. When roused her temper was as tempestuous as her brother's.

"You insignificant rat of a man!" she stormed fiercely. "Do you believe I would have endured the sight of you even this long, were it not for my brother here, and Mr. Drayton? Do you believe I'll remain alive one hour after they are gone?"

Mercy looked a trifle surprised.

"Do you know, my dear," he drawled, "I think you're devilish ungrateful! If Virtue and I were not so soft-hearted you wouldn't be here now. Oh, well, I like a girl with a spark of temper about her. You'll get over it. If you really wish to see the last of your heavy-weight brother and his pal, come along."

Turning, he strolled off toward that mosaic emblem, set in the northward pavement. The four convicts closed about the prisoners. A moment later, having escorted them a short distance in Mercy's wake, the guard drew aside. The handcuffed prisoners now found themselves standing at the very edge of the mosaic.

The colored marbles, beautifully inlaid, represented a huge chained eagle, pierced with arrows, and reaching vainly with open beak after a flying dove in whose bill appeared the conventional olive branch. On a scroll beneath three words were inscribed in scarlet letters:

"*Sic semper tyrannis.*"

They were the words of Booth, when he bestowed the martyr's crown upon Lincoln. "So ever to tyrants!" Incidentally, they were also the motto of a State; but the State was Virginia, not Pennsylvania. What could be their meaning here? And where was this "Pit of the Past" into which the prisoners were to be thrown?

The last question was immediately answered. On the far side of the emblem, Virtue, Mercy and their attendant bluecoats had grouped themselves. Now Virtue stooped, clumsily because of his fat, and pressed a spatulate thumb upon the round eye of the mosaic dove.

Instantly the whole emblem began to sink. It seemed hinged on the base of the scroll. A moment later and there was just a hole in the pavement, shaped like the emblem, and up from which struck a strange, reddish glare.

Edging cautiously closer, Drayton peered downward. Viola and her brother joined him. They stood motionless, the ruddy light striking upward upon their shocked, fascinated faces.

What they saw was a straight-sided pit, some thirty-five feet in depth. From top to bottom the walls were lined with tiny, ruby-colored electric globes. At the very bottom sat a squat, gigantic thing.

With shoulders and head thrown back, the face of it glared up at them. The mouth, distended to an opening of some six feet across, was lined with sharp steel spikes, slanting upward. The tongue was a keen, curved edge of steel. In its taloned hands the monster held two spears upright. A tail, also spiked, reared itself at one side, and the narrow forehead bore two needle-pointed horns of steel.

So the space at the bottom of the Pit was filled. Anything falling there must of necessity be impaled—if not fatally, so much the worse for the thing.

Trenmore growled in his throat.

"For sure," said he at last, "you murderers have gone to needless trouble! Why do you not cut our throats with your own hands? The deed would be fit for your natures!"

Virtue and Mercy only smiled complacently.

"Sorry you aren't amused," drawled the latter gentleman. "This little joke was not invented for your special benefit. Do you know who that is down there?"

"The statue of the devil you worship!" hazarded Trenmore viciously.

"Oh, no indeed! Quite the contrary. The statue of the devil *you* worship, my bellicose friend. That is the God of War, and as he can no longer stride loose about the world, we have made it convenient for his devotees to drop in on him. In other words, break the Peace of Penn, and you'll get more of war than you like. *Sic semper tyrannus!* Any man who assaults another is a tyrant by intent, at least, so down you go——"

"It was your police who attacked me!" accused Trenmore hotly.

Mercy's brows lifted.

"Was it? I had rather forgotten. That does spoil my parable, eh? But we shan't let it interfere with your invaluable opportunity to worship the God of War."

"Do you actually throw people—living people—into that vile trap?" Drayton's voice was incredulous. So theatrical, so tawdry seemed this Pit of theirs; like a stage dragon at which one may shudder, but not sincerely.

"We most assuredly do," smiled Virtue. He continued speaking, but his words were drowned and rendered indistinguishable by a great rattling roar, which seemed to rise from the open Pit itself. The prisoners instinctively sprang back from the edge.

There was nothing vocal in the noise, but if a bronze demon like that below should start into hungry life, just such a mechanical, reverberating roar might issue from its resounding throat.

The sound died away. "What was that?" demanded Trenmore sharply.

Mercy laughed.

"The subway, of course. The trains pass under the Temple foundations. You are the most curiously ignorant crooks that were ever brought in here. Where have you been living?"

Virtue glanced at his watch. "Mr. Mercy, if you are interested in their histories, would you mind obtaining them from the young lady later on? I'm due at a banquet in half an hour and I'm not dressed."

"Go ahead," shrugged Mercy. "We can finish without you."

Frowning, the judge shook his head. "His Supremity demands regularity in these affairs, and you know very well that the presence of the condemning judge is required here." Then he added in a lower tone, which nevertheless carried across the Pit: "I tell you frankly, Mercy, that he didn't like that business last week. You are growing too careless of his opinion, my dear fellow."

"Oh, he's an old—— Hello; there comes Lovely. Now we shall have to hold the execution till she has looked the prisoners over. If we don't, she'll be deeply offended."

"A lot I care," muttered Virtue. Nevertheless, he lowered his hand, raised as if in direction to the guard.

A woman was approaching from the doorway beyond the open Pit. Tall, slender, a striking blonde in hair and complexion, she was dressed in an evening gown of soft, droopy lines, seagreen and deeply slitted to show slender limbs clad in pale gold.

At first glance and a distance, Drayton fancied that "Lovely" well deserved her name. But as she neared two facts became painfully apparent. The color in her cheeks was not the kind limited by nature, and her golden hair, waved back under a jade-green net, was of that suspicious straw gold, easily bought but very seldom grown. Her features, however, were regular and clean-cut, and her eyes really beautiful. They were large, well-shaped, and almost the very green of her gown.

Smiling sweetly upon Mr. Virtue, the lady extended her hand to Mr. Mercy, and afterward swept the prisoners across the Pit with a cold, indifferent gaze. When it rested upon Trenmore, however, her expression changed. A sudden light leaped into the sea-green eyes. The pupils expanded darkly.

"What a perfectly gorgeous giant, Virty!" she exclaimed, turning to the judge. "Where on earth did you get him? Surely, you were not about to waste *that* on the Pit?"

"Why not?" His Honor bestowed another covert, annoyed glance upon his watch.

"He has already beaten up four of our blue boys," laughed Mercy.

"Indeed? How so?"

Mercy related the incident briefly, giving Trenmore full credit and even exaggerating his feats for narrative effect. The lady laughed, a silvery peal of light-hearted merriment.

"And you meant to throw all that away in the Pit! How extravagant you boys are. It's fortunate I came out here. Now, what I should like to know is this. Why hasn't at least *that* one," she pointed at Trenmore, "taken condemned right and entered for the contests day after to-morrow? Why didn't you, Number—Number, whatever your number may be?"

Trenmore eyed her, frowning.

"Madam, I can't so much as guess at your meaning. If there's some way out of this murderous business for my sister, my friend and myself, we'd take it more than kindly if you'll explain."

"Lovely," Virtue protested, snapping shut his watch, "I really must leave here immediately."

"Just a minute," she flung him, and called across to Trenmore: "You must know the laws!"

Believing that their fate hung in a delicate balance, Drayton intervened.

"We are strangers here. They haven't allowed us to speak or defend ourselves, but we certainly do not understand the laws, and we have not offended intentionally."

"Strangers! Strangers in Philadelphia?"

"Certainly. This gentleman only recently arrived from Ireland; his sister has spent the last few years in the West, and I myself am from Cincinnati."

The woman shook her head, looking more puzzled than before.

"Those names mean nothing. If you are really from outside the boundaries, how did you get in?"

Drayton hesitated. A diplomatic answer to that was, under the circumstances, difficult. Before he could frame a sentence sufficiently noncommittal, a new figure had thrust its way through the police guard and walked to the woman's side.

He was a man of about thirty-five, sharp-featured, cunning-eyed, and with a thin-lipped mouth which closed tight as a trap. Unlike Virtue and Mercy, the newcomer was attired in full evening dress. A light cloak, black and lined with flame-colored silk, was flung across one arm. In his hand he carried a crush hat.

Without troubling to salute her companions, and without the slightest evidence of interest in the meaning of the scene in general, he addressed the green-clad woman.

"Lovely," he demanded in barely repressed impatience, "are you intending to go out this evening or not? If you don't wish to dance, for heaven's sake, say so! I can take some one else."

She turned upon him a glance of indolent scorn.

"Do that, if you think best. All my life I've been looking for a full-grown *man* to share my responsibility under Penn Service. Now that I have found one, do you think I will let him be lost in the Pit?"

At this speech Mr. Virtue gave a sharp exclamation, and Mercy laughed outright.

"So that's what you're up to, Lovely! Cleverest, I'm sorry for you! Goodnight!"

The thin lips of "Cleverest" parted in an unpleasant smile.

"I always knew you'd throw me over if you found a chance, Lovely. You mean to enter your protegé for Strongest, I suppose?"

"Certainly."

"And you believe he will be able to supplant the present incumbent?"

"I know he will!"

"Ah, well, I shan't despair. You may close the Pit now, but it can also be opened again—after the contests. And what of these other prisoners?"

The woman laughed defiantly.

"They shall have their chance, too! Virty, I don't often question your decisions, do I? But this time I wish you to close your ugly old Pit and," with a glance of disdain, "*not* oblige Clever by reopening it."

Mr. Virtue glanced very dubiously toward the thin-lipped man. He appeared not at all enthusiastic. Mercy scowled.

"Don't forget me, please, Virty! I've a very personal interest in this execution, and even Lovely shan't do me out of it!"

"Oh, shut up, Mercy," broke in the woman impatiently. "I can imagine what your interest is. You're afraid this girl's brother won't let you have her. But the law is the law and they have their contest-right. You never think of any one but yourself! Virty, turn these people loose and I'll be responsible for their appearance Wednesday."

"Cleverest, are you going to stand for this?" demanded Mercy angrily.

But Cleverest, who had himself been eying Viola, now smiled a strange, fox-like, tight-lipped smile.

"Why not?" he asked simply. "If Lovely prefers the fellow's strength to my brains, what can I do but gracefully withdraw?"

The woman looked at him with a trace of suspicion.

"Such amiability is really touching, Clever. But I'll take you up on it. That thin chap can go in for Swiftest, I think, and as for the girl——" She frowned at Viola with a look of mingled dislike and reluctant admiration. "Oh, well," she finished, "the girl can enter the contest for Domestic Excellence."

Slapping his fat thigh, Virtue burst into a sudden roar of laughter.

"Splendid, Lovely! You have it all arranged, eh? Mercy, you and Cleverest are down and out! Take 'em—take your charming protegés, Lovely, my child; and shut up the Pit. Old War must go hungry to-night. And now you'll excuse me, Lovely. You've already made me miss at least one full course!"

"It would do you no harm to miss more than that," she retorted with a disparaging glance at his waist-line; but Virtue only chuckled without taking offense and hurried away.

TO BE CONTINUED.

DO YOU PLAN TO GO AHEAD?

IF you are out of gear, repair your own machinery. Don't go crying to some one else for help unless you need it. Talk with men higher up. Study every conceivable way of improving your standard of work efficiency.

Get off somewhere mentally and look back over your day's toil. What are you doing with it? Continually plan new lines of advance. Every opening higher up must find you prepared to fill it.

Don't be afraid that by working so hard in your present position you will be held there.

You can't work too hard if you work intelligently. Change your living habits if they need it. Such a move might increase your capacity a hundred per cent.

Unexpected

by Junius B. Smith

ROBERT BARBEE, attorney at law and representative to the State legislature from one of the up-State counties, perched his feet on the top of his flat-top desk and cast out puffs of smoke from a strong and ill-smelling cigar. The legislature had just adjourned, and Bob was well satisfied with his record as a member.

He had crowded through much legislation, some of it good, some bad, perhaps—the future workings of it would undoubtedly show—and among that which he himself considered the "goodest of the good," to use his own way of putting it, was a law for the compensation of those persons wrongfully confined in the State prison, as afterward appeared.

The inception of this law in Bob's brain was directly due to a case he had had at bar, wherein a man, duly convicted by a jury of his peers, of the crime of murder, with recommendation for mercy, had been sentenced to life imprisonment, had served twenty-odd years, and was then released when another, on his deathbed, confessed to the crime and completely exonerated the convict whom circumstantial evidence had placed behind prison bars. Bob had got him loose—which was

an easy matter, after the other's confession.

But the man who had served the prime of his life in jail, came out broken in body and spirit, penniless, a wreck, fit only for the poorhouse, where he eventually gravitated some weeks before his death.

At the time Barbee had thought what it would have meant to the wrongfully convicted man, had he been paid compensation for each day of wrongful confinement.

And the matter had buzzed in his head for several years.

At last, sent to the legislature, he drew a bill and got it enacted, covering just such cases. Briefly the law read that for each day any man was wrongfully confined by a sentence of any court in the State he should receive the sum of fifty dollars, the accrued total of which should be paid to him by the State upon the establishment of his innocence and his release.

The law was a good one and much of it was made in the papers, which explained it at great length.

And then nobody thought any more about it—nobody, that is, save Bartolio Kammenti, and his friend Stefe Gatsuras, who were nowhere near as foreign-looking as their names.

Kammenti was a crook. He would perhaps have denied that allegation, for he had not as yet let his crooked inclinations wander into the bypaths which leadeth unto ruin. Yet behind his scheming brain lay the dormant germ of a peculiar crookedness. He would not have taken your watch, nor have stolen funds intrusted to his care. He would not have committed murder, nor many other crimes. He made a distinction between injuring an individual and dipping into the public funds.

Nor was he a petty crook. All his life he had been waiting for an opportunity to do something really worth while.

He laid aside the newspaper account of the "Convicts' Compensation Law," as it had already been popularly dubbed, and sighed with firm conviction. Plainly he was turning something in his brain.

An hour later he gained admittance to the home of Stefe Gatsuras.

Stefe wasn't a crook himself. He didn't have nerve enough to be a crook. He was greedy, overly fond of the material things money would buy, a man who discounted his bills because he hated to see the other fellow get the money, penurious in the extreme, yet vainglorious and paradoxically extravagant when it concerned himself.

He was known as a "tightwad." Likewise he was known as a friend of Bartolio's. Just why they ever hooked up together no one knew. Nor did any one know why that friendship apparently parted—though a lot of people thought they did.

Kammenti laid the paper he had been reading, in front of the other's eyes. "See that article?" he said.

Gatsuras nodded. "I was just reading it before you came in. Sounds like easy money, making fifty bones a day for doing nothing."

"Nothing is right," Kammenti laughed. "All you got to do is bust rock, march in lockstep, be kind to the warden, and any other little trifles you may think of. But say, bo—it's easy money *after* it's earned."

There was a peculiar inflection in his voice that made the other look up quickly. "What mean you?" he asked, scanning Kammenti's features closely.

Silence came down between them for an instant, while Kammenti returned the gaze, seeming to study his man once for all at the last. And then he spoke:

"Would you like to make some money Stefe?"

"Would I? Say, does a duck swim? Is the earth round? Does a baby nurse? What's the idea?"

Kammenti's gaze lowered to the paper on the table.

Again silence came down between them, broken after a time by Stefe. "I get what you mean—but I don't. I'm not incarcerated for a crime I didn't commit—and besides——"

"You said something about easy money," the other reminded.

"Lord, yes—for the other fellow. I —I—well, what do you mean, anyway? Out with it. You've got something on your mind. Let's hear it."

"It were easy to commit a crime and afterward be guiltless of it——"

"You mean you want me to knock some one on the head, with the hope that afterward I'll be able to prove I didn't do it?"

"No, you chump—I thought you had some brains."

Gatsuras sank lower in his chair, with a shrug. "Very well," he answered. "Let's hear what you propose —seeing you're the brains of this organization."

"Thanks for the compliment. I'm not asking you to be on the inside looking out. I'm willing to do the look-step and stand the gaff, just so you'll help me put it over. There won't be a single element of danger in what I propose to do. I'm tired of working for two hundred a month, when I can lift that much in little more than half a week. And then it's taken care of for you. You get it in a bunch, where it'll do some good. You can live on the interest after you get out."

"I can—I thought you said I could be on the outside looking in."

"Oh piffle. Maybe I made a mistake coming here—only I thought you'd jump at the chance since there's—say —twenty thousand in it for you, if you help me."

At the mention of money, the eyes of the other glittered with an avaricious light. "And—I don't have—to be the goat?"

"No."

"Well—let's hear what you've got to say."

Kammenti took a cigar from his pocket and bit off one end. "You see I've doped out how we can beat that law. It's quite simple. I'll steal five hundred from you——"

"The hell you will."

"Easy, easy," warned Bartolio, hand-lifted. "Just wait till I explain. I'll steal five hundred from you, according to your say so. I'll go out and spend it—only it'll be my own money I'll be spending. But before I do all that, I'll go around pulling a poor mouth and trying to borrow from all my friends. I'll play I'm plumb busted.

"Then all of a sudden I'll go down the line, painting the town a deep vermillion—and I'll spend—just exactly—five—hundred—dollars. Do you get me, Stefe? I'll blow in five hundred little iron men—or rather its equivalent in bills. Then I'll subside with the info to a bunch of hangers-on that I've gone dry.

"See how it'll all check out when you set the law's machinery on my track,

saying you had drawn from the bank five hundred in bills, had brought it home, intending to use it as first payment on some real estate you intend buying, had laid it on the table, pending the arrival of the seller of this land, and that when your back was turned, I horned in on the pile.

"You don't discover it's gone until after *I'm* gone. Then you're tearing your hair and raving like a madman when this prospective seller arrives. But before he arrives, you've ditched that five hundred where in four or five years from now you can "discover" it and be filled with horror and remorse at what you have done. That lets you out on any charge of perjury that might otherwise be brought up against you.

"You see, absent-mindedly you slipped that packet of bills into an envelope with some other papers—and when you tell this to the authorities, in four or five years from now, I'll be turned loose, you'll get your rake-off, and— well, what do you think of the scheme?"

Gatsuras nodded as in agreement. "Some scheme," he averred. "I take no risk. You have all the inconvenience. I get twenty thousand for helping you put it over, and you want to stay in there five years——"

"Depends on what the sentence is," Kammenti cut in. "I'm not fond of staying there too long. I'll know about what my copper'll be and we can both figure it out to spring the innocence stuff a month or two before I'd be normally turned loose.

"I'll demand a new trial, as provided under this law, and in support of my petition will file an affidavit from you to the effect that you have made a mistake and falsely accused me. Then all I'll have to do will be to prove my innocence, as the State before had to prove me guilty, and—gadzooks! What is simpler? You get your cut. I live in luxury the remainder of my life, and everything is lovely and the goose hangs high."

"Listens good. Sounds simple. Is there any way you could fail? Have you overlooked anything?"

"Not a thing—and besides, you should worry. *You're* not the one doing time."

"Well, that being the case—you're on. But tell me of your plan in detail. I don't want to make a slip myself."

And so it fell out that one crook had made two crooks, and some weeks later Bartolio Kammenti was duly convicted, despite his desperate fighting, of stealing five hundred dollars in bills from his friend Stefe Gatsuras.

Time passed. It was irksome to Kammenti—yet he contented himself each night with the mental assurance that another fifty dollars, less Stefe's bit, were added to his fast-accumulating pile.

And then, when little more than three years had elapsed, he decided he'd had enough of prison life. It wasn't worth fifty dollars a day to be a convict. It was getting on his nerves. His face showed prison pallor. His bearing lost that assurance it had held prior to his loss of freedom, ambition was gone, and what, in the beginning, had been a money-making lark, developed into a nightmare.

His mental attitude was not helped by the fact that a guard, to whom he had taken a personal dislike, goaded him by harsh treatment into an infraction of the rules that resulted in solitary confinement for some days. Here he had plenty of chance to meditate, and in the darkness of his cell, he decided it was time to get out.

So at the first chance, he wrote a letter to Robert Barbee, attorney at law, asking that he come to the prison and see him. It would be such a joke—even though only he and Stefe could laugh—to have Barbee, the father of

this law, unconsciously assist in morally perverting its intent.

He smiled as he thought of the joke. Was the joke on Barbee—or the State? Perhaps on both. He had earned a snug sum. It would be constantly accumulating, pending the trial of his petition for rehabilitation. It was not as much as he had intended to earn by serving. But it was enough. Again he smiled. *C'est drôle!* as the French would say—it is droll.

Barbee came. Kammenti swore with much vehemence that he was innocent. He averred with all the impassioned appeal that lay in his name that he could prove his innocence—that Barbee, of all men, would dig up the evidence that would free him. He had not stolen the money—and therefore some explanation must be forthcoming—or Gatsuras were a crook. But why should Gatsuras be a crook, he argued. He had not profited by sending a man to prison.

"Yet you had a fair trial and were convicted," Barbee pointed out.

"Yet am I innocent," Kammenti swore. "See I will prove it to you. May I have your pen and a piece of paper?"

The other wonderingly complied.

Then Kammenti drew an order on a bank in another State, paying to Robert Barbee an even thousand dollars. "It practically closes my account," he said in explanation, "so it is all you will get unless you prove me innocent—when I will pay you another thousand."

The lawyer went away. He saw every person who had been interested in the trial—or endeavored to. He worked for a solid week, striving to discover some additional evidence that would enable him to entertain for his client a petition for a new trial. Without such new evidence, a new trial could not be given, and it were useless to make application.

Then he returned to see his client.

"Kammenti, I have petitioned the district court for a new trial, but unless I can file some supporting affidavits at least five days prior to the hearing on the petition, as provided in the law, your petition will be denied and no new trial given. I have raked this town with a fine-toothed comb, and I haven't been able to dig up anything new. Can you make any further suggestions that might give me a new start? So I can run down something to help your case?"

As he spoke, and the import of his words percolated through the other's brain, the convicted man turned paler than his natural prison color. He seemed to be dazed. Had something happened to upset their plans?

He had arranged with Gatsuras that when he was ready to get out, he would hire a lawyer, have him file a petition with the court, and among others incidentally call upon Stefe—which would be the signal for Stefe to get busy. Or maybe Stefe would get busy. Gatsuras had promised, however, that he would arrange to discover the hidden money within a few days after the lawyer visited him.

And he would have a very good reason for discovering it at that time. With a lawyer coming, insisting that Kammenti was claiming innocence, Stefe, in the eyes of others, might be pardoned for doubting to the extent of making a search of his premises, to allay the aroused suspicion that something might have happened to that money besides having it stolen.

Yet that had been more than a week now. Surely Stefe wouldn't wait that long before making the discovery and notifying Barbee. He could picture how they had planned Stefe should make that discovery. A few friends would call, as they were in the habit of doing quite regularly, the subject of Kammenti's conviction would be brought about in a natural manner—perhaps by the relation of the lawyer's visit; Stefe would talk about it, show them just where he had laid the money, describe in detail all about the case.

And then he would suddenly stand aghast—he had practiced simulating it until he had it down to a seemingly natural degree—they would ask him what was the matter—he would suddenly remember he had laid some papers down there beside the money— or was it *on* the money—and had picked them up later and put them in a telescoping envelope and had filed them away where he kept papers of no great value. Maybe—he would scarce dare to voice the newly aroused suspicion— maybe he had picked up the money along with the papers, not noticing. He would look. He had not looked at those papers since.

And then, accompanied by those who were present, he would go to this old box and search the papers stored therein and would find the money— would find it had never been stolen— that he had sent his friend to prison for a crime he did not commit.

Kammenti pictured it all in his mind's eye. He had coached Stefe, had rehearsed him for many days, until he felt Stefe would do the thing just right.

And now—perhaps Stefe hadn't yet had time to make the find. Perhaps, even, the lawyer hadn't seen him, though he had promised to do so, as well as to see every one else who knew anything about the case.

And then Bartolio Kammenti quite reeled and sank back to a seat at the words the lawyer next spoke, for they condemned him to serve out his term and without pay. What the lawyer said was:

"I called on Stefe Gatsuras—he died two months ago."

A Mystery Downstairs

By Francisco Curtiss

THE dull shadows of a January sky came bleakly through the cobweb-covered skylight, darkening the corridor as though long after sunset.

In my haste to leave the gloomy hallway I opened the wrong door and found myself in the dissection laboratory, a gruesome room on the fourth floor, covering the whole width of that end of the Anatomy Building.

A class of medical students were working diligently on several cadavers which lay on marble slabs or were chained up in grotesque positions. I stood there shuddering, unable to turn my eyes from these dead bodies which were wrapped and bound like Egyptian mummies.

A sudden jar caused the corpse of a large negro to slip from its awkward position and plop face downward on the table, sliding forward all the while. As he stiffened out, his only arm straightened over the edge of the table and pointed directly at me. Ten seconds I stood still, never looking away from the accusing hand that reached toward me, a tortured soul mocking me for my morbidness.

The students in the laboratory continued their work with the cold deliberation of a science harsh and unsentimental. I stepped back into the hallway and closed the door unnoticed—except by two pointing black fingers, the only ones on the hand.

When I was once more in the dusky corridor I saw, a few paces away, the door I had overlooked. On it was a plate with gilt letters bearing the name "Herbert Graham, Ph.D., Professor of Anatomy." I knocked and without waiting stepped into the anteroom of Professor Graham's office suite. A moment later the inner door opened and an erect middle-aged man entered, smiling with warm hospitality as he came forward.

"Say, doc, but I'm glad you're in!" I exclaimed as I enthusiastically gripped his hand. "I've had an awful time getting here."

"Just like your dad, aren't you? Wild and impulsive," Graham remarked as he gave me a friendly slap on the shoulder. "I shouldn't tell tales, but I was well enough acquainted with him when we were in college, so I know what I'm talking about. Guess he hasn't changed, has he? And you're here this semester to begin the law course?"

"I'm going to try it," I said grimly. "Anyway, I know definitely that I was never intended for a doctor."

Then much to the professor's amusement, I related my trying experiences in the laboratory, concluding with a melodramatic recital of the negro's pointing arm.

"You'd soon get over that—it's like stage fright. The boys work in there with as little concern as in a kindergarten. In fact, they play some quite unconventional tricks on one another. Right now I'm investigating a prank that went a bit too far—in fact, a very serious offense."

Graham rubbed a hand over his Vandyke as he concluded his statement, and an intent expression came into his eyes. He noticed my curiosity and as we sat down in the office he began to explain what had happened.

"Quite often I work here very late. Last night it was after midnight, when I was startled by a succession of screams coming from the direction of the janitor's rooms downstairs. He has a couple of rooms in the basement directly under the south end of the laboratory—in fact, the inner room comes almost under my office. I ran to the window and looked down, but the screams had stopped. A light was shining into the alley from the window of the inside room, and dim though it was, I thought I saw a man sneak around the corner of the building. I hastened downstairs to the janitor's door where I was joined by a policeman who had been attracted by the cries. We thought we heard some one moaning. We tried to force open the door, but it was locked securely. Then we ran around to the window from which the light was shining. It was open and together we leaped into the lighted room, revolvers in hand."

Here the professor jumped to his feet and slammed a fist on the table indignantly.

"What would you think of a gang of fellows who sought amusement by terrorizing children!" he exclaimed in a loud voice. "In one corner of the room, trembling and sobbing, was the janitor's child, a lad not over thirteen or fourteen. Next to the door that opens into a hallway within the basement there was a corpse seated on a chair, chained in a position facing the bed. In the middle of the top quilt was the huge black arm of a negro, recently amputated. It's the most inhuman thing I've ever seen. I can't imagine college men doing such work. I believe, that not thinking of the subsequent possibilities, the miscreants planned it as a spooky trick on the janitor.

"We tried to calm the boy, but he was too frightened to be readily assured, and as he and his parents, who are Sicilians, haven't been in this country long, I don't imagine he understood much of what was said. We got him fairly quiet and turned to the door that leads to the other room. We pushed it open and switched on the lights, but the room was empty and there were no signs of its having been recently occupied. There is an inside door in this room as in the other that opens into the hallway within the basement. We opened it and called loudly, but received no answer other than echoes. Across the hall is the door to the cold-storage room where the cadavers are kept, but we knew the janitor would not be in such a ghastly place at that time of night. We closed the door and returned to the room we had first entered, but the boy had disappeared. It's all very strange. I reported the occurrences to the dean, of course, as well as the police. I understand the janitor and his wife and child have not been seen to-day. I trust that now some of our humorists are well satisfied."

Graham shook his head disgustedly, while in awe I gripped the arms of my chair. The telephone rang, and as he stepped to the waiting room to answer it, I relaxed in my chair, observing the furniture and decorations of the office.

It was an unusually cheerful place, in that ancient nightmare of a building. Comfortable morris chairs were in the corners. There was an overstuffed davenport near a glowing fireplace. In the middle of the room was a library table, strewn with magazines in home-like untidiness. Shelves and bookcases hid the walls, and though the long rows of medical and scientific treatises did not interest me, I was pleased to see several sets of detective stories.

"I observe you are fond of Arsene Lupin and Sherlock Holmes," I remarked as Graham returned.

"Yes, I read them a great deal," he answered. "I am somewhat of an amateur detective myself—a very poor one, to speak truthfully, but it's my only hobby and keeps dull hours away. Although it isn't generally known, I work with the secret service quite often. My specialties are finger prints, identification, and handwriting. Rather a coincidence that it was Streeter, chief of the service, who just called. Rather peculiar circumstances—may be connected with the occurrences of last night. If you care for a bit of excitement, I'll share the downstairs mystery with you."

"Do I!" I exclaimed, jumping to my feet. "If you let me in on your adventure this time, you'll wonder how you ever got along without me."

"Streeter will be here soon, so if you'll pardon me I'll step over to the laboratory and run out the stragglers— it's after class time for Saturday afternoon anyway. We can't allow anybody else in the building when we begin our work."

The professor was not gone long, and when he returned he tossed a pair of black fingers on the table.

"The room is forsaken now," he said, "I found these little souvenirs over by one of the wash basins. Some practical joker cut them off your black friend's hand."

"Ugh!" I shuddered, and turned away.

"Don't let it bother you," Graham remarked. "You will see worse things if you associate long with detectives. Some queer cases we have."

A few minutes later Streeter arrived with several policemen. The chief of the secret service was a young man, sharp and erratic, observing every detail in spite of his restlessness.

"Tell you what," he exclaimed jerkily, "this is certainly peculiar. Know Rudolph Hoffman? Used to be in the supreme court? He left in his car for Delmonte last night—suddenly called away, important business. Never got there—found his deserted machine in the park this morning, colored chauffeur gone. And this janitor's kid that got scared last night and ran away— he's been working for the Hoffmans for a couple of weeks. The servants said he was terribly afraid of the chauffeur. Strange. What do you say?'

Graham sat down, looked steadily into the fireplace, constantly running his fingers through his hair. After some minutes he slowly arose, pulled out a table drawer and brought forth two automatic revolvers and a pocket flash light.

"I believe," he said slowly, "that we will learn more beginning right in this building. Have a couple of men guard the laboratory door in the hallway, Streeter—throw a cordon of police around the building and the three of us with an extra officer or two will search the janitor's rooms."

"As you say," Streeter answered snappily, for whatever his own procedure might have been, he regarded Graham highly enough to try the professor's method first.

Graham handed me one of the automatics, at the same time slipping the other and the flash light into his coat pocket. We were soon downstairs.

No one answered our hammering on the janitor's door and our skeleton key was useless, for the door was bolted or blocked from the inside. Iron rods formed a protective grating over the windows of the front room and we could not enter that way. So we tried the window of the rear room—from which Graham had seen the light shining early that morning.

The window was down, but unlocked and I had no trouble raising it. I raised the blind and Graham flashed his light in the room, which was devoid of occupants. I jumped down into the room and turned on the lights. Then I tried the door which connected with the front room, but found it locked. I looked around, but saw no evidence of disorder or recent habitation. All trace of the terrible scene of a few hours previous was gone.

"Perhaps the men that played that trick got frightened after what happened and returned to remove the corpse," I suggested.

"But I saw only one man— and a man alone does not do such things for amusement, though it is possible there were others I did not see," replied Graham. "Stay in there and wait till we break in the front door. Maybe we will find something. You can have an officer for company, if you like."

"I don't need any help—I'll take care of myself," I answered gamely, and I smiled grimly as I fingered my automatic, never imagining how a few minutes later I would regret my boastful words.

Graham and the others left as I sat in the chair that had been the resting place of the dead man. Grasping my revolver, I faced the door opposite the window through which I had entered; the door that opened into the hall beyond which was the refrigerator room where the cadavers were kept. Then I observed that Graham had closed the window after first pulling down the blind.

How slowly my friends worked! Seconds seemed like minutes, and in that solitude each minute dragged like an hour. My watch ticked louder and louder—louder and louder, until I was sure the sound would reverberate and echo around the room. Nervously I scraped a foot across the floor. There was a shriek! I leaped up holding my revolver tightly—my eyes were fixed on the white knob of the door that opened into the interior of the basement. It began to turn slowly, around and up. Chills ran down my back. Another creak on the floor! Some one was moving in the hallway. No, it was the latch of the door I heard. The doorknob kept turning. My heart pounded like a riveting machine. Now was the time—the latch was unfastened, the door would open and I would face that dead negro, back after his arm. Click! I was in darkness—the light was out! Then I saw him in front of me, grinning relentlessly through his dirty yellow teeth. Mechanically I gripped the butt of the automatic and pressed the trigger.

Bang! Bang! Bang!

Suddenly the light came on. In front of me was the closed door, marked by three bullet holes near the top. The doorknob still turned, faster and faster, until it was whizzing around. I reached forward and touched it. It was not moving. The reflection of the light combined with my imagination had been too much. Then when I saw that the door was firmly bolted, I was disgusted.

I went to the window and raised the blind. At least there would be no repetition of my childish fear if the electricity were again shut off.

I felt ashamed, but I would be a man! I deliberately turned out the light and stepped over to the door. I clutched my automatic, then quickly snapped back the bolt and stealthily turned the knob. There was pressure from the inside and the door was pushed open. Before I could shove back, a man was upon me. A ghost! But he harmlessly crumpled at my feet, a corpse. Again my nerves were terribly shocked, but I slowly recovered my self-possession. The cadaver placed in that room the night before had been leaned against the door, ready to fall on the first one who opened it. Somebody was playing the joke too well.

But I did not have time to philosophize. A puff of cold air, like the breeze off an iceberg, fanned my face a moment and was gone. Lingering after was the nauseating odor of a carbolic formal in solution. This time I was not the victim of hallucination. I had felt the presence of an invisible being, and to confirm that warning there had come the chilling puff of foul air. Some one in that black hallway had opened and closed a door, and I knew well it was not the janitor.

There was no mistaking the source from which that icy draft had come— the refrigerating room. But where in all that dark passage was the door? And who, thought I, but some madman would wander back and forth in and out of that dismal catacomb?

I pushed back the corpse, opening the door far enough to slip through into the hallway. There was a murky blackness all around, and the melancholy silence appalled me. I dared not hurt the madman, but I took a step down the hall to get out of the little light that came through the partly opened door. As I did so, I neglected to hold it open and it shut with a click. The oppressive stillness in that dark solitude was terrifying. Desperately I tried to open the door. It had latched securely and the doorknob was missing.

I was alone in a Stygian darkness from which there was no escape. I had not even a match. My automatic! What use was it, when that nocturnal monster could reach through the blackness and crush my throat with his skeleton hands before I could press the trigger. A revolver was no defense against the chimeras and apparitions that were conjured up in my disordered mind.

In that tomblike stillness the sound of my pounding heart would betray me as it drummed against my chest. My throat was so dry I could scarcely breathe. Those first agonizing moments were hours. I wanted to faint, to scream, to shoot the revolver crazily, to plunge madly down the hall, but I had not even the trembling strength to move had I dared. In my paralysis of fear, I remembered a maniac in a foreign country who had murdered people and sold their bodies. Perhaps some brutal moron was doing that very thing in San Francisco. Then my body would be worth as much to him as any other. But if it were an insane fiend with whom I had to deal, he at least was flesh and blood. I had protection, if I used it quickly enough. Then I heard a low humming sound, as of a huge machine muffled by many walls. Through my tortured brain there flashed a vision of the terrible pendulum in Poe's story. Perhaps this was even a more horrible instrument!

Then a light came on at the western end of the hall and I saw that no one else was there. In the north wall was the door which led to the refrigerating room, and almost opposite was another door which I knew opened into the front room of the janitor's apartment.

The peculiar murmur of the machinery ceased and instantly the light went out. My revolver encouraged me as I crept toward the west, feeling my way along the wall. At last I found the door to the front room, which was unlocked and I opened it slowly. My caution was unnecessary—there was no one there.

My friends were smashing in the outer door and had nearly broken through when I pushed back the bolt and opened it.

"What has happened, man?" cried Graham. "We were worried. We heard shots in this room and thought you were in trouble."

"You heard me shooting," I explained, "but it was in the next room instead of this, and I only imagined I was in trouble."

They listened intently while I told of finding the cadaver and about some one in the hall just a moment before myself. Graham showed great satisfaction when I spoke of the sound of machinery, and described the mysterious action of the lights.

"That helps a lot," he said. "As it is, we've made a lot of noise and have alarmed no one in the building, but we'll search the room and be as quiet as we can."

Graham stationed an officer at the outer door; the rest of us began a hurried examination of the room. Soon the professor showed us a sheet of paper lying among other foreign newspapers on a table. On this paper were two large reddish-brown finger prints and, below them, a small cross that was marked in the same color.

"Here's something," muttered Graham, "two finger prints and a sign marked in blood—the seal of some underworld organization. It was evidently placed here for the janitor and his wife to see before they entered the next room and found the cadaver and arm, the more emphatic warning."

Graham turned to me, saying, "Go up to the top floor and learn what the guards have seen or heard. Take one of the men in with you and see if anything unusual has happened."

I was not enthusiastic over visiting the laboratory, but determined to carry through my part, I did as the professor requested and ten minutes later was reporting back.

"The guards are certain they heard some one in the laboratory," I said, "and that nigger's moved. He was farther back on the table and he's got both arms now—both of them pointed right at me and he's still stretched out. The southwest window was the only one open and one of the faucets was turned on. But there wasn't any one there. We searched every place. Even the door to the elevator shaft was fastened some way so we couldn't open it."

"While you were gone, Streeter called up the Hoffman home," Graham informed me, "and I learned that two fingers of the chauffeur's right hand were missing, also that he had been employed there less than a month. Now what conclusion do you draw from these facts?"

"That's the chauffeur's body up there. Some one sold it to the university. The judge was killed at the same time and his body disposed of, probably the same way."

"No, no. That negro has been there a week. The chauffeur and Hoffman have been missing since last night only."

"Then the murderers cleverly substituted his body for the one that was there."

"No, it's the same body. Besides, we do not know that these men have been murdered. Your imagination is getting away with you."

"Then you think there wasn't some one in the hallway, or that I didn't hear peculiar murmuring noises beyond?"

"That part is plain enough. The noise is the sound of the elevator running between the refrigerating room and the laboratory. It opens on those two floors only. The strange action of the lights was caused by a circuit being made as the elevator stopped, probably upstairs. It is run by an electric motor and a short circuit occurred because of defective wiring. Of course there is some one beyond the hall and he has an idea of what we are doing. Your three shots disturbed him in the hallway after he had placed the corpse against the door. He went upstairs with the negro's arm and put it back on the cadaver. It had not been cut off when I was there yesterday, nor the fingers. When he reached the laboratory and replaced the arm, he looked from the window and probably saw a policeman or two near the outer door. Then he went to get a drink and left the water running. We'll go after him now."

Streeter called in three officers and posted one in each room, and detailed one to go with us. Then I borrowed a flash light and we cautiously entered the hall from the inside room through the door which I had opened before in a more daring way. To my surprise, the corpse which had fallen on me was gone. Graham took this fact as a matter of course, however, telling us that the person who had taken the arm away had also disposed of the body, removing it while we were in the front room.

We flashed our lights in the hall as we tiptoed toward the door that opened into the refrigerating room. We turned off the lights as the professor opened the door and we slipped into a vestibule. Graham slowly pushed open a door in front of us. The room beyond was dimly lighted and very cold. A familiar sickening odor burned my nostrils.

We heard the murmur of the elevator which became fainter and fainter as it rose upward. I wanted to push forward, but Graham warned me that we might have to deal with more than one person.

So we entered the room slowly and quietly, but there were no signs of life. Instead, everything in that gruesome chamber was suggestive of death. A row of ghostlike bodies in morbid shrouds hung along each wall of the sepulcher. I had felt dejected and gloomy when I entered the dissecting room upstairs, but in this cold tomb I was afflicted with a depression infinitely worse—a feeling of despondency crept over all of us, even the professor, who was so accustomed to this grim form of death. The heavy stillness so oppressed me that I could no longer remain quiet. I shoved Graham and Streeter aside and strode into the middle of that grisly cavern where I stood, peering through the pale light at the silent victims of bloodthirsty science. The odor of the preserving fluid was nauseating. It cut into the membrane of my nose, my eyes smarted. I felt weak and very sick. The lights danced up and down, and the cadavers whirled around my dizzy head.

Gradually my nerves became a little steadier, and at the whispered command of Graham I joined in an examination of the catacomb. I was close beside him near the north wall when he uttered a quiet exclamation. On a shelf, almost concealed by the bodies hanging in front, he had discovered a kit of dissecting tools, evidently stolen by the man for whom we searched.

"Look at this," said Graham, pointing to the side of the kit.

I looked and saw two fingers marks daubed in blood. I shuddered as I remembered that same sign on a piece of paper and I thought of those black fingers Graham had so carelessly dropped on his library table. We motioned for Streeter and the policeman. It seemed a little safer when the four of us were close together. Who could tell when those dead men would step down from where they hung! These thoughts constantly flashed through my mind. Then I would curse myself for a fool and temporarily regain my nerve.

I could remain quiet only a few minutes. My nerves were taut and ready to snap. Suddenly I walked away from my companions and stood alone in the middle of the room. My friends were separated from me by a row of cadavers as they continued to search the shelf. The dim electric light cast faint shadows around me as I looked toward a massive steel door, barred and locked securely. It was the entrance to the cadaver pond where the bodies were thrown into a solution to remain until the ghouls of science claimed them.

'Thank God," I muttered, "we don't have to look in there."

Then as I turned toward the door of the elevator shaft, the light went out, leaving the room coldly dark. The suddenness was a warning. I did not use my flash light, nor did the others flash theirs. In silence we waited.

Once more I heard the murmur of the elevator machinery and I faced the shaft entrance fearfully. The door clicked and I heard the heavy step of some one entering the room. My heart pounded erratically in my paralyzed throat. My knees trembled an instant, then my body became rigid and cold.

Suddenly the light came on, and I faced a huge negro. He was startled only an instant, then crouching viciously, like a gorilla, he came toward me, quickly traversing the twenty feet between us. I could not move and in my terror I forgot my friends, though I could not have cried out had I tried.

The giant negro raised a hand toward me just as the cadaver had done in the laboratory. One fact zigzagged through my disordered brain: Two fingers on that hand were missing!

It was this realization that brought back my senses. As the monster reached for my throat, I leaped aside and with astonishing coolness pointed my automatic. With a panther's quickness he was upon me, grabbing at my wrist, but too late! As he pressed against me, my weapon began to spit its little lead pellets. Together we fell on the damp floor. My companions reached my side as I crawled from under the brute. I arose unsteadily—but he was there to stay.

"You finished him," said Graham quietly, as he bent over the body. "Streeter, look in the elevator."

I was so dazed that I stood by dumbly, hands in pockets and shivering all over.

"Good work," said Graham as he gripped my shoulder. "Things will be easier now."

Then an exclamation from Streeter drew our attention. We huried to the elevator where he was bending over two bodies. Graham stepped in, but I had seen enough and could not help them remove the bodies.

"Just as I thought," Graham said. "Here is the cadaver that was in the janitor's room last night. The other is Hoffman. A blow on the head did it. Now we'll go upstairs and search the laboratory."

The elevator with its sinister hum rose with us to the laboratory, forsaken except for ourselves. The guards entered from the hall and we searched the room. We looked in closets, under tables, on shelves and in every possible hiding place, but found nothing.

"I give up," said Graham, in loud tones of disgust. "This is all for me— now we've got to get some of the laboratory assistants up here to remove the cadavers the boys were studying when I ran them out. If you men'll wait a minute, I'll finish the work on this one myself."

He picked up a knife and placed it firmly against a body that lay shrouded in gray cloth. There was a scream of pain and rage as it jumped up. I stood aghast! There seemed no end to the terrible things that were crowded into that last hour.

The cloth dropped down, revealing a veritable derelict of a man whose bloodshot eyes looked into a row of revolvers.

"Uh-huh!" exclaimed Graham triumphantly, "another murderer. A friend of the janitor's, aren't you?"

The captive nodded his head dumbly.

"The murderer of the judge! Aren't you? You're a murderer! Cut with it! Do you want to be hanged in the catacombs? Speak up."

"No, no," stammered the prisoner. "No murder—no murder. The nigger—he done it."

Graham was now a different person, harsh, cruel, and merciless—sweating the truth from this criminal.

"You lie. You are not the janitor's friend—you threatened him. Where is he? Where is his wife? Where's his boy? Don't lie to me! I'll let your chimpanzee comrade choke you. Norwood, take the elevator down and bring him up—get the chauffeur. He's told us everything. This man is lying—when that nigger finds he's being double-crossed he'll pull him to pieces."

"No, no, no—the nigger killed the judge. I wasn't there. He was going to rob him—hit him too hard. I wasn't there. I scared the janitor away. We wanted to hide the body."

Graham cross-examined him rapidly, with the cleverness of a great psychologist.

"Our police aren't fools. We know your game. We've got you. You threatened the janitor, didn't you, and made the boy work for the judge— made him spy through the house—kept

him terrified by the nigger. You couldn't rob the place—so you faked an outside message and got the judge started for Delmonte and the chauffeur murdered him. Talk up! Has Norwood started down yet—yes, just going —wait till he brings that orang-utan up here. Then you'll talk!"

"No, no, I didn't kill—I didn't kill."

The nerve-wracked man was trembling and his eyes bulged out as he spoke. "I didn't know till after. We were to rob. I wasn't there—he found me. We ran the janitor out and left a warning—the boy came back and saw we'd cut a couple of fingers off the hand. He remembered the nigger and it kept him scared. There was only two of us. The janitor's all right—they went to his brother's. I didn't kill."

Graham's manner suddenly changed, now that he had the whole story. I knew he disliked the mental browbeating that was so necessary under these circumstances, and I was relieved to see him smile. Streeter stepped forward to slip on the handcuffs and I moved toward the hall door.

There was a cry of warning as something whizzed past my head and a quivering stiletto struck the wall in front of me. I turned and saw the prisoner dash past the officers and run toward the open door of the elevator shaft. Without hesitating he jumped for one of the cables—and missed.

When I looked down, there was only a dim light shining through the top grating of the elevator, now at the bottom of the shaft, but it was sufficient to show the outline of a lifeless body.

ACCOMPLISHMENT

IT is not length but quality that counts in the game of life. Take this lesson to heart. It isn't the number of years you live that matters, but what you accomplish during that time.

Burnt Bridges

By Clarence L. Andrews

FROM behind drawn shades in the library alcove Homer Judson watched three persistent callers striving to gain admittance. The fact that one was Knowlton, his legal adviser, and another, Peter Bosworth, aircraft millionaire, gave him no comfort; the third man was Wardell of the district attorney's office, and the latter's presence argued for vigilant silence.

Occasional glimpses of an officer's helmet far down the driveway added to his uneasiness. Nor was that all—other helmets, he knew, would also be found at each entrance to the Judson estate.

He shook his head grimly, the chalky whiteness of his haggard features accentuated by the dark background of curtains. It was the age-old game of fox and hounds; and he, the quarry—winded, outgeneraled, exhausted—stood hopelessly at bay in his own home.

Two avenues of escape lay open to his choice. By risking an all-day wait, hidden in his lair as it were, evening would augment opportunity for a successful dash to his private hangar. Then, under cover of darkness, he could outdistance the blue-clothed hounds by flight in his *Eaglet*.

Or there was one surer way.

The three callers gave up their attempts to force an entrance and drove rapidly away in an open car. Judson watched the machine out of sight, the intensity of his emotions evidenced by twitching throat and jaw muscles.

When the car was no longer visible, he hurried to his desk from which he secured a large-calibered revolver. Removing two empty and four loaded shells from the cylinder, he pulled the trigger several times in quick succession. Satisfied that the action was flawless, he slipped six loaded shells into the chambers and pocketed the weapon.

Without seating himself he wrote a brief message on a sheet of note paper, pondered over it a moment or two, scratched out four words, added another line, then signed his name. This done, he surveyed the room from where he stood.

At length he crossed to the fireplace and attached his note conspicuously to the mantelpiece. Next, he stepped to the alcove for a final inspection of the now deserted portico, after which he seated himself by the hearth and drew the revolver from his pocket.

There was nothing theatrical about his actions; no smile softened the grimness of his features; each movement was performed in the precise manner of one whose purpose is both desperate and definite.

Lifting his eyes to the deep-framed portrait above the mantel, he studied its beauty intently. Constance Bosworth had been a wonderful girl, he thought—even more wonderful than the great artist had portrayed her.

His absorbing hope had been that some day she would reign as queen of his home; for her he had forced the money markets to do his bidding, had gripped and held the financial world by its throat that Constance might have riches no other man could bestow upon her.

And then——

Uncertainty shadowed Judson's countenance for the first time. The grave, pensive eyes of that canvas likeness seemed to regard him with a reproving look; some finer, hidden chord within him was stirred. Scarcely perceptible beads of moisture gathered on his brow; he appeared to shrink in his chair.

Long minutes ticked by before his gaze finally lowered to the quaint bronze clock beneath the portrait, then to his farewell message below. His breast swelled from a deep, indrawn breath as he elevated the weapon's muzzle till it pointed toward his right temple.

Vaguely conscious that it was then less than two minutes of eleven, he centered his eyes on the clock dial while his finger slowly contracted against the revolver trigger. His lips tightened at the same time; his entire body grew rigid in expectancy.

Noisy, quarreling sparrows alighted upon a near-by window sill only to vanish in terror when, an instant later, the concussion of a pistol shot jarred the window pane.

Almost on the echo of the shot Judson caught the sound of a door being opened, of swishing skirts and swiftly running feet. His right hand descended with extreme slowness, and pungent, grayish smoke floated from the revolver muzzle in an irregular spiral. A distorted smile of triumph, not unmixed with amazement, warped his face when the runner, a living counterpart of the portrait paused breathless before him.

"Homer! Oh, H-o-m-e-r!"

"Ah—Constance, I thought you were —how did you get here?" he whispered. "If you imagined you could save me, you're too late——"

"Too—late!"

Her eyes dilated in horror, a look which quickly changed to haughty disbelief.

"What hideous joke have you chosen to perpetrate this time? Not satisfied with trying to kill Herby and me, you would frighten me with you savagery!"

For reply Judson pointed to the threadlike stream of blood trickling down his right cheek.

Constance saw, and horror again returned to her eyes.

"Oh, Homer, how could you!" she moaned. "Had I the least inkling that your rashness would lead to tragedy, I would never have crossed your desire."

"Why waste such verbal salve upon me?" he asked leeringly.

"Are you even unkind enough to doubt me?"

"No, but I'm not convinced."

"Then what proof can I give you?" wearily.

"Die with me now!"

He held forth the still smoking weapon.

"That I cannot do!" she cried, drawing back in fear. "My life is not mine to forfeit."

"Rot!"

"Do you honestly think so? Knowing that you are now dying by your own hand, what do you imagine your self-murder has brought you?"

"Nothing else than the oblivion I crave."

"And why do you crave it?"

"Why! When life's bereft of riches, love, happiness, what's left? It's a nightmare—a shell of mockery like your own fickle heart——"

"You are unkind, Homer; yet, because of your delirium, I can forgive. You have chosen to escape those things which are but the refining test of life; blinded by your self-pity you are unable to foresee vast realms of anguish and woe of which Earth holds no store. It is the coward's way."

"Coward! Faugh! It takes nerve to do what I've done. It takes grit to face the end when you feel yourself growing weaker, to see the shadows settling for the last time. Soon everything will be shut out for all time—even you."

"And you feel no regret?"

"No," sneered Judson.

"You're not even sorry when I've hurried back to tell you my heart is yours entirely?"

"Humph! Your penchant for honeyed sayings shows no sign of abating."

"But, Homer, it's true——"

"Yes, no doubt it's true—after I've killed young Romaine, whom you would have in preference to me."

"How spiteful your egoism. I felt no love for Herby; he was sympathetic and considerate while you were selfishly unkind—but have you not been told? Your shot merely stunned him, his wound is slight——"

"Some more of your chaff, eh? I tell you I aimed straight at his sniveling heart—small difference it makes however—you'll go to him anyway. He has riches; mine are gone. Had you stood firm, I'd have made you the richest woman in the world; I was putting them all underfoot that you might be supreme—and at the most crucial hour I find you hobnobbing with that fop of a Romaine, scheming to break my power, eloping under my very nose.

You can thank the luck of fools that my shots did not get you both!

"Now observe the results of your treachery. To-morrow, profane hands will despoil the home I created for you —that wonderful picture of you up there will be stripped from its place. I can see you gloating over my downfall; others will gloat with you, my fickle beauty. But little I care now; another hour, and—pouf! Then you can bury me in the potter's field and be——"

"But, Homer, won't you listen? It is evident you've not heard the good news. You're not ruined, as you imagine; the market changed at the very last moment—you're richer now than ever before!"

"What!" shouted Judson, "are you telling the truth? Don't lie to me, Constance!"

Her hurt look maddened rather than shamed him. His sneering manner slipped from him like a cloak. Animal fear and utter selfishness blinded him to all but his own danger.

"I'm rich, you say—in spite of them all? God! What then have I done? A fool for haste"—he fell to cursing —"repeat your words, Constance; the truth—I must have it!"

"If you do not believe me, why not telephone?"—coldly.

"To be sure, the very thing—but, no. Another of your tricks to trap me, eh," he cried.

His harshness brought tears to her eyes; repressed sobs prevented her from answering. He tried to rise, but a weakness he had not yet noticed checked his effort.

"Don't stand there staring—do something—bring me a doctor—call the servants. You're not going to let me die, are you?" he muttered, cringing; then rage took possession of him. "I'll live, if only to spite you," he cried, his voice hoarse. "I'll not die—I must not die——"

By supreme effort he gained his feet, cursing wantonly as he cast the revolver from him. Like a maniac he brushed Constance aside and staggered to where he could view his face in the pier glass.

"Ah!" he said slowly, his face almost pressed against the mirror in his attempt to examine the self-inflicted wound. "After all, an unsteady hand has paid me well—I'm only scratched; I'm safe!"

Constance remained by the hearth, her awe-filled eyes following his every movement. He wheeled and strode to her side. A grin, made ghastly by his pallor, bared his teeth. Constance watched as if fascinated.

"Now I'll find out whether you're in earnest or not; repeat that promise, I say——"

"You must calm yourself, Homer. I'm only too willing to keep my word, but you're running a grave risk by becoming so excited."

"Excited! Not at all, my beauty. The risk is in delay——" He glided unsteadily in the direction of the telephone. "The bishop shall——"

Sounds of terrific pounding at the outer doors interrupted him. He halted, surprised at first; then a gleam of cunning crept into his eyes. The dormant savage within him was manifest as he whirled upon Constance.

"And you've been telling me the truth, eh?" he cried. "And fool that I am, I almost believed. The police are again at the door—hear them?"

"Are you sure?" she breathed. "You have not looked; it may be some one bearing the good news I told you of."

He darted to his post of observation, staggering back after one brief peek through the curtains.

"Come!" he commanded, beckoning her to the alcove. "See!" his whispered monosyllable sounded harsh and indistinct. "They're after me; a minute more and your betrayal would have got me. Watch me outwit the clumsy fools."

Seizing her hand, he half led, half dragged her through the house to the breakfast room. There helmeted silhouettes outlined against the curtained French windows sent him scurrying to the hallway, and to the kitchen. But as a means of escape the kitchen door was impassable; and, to his angry disappointment, the conservatory entrance was equally as well guarded from without.

Though the noise of attack increased, he neither halted nor relinquished his grasp of Constance's hand. Craftily he reconnoitered the situation by stealing from window to window. At last inspiration came to his aid—the coal chute was unguarded. Expressing his elation by a sharp oath, he rushed Constance down the basement stairs.

The chute was only large enough to permit one person to crawl through at a time. He entered first, dragging Constance roughly after him. Both emerged in open air unnoticed by the cordon of officers.

An expanse of lawn lay between them and the rose garden with very little shrubbery to screen his flight. Even the rose garden itself would afford slight protection against vigilant eyes. Once in the maple grove beyond, however, his chances would be bettered except at the high rubble wall which separated the grove from the hangar field.

With a muttered command for Constance to run he sped for the rose garden. She clung to his hand with listless obedience, though her speed failed to equal his own.

Midway of the garden Judson heard shouting at the house. Without looking back he knew it to be the cry of their discovery. He redoubled his speed but was soon hampered by Constance, now hysterical and stumbling. At the edge of the maple grove she fainted and fell.

Almost without halting he cast a look

over his shoulder, then cursed wantonly. Foremost among the rabble of blue-coated police and morbid citizens was a familiar bandaged head.

"The addle-pated fool, himself," he muttered, "and I thought I killed the puppy!"

Constance stirred slightly. He swept her up in his arms and went speeding on through the grove. Through the low-hanging, interlaced maple branches he could see the roof lines of the hangar. If he could reach it with just a half-minute margin to spare he could outwit them all—no speed was yet known that could equal the *Eaglet*. Once in full flight their capture would be impossible.

Clear of the maple grove he was confronted by the rubble wall. Unburdened with Constance it would have been no obstacle at all. Deciding quickly, he put forth all his strength and tossed her limp form to the top of the wall, swinging up after her with fear-born agility.

Back in the grove the pursuing officers were brandishing weapons but were not shooting. Young Romaine was within a stone's throw when Judson dropped into the hangar field and pulled Constance down after him.

To reach the hangar would expose him to gunfire should his pursuers choose to shoot, yet he struck out across the intervening space unhesitatingly. Half the distance was covered before the first officer topped the wall, albeit this lead was lessened dangerously by the time he entered the hangar and bolted the rear door behind him.

He deposited his still unconscious burden in the rear cockpit without strapping her to the seat. Time was too precious to waste in ceremony, and adjusting the spark, he hastened to open the huge sliding doors.

The hue and cry of pursuit was close when he whirled the propeller back one revolution. The motor caught with a snapping roar and almost before he reached and climbed under the cowl the machine went skimming from the hangar.

At the same instant the rear door was smashed from its hinges. Yells of rage rose from the throats of his pursuers though he failed to hear them above the roar of the motor. A flush of puerile exultation swept over him, but as the car began to elevate, realization that neither he nor Constance was clad for the cooler altitudes damped his joy.

And, too, the rush of air began to bother his injured head. He laughed, however, a derisive laugh, as recklessly he circled above the heads of his thwarted pursuers. After a dozen spirals which carried him higher with each turn, he bore away southward.

Constance, now conscious, shivered and moaned in her seat. Judson looked back at her crouching figure, then passed her the audiophone, motioning for her to adjust it.

"Now do you see what it means to try and corner me?" he questioned through the transmitter, a triumphant smile accompanying his words. "I've not only beaten those thick-witted sleuths at their own game, but I've got you in the bargain."

"Where—where are you taking me?" she asked tearfully.

"Anywhere that'll prevent your running away from me again—we'll live in a paradise of our own," he answered with an unnatural buoyancy of tone.

"But why did you not get my things and say good-by to mamma——"

He interrupted with an inane chuckle.

"Where we go you will soon forget all that's left behind. Neither care nor want will ever trouble you—my riches will buy every pleasure," he cried.

"But I have no wraps, and I'm so cold—and—afraid——" Her words trailed away in a sob.

Judson gave little heed. He was looking down upon the broken country below. Chancing to look backward, he yelled blasphemously. Far to the rear was another machine; and there was no mistaking the fact that it was in full pursuit.

High peaks loomed ahead. He mounted higher to clear them, the cold becoming more intense as he rose. His teeth chattered behind blue lips, and the fiery pain in his head increased to agony.

Another backward glance informed him that his pursuer was approaching at a speed greater than his own; other machines seemed to be joining in the chase.

Clouds drifted in fleecy banks above. By rising, he could benefit by their obscurity; yet the additional height would be a hazardous risk, considering his light apparel and weakened condition. But, with no other alternative, and without thought of Constance's comfort, he sent the machine soaring upward.

He regretted the move before he reached the desired height for a numbness began to creep over him. Although he realized that he was losing both mental and physical power to guide the machine, he fought doggedly to retain control of himself.

For safety, he began a rapid descent, at the same time exerting every ounce of will to keep from being overcome by dizziness. Below the cloud strata he nearly came to grief against a series of cloud-screened ridges. Tilting the elevator, he shot up again, avoiding disaster by the barest fraction of time and space.

With each successive escape, however, danger beset him in greater proportions. Puzzled to note that darkness was coming on at such an early hour, he gazed at the sky—and gasped.

Directly above, so close that recognition was easy, he espied Romaine's machine, with the latter peering down upon him. He fairly choked from cursing, raving because the revolver had been left behind, wondering what sort of craft Romaine possessed to have overtaken the *Eaglet* so soon.

The lust for battle revived his waning strength momentarily. He advanced the throttle to its limit, yet both machines drove into the gathering dusk, their speed equal and terrific.

Suddenly, to Judson's amazement, Romaine dropped a rope ladder from the upper machine and began to climb down it. Fascinated by the utter daring of the act, Judson could do no more than stare for a moment; then schemes of treachery grew in his mind.

He prepared for a sharp sweep to the right, but his hands, stiff and numb from the intense cold, refused to obey his will. Abject fear gripped his heart, he tried to concentrate his thought that he might break the spell which held him, his sensation was one of freezing.

Even the effort to turn his head was futile. A slight jar apprised him that his pursuer had set foot on the *Eaglet's* fuselage, and he steeled himself for his enemy's attack.

None came, a fact which filled him with hope. He wished that Romaine would come forward, or that Constance would say something. To know that help was only an arm's length behind, and yet to lack the power to call or reach for it, was an agony in itself.

He endeavored to speak into the audiphone; three times he shaped his lips to utter an appeal for help—then the stupefying truth dawned upon him— he was paralyzed!

A tremor passed through the *Eaglet*, after which the machine began to tip. A splintering, crunching noise, sounding above the roar of the motor, deafened Judson's ears; and the flying car collapsed

During the fleet instant of time that his nerveless body poised in space his mind quickened. Above, he could see Romaine steadily mounting the rope ladder with Constance strapped to his back. Then his last breath went out in a sigh as he began to fall.

The massive front door of the Judson

home burst inward with a crash under the onslaught of two brawny policemen. Wardell entered first, followed by Knowlton and a quartet of reporters. Without speaking, they gathered around the chair from which two death-glazed eyes stared straight into the painted one that looked down from the portrait.

"Well, gentlemen"—the district attorney bent forward to better view the blue-edged, powder-burnt hole by Judson's right ear—"you may call the coro- ner. Homer Judson's victims will survive, but his last shot went true!"

The lifeless bundle in the chair seemed to greet the announcement with a shuddering sigh, then the last twitching nerve relaxed; the revolver hand slipped from its resting place on the chair arm, the weapon dropped to the hearth.

And in the silence that followed, eleven deep-toned strokes tolled the hour from the mantel clock.

AMONG THE STARS

By Albert Owens

THERE, as I talked to you across the wire,
    The night drew close around us like a veil,
For I had found a single, singing trail
O'er which you came to me like living fire.
Then all the things that you and I aspire
    To win from fate like some romantic tale
    Fresh from a dreamer's pen, seemed dull and frail
Beside the beauty of a great desire.

And I who met you weeping once among
    The stars, your hair in darkened strands of light
That round your face like gentle fingers clung.
    Paused for a single moment in the night
To wonder if the songs that I had sung
    Found you with faith to dare the splendid flight.

Tales of the Double-Man

By Clyde Broadwell

IV.
Disentombed to Wed

Being a transcript of William Gray's verbal version of a most remarkable development in his mystic transcontinental metempsychosis with the body and soul of his other self, Arthur Wadleigh, of Cape Town, British South Africa.
—EDITOR.

I, WILLIAM GRAY, have gazed upon the dead body of my other self, Arthur Wadleigh, in a Cape Town burial-ground mausoleum!

For the better understanding of this startling statement by those who may read this and might not have read the preceding three tales published in THE THRILL BOOK, let me briefly rehearse the circumstances which led up to this dénouement in my strange two-bodied, two-souled existence.

When Arthur Wadleigh died and was placed unembalmed in a burial vault, it was believed by the scientists studying my double-ego problem that the occult link between myself and Wadleigh had been severed. But as I still experienced a mystic urge which sent my soul across the eight-thousand-mile interval between New York City and Cape Town, in vain efforts to enter and animate the body of my dual self, science became convinced that it was on the threshold of a still more startling series of phenomena in my case.

Every phase was reviewed and studied, especially with reference to the first symptoms of my plurality, when I, as William Gray, a Wall Street stockbroker, would fall asleep and immediately awake in Cape Town as Wadleigh; or, as Wadleigh, would fall asleep in Cape Town and immediately awake in New York as myself, William Gray.

A learned thesis on my case was read before the American Psychological Foundation by Doctor Mordaunt P. Dale, eminent psychic expert and fellow of the International Academy of Scientific and Supernatural Research.

The scientists there gathered were asked to make suggestions. The only one adopted was made by Doctor Vernon L. Barris, that I be taken to Cape Town. His argument was soundly logical.

"When Mr. Gray is in the same city with his other self, he at least may be able to sleep. Both will be subject to the same daylight and night hours.

Besides, both men being there—at least one, I mean, Wadleigh presumably being dead—science can study these phenomena the easier and better than with eight thousand miles separating the two physical bodies of 'The Double Man.'"

Consequently, urged by Doctor Dale and my own family physician, Doctor Marvin Porter, I arranged all my affairs and gave charge of my brokerage office at No. 4½ Wall Street, to my chief clerk, in my absence. Then in the company of Doctor Porter, Doctor Dale and several other scientists interested in my case, I set sail for Cape Town crossing the United States to San Francisco for the Pacific route.

Arrived in Cape Town, I expressed an intense curiosity to see my other self, and was taken to the vault where Arthur Wadleigh lay in his casket. This casket, it will be remembered, was sieved with holes to admit air and the lid also was left unfastened, so that Wadleigh, if he really were alive, could rise from the coffin without struggling.

I never shall forget the sensations that thrilled me as I raised this lid and peered at the face of Wadleigh. It was my own face—every feature of it, even to the mole on the right cheek near the ear! His dark-brown hair, slightly wavy, his blue eyes, his height and build, all duplicated my own. I lifted his left hand for the purpose of verifying a statement he had sent me in a letter replying to mine in the first days of our inter-transmigrations. Sure enough! The wart on my left thumb near the nail exactly corresponded with the wart on his thumb near the nail!

His body showed no signs of decomposition. In fact, he had every appearance of a normal, living man. I could not believe him dead, although there was no respiration, no pulse, and no slightest sign of life in the cold clay before me.

Beyond the scientific world, no one knew of my arrival in Cape Town.

I dreaded notoriety and willingly consented to disguise my features. Otherwise, as on a previous visit, when Wadleigh and I crossed each other's paths in mutual determination to see each other, but without achieving that result because mutual impulses on each occasion set his face west and mine east, going, and mine west and his east, coming, Wadleigh's friends and acquaintances would be certain to recognize me, and my stay in Cape Town would be marred by many unpleasant, if not actually awkward, occurrences.

Such an eerie feeling haunted me, having seen myself as I actually would look dead, that I became delirious and ill. For a week I lay in a semi-conscious condition in the home of Doctor Philip Spaulding, who had attended Wadleigh. Over me watched Doctors Porter, Spaulding and Dale, together with that renowned French genius, Doctor Lucien Trebaux, master of occult lore and psychic manifestations, who also had studied Wadleigh's and my case in conjunction with Doctor Dale.

When I recovered one week later, I was warned to prepare for a shock. I braced myself. I had need to do so.

"Mr. Gray," said Doctor Dale, deep sympathy in his voice, "Miss Elaine Brandon has become insane from grief at the death of Mr. Wadleigh, her fiancé."

I could feel the color leave my face. Elaine—insane! The girl I loved—had learned to love—when, as Wadleigh, I courted her in the arbor of her home! Great heavens! Had I not suffered enough already, without this fell blow at my happiness?

"Tell me more, doctor!" I cried.

"Miss Brandon went to Mr. Wadleigh's mausoleum to lay a floral wreath on his casket," explained Doctor Dale. "Her heart was breaking because she felt she had done him an injustice in disbelieving his story that he and you were one man, even though eight thousand miles apart. I hardly can credit the story she told, especially since she immediately became mentally unbalanced after telling it."

"What did she say, doctor?" I asked.

"It is so unbelievable," he hesitated, "and yet——"

"Tell me!"

"She placed the wreath on Wadleigh's casket, at the foot," said Doctor Dale. "Then she went to its head to gaze through the glass-windowed lid at the man she loved. He seemed so lifelike that she was not frightened. But as she stared, she says his eyes opened!"

"And then?" I cried as the physician paused.

"He raised the lid and took her in his arms!"

"Wadleigh" I asked, incredulous.

"So she says."

"What then?"

"She fainted."

"And——"

"Recovered. Wadleigh, she said, was lying in his casket, lid down, just as before! I can't believe it."

"Any other details?" I asked.

"Y-yes." Doctor Dale seemed embarrassed.

"Tell me all," I urged. "I'm the party most interested, you know."

"So you are, Mr. Gray," he agreed. "You may remember that especially constructed thermos bottles filled with liquid food were placed in the vault?"

I nodded.

"Well—they're empty!"

"Wadleigh lives!" I yelled. "I've told you hundreds of times I never believed he was dead."

"But he is dead, Mr. Gray. It is inconceivable that science should be mistaken. I believe Miss Brandon, in her insane frame of mind, ate the food. It is impossible to get anything coherent from her, now."

My mind thus reverted to Elaine, I experienced deepest grief for the sweet girl whom I had won by a semiproxy wooing. She had written that with Wadleigh dead she never would marry any other man, but I had vague hopes that I might win her, being such an exact counterpart of Wadleigh that she could not detect the difference.

Was my hope to be destroyed by her insanity? Was there no method by which she might be restored to reason? I discussed the subject with Doctor Dale and Doctor Trebaux. They both agreed that the only chance for Miss Brandon's recovery was for her to believe Wadleigh still lived.

To this end and for this purpose, I doffed my disguise and took up my residence in Wadleigh's house, the rear of which faced the rear of Miss Brandon's home. I recalled the many mornings, when, as Wadleigh, I had leaped the boxwood bounding our respective grounds, and kissed Elaine before going to the office of the London Ivory Company. Perhaps her mind might be restored by such a morning event repeated.

Elaine, consequently, was brought home from the private sanitarium where she had been taken, and was given her former room, which faced toward mine.

With beating heart, next morning, I went to my window, as I had done so many times before in the person of Wadleigh, and gazed toward the Brandon homestead. At her window stood Elaine, staring toward my window. I waved my hand to her. The distance was not more than one hundred and fifty feet. I could see her features— every dear detail of the loveliest face I ever have seen, unless I except that of my own lost fiancée, Erla Kingsley, far away in New York, who likewise had rejected me when I told her my strange story.

At first, Elaine evinced doubt, then interest, then eager yearning, succeeded by an ineffably wondrous brightening of eyes and sudden startled comprehension. The look of insanity fled and gave place to a perfectly normal expression.

I waved again.

This time, Elaine responded with a joyous salute, blowing me a kiss as well, just as she had been wont to do before tragedy blighted her life. Across the gardens I shouted:

"Meet me at the boxwood fence, Elaine!"

Back came her happy cry: "I'll be there!"

Happily I turned away from the window, rushed into the room I had allotted to Doctor Dale, and told him the joyful news.

"She's sane!" I cried. "Sane! Watch, doctor. I've told you, as I promised, so that you can study her condition."

Without waiting to hear his reply, I hastened out and down the stairs, through the hall and into the garden. I literally ran to the boxwood border. Elaine was just leaving her home and was walking toward me, her step sprightly, her face wreathed in smiles.

"Elaine!" I called, the yearning of my heart concentrated in my voice.

"Arthur!" came her glad cry—although I was William Gray.

Across the low-cut shrubbery I held out my arms. Elaine leaned toward me. We kissed. I can remember the thrill of that kiss now—shall remember it until I die!

"You were ill, Elaine," I said tenderly. "I was quite worried. Are you better, now?"

"Quite well, Arthur," she said. "Isn't it nearly time for you to go to the office?"

I evaded her question.

"I'm on vacation," I said truthfully enough. "May I breakfast with you. This bachelor dining is getting tiresome."

She rippled a laugh.

"You're always so ridiculous, Arthur!" she replied. "But you're perfectly welcome. Mother will be glad to see you, I'm sure."

I bounded over the boxwood and strolled with her into the Brandon home. Mrs. Brandon, who had been informed of our little conspiracy to win Elaine back to reason, met me with a motherly kiss.

"I'm so glad to see you, Arthur!" she cried. "I guess you were eating your heart out while Elaine was sick. She was quite delirious—Spanish influenza has that effect, you know."

"And is she entirely out of danger, now?" I asked, my voice tender.

"So Doctor Trebaux says—oh, here's Doctor Trebaux, now!"

I turned to greet the eminent French scientist. He was a wrinkled genius, to say the least. His forehead was seamed with deep lines. It was quite low. His hair came close down toward his eyebrows and covered much of his temples. But his eyes were the sharpest I ever have seen. With these he gave me a knowing look as I bowed to him, acknowledging the "introduction" spoken by Mrs. Brandon, although I had met the doctor before, as I have stated.

"So—our little girl is better, eh?" he murmured, turning to Elaine. "Let me see your eyes, closely, mademoiselle—so!"

He placed a thin, wiry hand to Elaine's chin and tilted her head so that her eyes were on a level with his own, he being slightly the taller. The most piercing glance I ever have seen he gave Elaine, telling her to gaze steadily into his own eyes.

What he saw evidently satisfied him, for he smiled reassuringly at Mrs. Brandon and myself.

"Entirely cured, Mme. Brandon," he said. "I needn't attend mademoiselle any longer. I shall give similar treatment to other patients—it worked so well in your daughter's case."

"Thank God—and you, doctor!" breathed Mrs. Brandon, while I echoed her remark.

"The wedding need be delayed no longer," he said slyly, and Elaine blushed rosily, squeezing my hand in returning my own pressure upon hers.

"Was I ill very long, mother?" she asked.

"Several weeks, Elaine. But it's all over now. You'd better rest, now, eh, doctor?"

"It would be well—er—er—yes," hesitated the savant.

"Are you in doubt?" asked Mrs. Brandon, suddenly terrified. "Isn't she well—really well?"

"What I really would like to see," he said slowly, "would be for Mademoiselle Brandon to take a vacation—go somewhere"—he grinned affably— "say, on a wedding trip—for a few weeks."

I understood his object. He wished to prevent Elaine from learning that Wadleigh actually lay dead in his tomb. She could not wed a dead man; I was the dead man's counterpart; he knew I loved her; she would love me, thinking me Wadleigh; no harm would be done. The plan suited me—more than suited me. I glanced toward Mrs. Brandon. She seemed dubious.

"It is best for mademoiselle," argued Doctor Trebaux. "Otherwise——" He shrugged significantly. Mrs. Brandon's dubious expression vanished in a sudden surge of motherly solicitude for her daughter who again might be stricken were the specialist's advice not taken.

"Well," she murmured, "if Elaine has no objections—of course, I haven't. I merely hesitated, as any mother will, to lose my daughter so soon.'

"You gain a son, madame," quoth Doctor Trebaux. "His reputation is unblemished—as you know."

"I've had such strange dreams," sighed Elaine. "I thought you were dead, Arthur."

I gazed at her with tender reproach.

"I have too much to live for—winning you—to die!" I chided, and rejoiced at the sudden surge of color in Elaine's cheeks.

"How soon shall they marry, doctor?" interrupted Mrs. Brandon, breaking in on my fond nonsense.

"Right away—to-morrow," he said firmly, "else I shall not be responsible for a possible relapse."

"But," objected Elaine, "I can't marry—to-morrow!"

"Why?" he queried, frowning.

"I haven't sent out invitations— haven't prepared——"

"Tut! Tut!" he scoffed. "You couldn't stand the excitement of a big wedding. You must have a quiet home affair, with only family members and a few friends present, mademoiselle. Is it to be? Or do you wish to relapse again into a sickness from which I cannot expect a second recovery?"

Elaine stared at him with wide eyes.

"Was I so ill as that, doctor?" she asked.

"Indeed, yes!"

"And I may relapse—if I don't marry at once?"

"Yes, mademoiselle."

"Then—can you marry me—to-morrow, Arthur?" she asked, turning to me. "Are you ready—do you care if it is only a little home wedding? You have so many friends, you know."

Was I ready to marry this sweet, blushing wonder woman? My eyes told her even before I spoke:

"Now—if you wish it!" I said ecstatically.

And so our wedding date was set for the following evening, at eight o'clock.

My sleep the night before my wedding day was fitful and disturbed by sensations hardly possible of description. Once, when I awoke to semi-consciousness, or, I might term it, a vague awakefulness, I can swear that I felt the lid of a coffin as my hands spasmodically reached out! It was quite gruesome. I can recall dimly wondering if I actually were animating the corpse of Arthur Wadleigh in his tomb. Who can say that I did not do so? Or that Wadleigh and I again had not become subject to that strange link of destiny which had caused our former marvelous metempsychosis?

Daylight came as a welcome harbinger of my joy that was to be. Ere the moon waned on this day's evening, I should have Elaine as my bride! Was ever man happier than I? I hummed gayly as I dressed. My face was fairly beaming with smiles of joy. I marveled at the change in my countenance when I beheld it in the mirror as I brushed my hair and adjusted my necktie. It was a transfiguration, compared to that unhappy day when I first noticed the streaks of gray at my temples caused by the horrors of my doubled-up estate. So also had Wadleigh been unhappy in the hour he also found himself growing gray. We were both young men—thirty-two years old only. But that sorrow was in the dead past, I told myself, swerving the channel of my thoughts toward the girl I was to wed this night. Immediately the nightmares of sleep were forgotten.

I rushed to my window. Elaine already was at hers, waiting to greet me. I waved my hand and blew a kiss to her across the garden greens and she reciprocated in kind. Then with light heart I turned away to go downstairs for my breakfast, usually set out by Wadleigh's housekeeper on the dining-room table.

Seated at the table, facing me as I entered the room, was my second self, Arthur Wadleigh—risen from the dead!

My nightmare had been no chimera after all! I actually had reanimated my kindred self lying stark and cold in death within an entombed casket! A thousand thoughts flashed upon me as I stared in open-eyed wonder at my duplicated human entity. Wadleigh likewise stared at me.

He had been insane when he "died," but his eyes now held no slightest sign of mental aberration. But he was pallid and I know that I also was waxen in color. The strange thing about this encounter was, that I felt no horror, but merely amazement and wonder. I did not shiver with dread; neither did Wadleigh.

We faced one another for fully two minutes without speaking—two men exactly alike, drawn thus mysteriously together from the ends of the earth, an antipodal distance of eight thousand miles!

His soul had been incarnate in my body; my soul had been incarnate in his body. We both loved the same girl—Elaine Brandon—who was to be my bride this night at eight o'clock—the girl whom I just had saluted a few moments ago across the garden space. Or had it been æons since I greeted Elaine?

My bridal night? Great heavens—no! It was Wadleigh's wedding night—not mine! I was an interloper only.

"Mr. Wadleigh?" I questioned, feeling such a query banal.

"Yes—you are Mr. Gray?" came his reply—in my voice!

"I am Mr. Gray. May I explain my presence in your home?"

"I can surmise," he replied slowly and sadly. "But you are welcome. Tell me about it, please. We are in the hands of some sinister fate. I had just entered and sat when you arrived. Martha—my housekeeper—seems to have taken as good care of you as she did of me. I was hungry and was about to eat when you walked in. Just to think—only a few minutes ago—ugh-h!" Wadleigh shuddered.

"I know," I said soothingly. "I knew you were not dead. How did you waken?"

"You woke me!" he exclaimed. "Then, your soul having stirred my soul into active being again, you fled the tomb—probably to fall asleep here. Am I right?"

I told Wadleigh of my weird nightmare and how my hands had touched a coffin lid.

"Unhappy men that we are!" he exclaimed bitterly. "Why are we such toys of destiny? You lost your reason; I lost mine. You lost your sweetheart; I lost mine——"

"No, Mr. Wadleigh!" I interrupted quickly. "You shall marry Elaine—to-night!"

Amazed, Wadleigh stared at me.

"Marry—Elaine—to-night?" he repeated. "Impossible!"

"But you shall, Wadleigh!" I cried, in supreme renunciation of my own happiness. "If you won't—*I shall!*"

"You?"

"Yes. Otherwise Elaine may become insane—*again.*" I was particular to emphasize the last word. He was quick to notice the emphasis.

"Again?" he asked.

"Yes," I explained. "She became insane after a visit to your tomb. She went to lay a wreath on your casket. She told a wild story of your rising and clasping her in your arms. She fainted. When she revived and returned home she told her story. Then she lost her mental poise. The scientists studying our case were called in. They decided the only plan to restore her to reason was by having her believe I was you. We tried it. The plan worked. Elaine was told that for several weeks she had been ill—Spanish influenza, you know—and that she had been delirious. She believed it. She mistook me for you. Then, for fear she should learn the dread truth again and become insane at the knowledge you actually were dead,

it was arranged that I should marry her to-night as yourself, Arthur Wadleigh, and go off with her on a prolonged honeymoon. I entered into the plan—for your sake, Wadleigh—and hers. And you're a lucky man to be alive—to wed such a girl! Think, man! To-night! Your wedding night!"

Wadleigh shook himself as though to arouse from some dream.

"That was mighty generous, Gray," he said. "But—you won her—it's your wedding!"

"Yours, old man!" I cried heartily. "I shall leave Cape Town, if the scientists permit. But say! I'm starved! Let's eat."

I sat opposite Wadleigh. Surely never on earth before had there been such a strange beginning of a wedding day!

Footsteps sounded on the stairs. In a few moments Doctor Dale, the scientific genius who had been studying our case, peered in at the door to greet me—and saw me in duplicate!

He started, rubbed his eyes as though to get the sleep out of them, then stared with unbelieving orbs at Wadleigh and myself.

I rose quickly and introduced Wadleigh to the savant, volubly explaining everything that had transpired.

"Then—this—this—means that you—you—you won't marry—to-night." His statement was more a question.

"Mr. Wadleigh marries Elaine to-night," I said smilingly, although my heart was leaden.

"Then, Mr. Gray," said Dr. Dale, "you must stay in Cape Town. Never, while you and Wadleigh live in this uncanny plural estate, should you separate for any distance that will mean day for one and night for the other. Otherwise——" He winked significantly as he paused, but neither Wadleigh nor I could get his drift.

"Otherwise?" I asked.

"Mrs. Wadleigh-to-be will have two

husbands—and that wouldn't be quite proper, would it?"

I stared; then realized. So did Wadleigh.

"Doc is right," said Wadleigh wearily. "But how can I expect Mr. Gray to be so generous?"

Deprived of Elaine, my heart was yearning for good old New York. This city of Cape Town suddenly had become hateful to me. But—Wadleigh had been cruelly dealt with. I could not resist the urge of his sorrow-stricken eyes.

"I'll stay here—until the link of destiny is broken," I said slowly. "God grant it be broken soon, or we shall both go mad—again."

"Well," interrupted Doctor Dale on the sudden silence which had fallen upon us after my fervent prayer, "now that this is settled—let us eat."

Despite his long "burial," Wadleigh was not voracious. Doctor Dale was quite curious concerning the emptying of the thermos bottles left filled with food in Wadleigh's tomb.

"Did you eat that liquid food we left for you?" he asked. "Or, don't you remember?"

"I have a hazy recollection only, of having left my casket, gone to the thermos bottles and eaten the food," said Wadleigh.

"Why return to the casket?"

"Some force beyond my control seemed to urge me back into it."

"Very strange—strange, indeed!" exclaimed Doctor Dale. "What was the sensation like?"

"As though something, or some one, were pulling me. It seemed as though I were subconsciously informed that unless I did lie in the casket I actually would die."

"Auto-suggestion, most probably," muttered Doctor Dale.

Wadleigh glanced at the clock on his mantle.

"I must go, gentlemen," he said, rising.

"Go? Where?" I asked.

"To the London Ivory Company in——"

"Sit down, Mr. Wadleigh," said Doctor Dale kindly. "Do you know how long you were unconscious?"

Wadleigh shook his head.

"Nine weeks!" exclaimed the scientist. "Plenty of time, then, for the office—after your honeymoon. Run over and see Elaine! Gray and I are going —to Doctor Spaulding's house again. Gray must disguise. Elaine must not know—until you both are out of this occult bondage and actually are yourselves again. Good-by, Wadleigh—a happy honeymoon!"

"And I wish the same!" added I, with hand outstretched.

Wadleigh clasped it tightly. It was the first time our physical beings had come into actual contact. Both of us thrilled weirdly. Actually it seemed we were shaking hands with ourselves rather than with one another!

"God bless you, Gray!" said Wadleigh fervently.

Doctor Dale and I had risen. All our effects were in the home of Doctor Spaulding, save a few odds and ends which we could take away later. We moved toward the door, Wadleigh following. My head was in a whirl. It was as though my physical shadow were following me, a fleshful shadow exact in color, height, stride, and voice to myself.

On the veranda I turned to Wadleigh.

"Good-by," I said, and walked with Doctor Dale down the broad steps.

Arthur Wadleigh was married that night. He and his bride still are enjoying their honeymoon "somewhere in Natal."

Will Elaine ever learn the weird circumstances that brought her a husband from the tomb of death? I wonder.

he Terror of the Rats

By Croyden Heath

SYNOPSIS OF PRECEDING CHAPTERS.

Jack Thornton, a young trial lawyer for a railroad corporation, has been "framed" by crooks and unjustly disbarred from practicing his profession. Unable to find honest work, isolated by his family, who believe him guilty of the crime of which he is accused, he drifts gradually to a penniless condition. At last, in a New York newspaper six months old, he reads an advertisement: "Have you physical courage? Have you health, brains, and resolution? Are you free of all family ties? Dare you try what most men could but would not do? Weaklings need not apply." Thornton answers the advertisement, is accepted by the man who inserted it, and is given his first test. Others follow, mysterious, exciting adventures, the forces behind which are incomprehensible to him. Finally he is furnished with money enough to make the journey to Peking, China, for some purpose unknown to him. Arrived there, he saves from the hands of two Chinese ruffians Joan Carrington, a young girl left stranded in China three years before, on the death of her father. She is now employed as secretary to an engineering magnate. So far she has gone in her recital to Thornton, when suddenly she stops, as if she had told him more than she intended. Joan and he part in the city, and the following morning Thornton is visited by the Chinaman who had inserted the mysterious advertisement in the New York newspaper.

Mr. Wang, as this Chinese calls himself, reveals the opportunity for which Thornton has been waiting—that of making enough money to clear himself of the charges which have made of him an exile. The Chinese also reveals that Thornton's father, a very rich man, has a deep interest in having his son, whom he believes guilty, rehabilitate his honesty and good name. However, Mr. Wang warns Thornton that this opportunity is fraught with more perils and difficulties than any other test that has yet been given him.

CHAPTER III.

THORNTON was awakened from troubled, disturbing dreams next morning by a Chinese boy at his bedside with tea, which was, so the lad informed him, "sweet as a sparrow's tongue." He noted that the porcelain had a painting of the god of longevity on it, so that he was able to drink to his own long life. Never before had this compliment been made him.

When he went later into the hotel lobby he was instantly aware of the changed attitude of the management. Where had been of late suspicion and inattention to his modest wants was now a servile readiness to do his bidding.

Thornton knew perfectly well that it was Mr. Wang's money which had brought about the grateful change, but what was it done for? How could he, John Thornton, of New York, help Mr. Wang, of Peking? And why had Wang spoken of others? Thornton shrugged his shoulders. Sufficient to the day was the evil thereof. Two nights hence at the Inn of Tatung he would know.

Meanwhile he was far more interested in trying to meet the pretty American girl. Why had he not obtained her business and home address? As he waited for a long procession of tiled carts, rickshas, and stout gentlemen astride of small donkeys to pass by he thought how strange it was that a girl of his own race should be here among the mysteries of this ancient walled city. What had an American girl in common with these subtle, secretive yellow people? He looked up to see a caravan of camels swinging by with long, slow, stately strides. Tall, heavy-coated camels, newly come from the wastes of Mongolia and Manchuria. He was conscious that he and this girl he had saved from robbers were of another nation and civilization. Sandgate had spoken once in his detached, slow manner of the awakening of China to her own great destinies and the growing impatience at the presence of the despised foreigners. Sandgate had told Thornton that every uprising, insurrection, or rebellion aimed at the foreigner had sprung into being without any warning the Europeans or British could sense beforehand. Diplomats and consuls were, and always would be, unable to know what was really going on around them.

Thornton found himself constantly thinking of pretty Joan Carrington. He had never been so obsessed with thoughts of a girl before. He was popular with women, and had passed through the many flirtations inseparable from the college life of a good-looking American with no haunting memories. This was different. There was a protective sense aroused in him when he thought how she had lain, pale and trembling, in his arms when the robbers had been put to rout. And she had pluck, too. Instead of fainting, as many might, she told him only that she was angry.

He remembered she said she was working for a firm which was German. That was nothing in the East, where British influence had always welcomed them and even helped them to establish their markets. Peking was sure to be full of German concessionaires. From the American consulate he might find word of the girl if he could satisfy the official he was a reputable citizen. There was the rub. The official might look on him coldly.

In the end Jack Thornton determined to put off investigations until he had met Wang and Wang's friends at Tatung and learned what they needed of him. He could not help being uneasy at the thought of their possible demands. He was not fool enough to suppose they wanted to meet him socially. It had been :t considerable expense that they imported him.

It was while he was wandering about the city, pondering on the problem of the suave Wang, that he was brought to realize the importance of the man. By this time the American was accustomed to the street sights of Peking. He knew, for example, that when mandarins went about they no longer used the sedan chair of other days. Mandarins had taken, instead, to riding in English carriages of the brougham or victoria type, glass inclosed, and removed from the rabble of the streets, but no mandarin would be content to be accompanied merely by his coachman. Each man of position must have his mounted escorts in their picturesque, long riding garments, round hats, and trailing scarlet feathers.

It was in such a carriage, attended by such an escort, that Thornton suddenly came face to face with the man he had first met in the lobby of a New York theater. The dress in which Mr. Wang made his nocturnal visit to the Hotel de Pekin was that of an affluent man. To-day Wang wore gorgeous raiment and was borne through the streets, looking neither to the left nor right. For the first time Thornton was assured that Wang was of the powerful.

It was dusk when the American entered the Inn of Tatung. The proprietor welcomed him courteously, hoping that he might be "full as a peony." Thornton had never before been so far from Peking, and looked with interest on the room into which he was shown and the curious scribblings on the wall. The longest of these screeds had been written by some previous occupant. "Enter your name here," said the jocular traveler, "for the competition as to which guest has risen with the most flea or bug bites."

It was quite dark when the host led him to a big bare room. In it were three Chinese gentlemen. Mr. Wang, no longer gorgeous in mandarin robes, but clad as he had been when he called at the Hotel de Pekin, bowed gravely.

"This is what you must do," Mr. Wang began.

"*Must* do?" Thornton repeated, frowning a little.

"Must do," said Wang again. "You cannot fail to realize that you have taken our money when you were at the Gate of Lost Hope. As an honorable gentleman, the son of an honorable father, you understand well what you did. To take money and offer no return for it is not the act of one whose ancestors are distinguished; it is the act of those who will '*kou lun*' and hold out empty hands for gifts. I found you when you had nothing. I exact a task of you. When it is accomplished you may return to your land and gladden your father's heart."

"You don't know my father," Thornton said, frowning.

"I know the heart of all fathers," Wang assured him impressively. "I know that when you return and show

him you are worthy to be his son he will embrace you."

"That may be," muttered Thornton, gazing at Wang's impressive and silent countrymen, "but how is it to be done?"

"When you do as we bid the way will be clear. Listen well to me, Mr. Thornton. I brought you here not by chance. I have made diligent inquiry into your life history. I know wherein you are weak and where you are strong. It is through your weakness we are able to benefit by your strength. You fell from a high position because plans of the railroad to be built from Peking to Lanchow were stolen from your custody."

"I wish I knew who did it," said Thornton gloomily.

"He is here in Peking," Wang said solemnly. "Be calm. Without me you cannot clear yourself."

"I'll do anything short of murder to get the chance," Thornton cried eagerly. "Who is it?"

"'There are some,'" Wang said didactically, "'so bad that their sins pickle and confirm them in evil instead of rotting them.'"

He turned to his two countrymen and spoke. They made regal, graceful gestures and spoke in their melodious Pekingese phrases. Then Wang turned to the American and began his explanations. Perhaps he consumed an hour in the recital. In the beginning he told the younger man something of the conditions of modern China.

It was the first time since Thornton had known Wang that he saw him moved out of his calm, smileless ways. Foreign concession hunters, whether German, British, or Americans, he declared, were the curse of China. More than anything, such men kept her back when it was the national will to progress.

Taking advantage of the rottenness of the administration, these concession hunters bribed mandarins to introduce them to ministers of state, and thus force on an unwilling people loans, grants, and monopolies.

This railroad scheme was a case in point. A German-American syndicate was determined to build it when China was perfectly well able to do so herself. Wang pointed out the recently opened road between Peking and Nank'ou. This road was built by Chinese capital and labor, and the two head engineers, Chinese both, were graduates of Yale and London.

"I was attorney for that proposed road," Thornton said dryly.

"That is why you are here," Wang said significantly. "Before I tell you any more you must swear by what you hold sacred that you will not betray us. I will tell you first that we only want for our country what your fathers won for America—Liberty."

"Am I betraying my own people?" Thornton demanded.

"You will be asked to aid in the punishment of an American citizen," he was told, "but it will help to cleanse your conscience. More than that, it will help to redeem your own good name."

As he listened Thornton learned what few foreigners ever do; he listened to a man high in the councils of a great secret society whose only aim was to give China back to the Chinese. He was told of the society in Tientsin which foreigners know as the "Society of the Red Door," but whose real name is "The Society Which Meets Injury With Retaliations." It was this society which had determined to drive out the accursed, blood-sucking concessionaires.

Wang was the head of the most powerful branches of the New China party. He had at his command resources almost limitless. Entranced, the American listened to those great societies of resolute men of which the West rarely learns.

He was told of the Sam Hop Hui and the Master of the Red Stick, who rules them, and the dread powers of the Society of the Sword.

Sometimes these societies, like the American Ku-Klux-Klan, pursued private enmities, but in the main they existed for that distant day when China would be free from foreigners and respected of the world.

"Where do I come in?" Thornton asked when the other had done.

"From to-night," Wang said rapidly, "you are George Fallon. You graduated from the law school of Columbia University in 1914. You are an unmarried orphan, born in East Boston. Your training in Boston and New York has been with politicians mainly. You have handled corruption funds with such skill that you have nothing to fear from the police. You have come to Peking to be confidential secretary to Adolf Jaeckels. You were engaged by William Jaeckels at the request of his brother."

"Fine!" gasped Thornton. "But as there is a real George, I suppose, where is he?"

Wang shook his head. There was sympathy in his voice.

"'As typhoons sweep the bamboo's sprays, so Death blew up his sleeve!'"

It was plain to the American that this George Fallon had not been removed idly. He was by this time thoroughly impressed by the organization which had mapped this one of myriad details with such freedom from failure. It was an uncomforting thought that unless he did what he was bidden some swift, noiseless fate might deal as ruthlessly with him as with Fallon.

After all, he was here, alone and unheralded, in a strange and unfriendly land. In America none knew of his coming and none cared.

"If Adolf Jaeckels, who isn't a fool, I assume, engaged this man he had references and something to go by?"

"You will find George Fallon's baggage and references awaiting you in the house of a respectable Scotch widow, where rooms have been reserved for you. Copies of the correspondence between the brothers Jaeckels relative to you, your ability, and the like are there, too."

"Suppose I fall down?" Thornton demanded. "I don't know a thing about East Boston."

"You must not make any mistake," Wang said suavely. "You will make nightly reports to me and receive every aid."

"It seems very strange to me," Thornton commented, "that a lawyer in politics in New York should want to take a job out here. You say the police had nothing on him?"

Wang understood the American idiom perfectly.

"George Fallon was mixed up in an unsavory case which concerned a woman. In a year or so he planned to return when the matter was forgotten. It was at the suggestion of his friends he accepted this opportunity."

"I'm understudying a scoundrel then?"

"A scoundrel working for a greater one," Wang admitted. "We know that Jaeckels is bribing certain of our countrymen here. He keeps no memoranda of such corruption. We know, for we have searched his office. It is too vast a business for one man.

"He needed such a one as Fallon, who was greedy for money, skilled in double-dealing, and anxious to be away from his country's jurisdiction. It will be your part to tell us with whom this Jaeckels deals. When we know all——" He made an eloquently expressive gesture. Thornton remembered the simile of the typhoon and the bamboo sprays.

But his spirits rose. It was work he could do without feeling ashamed. And Wang had hinted there was a reward in sight which might again allow him to stand before his fellows as an up-

right man. He felt, however, it was not politic to ask further.

"It's better than I thought," Thornton exclaimed brightly. "I'm ready to begin at once. Where shall I see you to make my report?"

"That you will never know," Wang told him; "perhaps in your office, perhaps as you walk the city streets, perhaps as you awake from sleep and think yourself alone. Make no confidants. Play your part with skill; forget you ever were named Thornton."

CHAPTER IV.

MRS. HAMILTON, in whose home Thornton was to spend many months, was not inquisitive. He often suspected her house had been chosen for just such a reason. When he arrived he was conducted to a room in which George Fallon's baggage was neatly arranged.

For long hours that first night he read through the private memoranda of that adroit schemer. That Death had "blown up his sleeves" seemed an equitable action. And there were some letters from a dead woman which would have brought bitter shame to any man. But they had been flippantly penciled by the one who had thought to escape.

Thornton read William Jaeckels' comments on George Fallon with amusement and eagerness.

"This fellow is about as slick as they make them," wrote William, "a good mixer, a hard drinker, and almost as selfish as you are. I have told him that you may want things done in a manner which would be outside the law here, but is all right in that God-forsaken land where he's going.

"He says if any yellow man can put over anything on him he'll take out his papers and sprout a pigtail. We can use this fellow, Adolf, but see he compromises himself. He'll have to read up international and company law when you get him. All he's done of late is to get thugs acquitted and get bail for crooks. His use to us is the knowledge of human nature. He knows when and how to buy a man. It's his job, and from what you say we need to buy yellow and white help if we're going to get that concession."

Undoubtedly John Thornton, member of an honorable family and decent beliefs, was engaged to understudy a very undesirable citizen. Ordinarily he would by this time have been worrying as to when and how he was to get to Jaeckels' office. But he was learning that his moves were mapped by other wills than his own.

He had been two days at the Widow Hamilton's house, during which he had learned a great deal of Fallon's past when a letter was brought in. It was only an unsigned note to say that he was expected at the Jaeckels' office, near the Ketteler monument in Ha-ta Mên Street, at ten-thirty next day.

Thornton had never kept an appointment with such vivid eagerness as this. The more he thought over the thing the more he liked the prospect of outwitting the monopoly-grabbing Jaeckels. He was shown into a big office. There was a large table, evidently Jaeckels', and a smaller one, which was later his.

An immensely fat, florid man in white drill was dictating to a slim, dark girl also in white. As the American stood in the doorway, either unheard or unheeded, Jaeckels put a fat, hot hand on the girl's arm. The American could see a shiver of disgust at the contact, but she kept on filling her notebook.

Then the fat man looked up.

"Come in, Fallon. What sort of a trip did you have and what do you think of this cursed place?"

Thornton could not get a glance at the girl, who hurried off. But the figure was so like that of the one who had filled his thoughts that he started to follow her. He was brought to his senses by the tug at his sleeve. The big, fat man was chuckling. He had a curious, thick way of talking, and he licked his lips a great deal.

"Now, now," he admonished mirthfully, "not so fast. She's mine. You can spend your evenings at the Circus Barowsky or the Arcade, but leave my little Plum Blossom to me." Jaeckels was still amiable, but the threat in his voice was unmistakable. "I should have thought you'd had enough of 'em after your little experiences."

"It seems so strange to see an American girl here," Thornton answered. He was confused and irritated at the thought that here in his private office, with a man like Adolf Jaeckels, a decent-minded American girl might have to pass her days.

It *was* Joan Carrington.

When he went to her side, after a long talk with their common employer, he saw the sweet face that had haunted him. She was vexed with herself later for showing him so obviously that she was glad to see him. But she could not help it.

Life pressed on her very hardly, and the passage back to her own country was difficult to save. Her little hoard had been expended a few months before, when she had been operated on for appendicitis.

Her every working moment was filled with dread of Jaeckels. Although he was an American citizen, he openly sneered at his adopted country and lauded that of his birth to the skies. That had been bad enough, but of late he had taken to touching her hand and arm as she took his dictation.

It seemed like the coming of new life and hope to know that her rescuer was to sit in the big room and share her labors. Surely the presence of a man such as this Mr. Fallon must keep Jaeckels within bounds. For a time, at any rate, it did.

Jaeckels was, above all, a business

man. At last he was able to talk openly, frankly, cynically about his schemes to as complete a crook as himself or his brother. He needed to be advised of American law. At this Thornton was infinitely the superior of the man he understudied. He had been for a year in the office of the district attorney, and the cases of get-rich-quick swindlers had given him a deep knowledge of their methods. Jaeckels listened with rapt attention.

"But we can do better here in Asia," he repeated again and again. "Stick to me, George, and be loyal and you'll make more than the big fellows ever would give you in Manhattan. My brother William's a British subject. He left London because New York offered him better pickings. Let me tell you this. He's leaving New York for Peking. That's what he thinks of our prospects."

"When?" the other demanded quickly. It would not be a happy meeting.

"In a couple of months," Adolf said.

"I've not seen any pickings," Thornton said after a pause of sheer relief.

"I've been trying you out," Jaeckels confided in him. "I can't afford to make any mistakes. My God, man, you don't know what's here for us! When I first came here I read something Sir Robert Hart, head of the customs, said about the land tax. He said it yielded twenty-five million when it should bring in, if it were properly managed, four hundred million."

Jaeckels made the motion of one squeezing something dry. "We must squeeze them scientifically. You and I can't do it alone. We must stand in with some of the officials. They get it principally by entering payments twice and padding the pay roll, but I've got something up my sleeve that beats it all.

"Listen. I know a minister of the Nung Kung Shang Pu—that's the min-istry of agriculture, industry, and trade —and that ought to be worth five millions in concessions if it's worked right. Now I'm not popular here, although I'm an American citizen. They've got nothing against me that could be put in writing, but——"

There was an eloquent pause. Thornton said nothing.

"You're a newcomer," Jaeckels went on, "and not mixed up in Pekingese affairs. What you have to do is to float around and spend money at the Peking Club and get favorably known. I'll put up the money. I'll see that you are introduced as the son of a rich friend who is sending you out here to get the edges rubbed off. Don't talk about business. The social end of it for you. Above all, do as I say. If you don't, back you go."

"That sounds like a threat," Thornton observed without smiling.

"That's just what it is," Jaeckels smiled. "Let's understand each other, Fallon. You think just because I weigh three hundred pounds and look soft physically, I'm soft mentally. I'm not. I'm hard. I'm unforgiving. I never forget an injury. I'm a bad man to cross." Then he smiled engagingly. "On the other hand, if a man's faithful and loyal I see he is rewarded. You understand?"

"Absolutely," said Thornton briskly. "You want me to play the social end of the game so I can lead them to your web. All right. When do I begin?"

It was hard work for a decent man to play his part with so complete a villain as Adolf Jaeckels. Hardly an hour of the day or night went by but Jack Thornton was tempted to throw up the position. But he held himself in for the reason that so much depended on it.

Some time during the twenty-four hours he made his report to Wang. It seemed he was doing well, for the mandarin praised his activity and promised him ere long the possession of facts which would clear him.

What made life bearable was the companionship of Joan Carrington. Often when Jaeckels believed him to be watching the ballet at the Circus Barowsky or wooing fickle chance at one of the gambling houses in Telegraph Lane, Thornton was with her.

He knew, without any possibility of mistake, that this was the great passion of his life, and because he wanted to offer himself freed from all shadows of suspicion he did not tell her how much he loved her. Had she but known it, this hesitation was his sincerest tribute. It was because she loved him unreservedly and with a strength of devotion that almost frightened her that she found it incomprehensible that he looked so much and said so little.

Jaeckels was growing more offensive every day. It would have been so simple to tell him she and George Fallon were engaged. One day her employer, casting discretion to the winds, poured out his passion for her.

"I love you, I love you," he cried thickly.

"That's nonsense," she said, springing to her feet. "You mustn't say that."

"Why not?" he demanded. "Is there any other man?"

Her crimsoned cheek gave him answer. His evil eyes glittered like beads of blue glass. Instantly he suspected this handsome young American.

"George!" he called loudly. "Come here."

Thornton strolled in leisurely. He could see something had happened to distress the girl he loved. "What is it?" he asked.

"Have you been making love to Miss Carrington? If you have you'd better cut it out. This is a business organization and I won't have it."

Joan Carrington's heart beat quickly. If she knew the high spirit and genuine nature of the man she loved this was the moment for him to put Jaeckels in his place.

For the moment Thornton could scarcely contain himself. He could see what had happened. The jealous intuition of the lover told him that, but he dared not risk a quarrel yet. Not an hour before his employer had outlined a scheme at once so boldly criminal that its complete possession would enable him to tell Wang all that the high-born Chinaman wanted to know.

It was now a matter of hours. In a day or two at the most he would be able to shake himself free from bondage and get back to his own country with Joan and honor. It was damnable that this thing should have happened at such a moment. To run with the hare and hunt with the hounds has ever been a difficult proceeding. He wished he had dared take the girl into his confidence, but Wang had been adamant. When he spoke he felt his voice ring false.

"What fool idea have you got in your head?" he demanded lightly.

"I'm telling you," retorted Jaeckels venomously, "to keep your hands off Joan Carrington."

"Forget it," said Thornton. "I want to talk to you further about that matter we discussed earlier."

His heart seemed to turn to water as he saw the pale girl shrink back as from a blow. He knew she must feel as Cæsar did when wounded by the dagger of Brutus.

"I won't forget it," Jaeckels exclaimed. "Before I talk business to you or allow you to be here, do you understand what I mean? If you don't I'll repeat it. You are not to have anything to do with this girl except in a purely business manner. You go your way when you're through here and she'll go hers. If you either of you disobey me you can get out. Do you agree to that, Mr. George Fallon?"

Thornton dared not look at Joan. He knew if he did his resolve would weaken. If only she could understand that this seeming treachery was being enacted for her benefit as well as his own!

The girl was young, friendless, and inexperienced. She saw only that the man she had idealized was, after all, a poor creature trembling before the wrath of his employer. When love should have lent him strength he betrayed only weakness. She turned her head away so that none should see the tears which forced themselves past the gates of her eyes.

"All right," said Thornton briefly. "I see."

"And you'll do as I say?"

"Yes," he said sullenly.

Adolf Jaeckels turned his attention to the girl.

"Your hero's got a bright yellow streak where his backbone ought to be," he sneered. "I wouldn't worry about him any more."

By a supreme effort she forced her voice to be firm.

"I won't," she replied, and walked from the room.

Jaeckels was still sneering when he spoke to the other man.

"I understand the temptation all right," he observed, "but this is where you keep off the grass. I never warn a subordinate twice."

Before she went home that night Jaeckels threw a newspaper clipping on the desk. It was from a sensational New York yellow journal and shrieked unsavory details at her concerning one George Fallon.

"When you've read that you'll be grateful to me," said Adolf.

Later she gave it back to him. She looked very white and broken, all the happy youth blotted from her face in a few hours of a working day.

"I am grateful," she said huskily.

Outside the office on Ha-ta Mên

Street, Thornton, despite his resolve to wait until all was cleared up, came to her side.

"All I ask," he whispered, "is that you suspend judgment. Don't condemn me—yet."

"I hate you!" she said, flushing. "I shall never cease to be ashamed at having known you. I shall never cease praying to forget you utterly."

From his window Adolf Jaeckels observed what happened. He chuckled. There had been many opportunities in his life to study feminine psychology. He was more amiable to Thornton now he had witnessed his rebuff. He even offered the younger man one of his best cigars as he talked over the secret matter concerning the bribing of a high official.

"If we don't get it some one else will," Jaeckels said when the scheme was outlined. "It's up to us white men to make hay before the Japs get into the game. When they do we won't get a look-in."

It was less than a week after Thornton's humiliation that his employer came to him in high good humor. His brother William had placed to his credit at the Peking branch of the Anglo-Japanese bank a half million of dollars. With this sum as a bait the brothers Jaeckels hoped to make themselves fabulously wealthy.

The first move in the game was a visit one night to the house of a Chinaman of position where would be gathered other native notables. Jack Thornton noted that although the misty night made recognition of streets difficult, Jaeckels deliberately mystified him by crossing his tracks and recrossing them.

"Spare yourself the trouble," Thornton said. "I've no idea where we are. I couldn't identify anything."

"It's not for you I'm doing this,"

the other whispered; "it's because others may be interested, too."

It was a rich man's house that they presently entered. There was the chapel for ancestral tablets and the spaciousness of the cleanly bare rooms was impressive. In the great hall four Chinese gentlemen were sitting at the teak guest table under a long Confucian motto. Through an opening Thornton could see the central court with its pond for brilliant fish.

He looked at the impassive faces of the men with interest.

They made none of the courteous gestures of welcome which such men would do to those of their own rank or guests whom they considered worthy of honor. Perhaps Jaeckels saw that his assistant noted this.

"They think about as much of us as they do of actors," he whispered. Thornton knew that the Brothers of the Pear Tree, as Thespians are termed, rank with keepers of opium dens and are denied social recognition. He felt humiliated at being associated with the perspiring blond man.

It is almost impossible to hurry Chinese of rank. Only one admitted knowing English, and his translations took an enormous time. Three hours were consumed in learning that for the consideration of a sum yet to be decided the concession Jaeckels sought would be his. It was complete victory.

Money was waiting at the bank. George Fallon was at hand to distribute it with craft, and his brother William would shortly be with him; William, who was his superior even in ways of guile.

That night Thornton could not go to sleep for thinking of the information he had for Wang. On his way back to Jaeckels' home he had memorized the names and positions of the four officials. They were all of importance, and none had been suspected by the New China party.

When Wang heard the last name of the four mentioned, his hands, so long and motionless, were suddenly turned into clenched fists. Thornton would not know that one of the guilty, on whom the seal of death was now irrevocably set, was his own brother.

"You have done well," said Wang. "You have accomplished that for which we brought you."

Thornton looked at him with the deep interest he ever felt toward this remarkable, inflexible, passionless man. He would like to have asked more of the methods by which the corrupt officials were to be punished.

"Shall I have to appear in a court of justice to give my testimony?"

"'Litigation,'" quoted Wang, "'is suing a flea and getting a bite for justice.' No. We shall deal with them more swiftly than that. To-morrow night I shall be here again."

Silently he slipped from the bedroom, mysterious in his comings and his goings.

Jaeckels was very busy next day. For the greater part of the time Thornton was obliged to remain in the outer office with Joan. Half a dozen times he made an effort to talk to her, but her haughty way of holding her head made him desist.

Presently her attitude ceased to hurt him. After all, this was the way a decent girl ought to behave to a man with Fallon's record. How was she to know the substitution?

He paused by the side of her desk.

"I'm going to marry you," he asserted, "and you're going to be perfectly happy."

Smilelessly she pointed to the inner office.

"If he hears you," she sneered, "he may come out and box your ears."

"So he might," Thornton agreed, still smiling, "but then again he might not. Listen to me, Joan Carrington. Before I marry you I'm going to offer you the spectacle of seeing him soundly whipped."

"Whom will you hire to do it?" she demanded.

"I've engaged myself in the star rôle."

She turned her head away and went on typewriting. She had been sobbing herself to sleep for a week now with a heart that she thought was breaking. She could never be happy again, she told herself.

Jaeckels had a big, roomy house near the Ch'ien Mên Gate. Men who were willing to meet him at poker were welcomed, and the stakes were high. There, too, were dancing girls from Barowsky's and champagne suppers on great occasions. Jaeckels had often talked of this place to his assistant, but so far had never invited him there.

"You'd better see it before I have to give it up," he remarked. "My brother is higher-toned than I am. He wouldn't stand for this place. He wants to make a splash in society. I like my house because no European or American ever comes near it unless invited. I'd like you to come to-night, Fallon."

"Some other night," said Thornton. "I'm tired."

Jaeckels winked ponderously.

"It's business," he said significantly. "I've had a message from one of the bunch, and terms are to be discussed. You've got to be on hand. It's mighty important. You have to get there early, remember. When it's all settled your place in the game is to be taken into consideration. You've got to collect for me just as you did for your political boss at home, only you've got to be a dashed sight slicker. If they get on to you I'll have to get another helper."

"You won't need one," said Thornton in a tone that Jaeckels did not like. "If they get *me* they get you."

"Do they?" said the elder man, and instantly set about wondering where a new assistant might be obtained.

He knew there was more danger in the undertaking than there used to be. The mighty nation had been used to systematic graft for a score of centuries, but was now suddenly awaking to a new consciousness.

CHAPTER V.

SEATED at her desk late that evening, Joan Carrington was startled by a knock upon the sliding door opening from the corridor. Before she could rise it had been pushed back and a man slipped in furtively.

He was above middle height, broad, and bullet-headed, and Joan thought that never had she looked into such a hateful face.

Quickly she took from the drawer of her desk a revolver that had been her father's and hid it in a pocket.

"What do you want?" she asked sharply.

"Mr. Jaeckels," he said. He spoke with a common intonation, and his small dark eyes roved from corner to corner as though fearing detection.

"Mr. Jaeckels has gone home," she said. "He won't be here until ten to-morrow morning. He lives on Ch'ien Mên Street."

The man was evidently a sailor on some American ship at Tientsin. Jaeckels often bought things from such men, stolen goods perhaps, but always at a bargain. But no sailor had ever made so free with Mr. Jaeckels' office. The man sat himself down in the vast chair, and took from his pocket a flask and held it to his lips.

"Samschu isn't so bad when there's nothing else," he observed. He looked about him with interest. "You the stenographer?"

"I'm Mr. Jaeckels' secretary," she answered.

"We'll get along fine," said the sailor. "I didn't know I was going to be so lucky."

"This office is closed," she said firmly, "and will not be open till to-morrow."

"You evidently don't know who I am," he said, faintly amused. "Why, little one, I'm George Fallon, if that means anything to you."

"You are certainly not George Fallon," she cried.

"Thought I was killed, I suppose," he said, smiling. "Well, little one, they had a tougher proposition on hand than they thought. When I got to Hong-kong I was invited to go out and sit in a friendly game over at Kowloon City. It was a friendly game all right. Over the entrance it said 'Auspicious Welcome.' "

The man who styled himself George Fallon suddenly woke to ferocious anger. "My God, when I think of what I suffered after I was left for dead I feel like killing every chink on sight. Some day I'll tell you about it." He looked at her curiously. "Why did you say I wasn't George Fallon?"

"Because Mr. Fallon is working here and has been for two months or more. He's at Mr. Jaeckels' house now. I heard Mr. Jaeckels ask him to go."

So startled was the girl at his flaming face when he heard this that she jumped up with a scream and the revolver fell to the floor. In a second he had pounced on it.

"I needed that," he said with an oath. "So there's some man here masquerading as me, eh? If there is it's the man who tried to have me put out of the way. I see it now." He broke the revolver and looked eagerly to see if it was fully loaded. "Six of 'em," he muttered. "He stands a swell chance of being able to pull that game again."

So dazed was the girl with the bewildering emotions of the moment that at first she could not comprehend her changed situation. If this coarse-faced man were indeed George Fallon, then the man she loved must bear another name and another past. Those loathsome revelations in the paper were not true of him. She had condemned him for another's fault. Fallon, watching her, alert for trickery and suspicious of every one, could not understand.

"Take me to Jaeckels' house," he commanded.

"I will not!" she said. What treachery could be baser than to lead this armed, violent creature to attack his fellow countryman!

"You will," he said, "or I'll raise such hell that you'll be sorry. What's it to be?"

She looked at the clock, and saw that it was yet early. It might be that the man she loved had not yet started from Mrs. Hamilton's house. If only she could take this new Fallon to Ch'ien Mên Street and then warn the other. She did not trouble to seek explanations. The newcomer was plainly puzzled by her readiness to what a moment before she had refused.

"I don't trust you," he said, frowning. "And I serve notice on you, I'm sore with everything in this damn country. Don't try any tricks."

"I won't," she said quickly. "I promise to take you to Mr. Jaeckels."

"All right," he returned more amiably. "That's all I want to begin with. If any one has been double-crossing me it's this fellow who calls himself by my name, and I can't find him too quickly."

It was the first time Joan had ever been to her employer's residence. He had often hinted that he would like her to come, but she had never shown any eagerness. Reports were rife of the type of gathering that met there. When the real George Fallon entered she slipped back into the street and made her way to Mrs. Hamilton's home, hoping to see the tall, straight figure of the man she had wronged.

She did not relish this visit because the Scots lady had rigid ideas about the proprieties, and it was now ten o'clock and the place in darkness. Looking up, Joan saw there was one light left in a room. And as she looked a man's form passed between the lamp and shade.

It could be none other than the man she had come to see. It was not difficult for one as slight and wiry as she to pull herself up to the balcony beneath the lighted window. As she did so the lamp was extinguished. She rapped gently against the shutter, but no one came to investigate the sound. Then, nerved by the necessity of seeing him, Joan pushed the window open and stepped down into the room.

As she stood there, hesitating, something passed silently behind her and closed the shutters. Then the lamp was turned up, and she found herself looking into the impassive face of a Chinese gentleman. In his less obvious way he seemed as much surprised as she was.

"Don't scream," he said in English as correct as her own. "I shall do you no harm."

"Where's Mr. Fallon?" she cried. "I must see him."

"I, too, am awaiting him," the unknown returned.

"How long have you been here?" she asked.

When he told her he had waited more than an hour she groaned.

"It's too late," she wailed. "They've got him now."

The Chinaman woke to vivid interest.

"You must tell me what you mean at once."

Directly he had heard of the coming of the real George Fallon and the meeting at Jaeckels' house, he made for the window. First he extinguished the lamp. The girl had determined that he was a man to be trusted. He had given her the impression of strength and courage. With the certainty that in

obeying him she was attempting to aid her fellow countryman she followed Wang.

CHAPTER VI.

WHEN Thornton left Mrs. Hamilton's he thought he had memorized the way to Jaeckels' house accurately. But it was night, and he lost his way and wandered in strange byways for an hour before he turned into Chi'en Mên Street and paused before his employer's home.

He was instantly admitted, and found himself very soon facing the Chinamen in a luxurious, gorgeously furnished room. It was a miracle of bad taste in a country of exquisite furnishings—exactly like Jaeckels', he commented.

Jaeckels looked at him curiously. There was an expression of triumph, Thornton thought. Evidently things were breaking right with him.

"You're late," Jaeckels said.

"Lost my way," Thornton responded, and looked at the four men of high degree.

They had cruel faces, he thought, hard, impassive masks that concealed God knew what immemorial vices. And they were content to betray their countrymen for filthy lucre. It was done everywhere, he supposed, in West and East, but Thornton was essentially honest and hated graft.

The next move on Jaeckels' part astounded him. The huge, fat man took an automatic pistol from his pocket and handled it lovingly.

"I cannot run," said Jaeckels, "but I can shoot with any man in China."

For the first time Thornton awoke to danger. In the almond eyes of these silent Pekingese magnates he sensed bitter hate. There was a tenseness in the situation that spoke of imminent peril. As the door was shut and he was covered by a loaded pistol and outnumbered five to one, any attempt at escape was impossible. He tried to pass it off easily.

"I cannot shoot worth a damn," he answered carelessely, "but I can run against any man in China."

"You'll never get a chance to prove it," sneered Jaeckels. "You've run your last race, Mr. George Fallon, and you've lost."

"What the devil are you talking about?" Thornton demanded. He wanted to know instantly. This fencing got on his nerves.

In answer a fierce-eyed man, dressed like a sailor, came into the room. If the others showed their dislike of Thornton this man's glance shouted it. He clenched his fists and made as though to spring at him.

"Not yet," Jaeckels said sharply.

"If he's spoiling for a fight," said Thornton, his spirits rising at the prospects of action, "let him have it. Turn that damned gun away and let him see what he can do."

"You keep where you are." the fat man commanded. "Meanwhile let me introduce you to Mr. George Fallon."

Thornton looked at him with interest. Those watching him were disappointed to see no sign of fear on his face.

"So you're the real Fallon," he commented. "From your press notices I can believe it."

He hoped the real Fallon would make a rush at him. In a rough and tumble there might be a chance at escape, which this hungry gun muzzle prevented.

"Not very careful of his personal appearance, is he?" Thornton exclaimed pleasantly. "Has an air of the salt sea about him. I don't think he'll be a credit to the old firm. He's hungry, Adolf. Look at him licking his lips. Feed the brute."

"Wait a minute," Jaeckels cried as the stranger tried to make a lunge at his impersonator. "Right now we want to know how he did it."

"Did what?" Thornton asked.

"Changed places with this man and had him almost killed in a Kowloon City gambling hell."

"They probably caught him cheating," Thornton explained. "Look at his blushing face. He admits it."

"Cut that out!" Jaeckels exclaimed angrily. "Haven't you enough sense to see that you're up against it? If I were willing to let you go Fallon here would want to get at you."

"He'll never forget me when I'm through," said Fallon.

"And if Fallon were merciful—which he isn't—you've got to reckon with that bunch there." He indicated the Chinamen of rank. "They can see through your game. You are not as happy as you seem."

Suddenly the Chinaman who knew English spoke. It was inevitably a Mongolian maxim. "'Antics are not always vivacity, as the fish on the hook can say.' This man must tell everything he knows. Unless he does we leave here with a poised sword over our necks. There are methods which we know." He permitted himself to smile faintly. "Methods which will make him open his heart as a sick child talks to his mother."

"That means torture," said Fallon vindictively, "torture that will break down any man's nerves. You've heard of Chinese torture, haven't you? Well, you're going to experience it. Tell me how you trimmed me in Kowloon."

"If I knew I probably shouldn't tell," Thornton returned, "and as I don't know I can't tell."

"He will tell you all," the Chinaman said with conviction. "Perhaps not at first, as he is strong and young; but later, when the sinews stretch and the nerves are plucked as one plucks the strings of the lute, he will answer your every question."

Still Thornton said no word and gave evidence of none of the creeping terror that came to him. They would torture him to make him tell of what he did not know. There was such certainty in the Chinaman's statement that he would make a complete confession. It was built on countless centuries of experience with men just as strong of muscle and stout of heart as he himself.

This, then, was the end. To come to shameful death in a far country. His relatives would believe him guilty. They would cease to talk of him and think of him only with resentment. And little Joan Carrington would never know that the love he offered her was clean and fine and worthy of her.

These men were determined on his death, he could see that. Even if he told them of "Wang" they would not believe that he did not know his real name and that of his companions. He was as one already dead.

"You'd better begin," he said. "I've nothing to say."

They bound him very tightly hand and foot. So cunningly were the bonds fastened that agonizing cramps seized him, so that he could hardly keep from calling out. And this was not even the beginning of the tortures that would soon commence.

He heard them arguing as to what place would be most secret and convenient. Jaeckels, it seemed, had little appetite for watching the punishment. He proposed to leave it to the Chinese and George Fallon. It would upset his stomach, he explained. The sight of blood invariably destroyed his digestive powers. But he pointed out that there was a vast cellar beneath the thick-walled house from which all noise of the outer world was shut off. It was full of rats.

The Chinaman who spoke English turned his slanting eyes on the bound man.

"That is well," he said smoothly. "We shall use them. You have per-haps," he said to Thornton, "read an English book which spoke of the use to which we put rats in our punishments? The writer knew so little. If you were to live you would be able to teach him so much."

It was indeed a vast and horrid chamber, this dark and dreadful space beneath the house. They placed him on a long table and he was only able to look at the damp ceiling. Around him he could hear the squealing of frightened rats.

"They're catching 'em," Fallon explained, coming to Thornton's side, "and putting 'em in a sack. The chink with the purple robe said he was glad they were half starved."

Fallon paused a moment. "I'm not great on this torturing stuff, but when I think what you made me go through down there in Hongkong when you tried to have me killed I'm not going to waste any pity on you. I'd rather have beaten you up first, but they're afraid I'd kill you."

Thornton, even in that moment, could laugh, but there was little genuine mirth in it. It was, rather, a last attempt to provoke a fight wherein he had a chance to escape.

"Oh, no," he explained, "they were afraid *you* would get killed. They know very well you wouldn't last two rounds with me. You're wise to have me tied up."

It was Jaeckels who pulled Fallon away, cursing and mouthing.

"Don't be a fool," he counseled. "Watch your step here. These chinks can make or break us. It depends what this faker tells. Keep your temper. You're not in New York, remember. I'm going before they begin."

Before they began Thornton heard Jaeckels' retreating steps. It must be very near now, he supposed.

A moment later he heard Jaeckels— from the top of the steps leading to the main floor, he surmised—utter a furious oath. Then there was the sound of many voices, rising high in anger or fear, and the cellar was full of men, Chinese all.

Not a thing could he see, but all about him were wrestling, fighting figures. Now and again he heard the harsh cough and indrawn breath which told him that a life had gone out as cold steel ran the body through. Above the din he heard George Fallon's voice. Then the harsh voice was stilled in the cough and indrawn breath.

It was Wang who cut his bonds.

When he stepped down from the table there was a dreadful stillness in the gloomy chamber. Fallon lay with the four Chinamen in the sprawling ugliness of violent death. And two of Wang's men were dead. It was a fearful sight, but it meant safety for him. Half hysterically he told Wang what had happened, of the torture threats, of Jaeckels, who could not bear to witness the punishment in which he had concurred. He wondered why it was Mr. Wang allowed himself that fleeting smile.

He pointed to the sack in which a score of hungry rats were fighting and squealing.

"It will perhaps appeal to Mr. Jaeckels' sense of humor that they will be his own rats who force the truth from him."

So Adolf Jaeckels was to fall in the pit he had digged for another! Thornton was wearied of this cruelty, of the mysteries of this old land to which he was bound by no tie of race, tongue, or tradition. He longed to be among a people he could understand.

"My father's house sounds pretty good to me now," he said.

"It is well," Mr. Wang returned with a smile of commendation. "You may now go to him proudly as a son unashamed and filial. Already he has proofs of your innocence. Go, and may you be as wide as a chrysanthemum border."

"It's not so easy to go," he reminded the mandarin.

"That is provided for," Wang said suavely. "The train to Tientsin leaves in one hour. Your ticket is already purchased. You will stay at the Astor House there until the boat leaves on the next day. You will be wise never again to set foot in Peking."

"I never will," Thornton assured him. "Am I to go back to my rooms?"

"No," said Wang, "it will not be necessary. Furthermore you will travel to Tientsin in native dress. I have such a costume here. There you will be safe if you keep within the Astor House. Also you will be wise to speak to none." Wang handed a package to the American. "Here are your tickets booked through to New York, and money which you have earned. I shall never see you again; years fly like arrows, one eager to pass the other to the mark. You will be happy."

"That's awfully good of you," said Thornton. "But I'd like to see a friend before I go."

"Miss Carrington will be guarded carefully," said the amazing Wang. "She will be sent suitably protected to her native land. You must not, for her sake and your own, venture near any place where you are known now. That is why you are to wear this dress."

Everything went as Wang had said. Rooms were reserved at Tientsin's best hotel, and he had in his possession tickets for the Mail steamer. But what puzzled Thornton was to find, on opening the packet, that there were three passages booked. An expensive way of hiding his track if it were done for that purpose.

After the breakfast, taken in his rooms next morning, there was a knock upon the door, a soft, timid knock. He had in his pocket the automatic which had been Jaeckels', and he gripped it. Although Wang had said little, he knew that there might be danger still.

It was Joan who came in.

"You!" he cried. "Oh, Joan!" Then he took her in his arms. "I said you were going to marry me and be happy ever afterward."

She told him that in an adjoining room was old Mrs. Hamilton, engaged by Wang to chaperon her to New York. At a moment's notice everything had been arranged. Wang had power, and his name was magical. He had bought the Scotchwoman's home, and she was going back to her childhood home in Inverness.

"It's magical," he confessed. "This Wang, as he calls himself, moves us like pieces on a board and we don't know yet what his real purpose is or what his name is. I wish I did."

"You do," Joan said, and whispered in his ear the name of the greatest power in all China.

"It's an honor to have been working for him," he exclaimed, "but as it's finished with I have other important things to do. I'm not supposed to leave this hotel till I make my run for the steamer, but you are a free agent. Now, sweetheart, you must do something for me. I'm anxious to have a heart-to-heart talk with an American preacher. I have grave doctrinal doubts which only a minister of religion can solve."

She looked at him in amazement. His tone was grave and his face smileless. Had the horrors of which he had just told her affected him mentally?

"Yes," he went on, "I wish for priestly consolation."

"You're not ill?" she exclaimed.

He took her in his arms again and covered her sweet face with kisses. "All I want to know," he whispered, "is if there's anything in Chinese law against our being married before the ship sails."

THE END.

GIFTS

By Roy le Moyne

WE'VE risen winged on the breathless night
    And gazed across the great expanse of sky
    Where stars sink flaming through the void and die
In final gasps of beauty and of light
Now all the giant echoes of our flight,
    In clouds of music that have thundered by,
    Are dwindling in a last despairing cry
Like some rare moment shrunken out of sight.

The splendid gift that makes our dream so sweet,
    That teaches us to find in beauty's thrall
The wasting chords that make you throb and beat,
    To have all life wait on your beck and call,
And rise up singing from the worst defeat.
    Maladi, yours the greatest gift of all.

The Kiss of the Silver Flask
By Evangeline Weir

OUTSIDE in the wind and the rain and the darkness a man looked through a window into the light and warmth of a glowing wood fire near which a woman was getting supper. His eyes followed her about the plain, bare little room, and not a movement escaped him.

A startling knock on the rough door brought the woman at once. She hesitated a moment, taking in the details, then stepped aside for him to enter. Without a word, he went to the fire, slipped off his wet coat and spread it across a chair to dry.

"It's a wild night, missus," he said, as he seated himself on a low stool before the blaze. "Tough on a man who has no home."

"The wind is high," she replied, going on with her work.

The man appeared to be deep in thought as he looked into the cheerful fire. He saw her cut the bread, go to the cupboard for a dish of cake, pausing to rearrange a set of platters against the rough back of the dresser. He heard a curious sound above the rain and the wind; a cry like that of an animal in distress. He saw her listen, hesitate, then slip a coat around her shoulders and go out into the darkness.

When she returned he noticed that the coat was gone. She stood by the fire, and, shaking the raindrops from her dress, explained that the wind had torn it from her shoulders.

"Husband coming soon?" the man questioned.

"The storm may detain him."

"Pretty lonesome up here among the hills."

"Yes."

"Live here all the time?"

She gave him a searching look and muttered something under her breath as she turned to scald the tea.

"Will you have some supper?" she asked, when the table was arranged to her satisfaction.

The man's eyes sought and held hers —his shrewd from long experience, hers defiant.

"Ain't you afraid, missus? I'm a rough man."

"Why should I fear you?" she asked in a voice like steel. "I am prepared to protect myself," and her eyes fell for a moment to the folds of her waist.

He made a mental note of it.

"If you will give me a cup of tea, I'll drink it here by the fire."

She did as requested, and the tea was so unusually good that he commented upon it.

"Your tea is good, missus; very good."

"How long have you been on the road?" she asked.

"A considerable time, missus. Sometimes it pays, and sometimes it don't."

"Why such a doubtful profession?"

He put a question. "Why do you live up here among the hills?"

"I like it."

"And I like the road."

"Which leads to prison."

"I take a chance, missus, same as you do in this lonely place."

"How did you chance to find this detached bungalow?"

"I have a liking for the hills. It began to rain and grow dark, and your light guided me to shelter."

She bent over to stir the fire, and he saw something slip from the folds of her waist and hang suspended from a thin chain. She concealed it quickly, her eyes searching his face as she did so.

Going to the table, she made an attempt to eat; but the food, with the exception of a cup of tea, remained untouched.

"It's good tea, missus," he said, with his eyes on the pot.

She poured him another cup, standing beside him as he sipped it.

"Thank you, missus," he said, handing her the empty cup. "It takes the chill out of my bones."

She put the cups and saucers into a small pan and carefully washed and dried them. As she replaced them in the cupboard she touched a platter, which fell to the floor. She immediately moved another in its place before she gathered up the bits.

Having disposed of the dishes, she pulled a blanket from a box and laid it beside him. His eyes asked a question, which she answered.

"I would not turn out a dog that sought shelter to-night. You may go to sleep there by the fire. You need not hesitate. I have no designs upon you."

"You are brave to ask a tramp to stay all night."

"I am almost as poor as you. If you see anything you desire you are free to take it."

Seating herself beside the table, she opened a book, but he felt that her eyes were continually upon him.

Outside the rain beat furiously upon the small bungalow, while the wind swept the trees with wild sounds terrifying to the usual woman. But she sat unmoved through it all, throwing wood from time to time upon the fire, then returning to her book.

Toward morning he went to sleep. When he awoke the woman had left the room, and the door of the cupboard was open. Hearing no sound, he crossed the floor and pushed aside the largest platter. Slipping his fingers over the rough boards, he forced a small opening and saw a box firmly secured against a panel.

It was empty, except that in one corner gleamed a wonderful diamond, lodged in a crevice as if caught there when rudely wrenched from a necklace. He put it in his pocket, his eyes glittering as he pushed both the board and platter in place and reseated himself before the fire.

The woman returned after a short time and, moving quietly, laid aside a muddy, dripping cloak. She made no explanation, and he asked no questions. She returned to her book, and thus the remainder of the night passed and with it the storm.

The man accepted the cup of coffee which she presently handed him, and gruffly thanked her for her hospitality. He then went down the steep, crooked trail, the woman watching him until he was lost among the hills.

Mrs. Temple was receiving guests when her nephew, George Field, arrived with a new man.

"Good evening, Aunt Amelia. Let me introduce my friend Gillis Dyson. I took the liberty of bringing him along without a formal invitation to either of us. Gill went to college with me, and helped your unfortunate nephew out of a good many scrapes."

Mrs. Temple held out her hand to the stranger.

"I thank you for saving the honor of the family. George is noted for his blunders at home as well as at college."

"I hope you do not mean that I have blundered in coming to-night without the usual note," George said wickedly.

"Do not mind him, Mr. Dyson; he likes to spar with his old aunt. Now, George, you are acquainted with all my guests, see that your friend enjoys himself."

"I see Aunt Crete here, and she looks stunning for a widow not yet four months old. Her grief has neither affected her looks nor her dress. Dropped her mourning rather soon, didn't she? Uncle George would be flattered to see how soon his loving wife recovered from her great grief.

Will you forget me so soon, auntie, when I pass on?"

"I'll hold your tricks in memory —you can always depend on that, if it be any consolation to you."

"Even a bad deed may erect a monument to a fellow!"

His aunt laughed.

"Mr. Dyson, do not let him demoralize you."

"I must pay my respects to Aunt Crete. I wonder if there might be a chance for me? You see, I have the money she sold herself to obtain and lost."

"George!" his aunt reproved. "I have no fault to find with Crete."

"Except that she did not keep her mourning on long enough. But that black and blue and silver thing is mighty becoming and covers a multitude of broken conventions."

His aunt had turned to a new guest, and his words were lost.

"Come on, Dyson, and meet the charming widow. If it wasn't against my training, I'd take a chance myself. Handsome, isn't she?"

Mr. Dyson was watching her with a perplexed face. He rubbed his hand across his brow as if trying to recall something.

"Aunt Crete, I am glad to see you looking well after a sad occasion. You look stunning in that new creation. This is my friend Mr. Dyson. Will you kindly take him off my hands while I go talk to some of the pretty girls?"

For an instant Mr. Dyson and Mrs. Field looked into each other's eyes; then she said lightly: "My nephew is incorrigible, Mr. Dyson. When you know him better you will cease to wonder at anything he does or says."

"My experience has been rather full; I went to college with him."

Again came the searching look in her dark eyes.

"Will you show me the conservatory, Mrs. Field? George has told me that

Mrs. Temple has a number of rare orchids."

"I shall be pleased to do it. Are you fond of flowers? Mrs. Temple has a superb collection of rare plants."

"How beautiful!" he exclaimed, as they entered among the mass of plants and vines. "It is like another world."

"I am glad you are able to appreciate such beauty. George calls them weeds. I wish George was more like you—well-balanced—he embarrasses me at times."

"He is a good fellow—true as steel," Dyson said in defense of his friend.

"But not master of himself as you are. I quarrel disgracefully with George, but I cannot imagine myself quarreling with or being bored by you. You would keep my intellect at its highest tension, and even a reaction would fail to lessen my interest in you."

"You flatter me."

"I am merely stating a fact. Do you read faces easily? I am sure you do. Now, George doesn't know a vain woman from a modest one."

They were among the orchids as she spoke, and she gave him the names and histories of a few rare ones. Bending over to bring a small blossom into a better light, a thin chain she was wearing caught in a branch, and a tiny silver flask slipped from the folds of her waist and rested against his hand.

"What a beautiful flask!" he exclaimed in admiration. "So minute in design, yet so perfect."

"It is very old!"

"Is it a perfume bottle? May I open it?"

She shook her head and held out her hand.

"It contains a powerful headache potion, and so precious that I rarely use it. It was given me in India by a man who distilled it from a flower little known."

She was watching his face as she spoke, but he seemed to have lost his interest in the trinket. She slipped it back among the folds of her waist.

"Be careful," she warned, "you will strike that rare one over your head. You are a tall man, remember. Not too tall, however; I like tall men."

"I am glad you approve of my height. I sometimes depreciate it myself."

"I see you and the merry widow have formed a mutual admiration society," George said to his friend when they were alone in his room. "Let me give you a piece of advice: Don't!"

"Why?"

"She isn't the real thing."

"I thought her complexion quite natural."

"Her skin is O. K., and she does not invest in hair goods, but she is a mere butterfly, sipping only from the richest plants. She is greatly interested in you. Wanted to know where you came from, and how long I had known you."

"And you said——"

"That she need not waste her smiles on you; that you were a poor devil of a lawyer struggling to keep a decent suit for important occasions."

"You were discreet. By the way, who was she before her marriage to your uncle?"

"I know but little about her, and I judge he knew less. He met her at Palm Beach among the gay crowd. Her unusual style helped her in the game, and they married two months later, much to her satisfaction. But it proved a losing game for her. Uncle died in less than a year, and had little money to leave her. It was entailed. She saw it all handed over to me. But she was game. Never a look or word betrayed her."

"She looks a cool one!"

"Aunt Amelia's home is open to her, and uncle left her enough to keep up appearances. She will soon find another fool to buy her dresses and diamond rattles."

"I find her interesting; I intend to cultivate her."

"Do not blame me if you get scorched."

"She knows more than you give her credit for, my friend."

"Wise or otherwise."

"Does your Aunt Amelia like her?"

"She flatters Aunt Amelia and gets well paid for the service."

For three weeks Dyson remained with George Field. Much of the time was spent at Mrs. Temple's, where he always found a welcome from both women.

One evening he and George called and found Mrs. Temple alone. The widow had gone to her room with a headache, much to the relief of his friend. Instead of leaving by the front way, they went through the garden to make a short cut to a certain street. Just as George was about to open a gate in the wall, Dyson put his hand on his arm and pointed toward the house.

They saw a woman in a dark coat and long automobile veil wound around her face and head stealing through the garden. She passed swiftly through the gate and closed it after her.

"We will follow her," Gillis Dyson said.

"You do not think——"

"No matter what I think. Let us shadow her. Be careful! See and hear all you can without arousing suspicion."

They dodged her up one street and down another until they finally arrived at the depot, where she was joined by a man who drew her into the shadow, then left her while he went inside to buy a ticket. Dyson motioned George to follow him.

In a moment the man returned and slipped a ticket into her hand.

"Nine-thirty," he said.

Dyson caught the words distinctly.

Then they separated, and the woman, after a few turns, went inside to wait for the train.

George stepped beside his friend.

"He bought a ticket for New York City—nine-thirty."

"Remain here, while I phone. You can watch her through the window. Do not allow her to slip from you."

He returned in a short time and said: "Go home, George, and be dumb. It is very important. I phoned to Bartin. Keep ready for a phone call; but answer no questions concerning this incident. If I need you the password is 'Diamonds.' "

"You do not mean——"

"I'll explain later."

They separated. Dyson shadowed the woman—followed her into the nine-thirty train—but lost her just as they pulled out. He was baffled and furious. He went to the conductor and explained matters, however, and the train was flagged at the first station. He then hired an automobile and returned to the depot he had just left. There he learned that an express for upstate had just left, and that the man who had purchased a ticket for the nine-thirty half an hour earlier had bought one for a little way-station in the mountains.

Dyson jumped into his car and put on all speed possible, arriving at the little wayside depot to find that the train had been flagged a short time before he reached it.

With the aid of an electric torch, he made his way up the rough, winding path of the hills. After a weary climb he came to an opening and saw a little bungalow clinging to the side of the mountain. He went slowly, cautiously now in the darkness. A light shone through the window, and he saw a woman take a small hatchet from a wood box, then open the door, shading her eyes with her hand as she peered into the darkness, straining her ears to catch the slightest sound. Having satisfied herself that she was alone, she did not enter but closed the door and passed around the corner of the bungalow.

Dyson crept around the opposite corner and concealed himself among the low-growing firs. He saw her stoop, and heard a sound like that of boards being torn loose; then a flash of many diamonds strung together. Holding an electric torch close against a board, she nailed it in place; she then examined her work, and being satisfied with the job, dropped the torch into her coat pocket and went inside the bungalow.

He again returned to the window and saw a magnificent diamond necklace, in two sections, in her hands. She dropped it quickly into a common brown-paper bag; then taking a bag of cakes from her coat pocket, she dumped them upon the necklace, and, twisting the ends carefully together, slipped it into her pocket, blew out the light, and went forth into the night.

Dyson waited until she had got some distance away before he investigated. He pried off the board she had so carefully nailed on, and found a space within. Moving his fingers skillfully, he found that the top opened, disclosing a small boxlike compartment. He then went inside the bungalow, moved the largest platter which stood against the wall of the closet, and found that it opened into it.

Satisfied, he followed the woman down the steep path. Like a winged thing she flew on before him. He could locate her by means of the torch which she was using. He saw the flash light of the down train, which pulled out before he could descend.

As he was about to enter his car, a hand was laid upon his shoulder, and Hough, chief of the detective force, stood there smiling.

"It's all right, Dyson. I arrested the man just after he left the depot, and knowing you were on the down train, I boarded the up train so as not to miss the woman either way. Bartin is on the train, and another of the force is waiting at the depot. I will return with you, and you can explain all to me. I have shadowed the couple for a long time, but have never been able to find the goods. When Mrs. Temple lost her diamond necklace I put up a new game, and you have worked it out fine. Now let's rush."

When the train pulled in, the suspected woman stepped from it, and withdrew into the shadow. As she did so, Hough brushed against her and secured the paper bag in her coat pocket.

"I have the bag with the diamonds," he informed Dyson, as he joined him. "Now we will ride to Mrs. Temple's and meet the others."

The suspected woman glided through the darkness until she came to the little gate in the wall of Mrs. Temple's garden. As she slipped the key into the lock, Bartin laid his hand heavily upon her shoulder.

"What are you doing?" he asked.

"I am about to enter a little private gate of which I have the key."

"I arrest you on a serious charge," he said, slipping the handcuffs on her wrists as he spoke.

"You are making a serious mistake. I am Mrs. Field, Mrs. Temple's sister-in-law."

"We will enter by the front way," Bartin said. "Will you lend me a hand?" he called to an assistant. "Mrs. Field refuses to go in by the front door."

Seeing the uselessness of resisting, she went quietly.

They rang the bell and asked for Mrs. Temple, who came down a little disturbed at being called from her bed in the small hours of the morning.

"What is the meaning of this unusual visit?" she asked, on seeing the three detectives, Mr. Dyson, and her nephew.

"Sorry to disturb you, Mrs. Temple, but I think we have at last found a clew to your diamond necklace which disappeared so mysteriously."

Then Mrs. Temple's eyes fell upon her sister-in-law's wrists.

"Crete!" she gasped. "Surely you are not suspected!"

"The phone rang after I had gone to my room, and I was called up to visit a dying friend up the State. I used the key to the little private gate in the wall so as not to disturb you. These gentlemen found me returning and mistook me for a thief."

"I have some convincing evidence," Hough replied, drawing out a paper bag, which he emptied on the table.

It was his turn to be surprised. It contained only a few broken cakes.

"Dyson, you saw her put the jewels in this bag?"

"I am not ready to accept your evidence, gentlemen," Mrs. Temple said coldly. "You seem to have made a serious blunder."

Dyson, with his eyes on the suspected woman, was thinking rapidly. Suddenly he looked down at her shoes, to which the mud still clung. They were fine, up-to-date walking shoes, but the heels were unusual—not in keeping with the general style.

"Bartin, I should like to examine Mrs. Field's shoes. The heels impress me as being unusual."

Bartin raised her foot, and Dyson tapped it with a small instrument.

"As I thought, it is hollow,"

He inserted a knife, pried a spring, and half of Mrs. Temple's necklace dropped to the floor. The other heel was opened and found to contain the other half.

"Crete!" her sister-in-law gasped.

"It means that Mrs. Field is one of the keenest professional thieves in this country—she and a man whom we arrested last night."

For the first time the trapped woman's eyes met those of Mr. Dyson. They were like a dagger, and ready to kill him in their intense hatred.

"I suspected you that night you sought shelter in the little bungalow. I was not fool enough to mistake you for a tramp. When I left the room the first time I warned my brother. The second time I removed the diamonds to a more secure place. When you came here with George I recognized you at once, knowing that you would finally track me down. Do you remember that I told you on that wild night, when you asked me if I was afraid, that I was prepared?"

With a swift movement of the hand they had released, she drew out a little silver flask and held it against her tongue; then it fell the length of its silver chain and dangled against her dress.

"Your prey has escaped you, Mr. Dyson; but you won the game. I bid you all good night."

Her head dropped against the chair; the powerful poison had done its work.

Mortier's Duel

by Jean Joseph-Renaud

The author, Monsieur J. Joseph-Renaud, who tells us this story of a mysterious duel, happens to be the champion fencer of France and of the world—amateurs and professionals included.

I AM going to tell you of an adventure which happened to me and which always makes me feel creepy as soon as I think of it.

My parry and thrust after a parry of *quarte*, with which, in a duel, I wounded the Italian fencing master, Carlotti, you remember? Ah, how the crowd talked of my calmness, the science I showed, my rapidity of action, the accuracy of my thrust, the way in which I seized my opportunity, and so on. I let them talk, for no one would have believed me had I told them that in reality my merit was very slight.

Well, the day before this duel—a most serious one—my own old fencing master, Lamotte, had been very ill for several months past. What was the matter? No one knew exactly, but he had never properly recovered from an attack of inflammation of the lungs, which affected his heart, and then he had diabetes on top of it all.

This was my seventeenth duel, and the poor man had not missed one of the preceding sixteen; his enforced ab-

sence this time must have been a grief to him, for he was very fond of me. It was he who gave me my first fencing lessons at school; it is to him that I owe my rapid parry and thrust. I had never joined any fencing school but his. Ah, he was not the white-livered, peace-loving sort of fencing master of to-day, who is terrified at the mention of a duel! His favorite pupils were the quarrelsome, bad-tempered ones.

I went to see him in his little house at Bois-Colombes. I had not seen him for some weeks, and I found him terribly changed, grown thinner than ever, with haggard eyes in a yellow face, and a hollow voice.

Evidently it was only a question of days with him now, poor fellow; yet he still got up and went for little walks in his garden. He had read the announcement of the duel in the papers, the duel I, Mortiere, was to fight with Carlotti, and he was deeply distressed to think that he could not witness it.

"I know, my boy, that you are not a bad fencer, and you are very quick to parry and thrust, but it always seemed to me as though I brought you good luck; no matter if I did not come near you, if I only looked on from a distance, I felt that my very presence brought you success.

"How are you going to manage to-morrow against the Italian? They say that the wretch is a first-rate swords-man. Ah, I shall eat my heart out! If to-morrow, by any lucky chance, I happened to be a little stronger, how glad I should be to come and see you fight once more!

"When I am dead you will have to get on without me, but it vexes me that, while I am still alive, you should stand up without my being there."

I assured the good old man that, thanks to his excellent lessons, I felt certain of wounding Carlotti, and I forbade him to make the smallest effort to come and see the duel, though I knew all the time that he was much too ill to do so.

Well, the next day, a little before noon—noon is always my hour—I arrived quite calmly at the "Parc des Princes" with my witnesses and a doctor.

It was ideal weather for a duel, warm, fine, and springlike, with a few fleecy clouds passing over the sun. The trees were covered with new little shoots, daisies whitened the grass around the bicycle track, and crowds of sparrows, rising from every bush, flew in the air like black specks against the light.

About forty French and Italian fencers were present. I undressed in the dressing room used by the cyclists riding in the races. I was smoking a delicious cigarette, and when you find a cigarette good just before a duel you are certain to wound your adversary. My witnesses won the toss, so all was going in my favor.

Carlotti is a shriveled-up little man of an olive complexion. He was per-fectly calm, and this made some impression on me. With his sword bound to his wrist with a strap, like all Italian fencers, he fell into a horizontal guard, and at the word "Go!" he immediately began to attack.

His blade was always faultlessly in line, and he made quick and persistent attacks till I felt as I did at my first lessons when I could not find a spot to get in a thrust. I parried well, but my thrusts never reached their mark, and he immediately gave a counter parry and thrust, at the same time pressing me back.

I was forced to fall back farther and farther, till, at the end of the bout, I was only six feet from my boundary line.

My witnesses did not think it a joke, I assure you. During our short rest I tried to think out a plan of attack, but my ideas were all mixed.

We were told to fall into guard again. I immediately attacked, hoping to press Carlotti back and thus regain some of my lost ground; but not only did he parry, but each time I nearly received his thrust. As for trying to rid myself of him by wounding him at the hand or the arm, that was impossible; his hand and arm were faultlessly covered by the "bell" of his sword.

He returned to his terrible attacks; I parried better than during the first bout, but I still found it impossible to get in a thrust. I knew there was something I ought to do, but what was it? I wanted to pull myself together and calculate, but my adversary gave me not a moment's respite. By the time the second bout ended I was almost done.

I could see by the faces of the spectators that they thought it was all up with me. My friends were grave. The Italians were exultant.

And what could I do? I had entirely lost my composure; I did not even try to calculate.

The duel began again. There was now not the eighth of an inch for me to fall back in. I should have to parry every attack without stirring. I withstood the first few, but my thrusts remained without effect, and the counter-thrusts of Carlotti came thick and fast.

I was gasping; my sword was a dead weight at the end of my worn-out arm; my left hand was hanging limp beside me; stars began to dance before my eyes.

By his repeated feints, by the way in which he seemed to be gathering up his strength, by a peculiar expression of his mouth, by the catlike stillness of his blade, which seemed to be slowly but surely driving home, I saw that Carlotti was going to attack and that he meant to finish me. I felt that all was over.

Just at that moment a neighboring clock struck twelve with dramatic effect—the hour of my death!

Pictures of my childhood began to rise before me—the house where I was born; the old market town, with its gables and posterns, built high above the violet-hued valley; the wrinkled faces of my parents bending over me when I was ill.

Yet I made a supreme effort, and tried to get round Carlotti. But in vain, for he barred the way, both to the right and the left. My attempt, however, prevented him from attacking.

At that moment, far away behind my adversary, I saw old Father Lamotte!

I only caught sight of him for a moment, of course, for I was kept busy defending myself, but I saw him quite distinctly; his face was frightfully pale, and he was leaning heavily on his stick. With his right hand he hastily imitated a *quarte parry,* followed by a *disengaging thrust.*

It was a revelation to me. To be sure, if my thrusts had been without effect, it was because, as soon as I had

parried, Carlotti followed automatically along the same line, and, as I gave a straight thrust, all my rapidity was useless, and not only did I not hit my adversary, but I exposed myself to the counter-thrust. At last I understood.

To a very evident feint of my adversary I replied by a *quarte parry* and then thrust home in *disengaging.*

"Halt!"

On the Italian's shirt, in the middle of his chest, a red spot appeared.

Perhaps this advice, given by pantomime, was not strictly according to rule, but Carlotti's seconds were two fencing masters, who gave him useful advice between the bouts. It was tit for tat.

While I was dressing I asked a friend to go and fetch Lamotte. But he was nowhere to be found.

As you may imagine, I told my coachman to drive round by Bois-Colombes, for I was anxious to thank my good friend at once.

But the appearance of the little house, as soon as I caught sight of it through the trees, filled me with surprise and a terrible presentiment.

Why were the shutters closed?

I hurried up the path; Lamotte's old servant, her eyes red with weeping, opened the door, and began sobbing as soon as she saw me.

To cut my story short, *he had not left the house!*

On the stroke of twelve a fatal syncope, caused by embolism, carried him off as he was taking a little walk in his garden and speaking of my duel.

Well, whom do you suppose I saw?

Who was it who gave me the advice which saved me, when I was already done for, defending myself blindly? A being of my imagination? I am very healthy-minded, and, besides, a being whom I had invented would not have been cleverer or cooler-headed than I. And I have never been subject to hallucinations. Then who was it?

Green Eye

By Augustin Lardy

SHE has always controlled me. Even when I was so young that I wore my hair upon my shoulders in long, golden curls—even then was I under her influence. There are some people I take an instant dislike to, and she was one of these, for there was certainly no other real reason for my detestation in the beginning.

No other person in Paris did I so dread, and to-day there is no person or thing in the whole world of which I am so afraid. She has but to express a wish and I hasten to gratify it. Should I hesitatingly suggest a course of action and should she disapprove, I instantly obey her whim. Her will is mine.

She is ugly as the Bastile and always has been so, I think. Hers is an ugliness so grotesque that it fascinates me, like the head of a gargoyle on the towers of Notre Dame. But it was not her ugliness that terrified and repulsed me at first. It was her right eye —an oblong, green organ in which the pupil is vertical like a snake's.

I say her right eye because she invariably wears a black patch where the other should be. Later, I came to dream about that other eye—weird dreams of an eyeless socket, black as the pit, from which a flame tongue, forked like a viper's, has darted out at me like a flash of evil. She needs but one eye, for the passion in that green orb leaps out upon one like lightning from a black sky. I have known her to fix my father—a man of daring and resolute character—with that eye of hers and make his will a flexible thing under her influence.

I really believe the old woman loves me passionately, and has never done anything deliberately to injure me. Indeed, everyone who knows us deems me insufficiently grateful for her guardianship. But I digress; to my story:

The first time I saw Madame la Gourmande I was about five years old. Until then my life had been the dream of a happy child. I lived with my parents in a private house set back a little from the Rue de Roche, and not far from La College Chaptal where I attended the lower school for the little ones. I remember it all as if it happened twenty hours instead of more than twenty years ago.

There I was then, as bright a youngster as any in Paris, and it is easy to imagine me with my slate, pencil box and a child's book or two strapped to my shoulders as a soldier carries his knapsack; a little red soldier cap cocked jauntily upon my curly pate; my hands in the pockets of the black apron all we schoolboys wore, and my red lips pursed in a merry whistle as I tripped down the avenue, one sunshiny morning, on my way to school. *Ma bonne* —my nurse, that is—did not accompany me because the school was so near.

Madame la Gourmande came grunting around the corner with all the grace of an elderly hippopotamus. We collided and I rolled in the gutter.

"Oh, le pauvre petit!"

She said it in a bass voice as she came lumbering toward me, her huge arms outstretched and her one eye with its serpent's pupil glittering greenly.

"Oh, le pauvre petit!" and she had picked me up and crushed me in to her saggy bosom which smelled of musk and mildew. She kissed me and her kiss tasted of onions and *eau de vie*, and her rough beard scraped my tender face. I struggled violently in the suffocating softness of her arms and breast. I kicked. I screamed. Finally she put me down and I danced away from her, furious.

"You—you—you!" I cried, unable to word my rage. My bare knees had been bruised by my fall, and as I rubbed them I grimaced at her. I was not more than five or six years old, you see, and as I was the only child I had been spoiled.

"My poor little one!" she said in that grating voice of hers. "My poor child! I am so sad you have scratched your pretty pink knees. Come hither and I shall give you bonbons. See!"

She advanced, fumbling in the capacious pockets of her black silk gown. She was a huge creature, broad as she was tall, this female Cyclops, and how old it cannot be said. She seemed to have no particular shape, for she bulged here and she bulged there and in the most unexpected places, too. Her feet were surprisingly small and even daintily shod, but her hands could have throttled a horse.

And her face—it was a nightmare of the damned. All I can do is strive to give a vague impression of her countenance. Her one glittering eye, and the patch of black over the other, would have made her hideous in any case, and in addition, she had a pair of mustachios which, if she had let them sprout, would have made the fiercest-looking gendarme in Paris thrill with envy.

Her mouth was a weird thing of tremendous elastic possibilities, and she was as snaggle-toothed as a witch and bearded like a pard. Perched on her head was an absolutely ridiculous little black bonnet tied with black ribbons under a chin as grim as the prow of a battleship.

"See!" she coaxed and held out a double handful of candies. I eyed them greedily, for mine was an unusually sweet tooth, but such was my revulsion to the old woman that I shrank instead of approaching.

"Naughty child!" she rumbled.

I stuck out my tongue at her and was horrified, petrified at what happened.

Out ran her own tongue and it wagged itself at me, its tip fully six inches from her mouth! Her one remarkably expressive eye gleamed with a green and venomous sense of humor, and I stared and stared as I saw the corners of her mouth slowly stretch until her face looked as if some one had severed the lower part of her countenance.

With a shriek of terror mingled with hysterical merriment, I fled. I did no work in school that day. I drew pictures on my slate of an indescribable face, split by a terrible grin, out of which rolled a Gargantuan tongue that wagged and quivered with astonishment at its own size.

And so ended my first meeting with Madame la Gourmande, the old woman destined to twist my life all awry.

The next day was Thursday, a day hailed by all French schoolboys with delight, for school does not keep that day. The Americans and the English give a whole or a half holiday on Saturday, and thus their little ones rest and play Saturday and Sunday together. But we French liberate our children from the prison of the schoolroom on Thursday instead of Saturday, for we believe it breaks the monotony of the week. Anything to escape monotony, we say.

Thus it was I sat that bright spring morning in the little garden in front of my home, wishing that I had some other little boy or girl to play with. A messenger lad whose uniform and cap with the gilt lettering, Bon Marché, declared he came from one of the largest department stores in Paris, appeared at the garden gate.

He carried a huge, thin cardboard box. My curosity was piqued, for I knew from the shape of the box it could not be another hat or a dress for my mother. And he was such a merry messenger boy! He winked at me as he asked if Monsieur Jacques Renan lived here. Jacques Renan! That was my own name. My father was Monsieur Charles Renan.

"*Mais, c'est moi!*" I cried, running to open the gate for him. But he would not give me the mysterious package. He wanted some older member of the household to sign for it, and so I took his hand, and, skipping in my eagerness, pulled him to the house.

One of the domestics signed his book, and not until then did I get my package. Father and mother were out, and so I shared the joy of opening the strange box with the servants. It contained a fine big hoop and a beautiful stick with which to roll it. It was just what I had longed for. Not until I grasped the stick did I notice a little piece of paper wound tightly about the handle. I slipped it off and found it a note, but as I could barely read at that age, one of the servants told me what it said:

"For Jacques from his fairy godmother."

The whole affair was assuredly most exciting, but I did not remain long wondering who was my fairy godmother. It was enough that I had a hoop and stick and that the day was beautiful. I paid not the slightest attention to the domestics' advice to stay in the garden—I have already said I was a spoiled child. In two minutes I had slipped the catch of the garden gate and was out in the street.

How wonderfully that hoop bounded and rolled! I guided it as if the stick I held were a magic wand. On and on I rolled the hoop, down one street and up another, farther and farther from home. Of a sudden the hoop, rolling a few feet in advance of me, wobbled and fell on the sidewalk in front of a squat, dingy house, oddly out of place in that splendid residential section.

A chill of fear shook me as I halted abruptly. As if compelled by some necromancer's power, my head slowly turned to the residence, and I found myself looking up at the old woman who was leaning from a window on the second story of her dwelling. She was smiling at me, and I thought her smile the hungry leer of some ogress.

"Ah, little Jacques," she rumbled, "I see that my hoop and stick have brought you to your fairy godmother, eh?"

So, it was she who had given me the toy. I might have known it!

"It is not polite, Jacques, to stand there silently like some mannerless peasant lad. You might say, 'Bon jour, Madame la Gourmande. I thank you very much for your nice present.' All well-born little French boys are polite, my little Jacques. I see that I shall have to take you in hand and teach you to be gracious."

Anger drove fear and wonder out of me. I hated this old woman with a hate certainly not born of reason. It was a thing purely of instinct.

"You do not answer, my little Jacques. How do you think I knew your name and where you lived, *hein?*"

In silence I stared at her.

"Ah!" She said it in the most knowing manner in the world, and she laid one tremendous forefinger alongside her shapeless nose. "Ah!" and her mouth began to stretch.

I did not wait to see it distend. I was too afraid that horrifying tongue would pop out and wag itself at me, and besides, her one green eye, cleft with a streak of vertical light, made me tremble.

Again I fled. Straight across the street I ran wildly, not seeing the taxi-cab spinning around the corner on two wheels and pure luck, driven recklessly as all cabs are driven in Paris, especially in those days when taxis were comparatively novel vehicles.

There was a bellow from the old woman in the window, an oath from the driver of the cab, a scream from some passer-by, and down I went under the wheels of the machine.

I regained consciousness in a hospital. My legs were broken and both collar bones smashed, and it would be a long time before I could move, I was told. I have walked with a limp ever since that day, for when my limbs mended, one leg was shorter than the other.

Father and mother were at my bedside when I came to my senses. It seems Madame la Gourmande had taken charge of me the moment the taxi struck me down. She had picked me up for the second time in my life and had commandeered the cab, driving like fury to the hospital where she had engaged a private room, a nurse, and had done everything to make me comfortable.

She insisted on paying all the bills, too, and browbeat my father in the matter, for he objected strongly to a stranger making any outlay for one of his family. The moment that she had placed me in the hospital Madame la Gourmande went to my home and notified my parents. From that moment commenced her influence with my people, which was surprising, for my father had been a military man, and his sweeping whiskers, ramrod bearing, officer's frown and commanding mannerisms imposed on most people.

My parents always respected Madame la Gourmande, and although they grew to like her as a sincere friend of the family, they were always a little in awe of her. It was her hypnotic eye, I suppose.

All my whisperings to my mother had no effect.

"Hush, Jacques," she would say. "It is wrong to dislike and distrust people because they are not beautiful. Madame la Gourmande loves you like a son, almost. At times I, your mother, am a little jealous of her love. She is very rich and can give you wonderful toys, and she has no relatives. Who knows, Jacques—your father cannot leave you wealthy as he would wish and Madame la Gourmande—— Try to love her a little, *mon enfant.*"

Gradually, in addition to my fear and hatred of this old woman, there grew up in me a violent superstition that every action of hers touching my life in the least was bound to result in harm for me. No matter how kindly her intention, the result was sure to be the same. Indeed, every thing that Madame la Gourmande did for me bore out that superstition, and the episode of the hoop, the taxicab and the hospital is but one illustration.

I remember cutting my left hand badly while playing in the garden of our home. I ran inside, frightened at the blood and crying with the pain.

Madame la Gourmande was in the room with my mother, and instantly both women were sympathy at once. But my child's mind blamed the family friend for the accident. I felt sure that if she had not been visiting us I would never have wounded myself.

Out of her huge pockets that seemed to contain everything one needed, Madame la Gourmande drew a phial containing some colored liquid. It was good for cuts and bruises, she said, and despite my loud objections, my mother made me hold out my hand while the old woman poured a few drops of the fluid on the hurt.

Immediately the pain stopped. I stared at her with round, frightened eyes while the tears dried on my face. That to me was but another proof of her witchcraft or her dealings with the devil.

That night my injury began hurting more than ever. It throbbed like a wounded bird one holds in the hands. The pain of it kept me from sleeping. I got out of bed, and, pushing open the long glass windows that led to a little balcony, stepped outside.

Moonlight bathed everything in a cool, white mystery. I looked up at the moon, which looked like the head of a huge silver nail driven up through the flooring of heaven. Her light broke softly upon my face, some of it falling upon my hand, seeming to do it good.

I unwound the bandage and held up the swollen member to the moon, waving it slowly, as if to wash it in her light. The pain abated. I walked to the end of the little balcony where I might watch the moon without craning my neck uncomfortably.

I shuddered as I thought Madame la Gourmande might be watching the moon at that very moment, and even as I thought, the balcony gave way beneath me and I fell headlong to the pebbled garden walk, many feet below.

This time I broke but one leg and did not pass into unconsciousness. My cries soon brought help, and in a few minutes I was back in my little bed, the center of an anxious group. Yes, Madame la Gourmande was there. My mother telephoned her and she had come instantly, late as it was.

She said she had been sitting up watching the moon!

There and then I resolved to be as polite to her as I knew how. It was fear—icy fear—you see, for I childishly believed her to be a sorceress of some sort. No one knew how old she was, and to-day she looks just as she did that fateful morning I bumped into her on my way to school.

The servants all feared and obeyed her, for with that all-seeing eye upon them there was little deceit and no petty thievery about the home over which she wielded an extraordinary power. I have heard the domestics whispering that Madame la Gourmande was widowed during the Franco-Prussian war, and so it is really frightening if one stops to consider her age.

Like the night, she never changes. Always is she gowned in her antique black silk. Always is that ridiculous little bonnet tied upon her head. Always does she smell of musk and mildew, and always does her eye glitter like a live green thing, while eternally does she wear that sinister black patch concealing a sightless socket.

And so, as I grew up with the dread of this old woman hovering like an evil dream over my life, the time came for me to decide upon the profession I would follow. My lame leg exempted me from military service and I had not the slightest inclination for business.

I wanted to be an artist, and as my incessant drawing had demonstrated my bent, and as my parents were quite well-to-do, they were willing that I should follow my inclination. But Madame la Gourmande said that artists led "disreputable" lives and that they seldom became "substantial" citizens. She decided the matter:

"I want the boy to be a doctor," she said.

But once again after that did I try to stem her will.

"I will not be a doctor!" I cried. "I am going to be an artist."

There was a scene. My mother left the room weeping. I stormed with a rage that surprised myself, and my father walked the floor tugging nervously at his waxed, military mustache.

"Very well," finally said Madame la Gourmande. "Let us give this colt his head. Let him try to win a scholarship at *L'Académie des Artistes,* and if he fails at the end of the year, he shall study medicine."

"Agreed!" I shouted. "I shall win!"

She held me with her eye.

"You will not succeed!" said she. "I will it that you become a physician. But you shall have your chance for the scholarship."

She kept her word, Madame la Gourmande. She arranged everything, and in a few weeks I was happy with charcoal and pencil at the art school. My work was sufficiently advanced to admit me to the life class, and there I seemed to make rapid progress.

Some whimsical old patron of the arts had endowed the school, making the odd provision that the examinations for the scholarships should consist of a few hours' work in class at the end of the year. The students were to sketch from a life grouping.

The day for the examination came. I had made fast progress in my work, and the household was excited regarding the possibility of my receiving the palm. Mine was a typical Parisian family—father, mother, child and one or two close family friends. The interests of the circle were turned in upon itself. It knew little other life. There is something intensely provincial and narrow in the life of such French families, even in Paris, the liveliest metropolis in the world.

I set out that morning, my face bright with hope. At the gate of our home I met Madame la Gourmande.

"Ah, little Jacques, you think you will win?"

"I am sure of it, *ma tante.*"

"You forget I have willed that you become a doctor. It is for your own good, Jacques."

I replaced my cap which I had doffed and fidgeted in my eagerness to be off.

Suddenly her one eye flashed its power into me.

"You will become a doctor, Jacques," she said quietly. Her glance still froze me some seconds after she had waddled into my home.

A feeling of the futility of everything settled like a fog upon my soul. I dragged myself to the classroom and hardly looked at the models. I knew it was useless to try and draw them. Of its own accord, it seemed, my hand began outlining a lumpy face with a startlingly powerful jaw. My pencil filled in a loose, shapeless mouth—the coarse lips rolled back in a grimace that disclosed stumpy, discolored teeth like snags in some foul, crooked stream. The nose was a bulbous thing that spread itself indescribably, and the eyebrows were shaggy and black, running obliquely across a streak of a forehead until they met over the bridge of the nose. The right eye glared like a cat's in the dark; there was a black patch over the other. A well-defined mustache crouched upon her upper lip, and upon her chin there were clumps of coarse whisker. A few gray hairs straggled about her head, on which perched a ridiculous little black bonnet.

I drew another picture. I sketched a bulging, massive figure with small, almost dainty, feet, riding furiously on a broomstick above the rooftops of Paris. She wore a tall, conical hat, and her face was an evil profile, black against a sickly bright moon.

The bell rang. The examination was over. I signed my name boldly to my drawings and left the room.

I had determined to run away.

Without returning home I set out. It was my intention to reach Marseilles and then smuggle myself aboard some ship for America. There were a few francs in my pocket, and I was not afraid, although but a schoolboy hardly well into his teens.

That night, with the roar of Paris miles and miles behind me, it seemed, I slept by the side of a broad highway which a peasant had told me was the road to Marseilles. It was nearly summer and the night was delicious.

The sky made a beautiful velvet counterpane, and my couch of mother earth seemed gentle and kind to my tired young limbs. The cool, soft kiss of the night wind closed my eyelids. I regretted neither my parents nor my home, and I fell asleep smiling up at the golden fleurs de lis of my coverlet.

The sun had been up hours before I awoke, stiff and sore from my night in the open. I was strangely dizzy, too, but there was a buoyancy in my bosom that was unwonted, and I had not walked far before I was singing a popular chanson of Paris:

"Il n'a jamais besoin d'un parapluie,
Quand le temps il fait beau.
Mais, quand il tombe de la pluie,
Il est trompé avec de l'eau!"

As the sun climbed, its rays grew fiercer and my head began to ache. The dizziness increased. I left the road to wander in a meadow fair with flowers, and there I met a farm girl with a huge yolk across her shoulders, sustaining two frothy pails of milk, for it was still early morning.

Of her own accord she gave me to drink, and drink I did, long and deeply. I left her staring at me as I again took the road. An old peasant, twisted and warped with the years like an ancient tree, passed me with his team of oxen dragging a creaking wagon filled with garden truck. I was interested in his withered, bearded old face, his blue smock and coarse, baggy trousers and huge sabots, filled with straw, and I would have liked to have handled the long, iron-tipped goad with which he prodded on his oxen. I walked by his side until he turned down a side path, and I watched him until a bend in the road hid him.

As I walked on an impulse for greater flight came upon me, and I quickened my pace, continually turning my head to survey the highway I had traversed. I lengthened my stride. Then I began to run, and I ran and ran, spurred on by nameless fright, until I fell senseless by the roadside.

"There he is, the poor, dear child!"

How that hoarse, rumbling voice penetrated my unconsciousness! Some one forced something hard between my lips, and a fiery liquid scorched my throat. I opened my eyes and found myself staring into the face of Madame la Gourmande.

It seems that when I failed to return from school, my people notified the police and devoted themselves to searching all Paris for me. Madame La Gourmande with her uncanny divination, took the road to Marseilles and had overtaken me in an automobile she had hired. It was inevitable.

The doctors later said I was suffering from brain fever brought on by overwork and excessive nervousness, but I, slowly regaining health in my little white cot in the Rue de Roche, knew far better.

The years went by swiftly enough. I gave up my dream of becoming an artist, and gradually came to take a careless sort of interest in my medical studies, eventually graduating comfortably at the bottom of my class. Before I was twenty-six I had become an interne at the Paris Hospital.

There I met Clemence Brecourt, a nurse. She was a quiet girl, with a calm, strong face and clear, fearless blue eyes. In her, for the first time, I found a human being with the sympathy necessary for me to bare my heart. Never did she laugh at my terror of Madame la Gourmande. She listened very seriously, when I told her my tale, one delicate hand frankly seeking my own.

We grew to love each other very tenderly indeed, and I, frail, limping, willess, came more and more to lean upon her and wonder at her quiet strength of character. She regarded my fear of the old woman in the light of an obsession, and encouraged me to plan some bold undertaking which would rid me forever of the old crone.

Alas, poor Clemence!

When my mother informed me that Madame la Gourmande had fallen ill and insisted on being taken to the Paris hospital where she could be attended by myself, it was as if a chill hand had closed about my heart. Then the next instant my bosom thrilled with a new and terrible thought.

"Courage, Jacques," I told myself. "One bold stroke and you will be a free man!"

Never before had I been so attentive to Madame la Gourmande. I showered the old lady with little kindnesses, and she was so elated with joy that I feared she would get well. It was I who arranged her transportation, and it was I who selected her private room. I made one mistake. Clemence requested permission to nurse the old woman, and I consented, stupidly enough.

Madame la Gourmande was in bed, looking up at me from under her shaggy brows when for the first time she saw Clemence and myself together. One swift glance from her one green eye and she had read our secret. She called me to her bedside as my sweetheart left the room.

"Jacques," quoth the old beldame, "Jacques, *mon enfant*, all thy life I have been good to thee. Now I am old, very old. I ask of thee my first favor, Jacques. Forget this pale-faced nurse of thine. She has neither birth nor social position. Assuredly, she can bring thee no dot.

"Now, for some time I have had my eye on the girl who will make thee a proper wife, *mon fils*. I know thy papa and mama will approve my choice, and I feel certain that thou, Jacques, will obey the wish of thy old godmother. I shall say no more for the present."

I did not answer. I stood smiling down upon her, but there was no smile in my heart.

Two days did Madame la Gourmande toss in illness. Two days and nights did she torture Clemence, for even in sickness the old woman's mind was cold and keen as ever. She insisted on the girl waiting upon her in the most menial capacities. Never did she lose an opportunity for an insult; always did she insist on the closest attendance.

The poor dear girl fell under the spell of the sick woman just as my father had done—Clemence who was so strong and self-reliant! Under the wicked eye of the older woman she became like some frightened little bird, hypnotized by a lazy old snake who held her paralyzed a while before the swift death blow.

On the third night I asserted myself for once and demanded that Madame la Gourmande release Clemence for rest. To my surprise the old woman gave way to my will and watched me with a cryptic smile as I placed two powders on the table by her bed.

One powder contained fifteen grains of strychnine; the other fifteen grains of aspirin.

"Your headache will return to-night undoubtedly, *ma tante*," said I, smiling like a guileless boy. "Take one of these powders. I hope you will not need two."

Why I left two powders, one deadly, the other harmless, I cannot say, unless it was from some desire to let the old woman's own hand unconsciously dice with life against death.

Did I feel any remorse as I sought my home that night? My breast sang like a robin hopping on the grass of the Champs Elysée.

Clemence, who was supposed to rest, that night, obeyed some impulse she could not define, and returned to the hospital, taking up her duties at Madame la Gourmande's bedside. Some power, stronger than her own will, drew her to her work, she told a sister nurse.

With her own fair hand she gave Madame la Gourmande one of the powders, and watched the old woman fall quietly asleep.

Worn by her vigil, my beloved's own head ached. She took the second powder.

She was found dead on the floor, while Madame la Gourmande slept the quiet sleep of one whose illness is broken.

And I? I care not whether I live or die. My always feeble will is hopelessly shattered. I have given up my practice of medicine. All my days I spend listlessly at home. I understand that Madame la Gourmande is arranging to present me to my fiancée she has chosen. No doubt I shall marry her.

OUT OF THE NIGHT

By Philip Kennedy

YOUR voice was like the echo of a song
    That floated to me from that wondrous hour,
Out from the night from love's far lonely tower
Beyond the pulse and beat of all the throng.
Such dreams as these make singing spirits strong.
    And mighty gods grow conscious of their power,
    Or touch with glory some dejected flower
Beneath the blind steps of a sightless wrong.

Love comes in calico or satin gown
    Out of the night with dainty tripping feet
And meets one in the shadows of the town
    Amid the tinsel music of the street.
I only know I dared not trample down
    A dream that was at once so strange and sweet.

The Fear

By Carleton W. Kendall

NEHEMIAH MORGAN, until some five months before his death, was my closest friend. He was a man of rare genius. His books, as all know who have read them, dealt with subjects far too abstract and deep for the lay mind to comprehend. He was a great thinker. His brain had that faculty for plowing into the depths of philosophy and of life; and from the nature of the malady it is only logical that it should have chosen him as its first subject.

About five months before his death, we happened to attend together a demonstration given by a certain Newi Gomiu of India. The evening was full of interest, as the man professed to be an expert in the tricks of the Hindu magicians. Nehemiah Morgan appeared to be in good spirits and studied the man with that impersonal, scholarly gaze of his, which he always assumed at any such affair.

At the conclusion of the performance, we went forward to meet the magician, and Nehemiah Morgan questioned him in regard to his belief in foretelling the future. He offered a demonstration, and my friend submitted. Newi Gomiu seated himself at a table, took a pencil in his hand, went into a trance, and proceeded to write. When he had finished, Nehemiah Morgan picked up the paper, read it, and handed it to me without any comment. It read:

You are afflicted with a terrible disease. It is the first case of its kind on this planet. You will die on January 27th of next year. The cause will be unknown.

Then it trailed off into unintelligible characters.

That was the last time I saw my friend. It chanced the next day I was called out of town to attend to some business in Chicago. Before leaving, I rang him up on the telephone, to say good-by, and after we had exchanged a few commonplace remarks, he complained of hearing a buzzing in his ears. Thinking it due to the telephone, I paid no more attention to it, but when I returned two weeks later and rang up his home, his housekeeper informed me that he was ill and had taken a run up to the Adirondacks for a change.

At that time I did not connect the buzzing in any way with his illness. In fact, the remark had entirely gone from my mind and was completely forgotten until, as I was getting up from breakfast a few days later, the telephone rang and my friend's voice sounded over the wire. He had just returned from the mountains and instead of regaining his health as he had hoped, he complained of nervous indigestion and the ever-increasing buzzing sensation in his ears. We talked for some minutes, and at the end of the conversation he mentioned for the first time the fear. He did not explain what it was, but made me promise I would not attempt to see him, and that I would have all letters and documents he sent me fumigated before I touched them.

That was the last I heard of him. Three days later I passed his brownstone residence on my way home from the office. It had the appearance of being uninhabited. The shades were drawn, and on the porch were a number of sun-browned newspapers. Wondering, I lifted the great brass knocker on the massive door and releasing it, it gave forth a heavy, hollow sound. No one answered, and, after repeating the performance several times without result, I left in dazed bewilderment to return home. After several fruitless attempts to reach him by phone, I came to the conclusion that he had left the city and closed his home indefinitely.

It was just four months and eight days later that I received word of his death on January twenty-seventh, together with the following document explaining the nature of the strange malady and describing the tortures he suffered while afflicted with the fear. The letter bore the postmark of a backwoods town in Maine. Further than that I have been unable to trace it.

In giving this statement, written in his own handwriting, I have had it carefully copied and forwarded to the printers in exactly the form I received it, except that in one or two instances I have condensed long descriptions of the repeated attacks of the fear. However, if there are any medical men who want to go into the case more thoroughly, I will be glad to let them examine the original manuscripts in my office. The document is as follows:

November 24, 1916. My dear friend Norman Humphrys: You perhaps have wondered, are wondering even now, at my leaving town without bidding you good-by, but at the time of my departure I was not myself. In fact, since this strange disease has come upon me, it is only in occasional flashes that my old self returns to its body and I can think of my friends and of my relations to society without being oppressed by that awful foreboding.

To-night I am myself, and while it lasts I am taking advantage of this state to prepare for you this document, telling of the symptoms and effects of this singular malady. The document you will receive after my death, and I direct that you use it in whatever way seems best to help prevent the spread of this unknown disease, which attacks only the best and leaves the ignorant untouched.

You will remember our visiting the demonstration of the Hindu magician, known as Newi Gomiu, on the evening of the twenty-fourth of last August, and you will probably remember his curious forecast of my future.

Up to that time I had felt no symptoms of the strange malady, save an occasional buzzing in my ears which I laid to a slight bilious attack. That night after returning home as I was sitting in my study reading—you know it was always my custom to read for an hour before going to bed—I felt a repetition of the buzzing, coupled with a peculiar nausea. For a moment I seemed to rouse as from a dream and my senses became keenly alert, then it passed and I felt all right again. However, before going to bed I took a dose of podophyllum and a hot bath.

In the morning I felt much better, with only an occasional spell of the buzzing in my ears. Yet when you telephoned just before leaving for Chicago, I was surprised to find that the buzzing sensation almost doubled in intensity when I listened through the receiver. You will remember that I remarked about it at the time. That afternoon I went for a drive along by the river, and in the evening I was able to do some work on my paper on "The Pluralistic Universe."

For the next few days I felt no repetition of the attack, and the affair entirely left my mind. I continued with my work as usual and enjoyed the best of health.

About a week afterward, however, I was afflicted with a terrible nightmare. Visions of horrible forms, and the impression of vainly trying to escape from their vivid clutches, crossing fathomless abysses on slender supports, scaling perpendicular cliffs— only to slip down, down with that sickening, falling sensation—all these I experienced with rapid succession. When I awoke in a state of nervous perspiration, there was a severe pain in the top of my head, and I felt the return of that buzzing sensation in my ears. In the morning the pain had left and was replaced with a nausea, but the buzzing sensation still remained.

Then came the fear.

I had just arisen from the breakfast table and was seated in the library bay-window overlooking the park. On this first attack it came slowly. I felt a certain numbness creep into my limbs, gradually rising from my feet like each succeeding wave of an incoming tide. At first I thought it was the beginning of a malaria chill, but I did not feel that chattering coldness which comes with malaria. Instead, it was more the sensation one experiences when one's foot has gone to sleep. It climbed higher and higher, up to my knees, my waist, and slowly I could feel the numbness creeping into my heart.

Strange to say, I did not ring for a servant, neither did I move nor shift my position in any way. I had perfect use of my limbs, although to move them was a wearisome exertion. The only part of me that seemed paralyzed was my brain. I could think clearly, yet I could not bring myself to act upon the thought. I was almost like a brain without a body. To move my muscles required the most powerful exertion on the part of my intellect.

I was that way for some minutes, then, with a rush, a super-consciousness came over me. My hearing was so acute that the buzzing of a fly on the windowpane roared in my ears like the thundering of an express train and jarred my whole nervous system. I had never realized the amount of noise around me before. The traffic in the street below, the roaring and thundering of the city, the servants moving in the rear of the house, were all magnified a hundred times, until the world seemed to be made up of only a variety of noises. Then the consciousness seized my eyesight. Colors became more evident, until everything I looked at was a riot of intense reds, or greens, or blues. The yellow colors, strangely enough, were of their normal intensity.

I closed my eyes, and as I did so I could distinctly feel the movements of the lids as they descended over my eyeballs. It was uncanny. I opened them again.

As I sat there in the library bay window, under the spell of that strange superconsciousness; feeling, seeing, hearing the new-old familiar universe about me—my sense of taste and smell did not become intensified during this first part of the attack—I felt a certain masterful exultation.

For the moment I was lifted above the life of mortals. But it was only for a moment, and during the subsequent attacks I never felt it again.

Sitting there with my eyes opened, I experienced the sensation of beautiful colors, glittering jewels, soft plays of light and shadow, purples, lavenders, magnificent temples, the hard flash of diamonds, the warm yellow of gold. Now I was in the center of an exquisite garden; then, as by magic, I was transported into the very paths of the sunset. I walked in Rome, in Egypt, in Assyria. I climbed marble stairways up to quaint Japanese temples made out of some effervescent substance. I trod the inlaid floors of great, arched chambers, and then dropped to the bottom of the sea and wandered among delicate marine gardens.

During the time of this hallucination I was keenly aware of everything going on around me. A servant entered and removed some old newspapers littering my study table. I watched the people passing on the street below and the automobiles as they spun along the gravel drive in the park opposite. Yet I could see, somewhere in the back of my consciousness, those beautiful visions. It was a delight, which in my moments of normality I like to reflect upon. By my description you will not feel what they were like. The scenes were too glorious for me to give you any adequate idea of how they impressed me.

My brain was still luxuriating upon the last of these visions—a gorgeous scene of tropical splendor, with snow-capped mountains in the distance and a riot of colored foliage and beautiful birds in the foreground—when, with the swiftness of a descending curtain, the scene was blotted out.

For a moment my senses swirled; then I was plunged into my first experience of the awful fear. The superconsciousness which I had felt before was as a grain of sand to a mountain, in comparison with that which surged upon me in that first moment. My senses which had become so keenly awakened before broke all bounds. My eardrums throbbed and vibrated from the roar around me until I could feel their very tissues tighten under the strain. I was aware of a thousand different noises—shrill, sharp, dull, heavy; the crunching of gravel under the auto wheels; the gurgling, surging intake of my own breath. Each one seemed louder than the other. The vision before me was of outrageous colors: bright, repulsive to the eye, intermingled together in a juxtaposition of blinding, glaring rays of light. As before, the yellow kept its normal intensity, but the reds and blues were so strong that to look at them nauseated me.

Then it was that I became aware of the sense of taste and smell.

I could taste the saliva in my mouth and it sickened me. To my nostrils came a variety of odors and scents which I had never before believed to exist. The smell of the carpet on the floor was distinctly heavy and odious. The painty smell of the furniture, the strong, pungent odor of the leather chair in which I sat, even the smell of hard substances such as iron and glass—all these penetrated to the delicate nerve centers in my brain and set my senses in a whirl of vulgar impressions.

The old world in which I had lived in partial consciousness became a mass of hurtling confusion. Noises, colors, odors, tastes, impressions, whirled together in conglomeration. My brain was overwhelmed. I could feel my own heart beat; could sense the expanding and contracting of my lungs. For a time it fascinated me, and I put my hands over my ears and closed my eyes so as to be better able to experience the sensation. It was like watching the slow, rhythmical motion of a giant bellows amid the roar and din of a huge blacksmith shop. The thump, thump of my heart reminded me of the pound of a pile driver. It was like some uncanny machine.

Then the thought flashed through my mind: What if the machine should stop?

With a new terror I strained my senses to catch the single beats of my heart as it pumped the blood through my veins. A large motor truck went by on the street below and the terrible roar of it completely drowned out the noise of the thump of my heart. Then it was that I felt the fear.

It seemed an hour before the truck passed and I could again catch the rhythmical beats. I knew that if they stopped I would be dead, and at the thought of death, my imagination, which, like the rest of my impressions, was in an abnormal state of acuteness, pictured, before my mind, black, horrible forms which surged about me like an enveloping swarm of gnats. I opened my eyes only to have my senses shattered with the blinding rays of light and the glaring, repulsive colors. The fear of death returned and I closed them again and listened with cold intensity for the rhythmical beats which denoted my existence.

What if they should stop? The idea crept through my brain like a fearful canker. I could feel a cold numbness stealing through my bones and my senses swirled into blackness.

I fainted.

When I came to from my faint, I was in my own room. Jenkins stood by my bed, and Doctor Horace was giving me a hypodermic. My sensations at first were as if a current of warm air had struck my body, striking my head first and gradually enveloping me in its warmness until it reached my feet. Then the buzzing sensation returned to my ears, but in a few moments left and I was myself again—all except for the fear.

From that time on I have never been entirely free from that awful, griping fear which overwhelms me during the attacks of the strange malady. Even as I write this, it takes all the power of my will to force from my brain that terrible consciousness of the action of my lungs and of the beating of my heart. In my normal mind I do not fear death, yet when the strange malady grips me the imminence of death appears to me like a huge dragon and chills me to the very bones. I have found that this fear of death is one of the more acute signs of the disease.

This first attack was on Thursday, and on Saturday night I left for the Adirondacks, taking with me Jenkins and one of the male servants. Doctor Horace had diagnosed my case as nervous indigestion, coupled with a bilious attack and brought on by overwork, and advised the trip up into the mountains for a few days. Poor old doctor; little did he realize the danger of the strange malady.

That trip to the mountains somewhat revived me. The sharp mornings of the oncoming autumn, the stinging, bracing air, the outdoor life, all brought me back to somewhat near my normal physical health. During my stay I suffered only once from a violent attack of the curious disease, and this spell lasted only a few minutes and was mild in comparison with those I experienced later. However, there always remained over me that imminent apprehension of death. Often I would find myself unconsciously drop into a listening attitude, counting the expansions and contractions of my lungs. Sometimes I would awaken in the night with a start, cold perspiration on my forehead, terror in my brain, and put in a half hour battling with my will to drive from my mind the terrible apprehension.

After a week and a half I returned to the city. The only physical symptom of the malady that remained was an occasional buzzing in my ears. True, my digestion was not in the best working order, but I suffered comparatively little from it. When I called you up on the phone I was in fairly good physical health; but always seething in my brain was that terrible fear that I would stop breathing or that the thumping of my heart would cease. It became a mania with me.

I consulted physicians, nerve specialists, metaphysicians, new-thought healers, psychotherapists and biochemists; but none could give me any relief. In fact, I even had an examination by an insanity expert. When he had given me various tests, he shook his head and pronounced me above normal. The thought of the helplessness of the situation appalled me.

The first indication I had of the contagious qualities of the disease was shortly before I returned from the mountains. I received a letter from Doctor Horace. It was written in a despondent mood, and he complained of feeling tired and partially losing his sense of hearing. He also mentioned the buzzing in his ears and the slight nausea. He inquired after my health and prescribed a change in my diet. The next time I heard from him was exactly three hours after I had been talking with you on the phone. He had shot himself in his office, leaving a note stating that he felt his mind gradually slipping away.

The shock of it brought on one of those strange spells. Jenkins told me

afterward that I lay as in a stupor for two days, answered all questions, carried on a conversation, and apparently seemed to retain all my normal faculties of thought. Yet during that time I can remember nothing, save the inky fear and a swirling memory of colors, tastes, odors, sounds, and sensations mixed together in confusion and dominated by a periodic beat—beat—beat. Unseen forces seemed to be struggling against my will to cause the cessation of that beat, and it was only with the most tremendous rallying of my thought powers that I could will my heart to continue. The intervals between my heartbeats were lifetimes in which I experienced all the terror and unnamed horror of a gripping nightmare. No wonder that when I awakened I was in a dazed condition, weak and exhausted.

I determined then and there to leave the city and to go into seclusion. Jenkins volunteered to go with me, and we left the next morning on the Portland Express for the backwoods of Maine. We have a little cabin here on the side of the mountain, and sufficient provisions to last until spring. I have my library and the reference books to continue my work on "The Pluralistic Universe," and hope to finish the paper in the intervals between the severe attacks of the strange malady. Always hangs over me the fear—horrible, gruesome, chilling. Even now I feel it and dare not write more to-night, for already the buzzing in my ears roars like the surf. My feet grow numb. I can feel the coldness creeping to my waist. My senses are becoming more acute. I must stop.

December 4, 1916. It is morning. The cabin is banked with snow and we are isolated from all the world. For the first time in many days I am able to think clearly and concisely. It is for that reason I write now. Jenkins has caught the malady, but as yet he has suffered only two short spells of the superconsciousness.

During these I had an opportunity to watch him. The only change in his physical appearance when he is under the spell is a slight heightened color just above the eyes. The rest of his face is pale. Curiously enough, none of the other servants who were with me caught the malady. From experiments and observations I have concluded it affects only those with a well-developed brain, and especially those whose memory can carry over a wealth of small details. It must be caused by some kind of a micro-organism which reacts upon the thought centers themselves.

December 6, 1916. I had a repetition of the terrible dream last night. The falling sensation this time was more distinct and vivid than before. When I awakened, I was at a loss to recognize my surroundings. The fear still hangs over me. It grips my vitals.

December 14, 1916. It is midnight, and I feel approaching another of those terrible spells. I cannot sleep. The buzzing in my ears racks my whole system. The crackling of the fire jars my eardrums and its brightness hurts my eyes. As I write I feel conscious of no other portion of my body save my hand and forearm. The scratching of the pencil is becoming unbearable.

January 9, 1917. Jenkins is worse. Last night he experienced the beautiful color sensations which I mentioned at some length in a previous description. These were followed by the fear in all its terrible superconsciousness. He is still in bed, weak and exhausted.

Myself—the fear has so racked my soul that I continually count the intakes of my breath. Imagine having to exert every tissue of your brain, willing yourself to breathe, to walk, to speak, and to perform all the ordinary functions of life. Even when I swallow a morsel of food, I am aware of its every movement from the time it leaves my mouth until it reaches the pit of my stomach. And at times the fear that I will forget to breathe so grips me that I am shaken with terror until I faint.

January 19, 1917. I am getting weaker. My spells of normality become fewer and fewer and farther and farther apart. For ten days I have suffered that icy fear—cold, gripping, terrible. Last night I had a repetition of the horrible dream with the falling sensation. Continually I count the rise and fall of my chest. My work will remain unfinished. I am doomed.

January 21, 1917. It is evening. The sunlight has been so strong to-day that I have been forced to cover the windows with blankets. Even then, the light has so racked my eyeballs I could keep my eyes open only for a few moments. I fear the darkness and its horrible mystery. A sickening riot of colors plays before my eyes and the saliva in my mouth tastes bitter and acid.

January 25, 1917. I am blind; I cannot see. The darkness falls about me like a velvet curtain, and I feel it creeping into my very soul.

The noise of the world is terrible. The fear clutches my heart. My breath comes and goes with conscious pangs. I feel the numbness creeping into my limbs. I cannot survive another spell. I fear I will forget to breathe—— Good-by

Do You Want to Earn Ten Dollars by Writing a Letter?

THRILLING EXPERIENCES

A NEW DEPARTMENT

We will award ten dollars with each issue to the reader writing us the best letter about some thrilling experience. Read the following announcement carefully before writing your letter.

WE read in the papers every day about thrilling experiences which people have had, but we seldom have an opportunity to obtain any side lights on the personal sides. There is no use in our repeating the old phrase: "Truth is stranger than fiction." We all know that it is. But wouldn't it be an interesting thing if we could read the actual, intimate accounts of those who have undergone some unusual experience that might have been harrowing, occult, mysterious, or unexplained? There are stories told of men and women whose hair turned white, as Byron wrote, "in a single night." Do you know any one who has had such a thing happen to him? Such events become far more enthralling when we can hear the actual account told by the one involved.

The world is so large a place, so much a matter of sharp contrasts and unknown things, that it is certainly possible for almost anything to happen. Rather than get these things second-hand, we are going to establish a department in THE THRILL BOOK where you or any other reader of the magazien can unburden to the public any startling experience which has occurred to you *personally* or to one of your friends. We are forced through space conditions to limit these accounts to five hundred words, but we are going to throw open our pages to all who can give us something extraordinary.

Sit down now and think over your life. It certainly hasn't been as humdrum as your neighbors claim it is. There has, at some time in your existence, been some experience, the unusual quality of which has perplexed you continually. For example, did you ever spend a night in a deserted house? We did *once,* and, believe us, it has been a burning memory ever since. Were you ever in a hotel when it caught afire? Did you ever witness some famous or terrible crime? Have you ever been in a terrific storm aboard a ship? Did you ever take a trip through some tropical country where few white men had ever been before? Did you ever participate in some free-for-all fight? Have you passed through any occult or mysterious experience that defied every known explanation? Did you ever see strange faces at night looking through a windowpane? Have you felt clammy hands touch your face as you walked along some gloomy road? Did you ever go through some nerve-racking hour that aged you ten years or so? Did you ever have some event in your life that convinced you that there was something in the belief that men do not pass out of the world when they die? Have you ever received any direct word from dead relatives or friends? Did you ever know any moment when something or other happened that convinced you instantly what a small atom in the universe the human soul is?

These and thousands of other questions have been interesting us ever since we inaugurated such an unusual venture as THE THRILL BOOK—the first magazine in America to print stories of occultism, mystery, and adventure, where the reader has an opportunity to share in the great ideas that have perplexed mankind since the days of Adam and Eve. It has seemed preposterous to us that no one has taken seriously the gripping subjects of occultism and mysticism which to-day are filling the minds of men like Sir Arthur Conan-Doyle and Sir Oliver Lodge. Nevertheless, it remained for THE THRILL BOOK to tackle a field without any rivals.

For the first time a large periodical has come out candidly and admitted that the American public has a mind all its own. It recognized the new tendencies toward the study of things unseen and unheard. It realized that people are everywhere to-day wondering about the thousands of men who gave up their lives in the Great War. Are they lost forever, they are asking themselves?

It will help materially in the understanding of these matters if THE THRILL BOOK opens its pages to an intelligent discussion of thrilling experiences which have come to our readers, thus opening the way to a clearer understanding of the tragic forces that control life and death. We want them to be truthful, straightforward, and intelligently done. We will either print them over the writer's name or without any hint of the author.

It is all part of the broad policy of THE THRILL BOOK—to stand behind the attitude of those who venerate Edgar Allan Poe, Ambrose Bierce, and many others who have seen clearly that all does not lie on the surface and that there are things which transcend mere logical explanation.

The human spirit is an eternity in itself. Life is so stupendous as to defy the rules of small minds or the understanding of the ignorant. We are here to print the sort of fiction that realizes this in its plots. We are the friend of those who want to be a little broader than the circle in which they live.

As a reader and believer in the ideals of what THE THRILL BOOK has stood for in the past year and what it plans to do, we ask you to write to us and tell us of those things that you do not understand, or of adventures in your lives of which there is no explanation, or which is of so startling a nature as to produce a real thrill.

From the letters printed in each issue we will select the best-written account of some thrilling experience and award the writer a prize of ten dollars. It is not necessary to use the typewriter. Make your communication brief, preferably not over three hundred and fifty words. The experience must be a truthful one and have happened to you or to some one whom you can trust to give an honest account. State in your letter whether you want it printed over your own signature or anonymously. We will not consider any unsigned letters, but will gladly follow your instructions as to the use of your name in print. The check for ten dollars will go to the prize winner promptly after the publication of the number containing the letter. The name of the lucky writer will be given in each case in the succeeding issue.

THE EDITOR.

Dreams.

THE Japanese believe it is dangerous to awaken a sleeper, in case the soul should be absent. We have often heard dreams discussed, but we must admit that so far we have not been convinced about the truth concerning their importance in our lives.

Nobody yet knows exactly what does happen when we are asleep. Doctors talk about blood pressure, but cannot tell why a lessened pressure should cause sleep, or what happens to our consciousness during that mysterious period—nearly one-third of our lives.

Some people have been known to intelligently answer questions in their sleep, but some authorities assert that sleep talkers and sleep walkers do not recollect what they have done after they are awake. The great Burbach states that children under seven do not recollect their dreams, though every one, children and animals included, all dream. Among grown-up people quite one-third cannot recall their dreams.

There are dreams and dreams. Not all are reliable as omens. Indeed, the only real difficulty is to decide whether your dream is a bona-fide message or is due to some ordinary physical cause, and quite without meaning.

No early dream is reliable, i, e., no dream that occurs soon after we go to bed, as the bodily processes, such as digestion, repair of tissue, et cetera, are still in process. An uncomfortable position in bed will cause a valueless dream; a crease in the bedclothes or in our night attire; a ray of light on the face, and many other similar incidents.

We must also remember that a mere jumble of odd adventure has no meaning, and also that some people are never reliable; something in their temperament preventing a true dream from manifesting itself. It is well known that watches vary according to the person who wears them; a watch appears often to be quite useless to its owner, but will keep perfect time when worn by some other person. It is the same with dreams; those with whom watches are thus erratic are quite useless for true omens.

Dreams that come to us near daybreak are the most valuable as omens, and it is generally held that if the sleeper is lying on the right side the dream will relate to the past; but if on the left side, then the omen refers to the present and future.

For our part we have read much about dreams in general, listened to many personal accounts of curious experiences in this line which other people have had, and also had strange dreams that perplexed and remained unexplained.

For instance, we have heard it said that it is most unfortunate to yawn in a dream; you will search in vain for health and success. To jump or break your way through a wall indicates some ultimate success. To walk on the top of a wall in a dream is also a fortunate omen.

There are hundreds of things of this nature, purely and simply omens that occur in our dreams. The question is, do these omens mean anything in a practical way?

We have all read of great generals who dreamed of victory or failure on the night before a battle and awakened to find it all too true.

There can hardly be any doubt that the future is often revealed by dreams. There have, of course, been many extravagant fictions palmed off as facts relative to dreams, but yet enough credible evidence exists of their importance to make any singular dream the subject of reflection and examination.

The subject is a vast one, many opinions to the contrary, but we feel sure that many readers of THE THRILL BOOK will be able to throw light on the subject. We will publish any letters not over five hundred words in length and which are serious attempts to bare the hidden meanings of dreams. Such communications will be read with interest by all who are seeking the truth about occult and not easily explained things of life.

The True Devotion.

BEHIND everything of value there must be a reason, cause for existence, purpose. Otherwise only failures will result. This is an age of intensiveness, sincere effort, close competition. Success requires conscientious application, knowledge of what others are doing, and how they do it.

Corporations exist because of certain individuals and combinations of individuals who have worked to a common end with amazing devotion.

To succeed greatly demands a great devotion.

In addition to our first element in this essay regarding work as a pleasure—in fact, demanding it to be so—we move a step higher; we are going to add devotion.

If we looked upon our work purely and simply as pleasure we might suffer thereby, as I have already pointed out. Pleasure carries no responsibility, but serious effort does.

Just because a man has an ax in his hand it doesn't mean that he must commit murder. He might just as well cut wood. And so with our opinion that work must be looked upon as a joyful undertaking.

I leave the rest to you.

Devotion is an emotion shared by beast and man alike; it is therefore one of the fundamental things. Devotion wrongly considered is often the means to a man's failure in life.

The clerk, for example, may have doglike devotion to a minor position, but I certainly don't respect him for it, if he intends sticking there.

The coldest sight imaginable is that of the shiny-sleeved clerk devoted to petty tasks. Whenever I enter a business office and look upon these fellows I feel sick at heart. Devotion to a false ideal is unworthy of any man. To be a narrow-chested idolater of sham ideals is a blow at mankind.

The clerk who idolizes his employer, even though he is a crook, surely deserves to be classed in the same category. On the same plane is the clerk who knows nothing of the bright side of the business and merely is devoted to his job because he is afraid to lose it.

However, devotion to one's own ideals is another matter. Once we undertake a line of work and are sure it fits our capabilities, then our devotion to it counts greatly in the result and facts.

Devotion, to my mind, is the wholehearted, sincere appreciation of a truth and the ability to follow it through any situation or chain of events.

When a man has decided upon the kind of work he intends following he must exert himself to the limit to attain his ends. It entails sacrifices, struggles, and the going without many superficial things that fill up the lonesome hours.

To the man or woman alone in the great city, or the farmer compelled to remain in the sparsely located section of the country, it is frequently hard to stick to a thing and carry it through to a fighting finish.

Many employees in the city are compelled to live in rooming houses, where the evenings are dreary and long and Sunday arrives with no hope of relief from the monotony. As we said a few lines back, this is an age of intensiveness. Could we ask for a more pitiful example than this of the reason why so many fail to succeed?

Think of the evenings going to waste year after year, while youth speeds by, leaving them facing old age and no independent income. They do not know the meaning of intensity. Their lives are thin, vacuous, idle.

Imagine that one of those people was given an opportunity to do the work he loved. What a change there would be! Alas, the average man dies without knowing half the possibilities that lurk in the human mind and will power.

Devotion of a sort exists for any work that we perform because personal pride enters in and provides all energy that compels us to move forward. Even the clerk wrongly placed knows devotion to his task, odious though it may seem. His fellowman is with him in the office. He tries simply because he would hate to fail. After a time he is deluded into falling into a rut by this same splendid emotion gone astray.

Don't spend your devotion upon work that does not fit you. Drop it, my friend, and put your affection on the right track. Don't waste any respect on things of a lower caliber than your own idea of yourself.

Don't be afraid of looking upon yourself with a favorable eye. This doesn't mean to go to a silly extreme. It means a common-sense appraisal of yourself as a marketable proposition.

If you were a storekeeper and continually apologized for the quality of your goods, do you imagine you would have many purchasers? It requires some publicity to put anything across properly. If you sit back in your chair chewing your thumb some one else is going to get away with the cake.

Devotion to your ideals and the candid, fearless carrying of them into effect is therefore a prima-facie fact. You might have many ideas, but if you let them lie around idle they would serve no good purpose.

I once knew a clever man who had the world's knowledge seemingly at his finger tips. He could quote from the greatest writers glibly. He was a hard worker, a good family man, an extraordinary personality, but at the age of forty he was only getting a salary of sixteen hundred dollars a year. His brain was like a lumber yard, piled high with uncut wood. He had never built anything with his knowledge. He was the sport of chance, the plaything of fate.

Devotion to your ideals, in consequence, is a working proposition. It means doing something for the things that you love. It means getting somewhere.

The cow is devotion personified, but it produces milk for others to drink, butter for others to eat, and calves for the butchers; what does it get for its devotion?

Capitalize some part of your devotion in the cause of self. Look out for pure selfishness. The open-handed man generates electricity, friends, opportunities.

The giver is the one who gets; to him who goes through life open-handed life responds with open hands.

Devotion, going a step farther, means devotion to something worth while in the eyes of your fellow men. It is the conscious paying of our debts to individual effort.

We cannot get away from another salient fact at this juncture. Devotion is the right state of mind to produce results. It is the generous expression of self in working terms. With two things in our minds, work considered as joy and devotion, to that pleasurable conception of toil we are well on the road to the third element, health.

American Fiction.

IF we were to believe the average magazine we would grow to think that the world consists mainly of superficial people who come and go across an unreal earth. The writer of fiction seems to think that all the mysterious elements have been explained away so thoroughly that there is no use in tackling them.

This attitude is not only a silly one, but it is leading us into bypaths of thought and feeling which are, curiously enough, neither true nor interesting. If we believe that the world is a simple, easily understood thing, and prefer to remain ignorant, all well and good. The fact is that the most of us do not relish the idea of living in the dark.

When you get right down to facts, even he who runs, as well as he who is too lazy to use his mind, comes finally to the realization that the universe is big enough to keep us wondering all our days. What lies on the surface is only a minor element in the big scale. Before birth and after death—what of these questions?

This is proven in the fiction field by the enormous popularity of such men as Poe, Bierce, and other writers of occult and strange stories. Perhaps the man who is most widely read in America to-day—that is, among the immortals—is Edgar Allan Poe. Why? Surely not because he was a master of English. There have been plenty of masters of English who couldn't have held our interest for as much as ten minutes in succession. It is because he had the courage to deal with the unseen, the unknown.

To all those who read "The Narrative of A. Gordon Pym" this fact stands out with refreshing singularity. The hero of that thrilling tale went so far into the mysteries of another world that even the mastery of Poe could not extricate him from his adventure, so he left him there. He refused to bow to any so-called "popular" taste and clear up the business by a false ending.

We meet this time and again in his short tales. "The Fall of the House of Usher, "The Pit and the Pendulum,"

"William Wilson," "Ligeia," and so on down the list.

We have been interested, therefore, in the fact that no other magazine besides THE THRILL BOOK has seriously considered this attitude of mind on the part of the public. The many stories which we have already published by unknown writers has convinced us that there are hundreds more whose work has been continually jettisoned by the periodicals. We want to see this work.

For example, in this number you will find a tale by Lillian Beynon Thomas, called "When Wires Are Down." We can say honestly that for suspense and mystery it is without an equal. And yet it had gone the rounds and could find no one willing to publish it.

"The Silver Menace," by Murray Leinster; "Unexpected," by Junius B. Smith; "A Mystery Downstairs," by Francisco Curtiss, and "Burnt Bridges," by Clarence L. Andrews—stories you will find in this number—are all out of the ordinary, entirely divorced from the average trend of present-day fiction and powerfully written.

As one reader said in a letter recently: "Thank the lucky fates that we have THE THRILL BOOK. At last an opportunity for the extraordinary and occult to find the light of day."

Thrilling Experiences.

DON'T fail to read the announcement in this issue of a new department which we are about to establish. It will be called "THRILLING EXPERIENCES," and will be devoted to the personal accounts of those who have had exciting, curious, and not easily explained adventures.

We have been receiving so many letters containing bits of personal history along these lines that we thought it was about time to collect the material and ask for more.

Soldiers, Sailors and Marines.

ALTHOUGH we have discontinued the department devoted to Soldiers, Sailors, and Marines, we wish to say that the officer who conducted it is always ready to offer his advice to any one who requests it. We will even print any letter that warrants general consideration. The officer in question has had quite a few years' experience in the army, and he has made a study of paper work, courts-martial law, and the customs of the service. Don't hesitate to make use of this opportunity to straighten out any tangle that may be worrying you.

THE EDITOR.

WILDSIDE PULP CLASSICS: PULP FACSIMILE SERIES

Series editor: John Gregory Betancourt

#1: *Spicy Mystery Stories* (August 1935)

Includes Robert Leslie Bellem, Atwater Culpepper, Ellery Watson Calder, Carl Moore, E. Hoffman Price, Jerome Severs Perry, Charles R. Allen, Arthur Wallace, and more

#2: *Ghost Stories* (June 1931)

Stories by Conrad Richter (best known as the author of The Light in the Forest) and E. and H. Heron featuring their psychic detective, Flaxman Low.

#3: *Spicy Mystery Stories* (February 1937)

The February 1937 issue features Robert Leslie Bellem, Lew Merrisll (Victor Rousseau, Hugh Speer, Justin Case (Hugh E. Cave), and many others — plus all the classic "spicy" artwork!

#4: *Strange Tales #7* (January 1933)

This issue features Hugh B. Cave's classic "Murgunstrumm," as well as stories by Robert E. Howard, Henry S. Whitehead, and many more.

#5: *The Black Mask #2* (May 1920)

The second issue of the classic mystery magazine, where hardboiled noir fiction was born!

#6: *Tales of Magic and Mystery* (February 1928)

The second issue of the classic mystery magazine, where hardboiled noir fiction was born!

#7: *The Phantom Detective #1* (February 1933)

The premiere issue of the detective-hero pulp!

#8: *Submarine Stories* (March 1930)

A reprint of a rare pulp magazine, featuring stories and articles about (what else?) submarines!

#9: *Sinister Stories #1* (Feb 1940)

A reprint of a rare pulp magazine, featuring stories and articles about (what else?) submarines!

– –

Yes! Please send me the following books, for which I enclose payment. (Or order online with a credit card at www.wildsidepress.com, or through your favorite online bookseller.)

☐ *Spicy Mystery Stories* (Aug.1935) - $19.95
☐ *Ghost Stories* (June 1931) - $19.95
☐ *Spicy Mystery Stories* (Feb. 1937) - $19.95
☐ *Strange Tales #7* (January 1933) - $15.00
☐ *The Black Mask #2* (January 1920) - $19.95
☐ *Tales of Magic and Mystery* (Feb. 1928) - $19.95
☐ *The Phantom Detective #1* (Feb. 1933) - $19.95
☐ *Submarine Stories* (March. 1930) - $19.95
☐ *Sinister Stories* (Feb. 1940) - $19.95

Mail to: Wildside Press, P.O. Box 301, Holicong, PA 18928-0301.

U.S. shipping: $3.95 for 1-2 books, $1 per additional book. *Shipping to other countries: please see web site:* www.wildsidepress.com

Name: _____

Address:_____

Address:_____

Email:_____